THE BASTARD

IN HER BOUDOIR

DUBIOUS MATES SERIES
BOOK TWO

CONSTANCE REMILLARD

HEADY PRESS

Cover Design by Black Dash Studio. Public domain image: *Portrait of Mary Matthews* (or Madame Julien-Francois-Bertrand de La Chère) by Marcel Verdier, ca 1843.

A bibliography of works quoted in this book can be found in the appendix.

ISBN: 979-8-9898865-4-8

Library of Congress Control Number: 2026907703

Printed by Heady Press. Philipstown, NY, USA.

With deepest gratitude to my alpha and beta readers,
whose feedback and support remain invaluable.

Special thanks to Kathleen,
for believing in this story from its earliest draft,
then using her keen eye to help polish it.

PREFACE

The novel uses two types of symbols to indicate breaks. The first denotes a lapse in time or location known as a scene break.

The second indicates a change in character point of view within the same scene.

***

All my books are 100% conceived and written by me, flesh-and-blood human, all my book covers designed by a human too. No AI, ever. You have my word.

This work also contains material which may be unsettling to some. If you wish to be forewarned, read on for a list of content warnings. If you prefer to read without spoilers, stop now and skip ahead.

The Bastard in her Boudoir is a romance set in three acts. Characters do not always act honorably toward one another, but as a work of historical fiction, their actions speak to norms held in the past. These actions also serve as plot devices.

This book contains: cursing, gambling, alcohol, tobacco, coercion, attempted assault (not graphic), kidnapping, drugging (laudanum), sex, dubious consent, elements of BDSM-style control (rules) and punishment (hand spanking, ruler), torture (not graphic, mainly flashbacks), PTSD, pregnancy, prostitution, and manslaughter (as self-defense, some blood).

To the best of my ability, these topics have been handled in a respectful manner true to the time period in which the story takes place. A few artistic liberties were taken, which I point out in my note to readers at the end. A glossary of regional and foreign words used in the story can also be found here.

~ *Constance*

ACT I

RULES & REBUTTALS

Learn from me, if not by my precepts, at least by my example, how dangerous is the acquirement of knowledge, and how much happier that man is who believes his native town to be his world, than he who aspires to become greater than his nature will allow.

Mary Shelley, from *Frankenstein*
or The Modern Prometheus, 1818

CHAPTER ONE

LONDON, SPRING OF 1839

"Fold." Milton laid his cards face down while the prig across the table gleefully gathered his winnings.

Tonight was going altogether well. Boring, even.

"Thank you, sir, thank you indeed!" The man beamed, his cheeks flush with luck. The old fool should walk, yet he wouldn't. In his head he'd already paid off his accounts, already ordered his titled friends a round of drinks at his club. It's what sixes and sevens always did.

They really shouldn't.

Milton leaned back in his chair and feigned defeat, proclaiming, "*Fortuna audentes juvat,* sir. Fortune does in truth favor the bold. Still, I'm not opposed to one last match before we call it a night, are you?" He arched his brow in a stare meant to sway, knowing the moment was his to plunder. The room had nearly cleared, though the hour was hardly late; this particular gaming hall would remain open for as long as he needed.

A perk of holding shares in an establishment owned by one's best friend.

His opponent hesitated and Milton narrowed his gaze,

willing this pathetic lord's backside stuck to its seat. Li had tipped him off, known all about the fellow's sorry state of affairs. No 'bees and honey' in this bloke's house. She also knew this man had daughters, one of whom was purportedly pretty enough—and proper enough—to be ripe for plucking.

The fellow chewed his mustache a minute longer before he pushed his earnings forward.

"*Vingt-et-un*?" Milton was satisfied his prey would no longer walk.

"Fine, yes. Why not?" The poor sod grinned, back in the game. His recent rush of victory had nicely warmed his veins.

"Excellent." Milton allowed himself to smile. "Your draw, sir."

They played another round, Milton counting all the while in his keen numeric head. He knew precisely when to time this fool's fall, and so game his desired end.

❧

Come morning, Milton made good on his win by calling at the lord's house.

"Bring me your daughters."

"B-both of them, Baron?" The pathetic toff quaked in his boots.

"Of course both of them," Milton snapped. "I must pick one, mustn't I?"

"Y-yes of course, I'll be but a moment." And off he scuttled.

Milton paced the man's drawing room. He hadn't liked the fellow last night, and he liked him even less now, but such was the way of the world. He needed a wife from a titled family, the more broke the better, and judging from the threadbare rug beneath his feet and moth-eaten drapes about the windows, this lord's family was ideal.

He hoped one of the daughters was passably fair.

"Oh, I beg your pardon." A bespectacled young lady abruptly popped her head into the room as Milton unwittingly met her eyes.

She flashed him an apologetic half-smile. "I am looking for my father, Lord Winthrop." She stared expectantly at Milton, who simply let his gaze appraise the lady's figure.

"He's just stepped out."

"Ah." Her smile tightened. "That is indeed unfortunate." She hesitated a beat before she entered the room and boldly took his arm. "Then I'm afraid you shall have to do instead." And the brazen miss proceeded to drag Milton out and down the hall.

He was so shocked by her behavior that he allowed himself to be led, his frown fast becoming a scowl. As they descended the servant stairs, he was about to berate her audacity when she placed a finger to her plump lips.

He chose to let the chit further surprise him.

She stopped him just outside the kitchen, her eyes pleading mutely at him through her spectacles, while a frail, female voice quavered from inside.

"As I told you before, Butcher Wilkes, the master's not in. Won't be till next—"

"An' a bold-faced lie 'tis, woman!"

From Milton's vantage outside the threshold, a barrel-chested man stood perilously close to a stooped, elderly woman he assumed was this household's cook.

"I'm past due me pay an' I'll not leave till I has it. An' if you'll not give it, I'll take sommat else fer it instead."

At which point the young lady inserted herself directly between the burly butcher and cowering cook, but not before pasting the most ridiculous, false smile upon her face that Milton had ever seen.

He remained just out of sight, transfixed.

"Mr. Wilkes, I apologize for keeping you waiting." She spoke with forced vigor. "Alas, it appears my father is indeed nowhere to be found. However, I can assure you I will come round tomorrow to pay in full what you are owed. You have my word, sir." She bravely met the man's eyes, though her hands trembled at her sides.

Oh, this was the *perfect* family from which to steal himself a wife, Milton thought, for to behold a respectable—albeit bespectacled—proper lady degrade herself before a mere tradesman was utterly delicious.

The butcher stepped forward and gripped the lady's slender throat. "I'll not wait more, miss. An' as yer dear papa ain't here, y' can pay me yerself, on yer knees, like t' other girls do." He promptly pushed her to his crotch, then gripped her head to thrust his hips at her face in a lewd manner. The lady began to beat at his legs with her fists, but he harshly snapped her neck back. "None o' that now, dearie." The butcher's leer deepened as he pressed his crotch closer. "*You'll* pay e'en if his lordship won't."

The cook screeched as she reached for a fry pan, making Milton, at last, shake off his stupor—thrilling though it was to see so common a drama played out not on a London back-street but in a lord's lofty home. He removed one kidskin glove with his teeth, then stepped into the kitchen to plant the butcher a facer, sending the man reeling and the young lady lurching back.

A gasp from the cook and a groan from the butcher diverted Milton's focus before he helped the lady up, who, to her credit, righted herself quickly, her look of gratitude almost embarrassing. He then tossed the butcher directly out the kitchen's back door into a courtyard, before he bolted the door behind him and acknowledged the cook with a nod. Only then did he take the young lady in tow to march her back in the direction from whence they had come.

"Kindly return me to your father's drawing room, miss," he instructed.

"Of course, sir." She kept her eyes averted, for modesty or shame he wasn't sure. He was only sure her bosom heaved nicely. "I must apologize for such unpleasant exchange and thank you for coming to my aid."

"You dragged me to your aid," he tersely told her.

"Yes, well, I hadn't much choice, had I?" she grumbled back.

Before he could retort they reentered the drawing room to find both her father and, Milton assumed, the lady's sister in wait. Lord Winthrop took one look at his daughter's disheveled state and froze. Not only was her hair mussed and spectacles askew, the lady's neck was blotched red from the butcher's thick thumbs.

"Lizzie!" her father sputtered. "Where the dickens have you been?"

"Apologies, Papa." Her lips thinned. "Butcher Wilkes stopped by to hassle Cook. *Again*."

"Well I hope you sent him packing." Winthrop huffed.

She bit her lip with a pair of pearly whites Milton found rather fetching. "Father, in your absence it was your visitor here"—she nicked her head at Milton—"who assisted me in sending Mr. Wilkes packing."

Winthrop begrudgingly met Milton's eyes. "I apologize, sir, for the manner in which my daughter so rudely—"

"Enough!" Milton cut him off, ready to be done with their polite charade. He removed his remaining kidskin, irritated he could not find the other. "I wish to settle matters. How old are your daughters?"

Both girls swiveled their heads at him, the bespectacled one fastest.

Winthrop swallowed. "Elizabeth has two and twenty, sir,

and Annabelle nineteen, both given the finest educations young ladies could possibly—"

"Turn around," Milton ordered both women. The one named Annabelle looked to the older Elizabeth in shock.

Clearly, their father had failed to inform them of his visit.

"Well, go on then," his lordship urged. "Do as the gentleman says."

Annabelle turned for Milton's perusal, while 'spectacles' stared him down, biting that plump lip of hers again.

"*Lizzie*," her father hissed, "do not embarrass me, girl."

Miss Elizabeth did not budge. "I will not demean myself by submitting to your guest's review, Father," she ground out, "especially when he has not deigned to introduce himself nor state his business with us."

Milton's lips twitched. "And yet the young lady was willing to demean herself in lieu of payment for the butcher's pleasure, if I recall." His eyes slid over her figure once more. "No matter," he scoffed. "I daresay I got a fair enough look at you then."

Her eyes blazed at him through her lenses; he did not flinch.

"As to my name, Miss Winthrop, it is Jasper Audrey, Baron of Milton, and as for my business, it is very simple, though I expected your father to prepare you for it." He shot Winthrop a glare. "I require a wife, and as your papa is in dire need of funds, I will pay handsomely for one of you."

If looks could kill, Miss Winthrop should have slain him on the spot.

"Erm, just how handsomely, Baron?" their father ventured, unabashed.

"I will forgive the three thousand pounds you owe me, Winthrop."

"*What?*" Elizabeth Winthrop burst out.

"No?" Milton arched his brow at her. "Four thousand then."

"No!" she got out, louder. "That is not what I—"

"Five thousand is my final offer, miss."

Disbelief marred Miss Winthrop's brow. "Father, you cannot allow this man to enter our home and so blatantly disrespect us by—"

"Purchasing a wife outright?" Milton met her gaze with amusement. "I believe I can, and will, purchase one of you, as your father agreed to as much over our game of cards last night." He watched her face fall. "However, as you are obviously not enamored of my suit"—he had her attention now—"I shall offer for your sister instead, who strikes me as more amenable in temperament."

***

Elizabeth gripped Annabelle's hand, unable to bear her sister's stricken expression a second longer. "Baron." She drew herself tall, willing her racing heart to calm. "My sister has not been brought out yet formally in society."

"Plenty of girls marry younger than nineteen. She is my preferred choice."

"Please!" escaped her lips. "Papa!" She turned to him, yet his eyes would not meet hers, the coward. The situation was so alarming, so unexpected, it simply *must* be a misunderstanding.

She gripped Annabelle's hand more tightly. "Baron, I beg you to reconsider your offer. Surely there are more suitable—"

"Miss Winthrop, having successfully haggled such high price for your sister, are you now proposing I offer for *you* instead?"

She could have sworn the man's ice-blue eyes sparked.

"I..." She madly deliberated in her head. If she did not act now, Annabelle would be lost, though if she offered herself, *she'd* be lost. Still, tomorrow was another day. She could solve the problem then.

"Yes." Elizabeth swallowed her panic and bowed her head. "Take me instead." Annabelle tugged furiously on her hand, but Elizabeth merely squeezed back, hard. "I should make you a better wife, sir, being older and wiser." She kept her head bent, not wishing to look at him but wishing to buy time to think.

"Hmm." He stepped forward to tilt her chin and stare into her eyes, just as the butcher had. "Wiser, perhaps. But not nearly as pretty as your sister."

Her body flushed hot with pride. "Surely you require your wife to be more than mere decoration." Her temper heated. "A wife must manage a household, and I assure you I—"

"She must also bear me heirs." His hands slipped to her waist, gliding low over her hips to boldly assess.

Elizabeth roughly pushed his hands off, but he quickly imprisoned hers in an iron grip.

"I have changed my mind, Winthrop," he announced to Papa. "I shall take your eldest daughter as wife instead, for four thousand pounds."

Annabelle gasped as Lizzie met the scoundrel's eyes in a bitter, bitter stare, his insult not lost on her.

"And now I should like a moment alone with my betrothed." His cold, cobalt gaze remained locked on hers. "Leave us," he ordered Papa, who hurried Annabelle out as fast as his scurrying legs could take him. Bella shot Elizabeth an anguished, parting look as she was dragged away.

Their father had failed them yet again.

The Baron, meanwhile, stepped back to take stock of her, his purchase. "You argue much." He crossed his arms. "But you appear robust in health, your tongue sufficiently sharp to suit my needs. I expect complete obedience from my wife, but will in turn keep her in great comfort."

"You … beast!" she cried, now that they were alone. "I shall never—!"

He pulled her up against his hard, lean form only to stare down at the rise and fall of her chest. "We will wed in one week's time, and when we do, your allegiance will be only to me. I do not require affection in marriage, but I do expect fealty. I am no beast, Miss Winthrop, and will honor the same wedding vows you, too, swear to uphold."

"No honorable man behaves like you." She skewered him through her spectacles. "And obedience is *granted* not demanded."

"Ah." He smiled. "My future wife would command my fealty too." He pulled her lower lip down with his thumb to expose her teeth. And then he leaned in, his breath blowing hot at her ear to send tremors down her spine. "Tell me, *Lizzie*"—too familiar, too fast—"does it not excite you in the slightest to have a man command you?"

Her breath hitched.

"Are you not, perhaps, the least bit aroused by my bold offer of marriage?"

She attempted to squirm free but was backed against her father's desk, his hand up her skirts before she could blink. "Get. Off. Me!"

"Shh, Lizzie." His teeth pulled at her earlobe now, making her heart gallop as his hand inched higher up her thigh, fingers tracing a frightening path along her thin drawers. "I merely need to ascertain you are indeed the maiden your father claims." He landed at the gap in her drawers, making her gasp outright.

"I see you *are* affected by me, good."

Before she knew it his finger slipped inside her shamefully slick channel, making her mouth fall open in a silent plea for help, her brain gone blank, voice utterly fled.

"I am delighted to discover you remain both chaste, Miss

Winthrop, and eager for our wedding night." He stroked her a moment longer, making her shake beneath his touch. "I promise you great pleasure, Lizzie, provided you obey me." He slipped his hand back out, smoothed her skirts, and righted her on her feet.

Elizabeth remained frozen in place, staring at this stranger who had just violated her so shamelessly. He straightened his cravat and then adjusted her spectacles, the finger he'd had inside her landing briefly on her nose.

"I shall procure a special license and arrange for a modiste to fit you for both your wedding dress and trousseau. The ceremony will be brief, the celebration after more grand. I see no reason for a long betrothal when the aim of marriage is, after all, pragmatic."

"Prag-matic?" She could barely speak, still weak-kneed from his assault. Her cheeks burned as if on fire.

"I require heirs, Miss Winthrop. Many, I hope." His eyes, hooded from their encounter, drifted lazily to her own. "And I assure you, I *do* now look forward to that process."

He took her hand and brushed warm lips across her knuckles before he let himself out.

Elizabeth Winthrop slid slowly to the floor in a none-too-elegant slump. She could scarce believe what had just been done.

CHAPTER TWO

Jasper Audrey, jack of all trades and new Baron of Milton, was a great many things, but a gentleman he was not. This did not plague him much. What plagued him was that he would never be a proper peer. Still, he was pleased with the outcome of his morning visit, knowing Miss Winthrop would help to right that grievous wrong. She was the perfect foil: respectable, titled, and of sufficient backbone to withstand the *Ton*. She was no wilting, simpering debutante and no simpleton either—more clever than her father by far. Though those spectacles were a shame. She might almost be called handsome without.

He considered her appearance as he strolled the leafy neighborhood streets, having sent his driver ahead so he might walk off his excess energy. He'd been honest when he'd deemed Miss Winthrop's sister more attractive, for the younger daughter had delicate, soft features and bright, wide eyes beneath a halo of chestnut curls. Elizabeth was almost plain in comparison: sharp, grey gaze to match her sharp tongue—not to mention ink-black hair pulled severely to her head. The sisters had looked unrelated, perhaps had different mothers even. Yet Elizabeth's person had excited him in ways he could not deny. His body had positively hummed in response to her own, and when he'd discovered her equally eager, he'd known she'd suit his bed. Those hips and arse of hers fair begged to be handled.

Milton's cock twitched and his step lightened just thinking about Miss Winthrop, realizing he had a week's time now in which to outfit his future wife and determine her course of training. At the very least she'd need a wardrobe and a lady's maid. At best he'd bring her to heel before they wed. Li would know whatever else a baroness required.

Yes, a visit to Li's to make the requisite plans and purchases was now in order. Though his missing kidskin still niggled.

It didn't matter. He'd buy another pair. Hell, he could buy as many gloves as he liked. There were perks to being rich as Croesus.

Elizabeth curled her body into a ball of misery and rage. Her life was crumbling about her, and all she could do was stew in her bedroom's window seat. Not even her beloved books and stories held escape, for she could concentrate on nothing but the memory of *that man's* unnerving blue dots piercing her when he'd lowered his price and demanded her hand in marriage.

That she should be wed to a baron so arrogant, so unfeeling and severe … *Oh!* She longed to punch his smug face the way he'd punched the butcher. Which only complicated her feelings, for in that instant he'd been a different man entirely, one who had defended her honor and come to her rescue. One who'd behaved nobly.

Though she'd all but forced his hand, she reminded herself.

She'd dragged the gentleman with her, knowing Butcher Wilkes would not take no for an answer this time.

Elizabeth's sigh held the weight of her soul, her thoughts careening every which way. Why was Father the pathetic creature he was? Why had her mother ever deigned to marry him? Or had she, too, been sold in marriage like Annabelle's mama? The thought briefly arrested. Papa had squandered her stepmother's income, his second wife powerless to control his gambling as he'd reduced the family to its piteous state. Which had led, of course, to Elizabeth's present piteous state.

Only why, in God's name, had Papa lied outright about her and Annabelle's ages? Elizabeth was nearly twenty-four and Bella close to twenty-one. He'd done them a disservice in this, too.

She sank her face to her hands, so angry she could not even cry. Nor could she deny that rotten baron had somehow, impossibly, roused in her stirrings of … No, she would not even *think* the word. She was a lady of virtue—at least, in deed she still was. She'd seen too much in life to proclaim herself an innocent. Butcher Wilkes was not the first man to assert himself. Elizabeth had escaped more compromising encounters than she cared to recall in her attempts to stall and sweet talk her way out of Father's debts. She knew the liberties men took, the filthy offers they made.

But no man had ever touched her as this baron had, in his finely tailored waistcoat and fancy kidskin gloves. His wiry frame had towered over her in the most egregious, commanding manner, as if he'd already owned her outright. And her own tremor of weakness, that revolting trickle to gut, right to where he'd…

She would *cease to think* on the intimacy of that moment, the flagrant, wholly inappropriate, absolutely—why, the man was evil incarnate! That ice-blue stare below his dark, pomaded hair had been so depthless, so fathomless, and yet … She shook herself to escape the memory of his eyes. Her spectacles had been no match for his scalding, searing gaze. And if she didn't figure a way out, she would be forced to stare into those eyes for the rest of her ungodly married life.

Elizabeth curled herself deeper into the window bench in her bedroom and peered into the black night outside, waiting miserably for sleep to come.

When it would not, she slipped to her desk, lit her small lamp, and pulled out paper and ink. She began to write. Not a comedy to distract Papa, not a drama for Annabelle to play the dashing hero or brave heroine, but a dark and dismal story of a lady trapped by circumstance.

London's dankest rowhouse housed the worst of the city's scum: a man more wicked than Beelzebub. Not even the low-life landlord knew his tenant's full name. He knew him only as the brooding baron, a shadowy figure who paid coin upfront each week for his room.

The baron had just settled his rent, smoke curling from the pipe dangling at his lip. He puffed a mix of opium and tobacco, the smell cloyingly sweet, his mouth a snarl when he grinned. It chilled the landlord's limbs.

"Go on, then," the landlord dismissed him, though his bones rattled and quaked. "Off with yer." Like always, his tenant's towering presence pinned the landlord to his seat.

The baron laughed a menacing, low rumble, then trod the narrow stairs back to his rented room. He stared at the girl who lay asleep in his bed, dead to the world, unaware of his wicked plans. She thought she was safe, thought he'd saved her from a worse fate. But once he ruined her properly, she'd be forced to marry him. And then his plans could truly take shape.

"Lizzie," Annabelle cried from the foyer, "Baron of Milton has sent you flowers! And a note!"

Elizabeth's heart sank. She'd recovered enough from yesterday's horror to swallow breakfast this morning, but flowers? She quelled the urge to vomit as she pushed her chair back from the table.

There was indeed a ridiculously profuse display of hothouse blooms in the foyer, utterly inappropriate given no shred of ardor lay behind the gift. The bouquet was a dizzying array of blue hyacinth and yellow marguerite, leaving Elizabeth only more displeased, for she was versed enough in the language of flowers to know her 'loveliness' had not charmed the Baron in the least, hyacinths be damned. And marguerites meant he'd 'come soon,' filling her with further dread. She ripped the note from her sister's hand.

> *Dear Elizabeth, I have scheduled your appointment at Madame LeBrecht's this afternoon for your dress fitting. My carriage will arrive promptly at two. I must insist you do not dally. —Milton*

She snorted. "Do not dally." Elizabeth nearly choked on the words, making Annabelle glance at her with concern. "*I must insist*, he writes." A harsh laugh tore through her. "I shall dally all right," she muttered under her breath, jaw clenched. "I shall dally as long as I well please."

She picked up his bouquet, opened the front door, and dumped the contents across the front step. Let him tread directly on his own blasted blooms when he arrived at two. Let him stand there and *wait*.

At precisely two o'clock Milton's carriage pulled up before Miss Winthrop's home. He straightened his hat before exiting his vehicle, then stepped over what appeared to be the remains of crushed petals on the doorstep.

He rapped the knocker twice and waited.

A footman ushered him in as Miss Winthrop was fetched, only it appeared the lady was not quite ready. Would he take a seat please, until she was?

He would not. Instead Milton paced the narrow foyer. He glanced at the clock. Ten after two. He paced more, his ire increasing with each tick of the hand. Soon it was quarter past, then nearing twenty after.

In a huff he took to the stairs, disregarding the footman entirely as he bellowed, "Miss Elizabeth Winthrop, I will not wait a moment longer!"

Magically she appeared, stepping out from what he presumed was the lady's own chamber. She clasped a book to her chest, looking wholly unprepared in but her house dress.

"Is that you, Baron?" Elizabeth pushed her spectacles up her nose. "I am sorry to keep you waiting, but I'm afraid today simply does not suit. Perhaps you might reschedule my appointment with your modiste for tomorrow instead."

Impudent chit. He grabbed her arm and hauled her downstairs past the footman, then promptly shoved her into his carriage with all the elegance of a tossed grain sack.

Sans bonnet or spencer, she righted herself on the seat, looking both stunned and fierce.

Milton yanked the door shut, pounded furiously on the roof, then turned to her with a glare. "You have deliberately provoked me."

"You have deliberately insulted me."

"Since when, pray, are flowers insulting?"

"When they are accompanied by not a shred of feeling, sir, but with a note of command, ordering me about as if—"

"As if you were my property already?" He continued to stare hard into her eyes. "Because you are, Miss

Winthrop. Let us not forget your father's word. And if you do not start following my orders this instant I can and will rescind my offer of marriage and take your sister in your stead."

She gasped.

"It matters little to me which one of you I wed, and I must say, I am beginning to wonder if I chose poorly."

***

Elizabeth froze, because the man seated across from her would crush Annabelle.

She swallowed her nerves and lowered her head, the rattling carriage making her stomach churn more than it already did. "I beg your pardon, Baron," she murmured meekly.

"Better." He still radiated anger. "But not enough. Beg me again."

Her eyes flashed to his, meeting therein a steely determination which again pricked alarm. She lowered her gaze once more, to settle on his tall, polished hessians, the sheer size of them forbidding. "I apologize for my behavior, sir, and beg your forgiveness."

He wrenched her across the carriage so that she found herself on her knees before his lap, her head snapped back.

"When I told you I expected obedience, I meant precisely that, Miss Winthrop. So either you do not understand the meaning of the word, or you require a demonstration of it. Which is it, miss?"

Elizabeth trembled. She would be wise not to cross her betrothed more until *after* they married, when Annabelle would be safe from his clutches. She swallowed her bile.

"Sir, I believe you just demonstrated your desire for obedience."

"Good," he told her, though his grip did not loosen. "Now remove those bloody spectacles."

"Sir, I do not—"

"If you cannot follow an order so basic, Elizabeth, then I *will* rescind my marriage offer."

She quickly pulled them off, unwilling to risk Bella's future on so simple a request.

His breath hitched. Unable to read his expression, she squinted at the Baron, now a blur, for the rotten man had just stolen her sight.

She was suddenly, unceremoniously lifted onto his lap.

"Look at me." His gloved hand turned her cheek to face him. "Can you see now?"

"Yes." She stiffened.

"Good." He leaned in for what felt like the start of a kiss when the carriage lurched to an abrupt halt, nearly throwing her from his lap. He gripped her close. "We've arrived," he told her gruffly. "See to it you behave."

She hastily donned her glasses as he pushed her off his lap and handed her down to his driver, to a boisterous London street.

CHAPTER THREE

Boot crossed comfortably over one knee, hat and gloves laid neatly beside him, Milton leaned back in his seat, a brandy in hand. He'd enjoyed watching his bride-to-be stripped to her smalls and measured head to toe. Miss Winthrop stood in the center of *LeBrecht's* fitting room attended by three comely maids, while the modiste displayed bolts of cloth for his approval.

Li, or Madam LeBrecht as others knew her, sat to his left thumbing a pattern book she occasionally thrust in his face. He'd known Li for years, and her staff knew him too—as well they should, considering Milton's own mother ran Li's other profitable business: prostitution.

He imagined Miss Winthrop's horrified reaction the day she discovered her husband's unsavory lineage. Then again, half his sodding blood was more blue than hers; she'd recover.

Li's maids threw him glances, for he was no stranger to their ranks. He'd grown up with whores and respected them for their ability to retain dignity in the face of pure debasement. And these three were whores turned seamstresses, though he suspected they still turned tricks on the side.

His mother had made sure Milton understood the difference between feigned deference and true submission, because after his sire's cruel dismissal of her, she'd never submitted her heart to another man. Of course she'd degraded herself plenty for men's pleasure, but it was for *her* coin, for survival. Even when Milton had been forced to grovel—clawing his way up the ranks at first wharf then warehouse, from sailing ship to gaming den, moneylender to investor—he'd retained his dignity. And damn well always would.

He'd make his rotten sire acknowledge his existence just as soon as he gained entry to the *Ton* thanks to a wife of the right kind. The bloody bugger still held too much influence in upper echelons to allow his bastard son a British baronetcy, but in Scotland they'd cared only for whoreson Jasper Audrey's money, not his birth. Which was why the deceased Baron of Milton's Scottish title and lands were now *his*.

With Miss Winthrop as his wife, he'd show London's toffs he was their equal. Though at present his betrothed could barely see the nose on her face. Li's maids had snatched her spectacles, reminding him of Elizabeth's defiance in his carriage, of how deliciously she'd knelt before him, hips flaring over a backside that begged to be slapped.

She'd passed his test spectacularly by showing such serious mettle, for he knew the *Ton* would taunt her for her unfortunate eyepiece. Still, if she could withstand him, she could withstand society's titters.

He peered more closely at his bride-to-be, whose nape flowed in perfect proportion to her skull, her neck in lovely concert with the rest of her torso. How in the world he'd never noticed the shape of a woman's head before perplexed him. Perhaps it was those spectacles hooked over her dainty, elfin ears, but she was like a lithe sprite from the waist up, and a lush Rubens from the waist down.

The last time he'd stared so intently at a woman in

LeBrecht's was when the Duke of Allendale had all but ordered him to seduce his future Duchess in Li's *Messieurs* room.

No, his conscience corrected. Wellesley had ordered him to protect and test, not seduce. He could still picture Lady Wellesley's stocking-clad calves and ample bosom, though Miss Winthrop was endowed enough not to disappoint.

Milton shifted in his seat, his trousers tightening as Li shoved yet another dress book at him. How many bloody gowns did one woman possibly need? Though he'd not question Li's judgment. She'd been remarkably astute over the years, enough that he'd trust Li with his life—and had.

***

Elizabeth stared into the blurry void that was her own private hell. She was wilting on a dais in the middle of a room surrounded by women nipping and tucking, squeezing and fussing like gnats. She was weak from hunger and worry and wanted nothing more than to run screaming from this shop, leagues away from this baron's exacting bearing and miserable marriage suit.

Being robbed of her sight made the experience all the worse, because she could see nothing beyond a close face, though she knew he was there, watching. He was choosing *for* her, too, outfitting her entire wardrobe without consideration of her own preference for color or style. It infuriated her, his obvious need to control. She would have to carve some shred of independence, some semblance of autonomy from him before he swallowed her entire being into his own.

Unless, that is, she managed to escape marriage altogether.

Elizabeth squirmed under his penetrating gaze. He was a blur of indigo across the room, the woman by his side a haze of red silk and inky hair. They were thick as thieves, the two, scheming up her wardrobe and wedding gown. *Her wedding!*

How she wished she had her spectacles, that she might shoot them dirty looks.

She stared in the direction of Milton's muddied blue person, hoping she radiated rage, when he rose and approached the dais to bat away the maids.

He slipped her spectacles over her nose. "You look as if you are about to faint." His hands encircled her waist. "You are also more attractive than I thought."

"And you are an even greater blackguard than I thought."

"I am indeed, Miss Winthrop." He laughed and drew her closer. "You amuse as much as you infuriate, a pleasant surprise indeed." He began to pet her. "You'll suit."

Elizabeth was shocked by his words and his pleasant male scent, close as he stood. He suddenly buried his nose in her hair, but she pulled from him. "You have taken one too many liberties, Baron. Have you no sense of decorum at all?"

"Admittedly none, Miss Winthrop, which is why I am in dire need of a wife."

She frowned. "You are a rake, sir, but at least you admit it."

"Oh I'll admit to worse than that." He grinned. "But come, you must dress so we may eat. I am famished. And after, I promise to leave you alone with the modiste, because I cannot bear to sit through more fittings. Who knew a wife required more uniforms than an entire regiment of soldiers?"

He helped her off the platform and into her modest house dress, which lay draped over a waiting chair. Elizabeth felt shy, though he'd seen her from every angle already. He hooked her efficiently from behind, as if used to fastening a woman's many small clasps.

Half an hour later, they were seated in a respectable tavern a short walk away, though the blasted man had ordered *for* her, a habit Elizabeth despised. She'd like to see his choice of meal taken from him. Yet she bit her tongue, biding her time and barely picking at her plate, eating next to none of the artfully arranged sandwiches before her.

"Are you not hungry, Miss Winthrop?" Milton devoured his without ceremony.

"Oh no, sir." She forced a smile. "I am ravenous."

"Then why do you not eat?"

"Because I dislike this watercress."

"Ah," he said. "Then you'll not mind if I…?" He reached across her plate to steal one.

"By all means, sir, be my guest." She rolled her eyes as he inhaled her sandwich.

"Pray tell me what you'd prefer, Elizabeth, and I shall order it for you."

"Goodness, do not trouble yourself." She motioned the waiter over. "I don't mind ordering for myself."

She was halted by his hand on her arm. "A gentleman always orders for a lady, Lizzie."

How dare he continue to call her Lizzie! "Well, as you are admittedly no gentleman, sir, I'm sure you'll not mind my ordering my own meal."

He tightened his grip while he snapped his other fingers, making waitstaff magically appear. "Be so good as to bring the young lady whatever her heart desires." His gaze locked on hers.

"Miss?" The waiter turned to her.

"A plate of watercress sandwiches, if you please."

Milton flinched but quickly recovered. "Why Miss Winthrop," he drawled, "I thought you did not fancy watercress."

"I fancy it when ordered correctly, sir."

Instantly his hand dropped to her thigh beneath the table, squeezing so that she jumped. "Try that again"—his reach crept higher—"and I'll be forced to punish your brazen attempt to outmaneuver me." His hand slipped between her thighs, to knead her there through her skirts, where he'd touched her before.

Elizabeth reeled from the intimacy of his action, though she would not be swayed. "Tell me, Baron, do you not long, sometimes, to let go of your perverse need to control?"

His hand worked her skirts more vigorously, making her cheeks bloom with heat.

"When you've lived a life such as mine, miss, you find it of great advantage to be in control." He pressed deeper. "At all times."

She gasped, but maintained her focus. "Is that why you purchased your title, sir?" She'd use what weapons she had, having pried the information from Papa last night. "What profession did you hold before acquiring your Scottish Barony?"

His jaw muscle twitched as he abruptly slid his hand off her. "Let's see." His eyes became slits. "Counting back I've been investor, swindler, pirate, prostitute, dockworker, gravedigger, and chimney sweep. Born, of course, a whoreson."

Elizabeth sucked in her breath.

"So I assure you, Miss Winthrop, the merits of being in control of my destiny are indeed *great.*" His eyes flicked over her as if she were a crumb on his plate. "I believe we've finished here." He threw down his napkin, pushed back his chair, and yanked her from her seat. Then he marched her out of the establishment, refusing even to look at her.

Elizabeth vainly attempted to slow her breaths as he dragged her down the street. Not only had she denied herself sustenance, she'd clearly struck a nerve. In fact, she was sorry she'd antagonized the man, now knowing his humble origin.

She placed her hand on his arm. "Sir, I should like to apolo—"

"Do not touch me without permission!" He shoved her

hand away so fast she winced. "You will finish your fitting alone, Miss Winthrop."

"Of course, Baron." She bent her head, confused that her attempt at repair had been so roughly rebuked. "I hope you will forgive my indiscretion."

He merely grunted in response before he left her at the threshold of *LeBrecht's*.

She found her own way inside.

❧

"Whadya do, miss? Prick 'is pride?" one of the seamstresses asked as Elizabeth suffered another fitting.

"More like she pricked 'is dick, Rose," tittered another, head at the dress hem.

"That man's got the finest prick I e'er—" the third maid started while the one named Rose elbowed her hard, declaring, "Mae! Not a word more!"

"Though I will say, he spent the first two hours starin' at 'er long enough t'—"

"Evie!" shushed Rose. "Miss Li said not to—"

"Please," Elizabeth implored them. "I have known Baron of Milton all of one day and am in desperate need of counsel." She turned her gaze on all three, having insisted this time she retain her spectacles. "Tell me all you know of him. Spare me no detail. And who is Miss Li?"

"*All* I knows of 'im?" Evie smirked. "That's hardly proper talk fer a lady, miss."

The others laughed heartily.

"I know he is a whoreson." Elizabeth would not mince words. "And that he was a gravedigger too." She would be bold. "Please," she pleaded, "if you will not tell me more, then I shall surely offend him again, and as I do not wish to—"

"Miss," said the one named Mae, "y' can scarce offend a

man as base as Jasper Audrey. 'Sides, his prick'll keep yer happy an' his money happier still!"

More laughter erupted.

"Aye," said Rose, "long as y' does exactly as he says, he'll keep yer in fine comfort, protect yer too. Always treats us girls well, no matter what t' others say."

Elizabeth's ears pricked. "What do others say of him?"

"Why, that he's a scoundrel, o' course! Some toff's bastard son, makin' off as better'n he is, lookin' down 'is nose at all them Cornwallises out t' cut 'im."

"You mean he is not respected in society?" Elizabeth guessed 'Cornwallis' meant lord in Cockney, or something less savory, perhaps.

"Now miss." Rose rolled her eyes. "He did right up an' purchase yer fer wife, did he not? Said one day he'd buy some shite gentry's chit right out from under the man's haughty nose." She laughed so hard she nearly sucked in the pin she held between her lips.

"*Rose*!" admonished Mae. "Stop natterin'. Can't y' see the poor girl's sweet on 'im?"

"Sweet on him!" Elizabeth nearly fell off the dais. "Why, the man's an utter *arse*!" She clapped a hand over her mouth; these maids were rubbing off on her. "How could you possibly imagine me sweet on him?"

Evie poked Mae, setting her into fresh peals of laughter.

Elizabeth remained annoyed. "Really, I cannot comprehend your—"

"'Cause he's so sweet in bed, miss." Rose winked. "Best there is, trained t' please a woman, if y' know what I mean." And she suggestively licked her lips.

Elizabeth was stunned by so lewd a gesture.

"'Tis true, he's the best, is Jasper." Evie piped up. "His own mum set Li's girls t' learnin' on 'im when he were a boy, an' later had 'im initiatin' all the innocents she got. Made sure her son gave 'em one hell of a good ride afore she set 'em loose in Li's whorehouse." She laughed. "An' I should know, as I were one meself!"

Rose gave the girl a friendly shove, then met Elizabeth's eyes with kindness. "Miss, only a whore knows what it's like t' sell her body, an' Jasp knows all the tricks same as us. Buggered men even, when he had to."

"He did," Mae said softly as the girls fell quiet. "For his mum he did."

"Only he'd not let 'em bugger him," Evie declared. "He'd let no man stick no dick up his—" But the girl stopped herself from saying more, watching Elizabeth's face drain blood.

"Aw now, it's not so bad, really," Rose attempted. "A hole's a hole when there's cash on the table. Don't matter if it's a man's or woman's most days."

Madam LeBrecht swooped in just then, skirts crackling in the stillness that had befallen the room. She frowned at her maids. "I hope you harlots have not been filling Miss Winthrop's ears with gossip about her betrothed." Her gaze pierced each one.

"No, ma'am," Rose answered. "We'd ne'er speak ill o' Jasp, you know that."

"*That's* Miss Li," Mae whispered in Elizabeth's ear. "She goes by both names."

"Well I am certain Miss Winthrop has had enough of you lot for today. Come," Miss Li told Elizabeth, taking her hand to help her off the dais. "Allow me to fortify you with tea before Jasper fetches you home."

Elizabeth was grateful to descend from the maids' chaos; her ears were still ringing with all they'd divulged. Miss Li's tea, however, was unlike any she'd taken before, for it was not simply tea, it felt like a ceremony instead. She sat upon the lady's floor, on woven straw mats hidden behind silk-screened panels, her cup no cup but instead a small bowl.

The lady was not of Elizabeth's world.

Miss Li poured tea in an elegant, slow manner, bowing before Elizabeth before she bowed before the tea, then raised her bowl reverently to her lips. Elizabeth followed suit, mimicking the gesture.

"Tell me something of yourself, Miss Winthrop." Miss Li stared into her bowl. "I should like to better know the woman Jasper will marry."

Clearly, this was no social chitchat. Then again, nothing about this day was as it should have been. Elizabeth was struck by the woman's overly familiar use of Milton's first name—Jasper—which the three seamstresses had also liberally used. She decided to be blunt.

"Baron of Milton offered an exorbitant sum for my sister's hand yesterday, ma'am, having swindled our father into great debt the very night before." She controlled her emotion. "I offered myself in her place, wishing to spare my sister a man like Milton."

"Ah." Li lovingly swirled the tea in her bowl. "A wise decision, Elizabeth. May I call you Elizabeth?"

"Of course," she answered, though Miss Li did not offer the use of her own name.

"Jasper is an old acquaintance of mine. In fact, I owe him my life. I am personally invested in seeing him well settled."

Elizabeth had no words to respond to this.

"He is under the mistaken premise, however, that power and wealth can buy happiness." Her gaze flicked up from her tea. "He also believes a titled wife will open doors which remain as yet closed to him."

Elizabeth had assumed as much, but this baron was marrying the wrong woman if he thought she might improve his standing.

"Which is why I am surprised he chose you," she finished.

"I more than urged him to reconsider, Miss Li."

"No doubt you did." She again peered into the depths of her tea. "Jasper is not a man easily dissuaded," she told her, "though you may be precisely the woman he needs."

"I…" Elizabeth hesitated. "Miss Li, I must ask if everything your maids just told me is indeed true about the Baron's past."

"Of course." The lady's clear, dark eyes met Elizabeth's without guise. "Jasper is who he is because of his past, as are we all, and you would be wise to embrace *all* that he is, rather than shun who he was." She blinked a moment, as if she shoved memories back. She forced a small smile, which gradually warmed until she beamed at Elizabeth, who gaped at how radiantly beautiful the lady had suddenly become.

"He will surprise you, no doubt, as you will surprise him." Miss Li's smile held. "But I should like to hear more, my dear, about your feckless papa and sweet, younger sister. And your spectacles, Elizabeth—they are charming on a face such as yours. Were you born with poor sight or afflicted by some childhood fever?"

Elizabeth realized the lady had no intention of telling her a thing more about Baron of Milton. In fact, for the rest of the interview Miss Li grilled Elizabeth entirely about herself.

CHAPTER FOUR

The baron's wickedness knew no bounds

Elizabeth poked her chin with her quill, hemming. The story was barely an outline in her head, directionless. It needed both defining and fleshing out. Yet it helped distract her from the wicked thoughts she would not admit to having. It was not *she* who'd dreamt of the brooding baron's lustful touch, but the ruined lady in her story who could not resist her evil captor.

She reread her last line, picking up where she'd left off.

The baron's wickedness knew no bounds, for this time he'd bound the lady's wrists, her tears flowing down her pale

"Drat." Elizabeth's ink smeared; she blotted the line as best she could, realizing she'd used the word 'bound' twice.

"Lizzie!" Annabelle's voice carried up from the foyer into Elizabeth's bedroom. "The Baron has sent more flowers. Red tulips this time!"

Elizabeth steeled herself for another of her betrothed's

wretched notes, in what was becoming a tired joke. She sprinkled pounce on the page, shook it back into the pot, then laid the sheaf atop her stack and headed down to breakfast.

My dear Elizabeth, I have determined a ride about the park with my betrothed in my new phaeton suits today's fine weather. I shall arrive at two and expect you, this time, to be punctual. —Milton

Punctual! she fumed. Well, two could play at this. She would indeed be punctual. In fact, she'd be more punctual than he would.

Elizabeth carried the man's disgusting, 'declare-his-love' tulips to the front entrance and dumped the lot upon the step.

Milton drove his new phaeton toward the Winthrop residence with uncharacteristic unease. He'd not intended to reveal his past to his betrothed so soon, but the way she'd taunted him at lunch, flaunting her birth in his face, had been insufferable. Miss Winthrop had demonstrated precisely what he hated about her class—and the very reason he needed her for a wife.

That he'd had to buy his title was a necessity he'd long resisted, because by rights a far greater title ought to have been his at birth. Some gentry chose to elevate their bastards' stations in life, but his spiteful sire had not. Milton's father was a different sort of 'bastard' altogether: a legitimate bloody prick.

No doubt sweet Elizabeth had been repulsed by his sullied lineage and gone crying to her papa last night to insist he dissolve their engagement. Only Winthrop would do no such thing; Milton had the man by his cobblers. It mattered little which daughter he wed, though Elizabeth's fierce glare atop her aristocratic neck, starkly profiled on Li's dais, had made his own bollocks ache.

He was still picturing Miss Winthrop's charms when he pulled up before her father's townhouse and lashed the phaeton's horse to the post. As he approached, he noted petals again stained the ground. He stepped over the blooms in his boots and was about to rap the knocker when the door opened to Miss Winthrop herself, dressed smartly, and on time.

"Why, Miss Winthrop, you—"

Her frown was severe. "You are late, sir." She pointed to the foyer's ticking long-case clock. "It is a minute past two and your note stressed punctuality."

He hid his grin behind a cough. "Elizabeth, your timeliness astounds, truly. I am so pleased you accepted my invitation for a drive, though I see my bouquets continue to—" his eyes flitted to the red dusting beneath his feet—"disappoint."

"Indeed, sir, coming as they do straight from a hothouse rather than from true-heated sentiment."

"Then I shall endeavor to do better." He extended her his arm. "Shall we?"

Miss Winthrop accepted. As they neared his gleaming phaeton, however, she abruptly stopped. "Goodness, I have forgotten my parasol, and it is much too bright to go without. I shall be but a moment, sir, forgive me." She headed back inside, leaving him to wait.

And wait he did, for the lady took her time to fetch said parasol, making Milton remove his timepiece from his pocket more than once.

At a quarter past two he began to suspect she'd not taken yesterday's lesson to heart.

When she at last emerged, she apologized profusely for the delay, though as he handed her up into his phaeton, she waved her parasol all too enthusiastically at the woman next door.

"Hello-o, Lady Stanton! I say, good day to you! Have you

met my intended? Do come and greet him. I simply *must* show him off."

Miss Winthrop swiftly stepped back down from Milton's vehicle, took his arm again in grip, and marched him determinedly in the direction of her neighbor.

What the devil did she have up her sleeve this time?

"Why, Lizzie!" the lady exclaimed. "Intended?" She clutched her hands to her formidable breast. "Since when are you betrothed, my dear, and to such a handsome gentleman?" The matron bent to scoop a wriggling pug into her arms, but not before giving Milton a saucy wink.

Christ, had he serviced her in past? Milton winced at the thought, realizing his wife would have to navigate a host of former clients he'd once taken for pay.

"Lady Stanton, this is my betrothed, Baron of Milton. He has offered me a ride in his fine new phaeton, is it not exquisite?" Elizabeth caught his eye, making Milton bite his tongue at her boldness.

"It is indeed a fine carriage, most fine." Lady Stanton appraised the vehicle. "Though I admit, I am not familiar with the Milton Barony. Is it—?"

"It is a Scottish Barony." Lizzie spared him further explanation, exactly as a wife should. "And how is Sir Wigglebottom today, Lady Stanton?" She tickled the rotund creature's chin, neatly changing tack.

"Naughty as always, Lizzie. *Very* naughty, aren't you?" Lady Stanton proceeded to regale them at length about her pet's adventures, making Milton's ears twitch. If there was one thing he hated more than pugs, it was ladies who waxed on in excruciating detail about their pets.

Not to mention fiancées who deliberately stalled.

He pulled out his timepiece, noting it was now a full five minutes *past* the half hour. He snapped it shut with a click loud enough Miss Winthrop flinched.

About time she noticed.

"Lady Stanton." He tucked Lizzie's arm in an iron-proof clasp. "I am exceedingly sorry to interrupt your stories of Sir Wigglebottom, but I really must see Miss Winthrop escorted to the park." He gripped her close. "I've a surprise planned for her, you see, which simply cannot wait."

"Oh?" The lady's eyes twinkled. "But of course, sir, don't let me detain you. It has been a pleasure to meet you." She extended him her hand, which he refused to kiss, it having been slobbered on by pug.

"Lizzie, dear, you must call on me posthaste, that I learn all there is to know about your handsome Baron." The matron shot him a sly, parting glance. "Tea perhaps, tomorrow?" she hinted, while he all but hoisted Miss Winthrop back into his phaeton.

"Tomorrow would be lovely, Lady Stanton, shall we say two o'clock?" Lizzie's eyes met Milton's and did not blink.

Devil take this girl, she needed training like he needed air to breathe. And he needed to regain control fast. He steadied his nearly shaking hands as he climbed atop and took the reins to urge the phaeton forward, at last.

He drove them in stony silence.

"You are quiet today, sir." Elizabeth attempted conversation even as she nervously licked her lips. Milton chose not to respond. She did not know him nearly well enough to be testing him at so furious a pace, which is why he let her stew a while longer in silence, in anticipation of his 'surprise.'

Milton had not intended to surprise Miss Winthrop today with anything but a leisurely drive about the park, to show her off to the *Ton's* promenading gossips. He'd purchased the phaeton for this express purpose, finding carriages like these ridiculous, but lords and ladies liked to show off their wealth, so he behaved just as frivolously.

He snuck a peek at his betrothed, who still worried her lips.

He imagined nibbling her plush pout until he had her panting beneath him like the pug had panted at Elizabeth's touch. Her thigh bumped his on the high, narrow bench, making his breeches pull taut. He gripped the reins tighter as she shifted in her seat, heat sparking. But when her palm abruptly landed on his leg he jerked, snarling, "Hands off!"

***

"Oh I—forgive me, I did not mean to offend." Elizabeth was quite caught off guard, for the Baron seemed unduly upset by her simply steadying herself.

He pulled the horse up, grinding the phaeton to a stop. "Did I not tell you *never* to touch me unless I gave my permission?"

"You did." She gulped. "Sir."

"And did I not express my preference for punctuality but yesterday too?"

"You did, Baron. I—"

"Yet you continue to do *everything* in your power to show me the very opposite of obedience and respect."

Too late, Elizabeth realized playing with fire would likely get her scorched.

"I do not think you understand what I expect of a wife, miss." He hopped down from the phaeton only to haul her from her seat and drag her in the direction of the woods, straight toward a thicket.

"Baron, please, you cannot—" She looked in desperation all about her, but not a couple or carriage was in sight. He marched her deeper into the trees where no one would notice them, find them, come for them. "Sir—"

"Not a word more, Elizabeth," he ordered harshly, "or your punishment will be that much more severe."

"*Punishment*?" she exclaimed, and immediately shut her lips.

She must lessen, rather than fuel, this man's wrath, though her own wrath bubbled just below her fear.

He dragged her into a small clearing, then plunked himself down atop a fallen tree trunk and hauled her, head down, across his lap. He raised her skirts full over her waist and gripped her bottom, causing Elizabeth to freeze, her mind falling blank.

She blinked as he pressed down on the small of her back and something hard pressed up against her belly. Then he struck her buttock with his palm, making her exclaim in shock, "What are you—?"

He struck again, her other cheek, his slap stinging, though he struck her through her drawers. Realizing, at last, what he was about, she began to squirm against his hold, desperate to escape the blows he now rained down in ever more heavy-handed smacks.

"Let me go!" she cried in horror. "You are … You are *hurting* me!"

Only the Baron did not heed her pleas. He continued to spank her, his blows harsh enough to start tears in her eyes.

And then, just as suddenly, he stopped to catch his breath.

Elizabeth remained over his lap, stunned, as his hand briefly, gently rubbed her smarting cheeks. Before he viciously tore her drawers in two, exposing flesh.

She thrashed with all her might to escape the Baron's clutches, but he held firm, the bulge in his pants pressing more deeply into her belly. This time he kneaded her blazing buttocks with a more controlled, rhythmic grip.

"I told you not to cross me, Lizzie." His voice brooked no argument. "I warned you I would punish disobedience, yet you flaunted it in my face." His hand still kneaded and stroked, eliciting an altogether different, strange feeling in her gut. "Had you but heeded my words and obeyed me, I should not have needed to punish you as I just did. And will again, if you continue to challenge my authority."

She bit her tongue, debating furiously how to argue her way out of this, fuming that any man should treat her like some misbehaving child. She was suddenly afraid he might do worse, alone with her in these woods.

"I know what you are thinking." His voice sounded off, gruff. "You think I am no better than a beast, to strike a woman's arse, then stroke her blushing cheeks." His touch, if possible, only intensified her body's inexplicable, irrational response. A moan escaped her lips, the sound embarrassingly wanton, needy almost. He pressed his hips harder into her belly. "But there are men and women aplenty in this world, Lizzie, lords and ladies finer than yourself even, who have paid me to strike them thus, begged me to beat their backsides raw, whip them naked and trussed, desperate for debasement."

She shuddered.

"I have seen the depravity of men, women, and children, Elizabeth, and nothing, I tell you *nothing* shocks me anymore. So if you think you can control me, tease or manipulate me into indulging your whims and becoming your puppet, you've another think coming." He inhaled a slow breath. "Do you understand me now, Miss Winthrop?"

She remained silent, her heart pounding in her ears, with fear, rage, and—

"*Do you?*" his hand urged, slipping between her legs to tease her aching center, wet enough he slid his finger inside again, forcing a different, more shameful moan from her lips. It was impossible she should now feel pleasure. Impossible! But she ground against his hand, despite her fear and loathing. Despite all better sense.

"Good girl," he crooned, making her abhor how her flesh craved the unseemly pleasure he now offered. His hand worked her deeper, stoking her inner fire, building sensations perilously, embarrassingly close, far too—

"*Beg me, Lizzie,*" he whispered in her ear, so near she felt the heat of his words while his hand kept her unbearably close to climax. "Beg for your release and just maybe"—his finger caressed her into fresh agony—"I will grant it."

Elizabeth wept, a cry rent from her throat which tore through her chest as she pleaded for release, reduced to utter, sodding servitude. Suffused with shame, she begged him for relief.

And in his wicked mercy, the Baron granted her explosive wish, right before he spanked her again, that much harder.

When it was over, her body shook, her thoughts an utter mess. The Baron merely gathered her sobbing person to his chest and kissed the top of her head.

Elizabeth cried herself silly on his lapels, weeping less for what her betrothed had just done and more for all she'd endured for years: her father's incessant lies, her mother and stepmother's deaths, the constant stream of moneylenders she'd been forced to deflect, marriage suits she'd fought to reject—all of it done to protect and shield Annabelle. Every past grief now came rushing back, flooding her with feelings so acute a knot of pain burst in a torrent of emotion she'd kept dammed up for years.

A wall inside her had just crumbled, and with it, a slew of old fears. All this had been accomplished with but a few harsh strokes of the Baron's steady hand, the irony of it not lost on her otherwise confused, conflicted mind. Elizabeth's soul felt undeniably lighter, as if emptied of a vast and weighty fog.

She lifted her head from his tear-dampened waistcoat to

say "Thank you" to the man who'd just handily spanked her bum. "I believe I may have … needed that," she clarified, exhausted.

"Hmm." He stroked her hair, which had escaped its pins. "Perhaps y' did, miss." His voice sounded different, softer. "I am sorry I hurt you, Lizzie."

"I am sorry I goaded you, sir."

"Hmm," he mused again.

"Mmm," she hummed in response.

They remained this way a while longer, each lost in thought as he continued to pet her. Somewhere deep inside, she did not want the moment to end.

"Elizabeth." He broke the spell. "Do you feel well enough now to—?"

"Yes, I am better." She righted herself on his lap, careful of her bottom, then stared up at him, close enough to notice his features had softened, relaxed. "My spectacles though. They must have fallen when you—"

***

"Christ, I forgot all about your blasted eyepiece." Milton berated himself for being so careless. He removed her from his lap, only to watch her wince as she settled on the rough log.

He searched for her lenses amidst the forest debris until *crunch*, he plucked a mess of bent wire and cracked glass from the ground, dangling the eyepiece before Elizabeth.

"Forgive me, Lizzie. I ought to have—"

"It is I, sir, who ought to have removed them the moment you…" She blushed an even deeper shade of red.

Milton sat beside her on the log and took her hand. "I shall purchase you another pair, no, three," he declared. "In addition to a spare, you shall have wedding spectacles to match your wedding dress. I should have thought of this before. I am an idiot not to have."

He heard her snort. Good lord, had she just giggled?

"You cannot possibly find this situation amusing, miss. Not after the—"

"Rather thorough spanking you just gave me?" She giggled again. "Forgive me, I cannot seem to hold back my feelings." More mirth bubbled out. "First I weep and now this need to simply … *Oh*!"

Fresh tears rolled down her cheeks from laughter so infectious he shook his head at her in disbelief.

"It is just…" She struggled against hysteria. "You must so desperately hate pugs, sir. Because the look on your face when Lady Stanton offered you the hand her beast had licked … *Oh*!" she burst out again, until he gave himself over to the same raucous relief.

"Miss Winthrop, I despise them." He chuckled. "I despise all small dogs, but pugs most of all with their—"

"Horrid, mushed-up, squishy faces," Elizabeth finished his thought. "I hate them too. I hate Lady Stanton most of all though." She instantly covered her mouth, as if shocked by what she'd just uttered.

A second later, though, she burst into renewed peals of laughter, and Milton found himself shaking his head at his betrothed, amazed.

"She is the most odious neighbor ever." Elizabeth struggled to catch her breath. "And in my great and awful stupidity I must now take tea with that … horrid woman tomorrow." She gulped more air. "Oh, why did I do it, sir? Why do I do the things I do?" Her laughter faded, giddiness receding as swiftly as it had begun.

Milton again took her hand. "We shall visit her together, Elizabeth. It is the perfect ploy. Why, I could not have devised a better plan myself. For she is a gossip, I assume, and what we need now is for all of London to know we are betrothed. Because our marriage will shock the *Ton*. You must prepare yourself."

"So you still intend to marry me?"

He had a mad desire to kiss the crease upon her forehead. "Of course, Miss Winthrop, why would you think otherwise?"

"Because you just…" She stared at him. "Sir, I do not think my sister would suit you."

He wanted so badly to taste her lips his loins tightened with lust. "Of course she would not suit. That is why I did not offer for her."

Her eyes grew wide, but she did not press him more, she looked away, shy. It was at once endearing and arousing.

"And may I ask what surprise you had in store for me today, sir, before I ruined it?"

"Oh, I should hardly think you ruined a thing." He did not wish to tell her the spanking was the surprise. "You have surprised *me* this day instead. Come." He stood to pull her upright, then helped straighten her skirts. "We must procure you new spectacles, but first we must fix your hair. You look a fright."

"I did not mean to anger you before, you know."

He began to fix her coiffure.

"In your phaeton, I mean, when I touched your leg." She paused. "It was not meant to provoke you as it so clearly did."

"I apologize for my reaction," he told her, "but I have been touched in ways I…" A crass cackle echoed maliciously in his head, bubbling from depths he kept well under lock and key. Milton's heart pounded in his chest. "It is best you ask permission first, always."

"Then may I touch you now?"

He extinguished a final flicker of callous laughter. "Yes."

She caressed the side of his face in a touch so tender he thought he'd perish on the spot.

"You are not the devil I thought you, sir." Her hand felt unbearably light at his cheek; he covered it to keep her from touching him more.

"And you are not at all the woman I thought you, Miss Winthrop."

❧

That night in her bedroom, Elizabeth's quill scratched a furious pace, sentences tumbling onto parchment with terrific speed. She left words half spelled, prepositions missing, articles dropping like the petals of some nodding, rain-drenched rose. Inside her brewed a storm, emotions threatening to crest. She wanted, *needed,* more of that unfettered peace the Baron had inexplicably granted. Until today the only way she'd known to quell her rage was to expel it onto paper. But now a new path had been delivered by her betrothed's heavy hand.

Her bottom tingled faintly, a reminder of the relief she'd not only welcomed but embraced, even if the man behind that relief still gave her pause. Baron of Milton remained frightfully exacting, after all. Yet what if he were less dangerous, wild beast and more the falconer who captured and then released? Elizabeth no longer knew with whom she dealt. She simply wrote her story, ink spilling across the page.

> *The baron's hand, heavy on the lady's head, stroked her as she clung to his legs, her head in his lap, weeping. She did not know herself, could not reconcile her grief with such intense, unchecked longing. Nevermore would she see her family—her siblings and her poor, suffering mama. She wept tears of regret, but also tears of joy, for he had given her a gift most unimaginable. The brooding baron had broken her spirit, but caused her to break free of all her chains. She*

could not bear his touch but longed to touch him. She could not bear his presence but longed to remain beside him.

Like the Sphinx he was a riddle she must solve to survive imprisonment. If she did not, the baron would consume her. Yet if she did…

No, he would consume her.

CHAPTER FIVE

Before settling in that night, Milton poured himself a brandy and grabbed *The Marriage of Heaven and Hell* from his stack of bedside books. Mutton lay beside him in his usual place upon the floor, the wolfhound's tail thumping for attention. Milton tried to read Blake's poems, but his thoughts returned again to Miss Winthrop's giddy laughter in the woods, to her peculiar expression of hurt and gratitude when he'd purchased her those new spectacles. She may come from finer stock than he did, but he knew hunger when he saw it. He also knew mistrust.

She was wary of gifts, and wary of him.

His mind replayed how he'd shown the young lady a needed lesson in control. He regretted taming her in the park, because one's future wife deserved better than a harried thrashing outdoors. Yet the manner in which she'd goaded and provoked had given him no choice but to make good on his threats.

He pictured her strawberry-red bottom and willed his cock to subside. He would have to teach her other, less pleasant lessons in the days leading up to their wedding, but he now feared those lessons less—feared their union less—though no doubt theirs would be a 'marriage of heaven and hell' just like Blake foretold.

He returned to his book, dogged by thoughts of Miss Winthrop. Her response to his punishment still surprised him. She may be a titled member of the *Ton*, but she was no lily-livered miss. She'd stood up to that butcher, stood up to her father, and repeatedly, it seemed, stood up to him. She would not cross him again though, of this he was certain. Nor would she willingly subject her sister to the demands he'd wrung from Elizabeth's body today. No, Miss Winthrop was up to the task of marriage. And she'd need her fortitude if she were to survive being both his wife and mother to his children. He needed her obedience, but he also needed her strength.

Both would test his mettle, much as he still needed to test hers.

"Lizzie!" Bella's voice roused her from her sleep. "Lizzie, you've another note!"

This time Elizabeth did not scowl at her sister's announcement but smiled secretly to herself, easing her sore bottom from bed to don her fraying banyan and make her way downstairs to breakfast. What message would the Baron deliver with this morning's bouquet?

> *My dear Elizabeth, I hope today's blooms better suit. I shall arrive at two and steel myself for rePUGnant conversation with your neighbor. Wear your new gold spectacles and I shall know you have forgiven me yesterday's liberties. —Milton*

She lowered her nose to sample the modest cornflowers winking from their vase upon the foyer's narrow table. They were as blue as his eyes and whispered their intention loud and clear: She would indeed be gentle with him today. She felt she could afford to, now that her feelings toward the Baron had shifted. He was still an impudent, randy whoreson, but he was clearly something more. Miss Li's words echoed in her head: *Accept the man Milton has been, not just the man he shows himself to be.*

She was admittedly now curious to know her future husband.

"What does he write, Lizzie?" Annabelle craned her neck across the dining room table to peer at Elizabeth through the door.

Elizabeth slipped the note into her pocket and proceeded in to breakfast, her thoughts awash with blue flowers. She did not share the missive with Bella but simply sat down to butter her toast, her mind replaying yesterday's events. Spanking aside, Milton had shockingly fixed her hair, a skill no gentleman she knew possessed. And when he'd driven them straight to an eyeglass shop after, he'd purchased her not two but *three* expensive eyepieces. A silver-rimmed pair to replace the one his boot had smashed, a gold-rimmed spare, plus mother-of-pearl inlaid spectacles commissioned especially to match her wedding gown.

She was about to take a bite of her toast, still overcome by her betrothed's generosity, when her father barked, "Lizzie!"

She looked up from her plate.

"Have you heard a word I've said?"

"Forgive me, Father, I am rather tired this morning," she lied.

"We must know whom to invite to this wedding of yours," he decreed. "And as Baron of Milton does not deign to answer my correspondence nor honor me with his presence"—he loudly harrumphed—"it is incumbent on you to ascertain the details."

"Of course, Papa, I shall ask him today."

He squinted at her. "Are those new spectacles you are wearing?"

Elizabeth stiffened. "Yes. The Baron took me shopping."

"Did he?" A gleam lit her father's eye. "And what else did he buy you, my dear?"

"A wedding dress and wardrobe, nothing of value *you* might steal."

His face flushed. "Elizabeth Winthrop, I did not raise you to be insolent."

"Of course not, Papa." She resumed eating her toast. "You scarce raised me at all."

She ignored her father's glare and Annabelle's searching looks for the rest of breakfast, instead recalling Milton's parting words from yesterday. He'd ardently pressed her hand to his lips at her doorstep to whisper, "You may wish to have a long, hot soak in your bath tonight, miss, lest your bottom still smart come morning."

"And *you* may wish to prepare yourself for pugnacious interview tomorrow with Lady Stanton, sir. I must warn you the lady's twin siblings, the Mrs. R. and Mrs. M., are even more odious than her pug."

He'd tapped her nose with the tip of one gloved finger. "I cannot *wait* to enjoy their company, Miss Winthrop, and yours."

At precisely two o'clock Milton stood upon a shockingly clean threshold, though he was ushered in by a different, more unkempt footman this time, who hollered crassly up the stairs, "Yer betrothed's 'ere, miss!"

He rolled his eyes at a household in such disarray, then tossed a coin to the lowlife dressed in livery. Had Milton not just forgiven Winthrop's gaming debt and more than paid back the man's losses with the sum settled on Elizabeth? Ample funds to keep a proper footman, pay off a leering butcher, and settle whatever other debts this lord had.

Unless Winthrop's affairs were in even worse straits than Li assumed.

Milton heard steps descending the stairs and looked up to see Elizabeth wearing her new gold spectacles. *One test passed nicely.* His heart leapt. *Now to see if she passes the next…*

He took her arm. "Miss Winthrop, you are a vision. I gather my bouquet was better received today?"

"It was, sir."

The small, blue cornflower tucked into her dark hair made him swallow. "Good." He patted her arm and led her out. "Only tell me quickly all I must know before we sit down with the esteemed Lady Stanton. I should like to be prepared for conversation as *pugnacious* as you warn."

She pulled something from her pocket. "Before we embark, sir, Cook found this in her kitchen, and I could only presume—"

"Thank you, Miss Winthrop, I have missed my kidskin. Though I thought, perhaps, you might have kept the glove, to remember me by?"

She blushed prettily. "I must warn you, sir, Lady Stanton shall undoubtedly ask how we met. We must have a story for her and her sisters to chew on, but it must not agitate."

"Ah." Milton squelched his grin. "What sort of story, do you think?"

His betrothed worried her lip again in such a fetching way he wished to hoist her back into his phaeton for another spanking foray.

"A slightly wicked story, sir." Those lips cracked a smile. "The *Ton* likes nothing better than a scandalous start to a marriage, though ours should not be too scandalous, mind."

Her brow creased. "I'd hate to see my sister tainted by anything untoward."

"Of course." He patted her arm in reassurance. "I shall think of something appropriately wicked, Miss Winthrop, have no fear."

She gazed at him with such newly trusting eyes he felt like a cad to deceive her. Instead, he brushed off the thought and bent his head to her ear. "And did you take that bath last night, Elizabeth, as ordered?" His arm dropped to her waist to slip low over her backside.

"Sir!"

"Did it soothe your aching bum?" He wanted his words to ignite her. "Because I admit I imagined you soaking in the water's warm embrace. I imagined every inch of you naked in your bath, the liquid caressing your heated flesh. You've such a lovely, lush bottom, Lizzie..."

She let out a squeak as Lady Stanton's footman opened the townhouse door and announced, "Baron of Milton and Miss Elizabeth Winthrop to see you, madam."

Twenty minutes later, Lady Stanton's parlor maid poured Elizabeth her third cup of tea. She'd been sipping for sheer nerves, though *why* she was so nervous she'd no idea. She'd visited her neighbor's home often enough.

Though never with her betrothed.

Portly Sir Wigglebottom panted at Elizabeth's feet, the dog's drool wetting her dress hem. She tried nudging him with her toe, but his squat little form would not budge. Milton sat close beside her, his masculine scent invading her nostrils in the cramped, stuffy room. Lady Stanton's damask drapes suffocated, her plush carpet too dark and too dense. When the Baron's hand promptly slid to Elizabeth's lap, the weight of his palm traveled straight up her thigh, making her only more skittish.

Did he mean to soothe or unsettle? And had the man no sense at how *improper* his hand's placement was?

"Lady Stanton, it is an honor, truly, to be welcomed so warmly into your home." Milton's teeth smiled, just not his eyes.

"Oh the honor is all mine, sir." The lady's lips pulled into a grin, her eyes flitting to her sisters, who stared stonily at Milton's hand on Elizabeth's skirt. "But now tell us, *do*, how it is you met our Lizzie, for she is not one to attend society's functions often. One is more apt to find her tucked into a window somewhere, her nose squarely in a book." Her laugh was shrill.

Elizabeth's teacup rattled her plate. "Indeed, Lady Stanton, you know me well." She took a hot sip and turned to Milton. "I am more inclined to lose myself in the pages of good fiction, you see, rather than in the fiction that is good society."

He squeezed her leg approvingly. "Lady Stanton, you must divulge more of my betrothed, for I know too little of Miss Winthrop's predilections."

"And how long *have* you known our Lizzie, Baron?" Lady Stanton's brow arched.

"Why, all of four days now, isn't it, dear?"

Elizabeth winced.

"Four days?" The lady's brow inched higher. "What whirlwind romance is this?"

Her sisters, as one, leaned forward in their seats.

"Well, I…" Milton smiled disarmingly at his audience. "Shall I tell them, dearest? You won't mind, will you?"

Alarm bells rang in Elizabeth's head, though she flashed him a sincere enough smile. "Oh, I trust you'll do our story justice, sir."

Milton patted Elizabeth's lap. "As I am sure you are aware, ladies"—the trio leaned further in to listen—"Miss

Winthrop's father is most keen on cards. So keen, in fact, I met him but a few nights past at the tables of an upstanding gaming establishment. And being, of course, an upstanding man myself, I let matters rest until the morrow, when I presented myself at his residence to collect my winnings. Only imagine who should greet me there instead of his lordship..."

Elizabeth's gut twisted as he left the three ladies hanging.

"Why, Miss Winthrop herself. Then imagine, if you would, my surprise when the young lady quite stole my arm and led me to her father's kitchen. In no time at all I was called to defend her honor before some scoundrel of a butcher come round to collect *his* debt. Indeed, Miss Winthrop was a veritable paragon of virtue when she thanked me for having come to her rescue, though I was astounded that a lady of her character should offer herself so wholly and unabashedly to one such as my—"

Lady Stanton's jaw dropped as Elizabeth's heart ceased beating.

"—self, and for such price as *she* negotiated on behalf of her darling papa." He let out an appreciative whistle. "Ladies, I was smitten. Nay, entranced. I did not hesitate to offer Lord Winthrop five thousand pounds for his beautiful, brave daughter, and was overjoyed to find my sum accepted with delight."

Elizabeth nearly cast up the contents of her stomach.

"And since that day, I have spent each and every afternoon in the company of my betrothed, overjoyed Miss Winthrop is to be my wife. I could not have dreamed a better match." He leaned back against the chaise as three shocked faces blinked back at him in horror.

Elizabeth violently pushed his hand from her lap, but that same hand pinned her forcefully to her seat.

With a choked gasp, Lady Stanton began to breathe again. "Elizabeth." Her voice trembled. "Is it true, dear, that you—

why, that you offered *yourself* to the Baron in lieu of-of payment for your father's *debts*?" She barely whispered the last word.

Elizabeth drew up every shred of pride she had. "I did indeed, Lady Stanton, offer myself in place of my sister, whose hand, I should clarify, went for Milton's five thousand whereas mine was worth a mere—"

"Elizabeth." Milton shifted in his seat. "I gave your father five for you, not four."

She refused to look at him. She could not. "Baron of Milton is overly modest." Her tongue felt like caked dirt. "For while I cannot deny my actions that day, I admit my motives were less mercenary in nature. You see, the Baron's exceptionally handsome bearing and oh-so-gallant behavior quite overcame my feminine faculties such that I simply *swooned* at the thought of becoming his wife."

Milton inhaled a hiss.

"I was so taken by his wealth of charm and bold powers of persuasion, ladies, that I'd have done anything to have him." She violently pushed his hand from her person to inch closer to the edge of the chaise, leaning forward so that her knees nearly touched Lady Stanton's skirts. "*Anything* at all."

The lady startled so violently Elizabeth took the opportunity to stand and nudge the pug from her feet. She continued to lie through her teeth. "And now if you'll excuse me, I really must check on Annabelle, as my sister's felt poorly all morning and I promised we'd call but a short while at your home. *Do* continue to regale the Baron of my penchants and pursuits, however. After all, you know me so very well, Lady Stanton. And as my betrothed is so enamored of your pug"—she was too angry to look at Milton—"I would not dream of stealing him from your company just yet. Good day, ladies."

She curtsied before making the fastest exit of her life, heading straight for her father's house and as far as humanly possible from the awful, utter scoundrel she was betrothed to.

Beast!

***

Milton discovered not only Sir Wigglebottom pressed firmly to his lap, but six eyeballs trained in great anticipation on his person. He was shocked by the way Miss Winthrop had just turned tables on him, utterly.

He remained, as manners required, fifteen minutes longer to listen to the three excruciating women wax rhapsodic about his future wife. He allowed the pug to drool upon his thigh. He even took the crumpet handed him to feed said pug small bites, letting it lap crumbs from his trousers with its leathery tongue. But the moment the room's clock ticked past the quarter mark he deposited the panting pug upon the chaise and excused himself.

A certain conversation urgently needed to happen.

"Elizabeth!" Milton bellowed five minutes later from her father's foyer. "Elizabeth Winthrop!" He blew right past the upstart footman. "Out of my way." He pushed aside her simpering papa, who withdrew at once, the coward.

Yet when he reached a door blocked by Elizabeth's sister, Milton stopped short.

"Miss Annabelle," he stated, "kindly step aside."

"Baron," she leveled at him, "Lizzie does not wish to see you."

His nose twitched as he stared down at her from his height. "Yet see her I must."

"I'm afraid I can't allow that, sir."

Courageous, he thought, but she'd soon cave. He tried a different approach. "I assure you not a hair on Elizabeth's head will be hurt once I enter her room. I wish only to converse with her."

"It is improper." Her face was too pretty for her frown. "A

gentleman may not visit a lady's bedroom unaccompanied, even if she is his—"

He stepped so close his waistcoat brushed her chest. "In case you hadn't noticed, miss, I am no gentleman."

She sucked in her breath.

"I can, however, give you my word no harm will come to your sister." The sheer proximity of his body made her finally step aside.

If only it were that simple with her sister, Milton thought as he pushed past Annabelle Winthrop straight into Elizabeth's room.

He took in her private space before he noticed her person, gazing out the window, back turned to him. His betrothed's bedroom was filled with books. In fact, the room looked remarkably like a library. Perhaps it had even been this home's library once. Books lined shelves which lined two mirroring walls, stacks of even more books piled upon every surface. Correspondence, too, lay about the space, amidst piles of parchment and ink.

Was she some would-be scholar or secret novelist? Never in his life had he seen a bedroom so decidedly *un*feminine. Its sole womanly touch was a small dressing table in one corner, pushed up against more bookshelves, with but a silver hair-brush and hand mirror laid atop.

"You are *despicable*." She spoke without turning, her posture ramrod straight.

"Come now, Elizabeth, surely you did not expect me to—"

"I expected you to be a man and not an arse!" She whirled about.

He took a step toward her. "I did nothing but speak the truth."

"Oh yes. After we'd agreed in advance to but a mildly colorful story to set them all aflutter." Her chest heaved with fury. "Instead, you chose to divulge the infinitely more scandalous, wicked truth. What a lovely wedding gift you have given me, sir." Her voice dripped venom. "What a ruinous gift you have given my sister as well," she seethed. "For now all future suitors will undoubtedly consider her just as willing to whore herself in marriage as I so clearly whored myself to you, for your rotten purse!"

Milton hardened. "Do not speak flippantly of whores, Elizabeth, given you are about to marry one."

Her eyes turned into saucers.

"I also advise you see your intended for how the *Ton* sees me: a degenerate, illegitimate bastard who purchased his title outright, a man so debased he must also purchase himself a wife. And then, Elizabeth, I urge you to imagine such talk as had I *not* told Lady Stanton the truth. Imagine, instead, I'd spun some sweet little lie about sweeping you off your feet, of making you fall so in love with me that you were blind to my defects, blind to my very origin. Imagine the rumors then as to your character, Lizzie, for surely the *Ton* would but deem you an ignorant chit, more foolish than even the lowest scullery who knows better than to allow a man as depraved as myself to seduce her silly."

He steadied himself. "Would you not rather they know the truth instead? That you acted nobly, honorably, in self-sacrifice to your family? Would you not rather the *Ton* see you as I did that day, as a woman of character and strength? For I have no intention of allowing society to degrade my future wife, Elizabeth. I warned you marriage to me would not be easy. I would rather be honest now and suffer both your scorn and theirs, than spin tales that will only come back to hurt our family worse, in years to come."

***

Elizabeth collapsed onto her bed, her hand gripping her

bedpost as the magnitude of his words sank in. She was indeed marrying a degenerate, a scoundrel of the worst sort, and the *Ton* knew it, would let *her* know it, and would unfailingly judge and abuse her sister in kind. He was doing her a favor to be so brutal now, even though it hurt like the devil to know she'd be an outcast, Bella treated little better. She'd agreed to this marriage to spare her sister, but it seemed she could not save her. Annabelle would bear the stain of this union too.

Bitter resignation swept through her.

"Lizzie…" He took a step closer.

"Don't." She shook her head, refusing to look at him.

"I am sorry," he told her softly.

"No." Her eyes met his, her insides quivering. "You are far from sorry, sir. You knew exactly what you were doing when you swindled my father, just as you knew precisely what to say to Lady Stanton and her sisters today. Everything you have done thus far has been calculated with intent. You may be some nobleman's by-blow, but you clearly have an agenda, and a wicked one at that. I don't know what it is you intend to accomplish with this marriage, but you care a deal much what society thinks, else you'd not be orchestrating things in such a backhanded manner. And I do not understand your need for what is beginning to feel decidedly like, well, revenge."

He visibly stiffened.

"Please, leave." She inhaled her next breath with difficulty. "Now that news of our betrothal will spread, there is no need for us to be seen together. And there is certainly no need for us to spend time together in order for you to pretend you remotely *care*."

He took a step closer. "I am not done speaking with you, Elizabeth."

"Well *I* am done speaking with you!"

For a split second the Baron looked stunned. But then he grabbed her face and forced a kiss that brutally invaded her senses. Elizabeth could barely breathe, his palms crushing her jaw as he angled her head for access. He devoured her in full, lips breaking free only to travel down her cheek and suckle her neck till she was sure that he had marked her.

When he finally pulled away, he held her chin so she was compelled to look at him. "I will see you each day until we marry, Elizabeth, and you *will* obey me in this. I am not done with you by a long shot, for you have rightly surmised I have plans. I have plans for us both. And you will neither thwart nor disrupt my plans in any way, else you discover more than my hand across your arse."

He turned on his heel and left, Elizabeth's soul so bruised by both his insult and assault she ached.

That night, she pulled out her stack of pages and picked up where her story had left off. She wrote like her life depended on it, for perhaps it now did. Perhaps the brooding baron mirrored her own bastard of a betrothed too close for what she wrote to be mere fiction.

Elizabeth had thought the two stories diverged, but plots blurred, the reality of her existence interjecting. Somehow she must expunge Baron of Milton from her breast, with the only tool she had: words.

> *The lady's limbs ached, bound as she still was to the brooding baron's bedpost. He'd abused her most cruelly when he'd savagely taken her lips. She shuddered at the memory, though her loins shuddered wickedly too. Fear and shame warred within her trembling, tattered heart. Would he ravage her completely? Steal her innocence for good? Did she wish for him to ruin her, or did she wish for her escape?*
>
> *She was but a pawn, a prisoner in his rented, soulless room.*

Wholly at his mercy, she raged at his abuse. To use his lips as weapon, a kiss to brand her flesh... She felt sure she'd die for excess of emotion, careening between the highs of heaven and lows of hell.

Soon, the lady had no tears left to weep. She closed her eyes, desperate for oblivion, and was slowly swallowed by a dark and dreamless sleep. Her chin fell to her chest, her arms falling slack, still lashed to the baron's bed.

CHAPTER SIX

My dear Elizabeth, prepare yourself for my arrival at one o'clock today. I should like to spend an additional hour reacquainting myself more deeply with your person on this, the fifth day of our betrothal. I have also scheduled you another appointment with Miss Li at two o'clock, to complete your final fitting and deliver you a needed refresher in manners. —Milton

She'd murder him, she would. She would murder him before she married him.

Elizabeth hoisted his outrageous bouquet of purple iris outside and crushed his clear 'I send a message' beneath her heel, rubbing his blooms—his person—out. Let him find her manners thus smeared across the front step when he arrived at bloody one o'clock.

She marched back to her bedroom, eschewing all breakfast, until a soft knock fell to her door. *Annabelle.*

"Lizzie, was he really all that awful?" Bella slipped in only to curl herself at the foot of Elizabeth's bed. "I tried my best to keep him at bay, but he—"

Elizabeth stifled a sigh. "Of course you did, dear, but the

man is not easily thwarted." She made a face. "I do not blame you, Bella. His every word and action is unconscionable."

"Well he cannot be all bad if he hates Sir Wigglebottom as much as you."

Elizabeth was in no mood for humor. "I briefly thought him amiable but was rudely enlightened." Her sigh escaped as a huff. "I must suffer this marriage until either he or I should die, and I simply pray *he* dies first. Then I might at least enjoy his fortune as his widow, living off the fat of his—"

"Lizzie, that is most unlike you. Why, I have only ever heard you speak of Lady Stanton in such coarse terms."

"Forgive me, Bella." Though inside, Elizabeth felt no remorse. "He brings out the worst in me, even as he presents his worst *to* me, served daily in his horrid notes and even more horrid bouquets."

Annabelle's eyes narrowed as she brushed a lock of hair from Elizabeth's neck. "Lizzie, did Stanton's nasty creature attack you yesterday?"

"The lady's pug does not bite, Bella, it merely slobbers."

But already Annabelle had pulled Elizabeth's braid aside, inspecting her neck to declare these were indeed bites, or welts of some sort, as if her skin had been—

Elizabeth flushed with shame, quickly pulling away. She was mortified by what she'd endured at the Baron's hands, or rather, his lips, yesterday. The devil himself had marked her.

"Lizzie, he gave me his word he would not hurt you when I allowed him entry to your chamber!"

Elizabeth barked a laugh. "*His* is no gentleman's word, Bella, which is why you must give me your word that you will steer clear of him until I wed."

"But surely he'd not—"

"I am sure of nothing when it comes to Baron of Milton." She reached for Annabelle's hand and crushed it in her own.

"Promise me you will not anger or displease him, for he can be most cruel, Bella. Most."

"Oh, Lizzie!" Annabelle flung her arms about Elizabeth. "Then I shall murder him, I shall. Like the heroine in your last play, I will dispatch him with my sword when I cleave his chest in two." Her arms rose to stab the bedclothes most dramatically.

Elizabeth's voice choked. Her sister was prone to histrionics, but to come to her defense in such a childish manner … Sweet Bella stood no chance against the Baron.

"I fear not even your fine acting can save me from my fate, sister. No one can."

❧

At ten to one Milton stepped over the crushed remains of yet another of his costly bouquets and rapped the knocker on his betrothed's townhouse thrice. The same disreputable footman from yesterday let him in without a word. He merely pointed Milton in the direction of the stairs, which he took two to a step, wrenching open the door to Elizabeth's bedroom to find her at her toilette, arranging her hair.

"Miss Winthrop," he announced.

She ignored his entrance and simply pulled a curl close about her neck, then with a snort of displeasure, knotted a silk scarf there instead.

"The curls suit you better. Remove the scarf."

"Go to hell." She finally acknowledged his presence.

Milton cooled his temper and his raging cockstand. He hadn't expected to be so affected by the smooth slope of her neck. He swallowed his lust, muttering, "Let us try this again. Remove the scarf, Elizabeth, as I should like the world to know you are mine."

She launched from her chair to attack him with her fists, pummeling his chest with a vehemence that, surprisingly, hurt.

Milton captured her wrists, holding her taut against his racing heart. "You have forgotten your very first lesson, Lizzie." He let his tongue trace the shell of one elfin earlobe. "Which is that I do not like to be crossed."

"I said, *go to hell*," she repeated, beginning to struggle in his grip.

"Hmm," he mused. "It would seem you have forgotten all your previous lessons. Pity." He took a step back but kept firm hold of her wrists. "Your second lesson learned, Lizzie, remind me, which rule is that?"

"You never stated rules, sir." She was breathing so fast he could not help but again notice her bosom.

He should not have.

"I did not think they needed spelling out. I thought you astute enough to glean them for yourself."

Her glare became a glower.

"Must I demonstrate them anew?"

"Rule two: do not be late. *Sir*," she spat.

"You do recall them, good. And lessons three and four, Elizabeth, if you would?"

"Do not goad, or touch you, Baron."

"Your memory serves you well. It seems only your execution of said lessons needs adjusting." He pushed her up against a bedpost, blocking her with his body, then released the scarf from about her neck before he loosened his own cravat.

***

Elizabeth felt blindsided. Not only had this blackguard just tied her to her bedpost, he'd shoved his necktie in her mouth, rendering her mute. That any man should truss and muzzle her like an animal was barbaric!

"Better, I think." He stepped back to survey her. "There comes a time when a man and his wife—or rather, soon-to-be man and wife—must settle matters between them. I believe our time has come, Elizabeth."

In vain she struggled against her restraints, rattling the bedpost just like the lady in her story. *Could this be happening?*

"It is day five of our acquaintance, yet you continue to try my patience. Deliberately."

She chewed his necktie like a horse champing at its bit.

"I admire your spirit, Lizzie, truly I do. It is what appealed to me the day we met, for you shall need that fighting nature when you face society's judgment as my wife. But between us—before me, your husband—it is not defiance I desire. It is acquiescence and compliance."

She thrashed against her bonds as Milton strolled to her door to turn the key, making her heart race even more. Did Papa know this man was in their house, alone with her in her bedroom? Who had let him enter unannounced?

Milton approached her from behind and began to slowly unhook her dress, causing Elizabeth's heart, if possible, to beat faster.

"You do not realize, Lizzie, that in compliance you gain far more than in defiance. You gain my ardor, my respect, and, of course, my trust." He undid the last clasp, pushing her dress off her shoulders. "You gain my skill, too, as a lover." He nipped the back of her neck with his teeth. "For a whore knows how to grant pleasure, Miss Winthrop, and I do not think you are immune to bodily lust. Are you?" His lips rounded her shoulder, his tongue tracing a path to the swell of her chest.

Elizabeth let out a strangled moan.

"I didn't think so." He stepped before her but allowed his hands, at her back, to now loosen her stays, pulling the cords even as his tongue dipped between her breasts.

A shiver wracked her flesh.

"Give me your submission and I will give your body what it wants, Lizzie. Let your mind go."

Her breasts tingled painfully in response.

"Are you wet for me yet, Miss Winthrop?" He nuzzled her neck. "Do you ache for my touch, sweet Elizabeth?" His hand squeezed one breast. "Surely you'd not deny your betrothed the right to explore." He yanked down her bodice in one fluid motion, releasing both her breasts at once.

"Buds as rose colored as your lips." For a long moment he simply admired her aching, pointed nipples. "Shall I suckle them, Elizabeth? Shall I taste your tips and make you spend?"

The man's voice, his words alone, drove impulses and sensations inside her which Elizabeth did not know existed. His hands began to knead her breasts until desire pooled between her legs, and then, *then* he traced his tongue across the expanse of one orb to inhale the tip, pulling her bud deep into his mouth until his groan of pleasure shot straight to her groin, making her gush.

"You see, Lizzie dear, if you learn your lessons well, satisfaction awaits. A wife, after all, should enjoy her husband's attentions, much as he enjoys hers. I promise you great pleasure, if you learn to obey. You must submit to your husband."

He abruptly stepped away to pull up a chair before her, seat himself in it, and then cross one leg over his thigh. She remained bound to the bedpost in anguish, her breasts exposed to both him and the room's chill air. He removed his timepiece and glanced at it, before he popped it back into his pocket and leisurely dragged his gaze across her, head to toe.

***

Bound and gagged, breasts puckered into two glistening points thanks to his tongue's labors, Miss Winthrop was more exquisite than Milton had dreamed. He could smell her arousal, knew she must be drenched for him. God, did he want to fuck this woman.

He stared at his bride's flushed face. "It is a quarter to two, my dear, and I do not wish to be late for your final fitting. Would you prefer to remain as you are, desperate for my touch, or will you nod your head and be my obedient wife?"

Her eyes blazed at him for answer.

"Nod once for yes, Lizzie."

She did not blink.

"Did you not hear me? I said—"

He watched her slowly shake her head, then shut her eyes in defiance.

Milton stood from the chair, sighed, and stepped an inch from her face. "*Why* must you make this harder than it is?" He cupped her cheek with his hand just as her knee came up hard into his groin, knocking the wind from his lungs as he doubled over in pain, roundly cursing, "*Fuck*!"

When he looked up, her eyes smiled at him above her gag.

Half an hour later, Milton stared longingly at his betrothed, seated across from him in stunning, stony silence. She flinched at each rut the carriage wheels hit.

He'd never been so aroused in all his life to have this minx knee him in the groin like a proper friggin' doxy. She'd been magnificent, his bride, even if he'd had to bend her over his knee for another stark spanking. He'd let no one, most especially not his future wife, beat him at his own game. Yet even while being thrashed she'd not cried once—not once!—and he'd not been gentle either. Afterward, he'd hauled her to his carriage, never mind her disheveled state.

He gazed at Miss Winthrop with not a little awe, while she returned his look with contempt.

"As for today's lesson, Lizzie, tell me, my dear, what did you glean from your time affixed to your bedpost?" He flexed his palm, still tingling from having tanned her backside.

"Not to knee you in the bollocks, sir." Her eyes flashed.

"A quick learner." He suppressed the urge to laugh. "I can scarce believe my good fortune in purchasing you for a wife."

"Nor mine for seeing you rendered *incapacitated*, sir."

Milton's laughter tumbled out, for she was stunning, this woman. She'd give the *Ton* a run for their money.

He could not wait to make her his wife.

***

She could not wait to skewer him with a poker. No, a dagger. Better yet, her heroine might kill him with a pitchfork. Three-pronged. Yes.

Elizabeth sat across from her wretched betrothed on her wretched, aching bum and wrote her story in her head, imagining all sorts of ways the brooding baron might be punished for his crimes. Of course his punishment must come at the novel's end, for killing off the villain any sooner was never good form. She could reform him, or make the heroine—the lady still needed a name—redeem his mortal soul by turning him from his evil ways, but she'd never liked those kinds of stories. Why must the lady reform the rake? Why must women be forever responsible for maintaining order and keeping the peace? Elizabeth was tired enough of managing her father, of putting Papa's moneylenders off. Milton was not the first man she'd kneed between the legs, but he was the first to make her weak-kneed with desires of her own.

Though she would, she *must*, ignore that disturbing thought.

The lady thrashed beneath the baron's weight, fearing for her innocence, if not her life. He wished to ravish her, and she, God help her, wished him to. Never before had she felt such a burning need for

No no no. That was *not* where this story should go!

Elizabeth shut her eyes and breathed. She ignored Milton's fierce glare boring into her across the rocking carriage. There was a pitchfork. The villain would bleed. How to place her heroine within arm's reach of the instrument? A hayloft. The lady would hide inside a barn and the brooding baron would find her, attempt to have his way with her and…

his hand slid up her legs, bunching her skirt so that the hay tickled her tender skin. Her thighs opened to him, yet before his hand could

The carriage lurched to a stop, nearly throwing Elizabeth into the Baron's lap. He righted her as their eyes briefly met, flames erupting in her gut, before the driver wrenched open the door and Milton handed her down.

CHAPTER SEVEN

"Jasper, do you think it wise to manhandle Miss Winthrop this soon?"

Li poured the steaming liquid in a graceful arc above Milton's bowl. She knelt on the mat across from him, her form as lithe as a cat. "I thought you'd wait until after the wedding to reveal your proclivities."

"It is better she learn now how I expect my wife to behave." Milton adjusted his position to match Li's, bowing low over his bowl before he lifted the tea to his lips with both hands.

She reflected the motion back.

"I am testing her resolve, and so far she has proven up to task, resourceful even."

"And did we not agree you'd offer for the younger daughter instead?" Her almond eyes flicked to his. "You surprised me when you showed up with the elder."

"I had every intention of offering for Miss Annabelle, but when I met Elizabeth—"

"You let your prick think for you." As usual, Li put him in his place. "It is bad enough I've lost Wellesley to that honey-haired duchess of his, but to lose you too…" She almost pouted.

Milton laughed, the sound ringing in the quiet of Li's tearoom.

"Do not jest, sir." She frowned, but her eyes returned his warmth.

"Li." He took her hand. "You will never lose me or Wells. We are family."

Li's smile hid her pain. "You shall have a family of your own soon enough, Jasper—the heirs you long for—just as Wells now has his firstborn, with another on the way."

"Another?" he asked. "Has he written to you? The damn fool can scarce pen me a note anymore now that he's ensconced in his Cumberland castle."

"He is currently in London, Jasper, with his wife, and staying with his mother. I saw them but two days past."

"Bloody hell," he swore. "And still he does not bother to write, the bastard."

"I believe *you* are the bastard." She looked amused. "Besides, it is likely Wellesley's duchess who would rather not see Lord Redstocking again." She smirked.

Milton bit his tongue. He'd not be made the butt of jokes for doing Wells a favor.

"Speaking of penning missives," Li returned to business, "are you going to invite me to your wedding? I have yet to receive a formal invitation."

"Blast," he cursed again. "I'll get them out today, and send Wells one too, since he's here. And bring your girls, Li. I'd like the church packed, for appearances' sake."

"As you wish, Jasper." Li bowed her head. "And as to the other preparations you spoke of regarding your intended?" She arched one elegant brow high upon her forehead.

"Tell your maids to be thorough." He did not hesitate. "Prepare Elizabeth as you would your finest whore."

❧

To her utter mortification, Elizabeth had been stripped completely bare. She'd begged *LeBrecht's* seamstresses to give her back her spectacles but was met with only laughter as the one named Rose guided Elizabeth's naked body to a lady's daybed replete with plush armrests.

Clearly, *LeBrecht's* was no reputable dressmaker's shop. Then again, with the man she was about to marry, nothing seemed reputable anymore.

Elizabeth's arms and legs were quickly stretched at her sides and her breasts lightly caressed. She was about to protest when silk skirts swept into the room.

"Miss Winthrop." Miss Li remained a blur in the distance. "As with all brides who visit my shop, you will be prepared for your wedding night in the manner desired by your groom."

Elizabeth opened her mouth to speak but was promptly interrupted.

"You will submit to my maids' ministrations"—those maids tittered behind their hands—"and after, I shall expect you again for tea, in order to educate you in other matters."

Elizabeth was about to ask what matters those were, but Miss Li's blur had already vanished. Then, to her utter humiliation, the maids systematically began to remove her body hair.

"Mark you already, did he?" Evie tsked when the three women helped Elizabeth flip onto her belly. "He's a might heavy-handed, but knows well how t' ease a body after."

"Aye," said Rose, "you'll not lack fer pleasure, luv." She laughed low in her throat.

Elizabeth started to speak when the third maid, Mae, whispered, "Biggest cock I e'er saw," sending them all into giggles.

Elizabeth's ears burned to hear them speak so intimately of her future husband. "Have you all had him then?" Hurt crept into her tone.

As one they fell silent.

"Well," she insisted, "*have* you?"

"Miss." Rose sighed. "We're whores, o' course we've all had 'im. And he's had plenty others 'imself. There's naught'll change that."

Elizabeth fought back tears. It shouldn't matter one whit that the Baron had slept with all these women. It shouldn't matter that he'd been paid to sleep with others too. None of it, absolutely none of it, ought to matter to her in the least, except for the threat of disease.

Fear lodged in her gut like a tapeworm beginning to feast.

Rose wiped a tear from Elizabeth's cheek. "There now, 'tis not so bad as that. Why, a man like Jasper's the finest catch a lady can nab! Handsome an' wealthy an' knows just how t' please. Now you tell me how many other girls're as lucky as you."

"Lucky." Elizabeth sniffed. "I'd have been luckier left a spinster than marry a man as base as—"

"Now look here." Rose peeled a strip of hair from Elizabeth's leg a little harshly; whatever poultice of wax they applied dried quickly. "I'll not have yer type speak ill o' Jasp. He's done yer a great honor indeed, askin' fer yer hand. He treats us whores better'n any o' them so-called gentlemen o' yer own class what visit. An' he'll treat you well too, long as you show 'im the respect he deserves."

"Respect?" Elizabeth raised herself on her elbows to frown at Rose's blur. "Is a man who tans a woman's backside *respectful*? Forcing her to submit to his every whim? What of his respect for *my* desires, ladies? What of my own free will and pleasure? What if I did not wish to be purchased for five thousand pounds, enslaved to his detestable—"

"*Five*?" Evie let out in a squeak. "He paid five thousand pounds fer yer ladyship?"

"Christ almighty." Rose sucked in her breath.

"Why, the wealthy friggin' bastard," Mae ground out, then cried, "I wish t' God a man'd offer so much fer me!"

The room chilled considerably as Elizabeth realized her error. "Forgive me, I should not—I should not have spoken as I just did. You have been most kind, to be so open with me about the Baron." She swallowed. "I did not mean offense. I most sincerely beg your pardon."

Elizabeth awaited their condemnation, only it did not come. Instead, a silk robe was laid across her shoulders and her spectacles placed back upon her nose. Three pairs of hands eased her from the daybed.

"Miss," Rose softened, "you'll have t' do worse t' offend the likes of us." She smiled. "Though we'll take yer apology with thanks."

Elizabeth sighed her relief as they led her to the dais, disrobed her once again, and began to oil her skin. Devoid of all hair but the locks on her head, her flesh felt alien to her, yet the process had not been too terrible. The maids next worked her body with sweet-smelling salves, their hands confident and firm. She imagined the Baron's own firm hands, for he'd touched her enough to grant her an inkling of what awaited her on her wedding night.

Though he'd touched her in callous ways too.

Elizabeth was wrapped again in the cool silk of the robe when Miss Li returned, this time with a hulking fellow two steps behind her.

"Finished, Rose?"

"Yes'm." Rose curtsied. "Cleaned up right nice."

Miss Li threw Elizabeth a critical look and addressed her staff. "Jasper will arrive in half an hour to fetch Miss Winthrop, girls, so we haven't time for tea, alas. Instead, I should like you to further her education, *tactfully*," she stressed. Her eyes flitted to the man she'd brought. "And with consideration to the lady's inexperience."

Evie giggled coyly at said fellow, who did not seem displeased by the attention.

"I look forward to congratulating you and Jasper on your nuptials, Elizabeth." Miss Li glided from the room. "Until then, I leave you in good hands."

By 'good hands' the lady apparently meant pure, debauched wickedness, for Evie unbuttoned the man's fall and proceeded to do what the butcher had intended with Elizabeth.

"Lordy, Mr. Damon, you've a fine prick." Evie licked her lips as she palmed the man's increasingly erect member in her fist.

Try as she might, Elizabeth could not tear her gaze away from his formidable endowment.

"See here, miss, how it grows t' me touch?" Evie grinned. "Nothin' to it, long as y' tease 'im nice'n steady."

"Not too steady, mind," Rose piped up, "else he'll pop 'is cork too fast, which *you'll* not want with Jasper, miss." She winked at Elizabeth.

"Show 'er yer trick," Mae urged Evie. "The one what gets 'em every time."

Elizabeth watched Evie push the man's trousers to his knees as Evie's other hand reached to cup his bollocks, kneading them until a groan escaped his lips.

"An' t' other," prodded Mae, making Evie grin more wickedly, the man jerking to her unexpected rear invasion.

"There, luv," she crooned. "That's it. Let Evie please you, just like Miss Li wants."

"Whadya do, Damon, t' deserve such fine service from our Evie?" Rose crossed her arms over her chest.

"I…" The man struggled to speak under Evie's caresses. "I dunno," he got out. "Said I'd been o' service to 'er. Said I'd done me job well an'—"

"An' what job might that be, sir?" Mae cocked her head.

"I don't right … *Jesus Mary Mother o' God*!" he let out in a roar of pleasure as Evie knelt to taste the man with her tongue.

Elizabeth's loud gasp made all heads swivel.

"Watch close now, miss," Rose instructed. "See how she uses lips an' tongue an' barely any teeth? Evie's best there is at fellatin'."

"Oi, better'n I'll ever be," piped Mae. "Though I've me own specialties." She smiled coyly.

Evie had by now swallowed the man entirely, making Elizabeth wonder how it was the maid did not choke, wondering how the devil it must feel to be so … filled.

Mr. Damon, meanwhile, looked fit to burst. His eyes rolled back in pleasure, his thick hands at Evie's head urging her to take him ever deeper, thrusting in a rhythm Elizabeth felt deep in her loins, sparking within her an alarming, wild yearning.

He cried out, loud, and shuddered as he held Evie there against him, around him. And then he slowly withdrew his still-wet prick.

Evie wiped her mouth with the back of her hand before she licked the length of him clean. She gave Elizabeth a sly smile, then pulled Mr. Damon's trousers up, tucked him back in, and fastened his fall. She gave his groin a little pat and stood.

"Nicely done, Evie." The Baron's voice surprised them all. "Damon." He nodded to the man as he entered, making Elizabeth and Evie simultaneously blush red.

"Come, Miss Winthrop, it's time you got dressed. I must return you to your father before he thinks I've spirited you to Gretna."

Elizabeth's entire body burned with curiosity as Rose ushered her behind a screen to help her from her robe into her dress. She ought to feel ashamed by what she'd just witnessed. Instead, she wished she'd seen more.

Milton took her arm when she emerged. He led her

straight into his waiting carriage, where she gingerly sat down to stare out the window, her thoughts flying hither and thither, scattering like barleycorn. Her mind returned to the hayloft in her story, adding new details she'd not considered before.

Those details alarmed her only more.

***

Milton willed himself not to grab and kiss his betrothed silly on their ride back. Those smart spectacles of hers perched on her pert nose above her long, tapered neck … The swell of bosom he'd explored in such stunning detail just this morning … Delicious images rose to mind even as his cock rose in response.

He continued to rake her figure with his gaze. "I'm sure you've had a trying day of it, Miss Winthrop, what with the final fitting you endured and such thorough baring of your flesh."

She remained stubbornly silent, staring out into London's darkening streets as if lost in private thought. Milton grinned. No doubt the lady pondered Damon's cock.

"I have just the thing to settle you, Lizzie." He spoke softly enough she wouldn't hear. "And shall deliver it to you myself, tonight."

Milton imagined the faint click of her room opening to him, his footsteps padding silently across her floor. She'd not see the coin he'd use to charm her father's footman to allow him entry to her bedchamber.

Lizzie would know none of this. She would only know once he arrived.

Elizabeth lay atop her bedclothes that night, unable to fall asleep. She felt raw and exposed, embarrassed not only by her new lack of hirsute parts, but by the ache of her bruised buttocks and the 'love bites' that still marked her neck.

The Baron's lewd insinuations and admittedly masculine bulk inside the carriage today had made her insides quake. Her eyes had traveled from his boots to his thighs to the bulge at his waist one too many times for her to think him the least bit handsome. He was loathsome only. *Loathsome!*

She was embarrassed, too, by her reaction to what Miss Li's maid, Evie, had done, because Elizabeth had been aroused, though she'd never let Milton know that. The fact he'd all but watched *her* watch Evie take that man into her mouth … *Oh!* She bit her fist, smothering a cry of fury and desire that maddened.

Elizabeth pressed her head into her pillow, pouring her frustration into the ticking in a string of smothered abuse: *that blasted, sodding, wretch of a man can go to the devil, the evil, filthy, whoreson!*

"Lizzie," a voice whispered low and sudden at her ear, making her freeze and cease her cursing. "I have brought you something." She rolled to her back and opened her mouth to—

"Shh." Milton's hand clamped down, silencing her scream. "You mustn't protest, darling, not when I've come to soothe your sore flesh." He dimpled a grin at her—how had she not noticed her devil had dimples?—then rolled her back onto her stomach and lifted her night-rail to her waist.

He sucked in a breath. "Oi, sweet, no wonder you're in pain."

She lay there in shock, arse bared to the very man who'd spanked it, as he began to rub something cool into one cheek, easing the sting considerably. He continued to apply salve to both halves.

"There," he soothed. "Better, yes? I should have instructed

Li's girls to treat you with this, Lizzie, forgive me. You quite upset my plans, you know."

"Plans?" Her voice remained muffled by her pillow, though her body relaxed into a delicious, dead weight as he kneaded more salve into her buttocks.

"Plans, yes," he told her. "You are continually disrupting them, my dear."

"I do no such thing…" Her eyes closed, his warm touch and deep voice lulling her into a relaxed, sleepy state.

"Ah, but you do, Lizzie." He pulled her braid to one side and tickled her ear with his breath. "You continually surprise me."

"Milton." She felt drowsy and scattered, half-lucid at best. "Why is Miss Li invited to our wedding? And do I dream you here in my room?"

"Because she is family," he told her. "And I am here because I wish to ease your pain."

"But she is not—"

"She is the family I *chose*, not the family I was born to. Just as I have chosen you to be my family too, Elizabeth."

"Mmm…" She moaned into the pillow, succumbing to his ministrations. His knuckles traced her jawbone, then softly trailed her neck, shoulder, and waist until he landed at her hip and slowly slid his hand across her bottom, pressing at her cleft before he lowered it between her now smooth thighs.

She slipped into delirium.

CHAPTER EIGHT

Elizabeth awoke with a start. She was still in her night-rail, but below the covers, her body felt decidedly less sore. She could not recall Milton leaving. Had she slumbered while he remained in her room? Perhaps she truly had but dreamt him.

She rubbed her eyes and spied a jar of salve on her bedside table. No apparition. He'd been as real as her thoughts, and every bit as wanton.

"*Lizzie*!" Annabelle cried from the foyer, no doubt announcing today's bouquet.

Elizabeth grabbed her spectacles and wrapped her banyan about her. Sure enough, a vase of wild, pink hedge roses, thorns intact, greeted her downstairs. Pleasure and pain. How apt.

> *My dear Elizabeth, it is time you met the remainder of my family. Dress your best and await me downstairs at a quarter to noon. We will take luncheon with my mother. I expect you not to disappoint. — Milton*

Post Script: You may inform your father our wedding will take place tomorrow morning at ten o'clock sharp in the church of St. Mary le Strand. I have taken the liberty of inviting your neighbors, the Lady Stanton, Mrs. R. and M., as well as Sir Wigglebottom.

Elizabeth's insides chafed. *Why, that scoundrel!* To invite Lady Stanton and her cronies, inviting even her blasted pug was—

"Lizzie?" Annabelle interrupted. "What does he write this time, sister?"

Elizabeth steadied herself. "You are invited to my wedding, Bella, you and Papa, tomorrow at ten. And today I am to call on the Baron's mother."

"Well, it seems only right you meet your mother-in-law before you wed."

You mean my whore of a mother-in-law? Elizabeth nearly spoke the words aloud, stopping herself just in time.

Instead, her eyes met Annabelle's. "Yes, I imagine it is time I met the woman who made the Baron who and what he is."

❧

At precisely quarter to noon, Milton stood upon a threshold noticeably absent of floral debris, bolstering hope his betrothed had come round at last. Moments later, Miss Winthrop greeted him politely, dressed suitably in a spencer and bonnet.

"I trust you slept well, miss?" he asked as he led her to his carriage.

"Very well, thank you," she answered primly, though her cheeks blushed as pink as his roses.

He'd pleasured her only enough to get her thinking last night, although he'd wished to ravish her completely. But Elizabeth deserved a virgin's wedding night. He could play the devoted suitor for one more day and be the sort of bridegroom expected by a fair maiden of the *Ton*.

Milton would never truly be that man, because he didn't want to be him. He did, however, want the kind of power men of society held. Wealth had bought him much, but only influence could buy him everything.

And he deserved no less.

With an eye to his mother, Milton surveyed his bride-to-be. Miss Winthrop's silver-rimmed spectacles matched her ensemble nicely. She'd folded her gloved hands neatly in her lap and looked the very picture of gentility. Though she did not look at him, at all.

He did not push his betrothed to speak, choosing instead to maintain restraint. He was curious to see how she'd react to his mum on this, Elizabeth's final day of tests.

After all, Miss Winthrop remained a means to an end—one he'd worked so long and so hard to achieve he wasn't quite sure what he felt now that end was in reach. Relief? Excitement? Dread? It was no simple feat to forge a dynasty out of nothing. But he would, with Miss Winthrop at his side.

He peered out the window and saw they had arrived.

"Your mother lives *here*?" she exclaimed, alighting from his carriage to stare up at the nondescript, brick townhouse situated on a perfectly respectable London street.

"Lives and *works* here," he corrected.

"Works?"

"This is Miss Li's house of ill repute, Elizabeth."

"But—"

"My mother runs Li's whorehouse the way a housekeeper runs an estate. Only one does not refer to her as a housekeeper. One refers to her as house *Madam*. Madam Audrey, to be exact."

Elizabeth paled.

"I can assure you, Miss Winthrop, little occurs here during the luncheon hour, as most whores remain abed still, asleep. You may encounter a few straggling guests, but I doubt very much you will be exposed to anything more salacious than my mother herself."

She stiffened on his arm, as if she balked.

"Lizzie." He gently pulled her toward the entrance. "Come now, you are braver than this."

***

Only Elizabeth did not feel brave in the least. She may well be marrying a whoreson, but she'd never entered a whorehouse in all her life. Yet before she knew it, they were ushered inside by a proper-looking footman who showed them to a formal drawing room to await the madam of this brothel, her future mother-in-law.

Within seconds, an arresting, dark-haired woman dressed in housekeeper black strode toward them.

"Jasper." She bussed his cheeks. "It is good of you to come." The lady did not deign to greet Elizabeth but only looked her over. "Not unattractive, but rather plain."

She proceeded to assess Elizabeth's every shortcoming. "Pity she wears spectacles," Madam tutted, "as they hide her best feature, the eyes, though with hips like hers she'll have no trouble birthing you heirs. You chose well in that regard, at least."

The woman behaved as if she, Elizabeth Winthrop, did not inhabit the very person standing right before the lady!

"And you've verified her maidenhood?" His mother turned to Milton. "You'll not be made a cuckold?"

Elizabeth opened her mouth in outrage, but the Baron stepped so close she felt his frame support—or warn—her.

"I assure you, Mother, Miss Winthrop remains as chaste as good breeding demands." His hand fell to Elizabeth's waist. "I could not be more pleased with my bride."

Elizabeth's nostrils flared. She would not let this woman rattle her. She'd hold her head high.

"Well I should hope so, given the sum you paid for her." Madam Audrey huffed. "You should have offered half as much for—"

Elizabeth pulled from Milton and stared the lady down. "I will not be discussed like a broodmare, madam, my appearance pored over without regard to my intellect. If you intend to treat the mother of your future grandchildren in such manner as this, ours will be no amicable relationship. In fact, I shall ensure your grandchildren have *no* relationship with you at all."

Madam Audrey blinked, then turned to ring the bell, ushering in a servant. "Martha," she addressed the girl rather than address Elizabeth, "we will luncheon now."

The maid's abrupt curtsy left Elizabeth only more outraged.

"Jasper, please escort your bride to the dining room," his mother ordered.

Milton took Elizabeth's arm.

What ensued passed in a blur, Elizabeth's jaw remaining clenched for the entirety of the brutal meal. For Milton and his mother conversed over the dishes as if she were not seated right beside them. They spoke of business and mutual acquaintances, of Miss Li and of money.

There was a great deal of talk regarding money.

What's more, Elizabeth had not a soul to turn to for sympathy; even the servants ignored her. Oh, they filled her glass and heaped her plate, but they performed these tasks with neither kindness nor contempt.

It was as if she had ceased altogether to exist.

Her mind hungered to comprehend *why* Milton's mother gave her the cut direct. Never in her life had she been so disrespected. Snubbed before by members of the *Ton*, yes. But her person—the Winthrop name—was at the very least always acknowledged.

Yet their behavior made her feel almost ashamed of who she was. *She*, Elizabeth Winthrop, of good standing and good breeding! Of high morals and expectations! Never mind her father had gambled his wives' fortunes and thereby his daughters' futures. Never mind she'd had to pawn, borrow, and sully her person by interacting with a subset of London's riffraff to keep her father from financial ruin. She, Elizabeth Winthrop, *was* somebody.

The longer she sat in mortification, the more she wished to flee. And the longer she stewed and chafed, the less she cared if Papa now had to scrape, cheat, and steal to return every penny this bloody baron had paid him for her hand. She would not wed this man tomorrow. She could not.

"I am leaving," she announced.

***

Milton's head snapped up as Elizabeth's chair scraped back from the table. She made for the door as his mother grabbed his hand to keep him in his seat.

"I warned you it was too much, too soon," she grumbled.

"She'd best get used to it, Mum."

"Only she needn't get used to it the day before her wedding." His mother pursed her lips. "You've been too hard on her, I can tell."

"Were you not equally disrespected and dismissed, all responsibility for your wellbeing, and mine, cruelly disavowed by her class?"

"Jasper," she chastened, "you are not your sire. I did not raise you to be such a man. And if you think that treating your wife the way I was once treated avenges past wrongs, you misunderstand entirely, son, what I wished to give you in life."

Milton pushed back his chair, irked by his mother's stern tone. He was not avenging past wrongs, he was *righting* them. Elizabeth must understand what she would face as his wife. She must be willing to defend his hard-won title, position, and interests, not to mention protect their children from insult. He was reclaiming his birthright—or as close to it as he could get. His mother's blood was just as good as his bloody sire's. He'd prove that man wrong or die trying.

Milton stormed from the table to retrieve what was his, but alarmingly found no sign of Elizabeth outside the dining room.

He began to push open doors, startling whores inside who either slept like the dead or blew him lazy kisses. He ignored them and hollered down the hall, "Elizabeth Winthrop, show yourself!"

Silence.

Once again, his betrothed infuriated, even if she'd behaved exactly as he'd wished. She'd held her head high as she'd stormed from their luncheon—a lady through and through. Elizabeth was the ideal mate for dealing with toffs, but damned difficult to manage otherwise.

Milton's ire grew as he pushed into more rooms. And then an ear-splitting scream pierced the air.

Lizzie.

He ran toward the shriek, tearing open more doors until he found her, and the man atop her.

***

Elizabeth had been toppled, a hand now smothering her cries. Fingers raked her thigh and shoved her legs apart, though she fought back with all her might. Still, she was no match against her assailant's awful weight. Despair laced her limbs just as the door flew open and her attacker was bodily lifted off her, hitting the wall with a thud.

"You bloody, sodding scumbag!"

Milton's face swam before her in a blur as thumps and grunts filled the room, the sickening sound of fist on flesh refusing to stop as her attacker fell limp beneath the Baron's repeated blows. Good God, he was murdering a man before her very eyes!

Three large fellows burst in to separate Milton from his prey, but Elizabeth found she could not cease screaming, her throat becoming raw, dry. Dark skirts swooped in to clap a hand to her mouth, urging *hush, girl, hush*! Those hands pulled her from the room as Milton's punches echoed in her head, the sounds so thick and awful she was suddenly, violently sick, tossing her lunch all over the hall floor. Hands swept her hair from her face as she heaved two more times and then collapsed, shaking, into the arms that held her.

Those arms rocked her gently and whispered words that only gradually, groggily made sense. *You fine, brave girl. My son's an arse and a half. I'll box his ears for bringing you here, I will.*

Madam Audrey.

Elizabeth was adjusting to reality when new arms lifted her away. She was carried to a room and smothered in an embrace, kisses rained on her head.

"Lizzie." Milton's voice cracked.

She did not answer. She sank into the safety of his strong, capable hold, though he smelled of sweat and rage. Never mind she'd wished to flee him not half an hour before.

She breathed, in and out, counting her blessings slowly, deliberately in her head. One, she felt safe. Two, she'd been spared. Three, Milton had come for her, protected her.

But he protected her only from others' attacks. Not his own.

"Luv, did that man—"

"Ruin me?" Elizabeth pulled from him, her sense of safety snapped in two. "Did he spoil your virgin prize, steal your purchased property?" She tried to disengage from him but he held her tight.

"That is not—"

"That is exactly what you meant." She pushed him away, hurt. "Because that is all I am to you. All I've been from the moment we met." Hot tears welled in her eyes. "So don't you 'Lizzie, luv' me, sir. I will not marry you tomorrow. My father will pay back every pound you—"

"Christ, woman. That is not at all what I meant, and even if—"

"If?" Her voice rose. "Even if I'd just been ruined you'd what—wait a month to make sure I was without child before you married me? Turn me out if I were?"

Milton's face bloomed red, but before he could reply his mother swept into the room, a maid at her heels.

"That is *precisely* what he'd do." Madam Audrey glared at her son. "My boy does not deserve you, Miss Winthrop."

Milton opened his mouth but was ignored.

"I shall escort you home." Madam nicked her head at the maid, who set down a pitcher and washbowl. Milton's mother held out her hand to Elizabeth, requiring her son to release her.

"Mum," he growled, "a word."

"Oh you'd like more than a word, boy, wouldn't you?" Her lips thinned. "You'd like a great many things, always have. But right now, you can *get out*."

Milton glared at his mother but obeyed.

"And Jasp." She stopped him at the door. "Clean up the mess you left, eh?"

She rang the room's bell, then sat Elizabeth down at a dressing table. Madam Audrey calmly brushed out Elizabeth's snarled hair in controlled, slow strokes while the maid washed Elizabeth's face and hands, inspecting her for scrapes and bruises.

"Tell me what happened, dear."

"I don't—" Eizabeth shook her head, trying desperately to refocus. "I asked a man to point me to the foyer, only he dragged me inside a room instead."

Tea arrived with biscuits, halting Elizabeth's speech. Madam urged her to eat as the maid knelt to stitch a rip at Elizabeth's hem.

Numb to her core, Elizabeth sipped tea and nibbled biscuit, tasting neither. How was she in this room, this house, in such disordered, dismal state? The cracked lenses in her spectacles fractured her face in the dressing mirror, distorting her world even more.

Another pair, ruined.

"Madam," she forced herself to speak, "why do you treat me now with kindness when before you"—she struggled to describe it—"blatantly abused me?"

The lady sighed. "Because Jasp asked me to, dear." She eyed Elizabeth through the mirror. "Surely you've noticed him putting you through your paces, testing you at every turn."

Truth dawned on Elizabeth.

"He's preparing you for what's to come, Miss Winthrop."

"But I—"

Madam stilled Elizabeth's scalp with the hairbrush. "He is preparing you for how harshly society will treat you as his wife." Her voice grew bitter. "It is how he is treated himself—how the *Ton* treats any they deem beneath contempt."

"But he was made a baron, Madam, with income and holdings which—"

"Exceed those of most nobles, yes. He's done very well for himself." Her voice held pride. "My son is indeed a wealthy man. But he had to purchase his title, Miss Winthrop, whereas your father was born to his. And therein lies all the difference. In the eyes of fine society, Jasper remains a bastard and a laughing stock. He could not even purchase a British Baronetcy but had to look to Scotland instead."

"Is that why he—?"

"He longs for what he cannot have, something no mother can give him. And he is too old and stubborn to listen to me anymore, that much I know." She coiled Lizzie's hair into a low knot. "*You,* however, impress, my dear. The rebuke you delivered us at luncheon was as cutting as our disrespect. I see why Jasper chose you for his wife."

"But—" Elizabeth's attempt to turn her head was sharply corrected.

"That does not mean he is deserving of you." Madam's wry dimples resembled her son's. "Which is why you are right to make him stew. He should be punished for pushing you so hard, and I can only apologize deeply, Miss Winthrop, for the assault you just suffered in this house. Miss Li and I tolerate no violence toward our girls. There will be consequences."

"So the man still—?"

"Lives, yes. Jasper doesn't kill if he doesn't have to. Simply beat him to a pulp. When you've lived the places we have, dearie, well, I made sure my boy learned how to fight."

Elizabeth was grateful for it.

"That man should not have been in this house at this hour," Madam continued. "We have rules and protections in place." Her tone betrayed real anger.

Elizabeth lapsed into silence as Madam Audrey finished tending to her hair. A moment later the maid finished at her hem. A second biscuit eased Elizabeth's stomach, yet before she lost courage she spoke the words that had sat her tongue all day.

"I cannot marry your son, Madam Audrey. I am sorry, but I cannot."

Madam adjusted Elizabeth's cracked spectacles on her

nose. "I know." She looked her in the eye through the mirror. "But you will. You'll marry my boy tomorrow, because Jasper Audrey always gets his way."

CHAPTER NINE

Madam Audrey herself escorted Elizabeth home in a hansom, having shown her how a little powder could readily hide a bruise. The Baron's mother thought of everything—except, of course, Elizabeth's desire to stop this marriage.

The moment she entered her father's house she marched to his study and laid forth Milton's character in starkly honest terms. But when this failed to move Papa in the slightest, she decried her betrothed outright, which only seemed to harden her father's resolve. Before she knew it, Elizabeth was railing at Papa, her nerves sapped of all control. By the end, she fell to her knees to beg him outright, and it was not in her nature to beg.

Still her father refused. He repeated in anger that she was promised to the Baron and nothing she might do or say would change that simple fact.

She suspected he had squandered her blasted bride price already.

Thus, Elizabeth did the only thing left her. She bolted from the townhouse, but her father's uncouth, new footman dragged her back upstairs, where she was shamefully locked into her room.

In despair, she fell to her bed, Madam Audrey's words echoing in her head: *You'll marry my boy tomorrow, because Jasper Audrey always gets his way.* Only what of her own dreams and desires? Why could Elizabeth never get her way?

When Annabelle was allowed in later with a plate of dinner, the footman locked her inside as well. The awful fellow now stood guard outside Elizabeth's bedroom on Papa's purported orders.

She refused the tray of food, scoffing when her sister proclaimed starvation never aided escape.

"Lizzie," Annabelle leaned close enough to whisper, "I shall come for you tonight after the footman falls asleep. I shall steal his key and release you so we may *both* flee Father."

Tears sprang to Elizabeth's eyes. "Oh Bella, how I wish…"

Her sister patted her arm with false assurance. "But now tell me of your day, of all that came before Papa locked you up. What is the Baron's mother like, Lizzie? What did she serve for luncheon?"

Elizabeth wiped dry her tears. "I admit I rather liked her, Bella."

"That is wonderful news, sister! Only why, then, did you—?"

"Attempt to call the wedding off?" Elizabeth snorted. "Because I cannot marry that man. He is … horrid."

"But I thought at times you had enjoyed his company this week?"

"Bella, you cannot imagine how base the Baron is. And I cannot even tell you any details lest I—" She broke off.

Annabelle's eyes were twin moons of concern. "Lizzie, what are you not telling me?"

Elizabeth shook her head and Bella's moons slivered into crescents. "What has he done that you cannot tell me, of all people? And why are you wearing powder on your face? What happened to you today? I will not rest until you—"

"It matters not." Elizabeth sighed, resigned. "What matters is that you will not be forced to marry the Baron. You will find a better husband than the bastard who will be mine."

It sounded like a line lifted directly from her story. Did life now imitate art? Had she written her own assault?

Elizabeth shuddered, all appetite fled.

❧

In the dead of night, a form slipped into Elizabeth's bed, hushing her with lips and hands before she knew her up from down. Her betrothed's muscle overpowered, but her tongue could still protest, "You've no business being here!"

Milton enveloped her more tightly in his arms. "I've come to apologize, Lizzie, before it's too late."

"Too late?" She harrumphed. "It is indeed too late for you to—"

He silenced her with his mouth, his kiss sinking deep into her bones, settling there a sweetness that scalded. Then he wrapped his lean frame about her own, tucking her head beneath his chin as he radiated warmth. She was again struck by the same odd sense of safety she'd experienced just that afternoon. Only this time she was not reeling from a stranger's violence. She was reeling from her betrothed's molten kisses.

"Elizabeth, I must apologize on the eve of our wedding, because you've passed every test I gave you with aplomb. And I was not gentle in my testing. My mother has berated me enough on your behalf for my conscience to burn, yet the trials I set you were necessary."

Trials?

"The moment we wed, the world will treat you with as much disrespect as it does me, and you shall have to be very brave to withstand it—braver still once children are born. You must defend them against society's cruelty."

His words reminded of his mother's, yet *why* he was so hell bent on gaining entry to the gentry when he had enough wealth to—

"I have worked very hard to prove myself, Lizzie." He continued. "For thirty-five years I have fought and clawed my way to where I stand, and I will not give up what I've achieved. With you by my side, the mother of my children, I will forge a dynasty to last beyond my death, elevating my heirs to their rightful place."

Was *this* his idea of success—heirs?

"And I will let no one, ever, harm you again, Elizabeth. That man was the exception, not the norm, at Miss Li's brothel. My mother and Li take unparalleled care of the women who work there. They tolerate no violence or coarse handling, or any—"

"Do you mean to say they run a respectable whorehouse, Milton, or merely a reputable one?" She could not help but nuzzle her nose deeper into the hollow of his throat to more fully savor his scent.

"Both. Li maintains the most respectable bawdyhouse in our fair city, with only the finest, most impeccably trained whores money can buy."

"Whores you do not visit yourself?"

He stiffened, but then his hands began to tickle her beneath the covers. "You think I have not tasted of those fair courtesans myself?" He cupped her breasts through her night-rail, making her suck in her breath.

"No, I—"

"Do you think I have not *worked* there, as one of Li's paid male courtesans?"

Elizabeth froze.

"Because I have, Lizzie. It is where I learned how to service women deserving of pleasure. And you, my dear, are this night wholeheartedly deserving."

Milton slipped low upon the bed and slid Elizabeth's night-rail up her legs. He nudged his head between her thighs and proceeded to consume her in such exquisite, bawdy manner she took leave of all her senses, flesh succumbing to his skilled lips and tongue until she could not keep from crying loud his name in heady rapture.

She hadn't known such act as Evie's could be done to woman too, but oh the bastard did it well. So very, very well.

Elizabeth's loins shook, her muscles trembling still, sapped of all strength. Miss Li's maids had not lied, for Jasper Audrey did indeed know how to grant great pleasure. Yet the man also granted pain. Though she would forget that pain in this moment, and simply bask in his gift.

She shut her eyes, exhausted by bliss.

***

Milton crawled in beside Elizabeth and lapped beads of moisture from his betrothed's flushed skin, then stroked her feverish forehead. He'd just broken her last defense, using gratification to overpower, sheer sensuality to persuade. She would marry him tomorrow; Miss Winthrop had been swayed.

He nuzzled her lovely neck, content. It was not a feeling he often experienced, especially not after disastrous events. He remained furious at himself for endangering her today, yet hopelessly aroused by her now sleeping form, wrapped snug in his arms, safe.

His.

Tomorrow could not come soon enough.

His hand stole possessively to her breast, the other gripping her hip as he stroked the lovely swell in anticipation of his wedding night. He pushed his cockstand against her lovely, round arse, desperate for contact. He did not deserve this woman for his wife, but he hoped he'd made her feel deserving this night. Small consolation for all she had endured, yet how else was he to show her he wasn't a complete cad?

Tongue her a pretty speech, rather than tongue her pretty cunny, he berated himself.

Milton cursed his crass, pathetic self. He vowed right then and there his wife would lack for nothing in their marriage, though the one thing he could give her least, was what he secretly wished to give her most: himself.

CHAPTER TEN

When Elizabeth beheld the bridal bouquet Annabelle delivered along with breakfast that morning, the Baron's late-night visit still fluttered low in her belly, a reminder her bridegroom appealed on one level, at least. That she'd remained chaste for her wedding was a truth his white lilies could attest to, though severe misgivings still eclipsed her carnal interest in the man.

Better wedded to her books, than made his bride today.

While her sister hid her worry behind banal pleasantries, Elizabeth forced herself to eat from her tray. Her nerves were about to fail her when a knock announced the surprise arrival of Miss Li's three maids. Rose, Evie, and Mae proceeded to help powder, perfume, and lace her into her bridal gown.

When they'd finished, Rose handed her a small box with a note from the groom.

My dear Elizabeth, I trust you are refreshed after last night's rest. I admit I enjoyed watching you sleep. I enjoyed quite a few other moments even more. I hope you enjoy your wedding spectacles. Do try not to break them. You go through eyewear like other women go through gloves. I await you at the altar in eager anticipation of your vow of obedience, and in desire of all to come. Yours forever more, Milton

Obedience! Elizabeth crumpled the note in her fist. How like him, to add a barb to what might otherwise have been a charming message.

She shoved the wadded note into her dresser drawer and untied the oblong box. Inside, wrapped in tissue, lay the most beautiful pair of spectacles she had ever seen. Gold-filigreed wire encased the lenses with shimmering strips of mother-of-pearl inlaid at each temple. And where temple met lens, a tiny diamond winked back. Exquisite.

"Lizzie, *do* put them on," Annabelle gushed. "I've never seen anything like them."

"Aye." Rose's eyes misted. "He's sweet on yer, lass. That cost 'im a mite."

"More'n a mite, Rose." Evie laughed. "More like a might many pounds!"

"An' a might many favors he'll be expectin' on his weddin' night in return." Mae giggled.

Elizabeth's cheeks heated. "They are lovely, yes," she murmured, admiring them in the mirror.

By the time Miss Li's maids had finished with her, she looked the very picture of a presentable, bespectacled, London society bride.

St. Mary le Strand's pews in London's West End had cost Milton a pretty penny to bedeck with fragrant, snow-white lilies—the bloom he'd chosen to declare 'my love is pure.'

Though love, of course, played no part in his marriage.

He paced the church sanctuary in anticipation of his bride.

The guests had all arrived, including those he'd hired to make their wedding appear sufficiently grand. His side of the church was filled with well-dressed whores and sailors, his bride's side with well-compensated actors. He'd even paid a few London rags to report on the event. And of course Lady Stanton sat front and center, pug wriggling on her lap.

She caught his eye and waved; Milton pretended not to see her.

His friend, Wellesley, had brought his wife, the Duchess of Allendale, who did indeed look very pregnant. Milton was surprised the lady had ventured out. Wells's mother, the Grand Dowager, had also deigned to attend, for which Milton was exceedingly grateful. She lent an air of respectability to any gathering; he'd thank Wells later for such a generous gift.

And there sat Li beside his mother, looking decidedly put out, but then, when did she not? His thoughts veered to all his wedding portended, to his arduous journey here. One step closer, and all he could think was: Would Elizabeth now accept him? Would she even grow to like him?

It was a childish thought, one he quickly dismissed. For he'd wooed her enough this past week and slaked her lust just last night. She'd succumbed to his vulgar talents and displayed an appetite for earthly delights, open, he now hoped, to more intense experience.

She had only to keep her appetite for him, for tonight.

He tamped down his lewd thoughts, willing his cock to also stand down. He had a ceremony, luncheon, and dance to get through before more amorous distractions might be enjoyed. He must first make Elizabeth irrevocably *his*.

He looked up and saw his bride approach down the aisle. Breathtaking.

***

Papa held Elizabeth steady, and good thing that he did, because her legs were jelly as she entered the church. The closer she got to the altar, the more her limbs rebelled. She couldn't do this, it was impossible to move forward. Yet somehow, miraculously, she did. She stared straight ahead, unable to meet the eyes of guests she passed, row upon row of people she did not know. She didn't want to be the center of their attention, of this ceremonial charade. Their stares felt like arrows piercing the armor of her gown with each labored step she took.

Elizabeth wished to run, screaming from the church; her father merely patted her hand.

As her panic grew, her breaths stuttered in her chest. She gulped air as the room tilted sharply and the altar swam dizzyingly before her eyes. In the nick of time, the Baron turned and locked her in his stare: a flicker of calm, of hope.

No more, no less.

Air filled her lungs, as if she'd silently gasped. Her breaths propelled her forward and not once did Milton's gaze waver.

When she reached the altar, her father let her go. The Baron's warm grip steadied, his smile genuine.

The ceremony passed in a blur—Elizabeth's fine new spectacles notwithstanding. Already, she sat atop her husband's phaeton, unable to recall how she'd gotten from altar to carriage, a handsome white gelding pulling them through the streets, for all of London to see.

She was, God help her, *married*.

Elizabeth waved to passersby, performing her new role, and Milton, seated right beside her, appeared well pleased. When he stopped them before an impressive, limestone-embellished dwelling, he jumped down to hand the reins to a groom before he helped her alight. Rows of staff stood outside the house to welcome them inside, but before they'd even reached the front door, he scooped her into his arms to carry her across the threshold, into her new life.

Inside, he planted her on her feet and kissed her roundly. She was overcome by both his ardor and the sheer scope of the entrance hall: the massive, ornate staircase, tall potted palms, enormous Baroque paintings, and more rows of servants lined up against the walls.

"Welcome to your new home, wife." Milton grinned.

She blinked, disbelieving wealth like his was real.

"Our guests will arrive shortly, Elizabeth. We will greet them in the parlor for our wedding luncheon and afterward, there should be time for you to rest before the dinner and dance. My mother and Miss Li arranged for everything; we need only mingle. You can do that, can't you?"

She blinked again, overwhelmed.

"Lizzie?" he demanded.

"Yes, yes of course I am capable of mingling, Milton. I am simply stunned by your … abode." She stared up at the gilded ceiling, the sweeping arches. Good God this man was—

He laughed. "Why yes, *Lady Milton*." He used her new name, which sounded very strange. "Your husband's filthy rich. Get used to it, darling."

He led her straight into his parlor, where, like his wealth, Elizabeth knew she'd be shown off too. And she was, just as soon as guests arrived.

"My congratulations, Baron, Lady Milton." The Dowager Duchess of Allendale peered one second too long at Elizabeth's spectacles.

"Your Grace, it is so good of you to come." Milton bowed as Elizabeth dropped into a curtsy.

"I promised Roland if he gave me grandbabies I'd acquiesce more often to his demands." She side-eyed her son, the Duke.

"Mother has been pleased with me only since I married." He put his arm about his very beautiful, and very pregnant, wife.

"And my husband, Lady Milton, is a rake of the worst order." His Duchess smiled warmly at Elizabeth. "But he's an honest rake, I'll give him that."

Elizabeth fell into another deep curtsy, her eyes resting on the lady's midriff. "Congratulations, Your Grace, on your impending joy."

"Joy, yes." Her Grace sighed. "With a two-year-old at home, Lady Milton, there'll be more work than joy once his sibling arrives."

The Dowager's lips pursed.

"But never mind all that." The Duchess promptly took Elizabeth's arm. "I should like to learn more about *you*, Lady Milton, as I know a thing or two about your husband already." She flashed Milton a tidy grin. "I am going to steal your bride, sir," she told him, bold as anything, "but I promise to return her to you relatively *unscathed*."

Elizabeth could not believe her husband's paling face, nor how quickly the Duchess swept her into an alcove. Her Grace eased herself onto a bench, cradling her belly. She was a striking woman with hair the color of burnished gold, her figure, even with child, of stunning proportions.

"Tell me, Lady Milton, was your husband as insufferable as mine throughout your courtship?"

Elizabeth's jaw dropped.

The Duchess leaned closer. "I am not as you think," she whispered, "and suspect you are not either. Call me Charles, please. May I call you Elizabeth in return?" Her smile was warm and inviting.

"Charles…?" Elizabeth tripped over the name, confused.

"It is a boy's name, but it is mine, nonetheless."

"Call me Lizzie, Your Grace," she blurted.

"Lizzie." Charles smiled. "I like it." She instantly put Elizabeth at ease. "Our husbands are good friends you see, and I hope we will be too. In fact, they go far back in friendship. I assume you've met their other good friend, Madam LeBrecht, or Miss Li?"

"Yes," Elizabeth answered, thinking here, at last, was someone who might reveal something of her husband's past.

"I met Li while the Duke pursued me, Lizzie, and have grown to respect and appreciate her friendship with my husband, though I disliked her immensely at first."

"Disliked, Your Grace?"

"Lizzie, you needn't 'Your Grace' me when we speak in private."

"Forgive me, Charles."

"Roland and Jasper were once rivals for Li's affection."

Elizabeth inferred Roland must be the Duke's first name.

"It is how they became friends, the three of them." The Duchess's face sobered. "Our husbands may have colorful pasts, Lizzie, which do not sit well with society, but it does not make them bad men. In fact, it makes them better men than those of the *Ton* who appear to be upstanding, but in truth are not."

Elizabeth stared at the Duchess with increasing awe. "Your Grace—Charles," she stumbled, "may I ask if you married the Duke for love or—?"

"For coercion?" Charles's lips pursed. "It was a bit of both, but that is a story for another day." She squeezed Elizabeth's hand. "Is he very beastly, your Milton?"

"He is..." Elizabeth was unsure how to answer this woman who gazed at her with such sincerity.

"Whatever you tell me, I shan't judge."

"He is..." She tried again, and in a rush it tumbled out.

"He is a beast and a terror and yet at times alarmingly tender, such that I do not know how to reconcile my thoughts of him in the least."

"Well." The Duchess adjusted her seat, taking her time to answer. "It took a good while for the Duke and myself to reconcile, Lizzie, but it was worth the hurdles. I love my husband deeply."

Her admission shocked.

"It is hard to look past hurt," she told her. "It is also difficult to meet another's anger and pain with gentleness, something I learned the hard way with my Roland."

In that moment Elizabeth believed the Duchess understood her better than anyone on earth.

"Lizzie," Charles told her, "do not hesitate to write to me, should you need a friend. I am not often in London, but am happy to correspond. I suspect you've a long journey yet with your husband, one I hope ends happily for you both."

Elizabeth was intensely grateful. "I cannot thank you enough for your offer of friendship, Your Grace."

The Duchess beamed another brilliant smile. "Good, for I fear we must return unto the fray." She looked across the room at the Baron. "I wish you luck." She sighed. "It is not easy to wed one who wishes to prove himself, is it?" Her gaze fell on her own husband, in conversation with a third, swarthy-looking gentleman. "They are pirates, these men, to steal our hearts." She looked Elizabeth squarely in the eye. "But they are admirable pirates, men worthy of love."

And with that, the Duchess of Allendale steered them back to their respective mates, who were busy ribbing the other fellow as if they'd known the man for years.

Over the course of their wedding luncheon, the room grew ever more boisterous. Despite the presence of the Dowager Duchess of Allendale, the meal devolved all too quickly into merriment—and not the sort enjoyed by the *Ton*. Elizabeth spotted her father and sister looking scandalized at their end of the table. They seemed unsure how to comport themselves amongst guests who ate and drank with gusto—not to mention ladies who draped themselves across gentlemen's shoulders, or landed directly in gentlemen's laps.

Not knowing how to ease matters, Elizabeth simply tolerated the loud, spoon-to-glass toasts her husband appeared to revel in. Yet the moment lunch finished, she sought Bella and Papa.

"Lizzie." Annabelle spoke guardedly. "Who *are* these people?"

"Acquaintances of my husband." Elizabeth glared at Papa. "I told you the Baron was no gentleman."

Her father shifted on his feet. "I think it best I take Bella home early, Lizzie. In fact—"

Only Miss Li appeared serendipitously at Papa's side, slipping her elegant arm into Lord Winthrop's to lead him away in close conversation. Unsure of the lady's motive, Elizabeth was nonetheless grateful to be afforded a moment alone with her sister.

"Annabelle, do *not* let Papa bully you into anything now that I am wed. As soon as I am able, I will get you out from under his thumb. With my position now as married lady I should be able to provide you with a season when you come of age next month. Or barring that, I'll find the means to send you to live with our cousins in Durham."

Annabelle frowned. "But Lizzie, who will care for Papa if I, too, leave? With no one to reconcile his books, how will Cook manage the household finances?"

"He can care for himself, Bella, and high time he learn

how." Elizabeth had never understood her sister's soft spot for their father, but she well understood Bella's concern for dear Cook. She'd make sure the woman who'd raised them was provided for; the Baron could hardly begrudge her that.

Annabelle brushed tears from her eyes. "I don't like this one bit," she muttered. "Whatever shall I do without you, Lizzie?"

Elizabeth swallowed her grief, willing herself to remain hopeful for Bella, though she realized with a sinking heart they would be parted now for good. "You shall be strong and brave and smart. You shall be all these things, Annabelle, because you already *are*." She gripped her sister's hands. "Have faith and visit me often, as I will visit you. And keep me apprised of Papa. I'll not have him sell you, too, into some miserable marriage for a sum he'll only gamble away. I won't allow it. I will not."

CHAPTER ELEVEN

Annabelle Winthrop twisted her skirts with unease. The festivities had grown only more unruly since Elizabeth's parting words, leaving her unsure how to conduct herself, or whom she might even converse with. She wished Lizzie had not abandoned her, but as the bride, her sister was expected to broadly socialize. Annabelle hid herself in a corner of the room, awaiting Papa's return, when a man sidled up, weaving on his feet.

"An' why ain't *you* partakin' in no fun, miss? Why, you're prettier'n all th'—"

"She's not one of Li's," a gruff voice interrupted. "Christ, man, have some sense." Annabelle's tawny-haired savior sent the drunkard stumbling with a firm shove. "Not the brightest chap, I'm afraid," he apologized, straightening his suitcoat.

"I am in your debt, sir." She'd not felt her heart thudding till now. "And am grateful for your assistance."

The gentleman flashed her a sparkling smile. Not only was he smartly dressed, he did not reek of drink. An anomaly in this crowd.

"And as you are clearly *not* one of Miss Li's ladies, I presume you are with the bride's party instead?"

"I am her sister." Annabelle was relieved to be conversing in a civilized manner.

"Then I shall remain steadfast by your side Miss—Winthrop, is it?—to scare off further untoward advances."

He charmed her not a little with his fine manner of speech and equally fine appearance; she suddenly found her heart thudding for altogether different reasons.

"Thank you, sir. I am sure my father shall return shortly."

"Lord Winthrop, I presume?"

"Do you know him?" Annabelle was instantly suspicious. Papa knew too many gentlemen of a certain type.

The man's lips twitched. Sculpted lips, neither thin nor thick. She really should not notice.

"I do, Miss Winthrop, as he regularly frequents my establishment."

"Your establishment?"

"Yes, I own a—"

But he was cut short by Papa himself, who'd appeared like a burr at Annabelle's side.

"Bella, we are leaving." Her father took her arm in a close grip. "I've bid farewell to Lizzie and the Baron so we needn't—"

"Lord Winthrop." The gentleman stepped forward. "I was just making your daughter's acquaintance."

Papa seemed instantly on his guard. "Harris, I did not expect to find you here."

"Didn't you?"

"No, I—"

"The Baron and I are old friends, sir. Business partners. Surely you knew that."

Her father's face flushed. "If this is a matter concerning my account—"

"No, no, not at all," the gentleman assured Papa but met Annabelle's eyes. "I never mix business with pleasure, my lord, though meeting your daughter has been a singular pleasure indeed." He took Annabelle's hand and smoothly kissed it, her father's face a cloud of fury. She felt a hard edge press her glove as the gentleman kept her hand prisoner a moment longer than was necessary. And then Mr. Harris smiled pointedly at Annabelle.

His teeth were slightly crooked, one jagged, as if he'd bitten off something hard. It gave him a slightly feral look, though not menacing. Intriguing.

"I hope we meet again, Miss Winthrop." His eyes locked on hers. "Happy to be of service, should you ever find yourself in need."

She flushed as he released her hand, then quickly slipped his card into her dress pocket to hide the indiscretion. Mr. Harris clearly knew her father, and knew him in a way she felt sure was not entirely above board.

***

Harris stepped away from the girl and immediately sought Jasp, who took one look at him and asked, "You met the sister, then?"

"Oi." He nodded. "Jam tart, that one."

Jasper's brow furrowed.

"Not that I were lookin'," he added. "But I see yer concern. You sure about this, Jasp? Meddlin' in some lord's affairs rarely leads to—"

"Arty, you know the girl's addle-pated father, and you've just met my wife. What do you think is going to happen to Annabelle Winthrop if I *don't* intervene?" His face soured.

Harris chewed his lip. "I'll keep me eye on ol' Winthrop, but I can't be there at every turn."

"I simply need you to keep her safe until I can arrange a proper marriage."

Harris shook his head. "Inform yer lady wife, Jasp. If she's not in the know then—"

"If Lizzie is at all in the know things will go south decidedly fast. You've no idea the temper on that woman."

Harris laughed. "Temper? *You,* Jasp, marry some blueblood with a temper? Why, this day can't get no better!"

Jasper glowered, like he usually did, but Harris took no heed. He'd known his best mate all his life, having grown up with him in the East End, a whoreson like himself.

And he made damn sure Jasper Audrey never forgot it.

Because climbing ranks was something Harris had never understood, though to be fair, he didn't know his own sire, and frankly, didn't care. Still, Jasp had enough blunt now to live the lap of luxury. Hell, he'd set Harris up in business, God bless. But marrying this fancy lady and interfering in the fancy sister's affairs wasn't right.

He'd do his bit to help his friend, but he didn't have to like it. Though he did like the look of yon miss—some toff was sure to snatch her up. Jasp would have no trouble marrying the young lady off, provided her old 'pot and pan' didn't auction her to a high bidder first.

Elizabeth felt dizzy. She longed to lie down and escape the boisterous voices which all clamored for her attention. Hadn't Milton promised her a rest before dinner? Were all weddings so exhausting? She'd lost count of how many colorful 'characters' she'd met.

She edged her way toward a door, hoping to find a room she might lie down in. She slipped inside, eyes landing greedily on a chaise. She headed straight for its soft cushions when noises ground her steps to a halt.

Two guests pressed into a corner seemed wholly unaware she'd entered the room. Worse still, they looked as if they were, well, rutting! A man stood behind a woman, skirts lifted to her waist, his hands angling her hips as he thrust against her in that same rhythmic motion Mr. Damon had used to avail himself of Evie's mouth at *Madame LeBrecht's*.

A hand clapped over Elizabeth's lips as her husband's voice whispered, "Come away, wife, give the lovers their privacy. There'll be time enough to watch some other day, time enough for our own play."

That same hand left her lips to brazenly trail its way to her bosom, making Elizabeth arch her torso back against his own. He lowered his head to her neck as he ground his hips into her bottom, palm gripping her bodice.

"Lizzie, you wanton—" Milton broke off, his breath hot on her skin. "Come away now, quick, before I lift your skirts too. Let me show you to your bedroom, though God knows I ought to find someone else to take you there instead."

Their walk upstairs passed in a haze, Elizabeth's senses remaining heightened from the encounter, though Milton did not speak or touch her more. He merely showed her inside a room.

"You may retire here until dinner. Your lady's maid will rouse you when it is time to dress." He began to undo her wedding gown's numerous hooks.

"I'm sure I can manage, sir, you needn't—"

"Allow me to assist you, wife." His tone, as usual, commanded.

Elizabeth ceased further protest, for why should she now resist? As husband he'd every right to undress her, every right to take her right this minute if he wished. She flushed to recall what she'd seen in that room, the sounds made, the motions of bodies in sway.

Her dress fell to the floor as Milton gently unlaced her stays. Before she knew it, her corset slipped free and her head fell back against his chest, his chin resting atop her head.

***

Milton held his wife a moment longer before he scooped her up and laid her on the bed. His eyes traveled up her white, stockinged legs to the V visible beneath her all too sheer, clinging shift.

He wrenched his gaze to her face to remove her spectacles, then pressed a kiss to her brow and a firmer one to her lips. And then he stepped from her room into the hall, directly into Li's path.

The lady took his arm. "I feared you were up to no good." She marched him down the hallway, and then down his grand staircase, one blasted step at a time. "Patience is a virtue Jasper, you of all men know this."

"I am not without willpower, Li."

"When it comes to your bride, I fear you may be."

He harrumphed as they entered the ballroom, Li making a moue as she surveyed the guests cavorting about, some of whom careened unsteadily across the room.

"This is not at all what your mother and I envisioned." She angrily snapped open her fan.

"Honestly, Li, can one expect anything less from a party of pirates, whores, and thieves?"

"I suppose not." She grimaced. "Though thankfully this is a private party devoid of gossip rags."

"Who said I didn't invite the rags?"

"Jasper!" She smacked him with her fan. "You will ruin your poor wife's reputation before she's even—"

"Elizabeth's reputation was ruined the moment we wed. It is better this way. Let them know whom she married, and let her know who her husband is."

"Yet you take offense when they snub you—as they'll snub her now too." She huffed. "There is a proper way to go about these things, yet time and again you choose the opposite."

"I'll not hide who I am."

"No one is asking you to, Jasper, but—"

"No." He cut her short. "My father will acknowledge my existence."

"But Jasper, the man will never—"

Milton walked away from Li. She believed he was intentionally making things difficult for Elizabeth. What she didn't understand was that he *needed* his wife to succeed, to triumph in her role.

Everything he did was to prepare and protect her, because everything he'd long sought was at last within reach: title, wife, influence, heirs. He'd never be a duke, but he could run in dukes' circles, use his wealth to thwart endeavors, access persons of importance in ways previously denied him.

Milton could and would make his sire sit up and notice, and then he'd make that man's life a living hell. In the meantime, he was rich enough to throw himself a goddamn party, the sort of party befitting of a whoreson. The few toffs who'd deigned to accept his invitation would tell those who had declined just how filthy rich he was, rich enough to flaunt his illegitimacy in their faces.

Besides, even if he'd done every last thing right, put on the most proper wedding dinner and dance in all of London, they'd still have scoffed behind his back, tittered behind their fans. The *Ton* found fault no matter how hard he strived to fit in. Why not give them what they already all assumed?

His wife would win them over. She'd add the poise he

lacked. Elizabeth would put them in their place and shine where he did not.

She was crucial to his plans. He needed her like he needed air.

❧

Dinner devolved quickly into dancing, only it was not the sort of dancing Elizabeth had been taught. This was peasant dancing at best, and at worst, drunken tromping about. Guests who were also musicians had struck up a jig, to which couples leapt and twirled about.

"Word of warning, my dear: prepare to be manhandled." Madam Audrey had appeared at Elizabeth's side. "It's tradition amongst our folk for a man's bride to be passed between his friends."

"Passed?" Elizbeth was appalled. "Why, I've never heard tell of such custom as this, madam. I most certainly will not be—"

But already she'd been nabbed, her mother-in-law's parting smirk flashing. Elizabeth was suddenly tossed across the floor, spun silly in various men's arms. A hand at her waist, a hand on her arse, she was flung this way and that, like a ragdoll. Pulled to men's legs and tighter still to men's chests, the speed of the jig increased the room's shouts and stomps to an alarming, fevered pitch.

Until she fell into familiar hands.

Milton righted her in his grasp, snapped his fingers above his head, and the music changed at once to a slower, more sultry tune. It was no song she knew, but her husband's sure feet led her in step.

The lyrics, however, were another matter.

"Sir," she hissed. "This song is … Why, it's—"

"*The Lusty Young Smith.*" Milton chuckled. "'Tis played at all weddings."

"Milton, no such song is played at all weddings." Her cheeks scalded as the next verse rang out.

Red hot grew his iron, as both did desire,
And he was too wise not to strike while 'twas so.
Quoth she, "What I get, I get out of the fire,
Then prithee, strike hard and redouble the blow."
With a jingle bang, jingle bang, jingle bang, jingle,
With a jingle bang, jingle bang, jingle, hi ho!

He lifted her high at *hi ho!* and grinned for exertion. "Well, 'tis sung at *our* weddin', darlin'. Our guests'll expect I strike hot at yer forge!"

Elizabeth's ears burned at her husband's crass language, while the song's verse, and tempo, grew bawdier still.

Six times did his iron by vigorous heating,
Grow soft in her forge in a minute or so,
And as often was hardened, still beating and beating,
But each time it softened, it hardened more slow.
With a jingle bang, jingle bang, jingle bang, jingle,
With a jingle bang, jingle bang, jingle, hi ho!

Again, she was lifted, and when brought down, tipped low. "And I'll not apologize fer wantin' to show off me new wife neither." She gasped as her husband pulled her up fast, the audience roaring with hoots and hollers. "Shall we give 'em a taste o' what's t' come, luv?"

Milton looked like the devil, his blue eyes bright gems, speech slipping into that of a wholly different person. She tried to protest, but he flipped her over his shoulder and cupped her arse with his palm. The room erupted in whistles and laughter as he spun her rump high overhead in his arms, the verse now altered so the Smith was named Jasper, his damsel named Lizzie. The tempo reached its peak as Milton landed her on her feet, then bent her back in a kiss that was … masterful.

Elizabeth's head reeled.

When he finally let up, he bowed to his brethren, the room awash with fresh cheers. "To Jasper!" they shouted. "The bastard's done wed! Huzzah to the Baron, our whoreson, our lad!"

Milton again threw Elizabeth over his shoulder, bidding the crowd good night. He carried her off, to complete the final act.

CHAPTER TWELVE

"Strip," he commanded.

Elizabeth stood in her husband's bedroom, stunned.

"I am not your whore," she snapped.

"No, you are my wife, and as such I will not pay you to strip before me, I shall order you to instead."

Her thoughts scattered like mice.

"Lizzie, I have demonstrated before what happens when you do not obey me, and I want to be very clear how our marriage will work. You will obey me in the bedroom, and I shall reward you with great pleasure. If you choose not to obey me, you shall be punished instead, at my pleasure."

She was again shocked, for this was not the man who'd granted her bliss just last night. This was the man who'd tied her to a bedpost and roundly thrashed her; he was likely capable of worse.

She recalled the Duchess of Allendale's words to her but this very afternoon: that it was better to meet anger and rage with gentleness, though the concept felt far removed from present circumstance. *Very*, very far.

He was testing her like he had all week. And if she passed

this last test then … Elizabeth's mind opened. If she passed this new test, then perhaps he'd not test her more. Perhaps he'd allow her some leeway, some freedom. If she acquiesced now, she might gain what she wished later, when it mattered more.

She dropped her gaze, training her eyes on his familiar shining hessians, and began to unhook her dress. She sensed him watching hungrily as her fingers continued their work.

Once her dress dropped, she began on her stays, fumbling at the lacing. When these dropped too, she paused.

"Pray do not stop, Elizabeth." His voice simmered. "The view only improves."

She steeled her nerves, for she'd never stripped naked before anyone but her sister and servants. Still, he was her husband; she would see this task through. When she stood before him in only her stockings, Milton let out a hiss of air.

"You are breathtaking, my dear." He continued to look his fill. "Now on your knees before me; that is how a wife greets her husband before he takes her to bed."

Elizabeth's eyes flashed to his, which remained hard as glass. She worried he might hurt her, though he'd not hurt her in the least last night. He pushed her down with his hands, making her kneel before him as he tipped her chin.

"Take down your hair."

She obeyed, pins scattering to the floor as her braid fell free, which he grasped, pulling her head back until her body arched, breasts pushed out. His other hand played with their tips until they peaked. Until she bit back an embarrassing moan.

"Now place your hands to your sides, palms flat to floor. Yes, like that. Open your legs, do not close yourself to me. When you come to my bed at night this is how you will present yourself, naked but for your stockings, braid down your back, breasts thrust forward and thighs parted.

She inhaled a sharp gasp.

"Does it not arouse you, Lizzie, to give yourself to your husband? To grant me ownership of your flesh? You are exquisite in your submission."

She was ashamed of her slick thighs, humiliated to imagine she might *enjoy* presenting herself in this lewd manner. She was not that sort of woman.

Elizabeth burned with unbearable anticipation while Milton surveyed her kneeling form from every angle. And then he positioned himself before her, his waist at her head, tilting up her face again. Inside, she was a bundle of nerves, while he reflected back only calm. And lust.

"You will take me in your mouth first, Lizzie, as you observed Evie do at *LeBrecht's.* Undo my fall and caress my cock, bring me to completion. You will taste my seed before I claim your maidenhead. In time, there will be no part of your body I will not take, and so own."

Elizabeth's heart beat so furiously she could not keep from trembling.

He stroked her cheek, then gently palmed her face. "Do not fear this, wife. I took care to remain free of disease, despite my sordid past. When I did not sleep with virgins, I used French letters for protection. I would not endanger my ability to sire children, nor endanger my wife. I will be gentle with you tonight, but only if you obey me."

He forced her again to look up at him; she had no idea what French letters were.

"Now do as you are told." He removed her spectacles before he pressed his crotch to her face.

And God help her, Elizabeth did.

***

Milton wasn't sure he could withstand his wife, because her innocence nearly rent him in two. He suppressed his tender urges, buried them, in fact, to administer this final test.

Because he'd not be married to a woman who defied or denied him physically.

Milton knew that if he mastered Lizzie's body he had a chance in hell of mastering her mind. Yet the unschooled manner in which she caressed his cock pierced him to his core. She was every bit the aristocrat taught to fear and revile men such as he—yet here she knelt, fumbling to pleasure him with virgin lips and tongue, allowing him entry to her hot, wet…

He came too fast, spilling down her throat as he forced her to swallow, ashamed he'd lasted such a short while on this, her first time.

He beat back the jeering voice in his head, instead folding her in his arms right there upon the floor. He unwound her thick, black braid so that her locks flowed like ribbons to her dimpled buttocks, then stroked those lush swells, knowing the curve of cheek beneath his palm, how her perfect twin globes warmed to his strikes. Milton began to harden again with desire. He'd have to pace himself to last, because he was damned if he'd now rush what he'd anticipated since he'd first laid eyes on his wife, on her knees before that butcher in her father's kitchen.

He'd wanted her then, badly. Wanted his own fine lady to debauch whenever he wished, until every haughty trace of noble blood that flowed inside her veins was his.

And now, at last, he had her.

***

Elizabeth lay limp in her husband's arms. She felt uncouth and unclean, his seed's bitter taste lingering on her tongue. She wanted to weep but found no tears, no sound. Instead, she felt demeaned by the very act she'd found arousing when she'd watched Evie pleasure Miss Li's man. She knew not why she felt such revulsion now, she knew only that she'd done wrong.

No. *Been* wronged.

She remained motionless in Milton's arms as he stroked her long locks. She waited for his next order, next punishment, to come, yet her husband only praised. He pulled her to her feet, placed her spectacles back on her nose, and settled her gently onto his bed.

He fetched her a brandy which she downed in one gulp, cleansing her mouth, while he sat at the bed's edge, watching. Waiting.

Elizabeth no longer felt shame—though she still wore only stockings and her husband remained yet fully clothed. He'd debased her so thoroughly, what more could he take? Her pride?

He refilled her glass and she sipped more slowly, savoring the drink's fiery spread to her numb breast. He traced her nose with his finger—"You have given me great pleasure, wife"—then slowly unbuttoned his shirt. "I shall return the favor." His voice was dark with desire as his shirt fell away, revealing a muscled chest peppered with vivid, angry scars.

The scars alarmed her, but inside her breast Elizabeth felt cold to her core. "It matters not what you do to me, sir, for you have robbed me of my innocence, made me more whore than wife."

His eyes flashed blue-black. "Do you think that is *all* a whore gives of herself, Lizzie? To swallow a man's seed?"

She looked away; his gaze was too ferocious, too desperate almost to withstand.

"I have not begun to make you my whore, wife. You do not realize the depravity I am capable of."

"And is that what you desire, Baron?" She finally pushed back. "Is that all marriage means to you? Subservience, debasement, *degradation*?" Elizabeth's gut ignited, though she quickly doused the flame. "That is not marriage, sir, that is servitude at best. You may be baseborn, Baron, but you presented a better version of yourself to me in courtship than you do now, on our wedding night."

His eyes narrowed to slits, yet she willed herself to remain indifferent, to prove he could not hurt her. "I did not expect affection from you," she continued, "but respect for my person I did, in truth, expect. And if I must continue to suffer the man you've just shown yourself to be, I pity the children born of our ill union, who will discover in you a beast of a father, instead of a gentleman."

Milton pinned her wrists to the bed so fast his weight robbed Elizabeth of all air. All self-control escaped her as she berated him with the only part of her still free: her tongue.

"You wicked, bloody—!"

***

He stole her curse in a kiss of fury, then raked her flesh with his teeth, attacking skin with nips and licks. He ravaged his way down her shaking body, then rid himself of his breeches at the foot of the bed.

Milton would show this lofty hussy who was master of her world, if it was the last dastardly deed he did. He'd render her senseless with desire, then grant her no release. Because he, Jasper Audrey, would let no blueblood make a mockery of him.

Yet her gaze blazed orange in the glow of the room's crackling, spitting flames, her eyes lit by a fire that matched his own unbridled lust. Milton paused his attack not to stop his assault—he'd force pleasure from flesh the only way he knew how—but to separate mind from body, to detach his soul from what now occurred. He knew how to float, how to assess from a distance. Yet the man he looked down at…

That man was no better than his own bloody sire.

He slammed back into his body, quelling the awful urge to do his wife harm. He was better than this, damnation. She deserved better on her bloody wedding night. He'd not initiated his mother's many virgins in such crass manner as he now treated his wife. *Fuck!*

Milton slumped atop Elizabeth, the beast fled his breast, his spirit dead. He could not move. He barely breathed.

"Baron," she spoke at last, her tone this time devoid of judgment. "Clearly I have provoked you, as I've done so oft before."

He made no attempt to respond.

"Rule number three, *do not goad,* was it not, sir?" She paused. "Milton?"

He only nuzzled her nape, inhaling her scent, so sweet.

"Jasper?" She timidly spoke his name. "Are you … alright?"

"*Fuck, Lizzie.*" He exhaled the expletive hot onto her skin. "My mother was right." He sucked in his next breath, returning to himself. "I don't deserve a woman filled with your fire and light."

"You *don't* deserve me," she agreed. "But you have me."

He ceased to breathe.

"So what will you do with me, husband?"

Milton lifted his head and met his wife's eyes with raw determination. "I am going to pleasure you like you've never been pleasured before, woman."

***

And he did. For Elizabeth was being eaten alive, every inch of flesh kissed, bit, lapped, and laved. *This* was what Li's maids had meant when they'd told her Jasper Audrey was magnificent.

He played her like a fiddle, trite as that might sound, for her body was, in truth, his instrument. He began a slow, surging tempo, attuning her nerves to his touch as he stroked her breasts into peaks. Heat ignited a blaze deep inside her groin, for the man did not cease, though she begged him for release.

"Not yet, Lizzie." He dipped his head to her bosom again. "Wait." He inhaled a nipple, suckling with lazy vigor, as though he'd all the time in the world when *she* had no patience, no sanity left at all. Her senses screamed for more, *now,* while his hand at her other breast plucked a pulsing pizzicato. Until he released her nipple to the air—*at last!*—then bent his head to devour the other.

A drop rolled down Elizabeth's hot face. Did she weep? Did she care? The sounds emanating from her throat rang more animal than human in her ears.

"Darling," Milton teased as he released her aching bud. "Your impatience is a treat, your tears a delicacy, the gift of defeat." He sampled her damp cheeks. "I cannot wait to sink myself inside you, but you must be ready for me first. Slow down, my sweet."

Elizabeth was well past waiting. She pulled him to her, only to have him roughly shove her arms above her head.

"No touching," he growled, the devil in him returned. "You will not control or distract me. Lie back and take your pleasure, Lizzie. Do not touch," he repeated, then thrust his tongue down her throat.

She groaned in pure frustration, for it killed her not to touch, but her tongue, at least, was allowed to dance with his. Their lips tangled in passion until he overpowered her again, attacking breasts and belly with teases and licks, before he landed at her quim, where he'd exhausted her just last night—and why Li's maids had so thoroughly stripped her.

Milton settled between her thighs and played her with virtuoso skill, making her arch right off the bed. His fingers pried her wide and stroked her every crease, slid voluptuously over slippery flesh. Back and forth he played her: faster, slower, pressure, release.

"I am ready, Milton, do not wait," she panted, desperate.

"Patience, woman." His breath tickled as he traced and tongued her cunny till she could take no more.

Without thinking, she grabbed his hair and shoved his face more deep, but he violently pinned her arms above her head, looming large over her body, nostrils flaring.

"Do. Not. Touch." His expression was grim, twisted. "If you cannot control yourself, Lizzie, I shall be forced to restrain you."

Her heart skipped a beat. "Then bind me, Milton. I cannot help but touch."

He grunted as he grabbed silk neckties from his dresser, affixing her arms to the bedposts in a flurry of action, testing the ties for tension. Fear flickered across his face, but just as quickly disappeared. "I'll go as slow as you need, wife."

"I am not afraid," she answered.

"But you should be, Lizzie." Their eyes met. "You *should* fear your husband."

She did not, though he pushed her thighs wide and slid his fingers deep inside. She gasped at his invasion, yet she trusted Milton now, despite his words. Perhaps she trusted him because of them. His fingers curled and stroked until he brought her just within reach. Just…

Elizabeth thrashed against her ties, grateful for their hold. She relaxed her legs to greet him as he slid his hips between, eager to be let in.

With slow and steady pressure, he gently entered and stretched. He bent his head to her ear and asked, "Lizzie, may I?" as if *he* were the one in pain.

"Yes," she hissed and he thrust, his reticence gone. The burn warmed to a glow as he drew back and impaled her once more. She felt breached yet somehow starved for more.

"Move with me, Lizzie." Hot breath grazed her earlobe. "Join your body to mine in dance."

She shifted her hips, and he slid further in, making her grit her teeth and gasp.

"God help me." Milton groaned as he pulled back out. "Forgive me, Lizzie," he whispered, before he fucked her with full force.

CHAPTER THIRTEEN

Elizabeth awoke to images which dizzied, and for a moment those images felt not like dreams but like reality. Her wedding night came crashing back, making her flush to her toes.

'Fuck,' she realized, was indeed a fine word.

"Good morning, wife," Milton's deep voice rumbled as he leaned over to kiss her nose. "How does it feel to no longer be a virgin bride?"

She stretched her body like a cat, every inch of her gloriously sore. "Well used, husband." She sighed. "And most thoroughly pleasured."

"Good." Milton's hand boldly traveled beneath the covers, to right between her legs.

Elizabeth gulped.

"I am pleased I brought you pleasure." His hand stroked her awake. "I think I'll have my bride again." He pulled back the covers to bathe her in sunlight, then raised her hips to enter her once more. Her breath caught as he pressed her hands again above her head, in undeniable control.

She fell into his motions, though he was large and she still tight. She'd learned last night to relax her body and remain open to him, for if she did he would not hurt her.

She arched her hips to match his rhythm as he nibbled the shell of her ear.

"I expect you to acquiesce whenever I ask, Lizzie, and I warn you, I will ask more often than is seemly." He thrust harder, making her moan, much too eager. "I am going to fuck you often, to ensure my seed takes root in your womb. For I long to see you as round and ripe as the Duchess of Allendale looked at our wedding."

He pushed her legs wider, hitting her sweet spot now. She spiraled higher, reaching for that all-consuming peak she knew he'd grant.

"My prick at your cunt, my lips at your teats…" He groaned between thrusts. "I am impatient, wife, to get you with child."

Her breaths stuttered at his crass language.

"Does it arouse you, Lizzie, to imagine me in you even as a babe grows inside you? I should like nothing more, Lady Milton, than to fuck you while pregnant. Would you like that too? Tell me." He forced another gasp from her lips, the sensations increasing in intensity. She'd do anything to gain her end, that moment when—

"Tell me what you want, Lizzie. Tell me, and I will give it to you."

She could not speak. He'd rendered her senseless, again. His lurid words only fueled her inner frenzy, which the rake surely knew, else he wouldn't do it so adeptly. He made her shiver with each thrust, made her tremble with—

Yes, yes!

"There," he crooned as Elizabeth flew to heaven and back. "You've shattered again much too soon; you must delay your climax, wife. You must learn to come on my command."

Her breath caught as he spent his seed deep into her core and collapsed, sated, atop her.

Her husband began to lightly snore.

❧

Elizabeth dreamt new swirling bursts of color, or was it sunshine that blinded her sleep? She wriggled deeper into the bed's warmth, wrapping her body more tightly into the covers, when something cold and wet shoved straight into her armpit.

She sat bolt upright, accosted by the biggest, most insistent wolfhound she'd ever—

"Heel!" shouted a voice from the door. "He'd not be contained a moment longer, Jasp. We waited long as we could, honest."

Elizabeth clutched the bedclothes to her chest.

Meanwhile, a hound snuffled and sniffed her roundly, whiskers tickling flesh in places her body had never been licked by dog, let alone human, before last night. The creature's tongue lapped her up; she could not help but laugh.

"Gerald, breakfast, and a bath for my wife. Mutton may stay … for now." Milton grabbed the dog in a headlock to pull him off Elizabeth. The wolfhound licked his master's chin.

"Right, then." The butler left as Milton wrestled the beast off the bed, ordering, "Down, boy! Sit."

The dog at once obeyed.

"Mutton?" Elizabeth asked. "However did he get such a name?"

Milton snapped his fingers and the dog trotted up to lay his head atop the coverlet, closing his eyes in ecstasy as his master worked the fur behind his ears. "Is it not obvious?" Milton turned the dog's head, pulling out tufts at either side of snout, a perfect pair of muttonchops.

She laughed. "I see now, yes. He is gorgeous, Milton. How long have you had him?"

"Mutton and I go back to when we were both more starving mongrels than sleek wolfhounds." He continued to scratch the dog's ears as Elizabeth leaned across to pet the fellow.

"Your taste in dogs runs large, I see—in contrast to the Wigglebottoms of the world."

"Mutton gobbles pugs in one bite, *don't you, boy?*" His tone shifted when he spoke to his hound. She could not believe her husband had a soft side.

"Which reminds me, Lizzie, I invited Lady Stanton to congratulate you today."

"You—?" Elizabeth was immediately distressed.

"Expect a list of callers this afternoon, all eager to greet the new Lady Milton. Enough wardrobe has been delivered that you should have a few ensembles from which to dress. I'll send a cart to fetch your belongings from your father's house later today."

She continued to stare at him.

"May I ask why you look so put out, wife?"

She debated how best to respond. "Because as lady of this house, sir, it falls to *me* to determine the handling of my social affairs, such as my calendar and dress."

Milton continued to stroke Mutton. "Elizabeth, I thought we went over your position during our courtship. Surely you recall the rules I taught you."

Her disbelief only grew.

"Recite them for me," he stated calmly.

Elizabeth frantically reviewed all she'd learned over the past tumultuous week. "Do not cross you."

"That was the first rule, yes. Number them for me, Lizzie, there should be six."

She inhaled a breath. "Do not insult by being late. Two."

"Continue…"

She fired off the rest. "Three, do not goad. Four, do not touch your person without permission. Five, do not try your patience by kneeing you in the bollocks." She bit her lip at this. "And six, do not disobey."

"Excellent. I will point out rule number six is the same vow of obedience you swore to uphold before God and our wedding guests. Therefore, there can be no question, on your part, as to how our marriage will work."

Nowhere in his list was there a rule explicit to social calendars or manner of dress, however.

"Husband." She chose honey to catch this fly. "I do recall, in detail, your rule concerning obedience, and as I have obeyed your every wish both during and since our wedding, I believe I am now entitled, as befits a baroness, to see to my own dress and possessions, as well as my own calendar, these being nowhere expressly stipulated in your six rules."

"Hmm." He scratched Mutton's chops.

"You must grant me certain freedoms, husband, if you wish our union to be an amicable one."

"Hmm."

"Respect is earned, sir." She spoke carefully. "Granting a wife some allowance would go a long way toward—"

"Earning her respect?" he finished, Milton's handsome lips twitching.

"Yes."

"Hmm," his chest rumbled.

"Milton…" she began.

"Yes, darling?"

"Do you think I jest?" Elizabeth grew anxious.

"Oh no," he told her, lips now smirking. "I think you are entirely in earnest, Lizzie, which is why I am earnestly contemplating your request."

"Contemplating?"

"Hmm."

"Jasper…"

"Elizabeth, I did not give you permission to use my first name."

"But we are married, and married couples may address one another by their—"

"You see, this is where we seem to differ in our interpretation of my rules," he stated coolly, all mirth vanishing. "You are under the impression rules are negotiable, and I am under the impression that as my wife, you are now my property, along with any other property you bring to our marriage, such as personal possessions, which include, of course, the body you possess. And as such, I am legally entitled to do with my property what I will. Is that not what British law states here in England, when a woman marries?"

She glowered at him, for she knew this legal truth, a truth which burned as hot as coals here and now, beneath her husband's thumb, as it had under her father's.

"Therefore, wife, I am respectfully contemplating your request, while knowing it is completely within my rights to deny it. In fact, it is within my power to demand you address me as 'Master' rather than by my first or last name even. Would you like that, Lizzie, to call me 'Master,' as reminder, perhaps, that I *am*?"

He'd said this so quietly, so calmly, she felt slapped.

"Elizabeth," he prompted, "I should like an answer, and I'd rather not have to demand it."

She hoped her gaze sliced him clean in two. "I think you are the devil himself to treat *any* soul the way you treat me."

Only instead of taking offense, Jasper Audrey, whoreson, threw back his head in deep, delighted laughter. "Why Elizabeth, that is the most honest thing to come from your mouth yet! At last you know whom you married: the devil himself. Welcome to my world, wife."

Elizabeth hadn't time to retort because breakfast arrived just then, wheeled into her husband's bedroom on a cart. She refused to look at him while she ate. Instead, she lavished her attention on Mutton and snuck him tidbits from her plate. She did not care if Milton disapproved.

He sent her to her room once she had finished, through the adjoining bedroom door. There, a slew of servants finished pouring her a bath.

As she settled into the tub, her new lady's maid, Ginny, arranged Elizabeth's toilette. Elizabeth barely listened as the girl prattled on, her mind a mess of thoughts, least of which was that she'd have her own maid. For years she and Bella had simply assisted one another. She prayed this marriage would keep Annabelle safe. At the very least she might give her sister finer items to pawn, for the Baron's house dripped with expensive taste.

She slipped beneath the water, Ginny's chatter now a muddied hum. How in the world would she convince Milton to grant her greater freedom? Miss Li's maids had sung his praises, and he was skilled in bedsport, to be sure. Yet he did not treat her, his wife, like he treated others. Why, he treated whores, for God's sake, better.

And in a flash it came, his motive clear: Her husband had not married her to improve *his* social standing, he'd married her to settle a score with the *Ton*. And she—insignificant, bespectacled Elizabeth Winthrop—would now be proxy for every insult ever rained upon Jasper Audrey's whoreson head.

Elizabeth gasped as she came up for air. She was being punished for the sins of society, subjected to the same snubs shown him. For hadn't Milton's mother been cast off by whatever lout for lord had fathered him?

She'd be her husband's scapegoat in society, doomed to fail.

With a wretched sob she drowned herself again, to hide from her bleak future, for where could she possibly go? What recourse did she have? She pitied herself a second longer before she vowed to make a plan. She'd not survived her blasted father to succumb to a bloody husband instead. But to carve a path forward she must learn *why* Jasper Audrey wished to punish her for punishments he'd endured in the past.

"Done then, miss?" Her lady's maid asked as Elizabeth resurfaced.

"Yes, thank you." She stepped into the soft banyan held out.

"Jasp work yer over last night?" Ginny grinned knowingly.

"And have you had him too?" Elizabeth bit back. "Tell me, has my husband hired an entire household of whores?"

The girl's face fell. "Beg pardon, ma'am, fer speakin' out o' turn." She quickly toweled Elizabeth's hair dry. "'Tis me mum Jasp knew. Did her a good turn, hirin' me on here. We ain't all of us former whores an' thieves, but Master Milton don't look down his nose at no one in need. You'll not find a more loyal staff in all o' London."

Elizabeth was at once contrite. "I—forgive me. I should not have assumed. Nor do I know the Baron well enough to judge his actions." She wrapped the robe tighter about her.

"Oi, y' sound like any lass just married, ma'am."

Was Elizabeth's slight so quickly forgiven?

"An' I'm sure he's not an easy man as 'usband, you bein' his better'n all."

"Is that how others see me? How staff see our marriage?"

"See *you*, ma'am?" Ginny's forehead creased. "Well, sure there's more'n a few as can't figure why Jasp'd want t' marry you instead of his own kind." Her frown deepened. "Rumor has it he paid a small fortune for yer, ma'am, an' no offense t' yer person, but he could've had th' fairest whore fer wife, had he wished."

Elizabeth hid her displeasure.

"So if you're askin' *my* opinion"—Ginny laid a dress out on the bed—"either Jasp's lookin' t' move himself up some rungs by marryin', or the man's sweet on yer, ma'am." Her eyes sparkled. "Mayhap a bit o' both."

"Oh it is decidedly the ladder he wishes to climb, Ginny." Elizabeth grimaced.

"You so sure, ma'am?" The maid grinned. "'Cause I'm guessin' he climbed yer ladder more'n a few times last night!" She laughed heartily.

Clearly, no amount of training would make this girl respectable.

Elizabeth subjected herself to Ginny's ministrations, but took offense when the maid refused to fetch Elizabeth's drawers.

"I'll not go about this house without smallclothes," she informed her tersely.

"He'll not like it, ma'am." The maid clucked. "Jasper gave strict instructions on how t' dress yer ladyship. I'll not take blame fer orders *you* choose t' disobey."

"Disobey?" Elizabeth was livid. "You listen to me, Miss Ginny. As *my* lady's maid, you will obey my orders when dressing me, not the Baron's. If he takes umbrage with you, you tell him to speak with me." She stared the girl down. "I will not dress sans smalls."

Ginny grudgingly fetched Elizabeth's drawers, muttering, "As y' wish, ma'am."

CHAPTER FOURTEEN

Elizabeth sat at her spacious new desk to pen a few necessary letters. Her room contained a dressing table, two armoires, a dressing screen, chaise, two armchairs, washstand, four-poster bed, and yes, modern plumbing. It lacked but one thing: books.

She hoped her precious collection would arrive soon, along with the rest of her more meager belongings. Her writing portfolio, at least, she'd tucked into her wedding chest. She itched to continue the brooding baron's story, but she had more important missives to compose right now.

Elizabeth wrote first to Annabelle, to assure her she'd survived her wedding night; no more detail than that. She wrote to the Duchess of Allendale next to thank her for her counsel and boldly request an audience before Her Grace left London. Then she wrote to Miss Li and to Madam Audrey, asking each to call at their earliest convenience, as she wished to discuss her husband's—

Elizabeth crossed out the word 'proclivities' and wrote 'history' when a knock interrupted.

"Ma'am." The Baron's butler, Gerald, poked his head inside. "Your first caller has arrived."

"Already?" She twitched. "But it is barely—"

He nicked his head at the clock and Elizabeth jumped. Where had the morning gone?

"Goodness." She gave him a tight smile. "May I ask who calls?"

"A Lady Stanton, ma'am, and her"—Gerald hesitated—"pug."

"In that case, Gerald, you may inform the lady I am unable to entertain her this morning but will call at her home later this week. Let me know when other visitors arrive."

Gerald frowned, then bowed and left.

Elizabeth returned to her desk, only to be interrupted minutes later by another knock.

"Ma'am." The butler poked his nose in once more. "The master wishes to see you downstairs."

"Tell him I am currently engaged but will be down presently."

"You sure, ma'am?"

"Yes, Gerald, I am sure." Elizabeth returned to her escritoire, thinking Gerald was a rather odd sort of butler. She'd expected a *Very good ma'am* or *As you wish, ma'am* from him instead.

Five minutes later her husband stormed in, ready to pounce. "Did Gerald not deliver my order?"

She cleared her throat to hide her nerves. "He did. But as I was in the middle of correspondence, I did not think you'd mind if I were a few minutes delayed."

Milton stepped inside. "Did he not inform you Lady Stanton awaits?"

Elizabeth did not wish to cause Gerald any trouble. "He did, sir. I have decided to call upon the lady myself later this week."

Milton stepped closer.

"I will not entertain her," she told him firmly.

"Yes, you will."

"Sir." She swallowed. "I obeyed your wishes in full last night, as expected of a wife. I find it only fair that for every favor I grant my husband, he grant me one in return." The idea had just popped into her brain.

"Did I not do you enough favors last night in bed, wife?" Her husband prowled toward her.

"Those were not favors, those were … they were …" She did not know what to call what he'd done to her flesh, but he was making that flesh tingle and prickle the closer he stepped.

"No?" Milton cocked his brow. "You did not enjoy my attentions last night?"

Her face heated. "That is not what I said. You are—"

"I am attempting to ascertain the position of your argument, Elizabeth, though I can think of a few other positions I'd like to argue you into." His eyes swept her day dress in a lurid caress.

She inhaled sharply. "Milton, please. I do not wish to continue a friendship with Lady Stanton now that she is no longer my neighbor. You know what she is like. Why insist that I—?"

In two strides he hauled her from her seat and propelled her out the door and down the hall in a vice-like grip. "Must I remind you again, Lizzie, of how our marriage will work? As my wife, it is your duty to further my position in society. I married a well-bred young lady who would not dream of disrespecting her congratulatory callers. Lady Stanton must experience you blissfully wed, enamored of your husband. No, *enraptured*, I think."

A maelstrom bubbled up in Elizabeth's breast.

"You will play your wifely role, and if you play it well—*if,* my dear—I will reward you with more favors. Will that satisfy your persistent and perverse need for *égalité*, wife?"

"Fine," she spat, her insides steaming like a Russian samovar. "But your favor had better be great, sir, because enduring Lady Stanton is a very tall order."

"Oh, Lizzie." He chuckled. "All my favors are great, dear. Huge, in fact." He shoved her into his parlor and proceeded to fawn all over their horrid guest, who seemed delighted by the Baron's attention, but most especially by his obscene wealth.

"Why, Elizabeth, I can scarce believe *you* are now mistress of such impressive house as this!" Lady Stanton's eyes had not stopped appraising Milton's lavish decor, or the devil himself.

"Neither can I." Elizabeth forced a smile while she sat upon the settee, taking her husband's hand in her lap in order to crush it. "But I am very happy, Lady Stanton, *most* happy indeed." She forced her smile wide, squeezing her husband's hand as hard as she could.

"Let's not get carried away, dear." He squeezed back, painfully. "We wouldn't want to give Lady Stanton the impression *all* is milk and honey in our marriage, now would we?"

Elizabeth's gut did a flip.

"Was it not just this morning, Elizabeth, that you questioned my authority and wished to dismiss your callers for the day?"

Elizabeth's jaw locked before it twitched.

"Why, Lizzie." Lady Stanton's lips creased into a line. "You *must* receive all callers. It is *de rigeur*. Did your mother not—?" She clapped her hand to her mouth. "Forgive me, of course she'd not have … That is, she left this world too soon, my dear. I ought to have seen more to you after your stepmother also passed. I ought to have prepared you and your sister better."

"It is never too late, madam, for us to repair my wife's shortcomings," Milton chimed in.

Elizabeth would murder the bastard. She'd—

"Quite right, Baron, *quite.*" The odious woman nodded her agreement.

"Oh look, Milton, darling." Elizabeth longed to cuff her husband one. "Sir Wigglebottom has taken a fancy to your boot." Sure enough, the pug was humping his hessian.

Milton tried to shake the creature off, disgust flitting across his handsome face, before Lady Stanton scooped her pet into her lap.

"Naughty boy!" she scolded. "Have you no shame?"

The pug merely licked her powdered cheek.

Elizabeth took advantage of the distraction. "Lady Stanton, did you know my husband has a wolfhound? An enormous, gorgeous, fellow. Perhaps your pug would like to romp with him while we chat?"

Lady Stanton looked appalled. "A dangerous wolfhound, here in your house? When you know Sir Wigglebottom accompanies me everywhere? I should have been forewarned." She huffed as she stood. "I must take my leave at once, Lady Milton, before my poor boy gets *eaten.*"

Both Elizabeth and Milton rose from their seats, though the Baron's words stopped the lady at the door. "I apologize for not mentioning my hound sooner, madam, though I hope you will visit us again, perhaps sans pug? If only to assist Lizzie in completing her education. We wouldn't want her failing in society where her deportment remains lacking."

Elizabeth's attempt to crush her husband's boot beneath her heel failed.

"You may count on me to assist, Baron." The pug squirmed in Lady Stanton's arms. "I consider it my duty to see Elizabeth fully settled in her new role as Baroness. I should like to see her sister settled too, and soon. After all, we neighbors must look out for one another, mustn't we, Lizzie?"

Elizabeth swallowed bile. "I should like nothing better, Lady Stanton."

The moment the lady exited, Elizabeth whirled on Milton. "Is it your intention now to goad *me*, sir, at every conceivable turn? Because it certainly feels like it, inviting that woman to tutor me in etiquette when I have repeatedly expressed to you my distaste for her company."

"My rule against goading, Elizabeth, applies only to yourself. Though I will clarify that I do not, in fact, goad. I strategically position to elicit sympathy from a woman who loves to gossip, so that her visits here report to society how swimmingly well we get along, and how filthy rich I am."

Everything he did was calculating in nature, Elizabeth thought, nursing her resentment as she chewed her lip.

"You are quite attractive when angry, wife." His eyes glowed alarmingly. "Shall I return you that great favor I promised?"

Before she could tell him to rot in hell, Gerald appeared. "Your next caller's arrived, Lady Milton. A Mrs. Ogilvy, ma'am."

Milton's gaze remained locked on Elizabeth. "Show Mrs. Ogilvy to the picture gallery, Gerald, to buy us some time."

"Very good, sir." The butler vanished.

"I see." Elizabeth was now livid. "So Mrs. Ogilvy can wait, but Lady Stanton could not? Just what are you playing at, sir? I should like to know the reason why you—"

He spun her about to press her up against the sideboard.

"Would you like that favor or not," he whispered gruffly into her neck, his hands reaching up her legs until he muttered "*Fuck*!" and cursed Ginny roundly.

"Unhand me!" She tried to push him off, but he only bunched her skirts higher, telling her to hold them up, damn it, as he yanked her drawers clean to the floor. He ordered her to step out, *now*, before he flung the offending garment clear across the room and landed a smack to her bared backside.

Elizabeth found herself in the awkward position of being

arse up against a table of decanters, forced to hold her skirts high, naked below her waist but for her stockings and slippers.

"Let me guess," Milton growled. "Ginny relayed my order, and you ordered her the opposite."

Well, yes.

"There is a reason why you've no need for drawers, Lizzie, and that is because I shall have you—and reprimand you—whenever and wherever I wish. If it should take longer than a month for you to become pregnant then of course you'll don rags, but otherwise you will remain naked at all times beneath your dress, whether at home or away, available to me. Do I make myself clear?"

"*Bastard*," she muttered, mortified by the position he kept her in.

"What was that, wife?"

"Of course, sir." She seethed.

He slipped his hand *there* to find her, damnation, wet. She did not like how her body betrayed her rational mind one bit.

Milton gripped the nape of her neck, while his other hand began a wicked dance between her thighs. "I think we have just enough time for that great favor, wife. Shall I fuck you now to improve your mood?"

Elizabeth's loins ached with greed, but she *would not* answer yes.

Would. Not.

"Come now, Lizzie, I can hold you here in agony or give you what you want. You need only say it, darling. Say you want a fast fuck, sweetheart. Say it and my prick will grant your wish."

Inside Elizabeth, two minds warred for control—sane, rational Lizzie and wanton, insensate Lizzie. The two shouted at her, equally insistent.

Milton slid a finger into her throbbing flesh. "Say it, luv. I know y' want me." He dared her to defy what her person desperately craved.

"Y-yes!" she stuttered in anger, legs shaking under his touch. "Yes, blast you, Milton. *Fuck me.*"

***

Oh, it was delicious to fuck one's own wife in one's own parlor: a sinful, sumptuous delight. Milton thrust with abandon into her molten cunny—a cunny he owned, and a cunny that craved cock as much as that cock craved her.

She was perfection, his Elizabeth, a precious lady wholly his to plunder, obedient to his every beck and call. Last night she'd exceeded his expectations. He'd wanted to stay in bed with her all day.

Alas, the world would not wait.

He fucked his lovely new wife good and long there in his parlor, and once he'd shot his seed—taking root, he prayed—Milton buttoned his fall and smacked her arse before he lowered her skirts. He turned Elizabeth around to adjust her crooked eyepiece and noted the tiny beads of sweat covering her forehead. The scent of her arousal lingered in his nostrils as he leaned in to lick her cheekbone.

"You are a delight, wife, better than a plate of hot, puffed pastry. I hope Mrs. Ogilvy is impressed by you. I daresay she'll admire your glow." He kissed her slowly, deeply, pulling her lips with his teeth.

He liked how he made her breaths increase.

"And Elizabeth, I should mention Mrs. Ogilvy is a former patron of mine who knows my penchant for flesh. You needn't be embarrassed by anything she shares or asks."

His wife blushed a shade maroon.

"I believe we are equal again, tit for tat, Lizzie, or favor for fuck, yes? That *is* how we determined this marriage would work, is it not?" He flashed her a grin as he quit the room to leave her with her next caller.

He'd leave her alone with the next three callers too, having handpicked today's guests to report back on whether his wife was loyal. Because he trusted Elizabeth only as far as he could fuck her, though she was getting good at that—fucking. No, she was a delight. The purpose of intercourse was to secure an heir, but he was eager to screw his gorgeous wife for entirely different reasons.

Fucking was a bonus to being married, and fucking without a French letter was divine. Too long he'd denied himself that joy. He could not wait to bury his cock in his wife again.

He did not trust Elizabeth, however, because she still did not trust him. She was a slippery eel with a mind of her own and far too much pluck—pluck which consistently overruled her more rational self.

Maybe he should invite her to join his discussions with Kilpert.

No, Milton thought, he'd keep his tutor for himself, nor did he want his lack of education made even more apparent. He'd find someone else to handle her all-too-curious mind. Not handle—subdue. For now, he'd let her stew. She'd sip tea with Mrs. Ogilvy while his seed trickled warm down her thigh, her cunny pulsing from his pounding, leaking wet spots into her skirts as a reminder she was *his*.

"So you are the new Lady Milton." Mrs. Ogilvy's elegant cane scraped the floor as she eased herself into a chair.

Elizabeth stared blankly at the lady, who patiently waited for Elizabeth's brain to regain sense. She did not know whether to laugh or cry at the position her husband had just put her in. He was Lucifer himself: a wanton, fallen archangel so smug, so wicked, she wished to slap his handsome face.

He'd also made her shatter so exquisitely her body still thrummed with pleasure.

Elizabeth thought she recognized her guest. She'd seen this woman before. Only where?

"Lady Milton, is it *necessary* for you to wear those spectacles? I took Jasper for the type who'd—"

"Wed a more attractive woman?" Elizabeth finished Mrs. Ogilvy's sentence without batting an eye. "You are not the first, madam, to find my appearance lacking."

The lady broke into a smile. "But as for spirit, well, it's clear what Jasper sees in you." Her eyes twinkled. "Tell me, is he still devilishly good in bed?"

Elizabeth nearly choked but got hold of herself fast. "Mrs. Ogilvy, in what capacity, may I ask, were you in past 'patron' to my husband?"

The lady barely suppressed her grin. "Why, as a lover, Lady Milton. What other manner of patronage should a woman my age offer a young stud like Jasper?" Her laughter tinkled like tiny bells Elizabeth wished to rip from the air and shove down the lady's throat.

She quashed the urge, surprised by her reaction. "Then I must thank you, madam. No doubt your patronage helped facilitate his purchase of me."

"Purchase?" The lady's brow arched. "How quaint, to think Jasper—"

"Yes, madam, it appears that while you needed to pay the Baron for his skills as a lover, he paid for the *privilege* of becoming mine."

"Oh ho!" Mrs. Ogilvy burst again into laughter. "Bravo, Lady Milton, *bravo*!"

Elizabeth was so stunned she simply leaned back in her seat and stared daggers at the woman.

"My dear." The lady patted Elizabeth's lap in a friendly gesture. "Of course he paid handsomely for you. Why, just look at you! Utterly unafraid to put an old bird like me in her place. Well done, Baroness, *well done*."

Elizabeth was still stymied, but after suffering similar encounters with her next three callers, she had an inkling why Mrs. Ogilvy had congratulated her. Her husband continued to test her, only this time, she might just have passed muster.

She'd also gleaned how Milton had lost his Cockney accent: He'd traded Mrs. Ogilvy hours in bed for hours of lessons in diction. No coin exchanged.

CHAPTER FIFTEEN

Elizabeth's remaining few possessions and books arrived the very next day, accompanied by a brief note from Annabelle, bless her. Only wherever was she to put them? Unlike her old bedroom, her new quarters had no bookcases. She stared at the two chests resting in the foyer beside four footmen and Gerald, who awaited her order.

"Bring them to my room for now," she told the butler.

"Bring them to the library, Gerald." Milton's voice called down from the upper landing. "That is where books belong."

"I should like to sort them in my private chamber," Elizabeth objected.

"So you can hide from me what you read?"

She wished to hide from *him*, but that was neither here nor there. "I am not ashamed of what I read, sir."

He looked down at her, into her almost. She imagined he was picturing her naked, because last night he'd made her lie very still upon his bed as he'd slowly stared his fill. His scrutiny had thoroughly unnerved her, but also made her tingle, like it did even now.

"Allow me to show you my library, Elizabeth, that you may

assess my collection and determine it worthy of adding your own." He motioned for her to follow.

She trudged up the enormous staircase, two steps behind him as he led her through his cavernous townhouse—a home she had yet to fully explore. Yet when Milton pushed open a pair of weighty double doors, Elizabeth gaped.

"I take it you approve my sheer quantity of books, but do you approve their contents, I wonder?"

Row upon row, shelves floor to ceiling, his library stole her breath. Light streamed in through south-facing windows, reflecting a dome of cerulean blue. Unlike the rest of her husband's residence, his library was not overly ornate, its chairs and tables more utilitarian than decorative. A stunning Persian carpeted the floor with birds of turquoise nesting in leaves of verdant green, all woven into the rug's dark maroon fibers.

The smell of leather and parchment pricked Elizabeth's nostrils. What adventures lay await betwixt the many pages here? What worlds remained uncharted, what art unseen? She must tread lightly in such a holy space, though like a magnet, the stacks called to her. *Escape.* She ran her fingers over spines embossed in lettering proclaiming Shakespeare, Chaucer, Dante, Sappho. Euripedes smiled back. Science. Mathematics. Latin. Greek. Geography. What riches Milton had! And what was this *One Thousand and One Nights* she spied?

"Does it suffice, Elizabeth?" His voice pulled her back.

"Sir, I am bewitched."

She pulled those *Nights* from the shelf to slowly turn the book's pages, a universe in ink, ripe for plunder.

"Good." His voice again interrupted. "I'll have Gerald bring your chests up. You may show me what volumes you've brought."

"I—"

"*Elizabeth.*" His tone warned. "I should like to know what my wife reads."

She swallowed, not in fear this time, but pleasure. Would he approve her paltry collection? Surely the man read, if he had a library like this. Or was this room merely meant for show?

She thrust her nose back inside the book she held, surprised by how her hands trembled. It was too much to hope her husband shared her love for the written word.

A minute—ten minutes? an hour?—later, Milton returned with the footmen carrying her heavy chests. These they deposited beside a long reading table.

The Baron bent to undo the latch on one.

She shut *One Thousand and One Nights*. "Allow me to assist, sir."

"Elizabeth, there's no need to—"

Their heads collided and she tumbled, inelegantly, to the floor.

Milton helped her up. "Are you always this addled around books?" His hand steadied her as she dusted herself off.

"No." She flushed. "Just … nervous."

"Nervous around your husband?" His mouth twitched. "Why Lizzie, I am flattered."

She took courage. "I've known you such a short while, sir, and in that time we've—"

"Had our share of disagreements, yes. But we've had our share of enjoyment too, have we not?" His smoldering look sent her insides galloping.

"What I meant was, I know little of your interests—outside the bedroom, that is."

Their eyes met.

"What do you like to read?" she asked, her hopes all pinned on this one question.

He began to pull her books from the opened chest, glancing at the titles. "I've not had much time for study, Elizabeth, so that is hard for me to answer. I like what I've read of philosophy and mythology, though. And history. I should like to learn another language someday, to expand my reading."

"Which?" she asked.

"Which do you know?" He looked up.

"Italian and French."

"I'll start with French." He averted his gaze to pull out more books and stack them on his table. "I would like to read your collection, with your permission. You, of course, may read any book you find in my library, which I admit was compiled with paid guidance. Unlike men of your class, I did not have the luxury of a university education."

"Neither did I," she grumbled before she realized what she'd said.

His lips curled faintly in response, but he made no snide comment as to her sex. She was grateful for this and equally gratified he'd asked *her* permission to read her books. Such small acknowledgement of her person quietly thrilled her.

"What should I begin with?" He continued to peruse her collection.

Elizabeth opened the second chest and searched for Ovid's *Metamorphoses*. "This."

"That I know." He smiled. "Pick another."

She handed him *Les Liaisons Dangereuses*.

"I cannot read French, Lizzie. Not yet, at least."

Right. She rummaged until she found *Ethelinde* by Charlotte Smith.

"Fiction?" he asked.

"Yes." She hoped he'd like it. "You might appreciate the antihero."

He flipped to page one. "Mind if I skim this while you unpack?"

"Not at all." Her heart beat faster, curious as to what he'd think of the orphaned Ethelinde and the men who pursued her. What did he think of her, his wife?

"Hmm…" He mulled as he wandered to a window, seeking better light. For a moment his profile evoked the book's most villainous rake, Davenant.

Milton settled into a wingback and Elizabeth stole glances at his serious, handsome face. She liked the sharp planes of his cheeks.

She continued to unearth her beloved books, relieved to find all accounted for. She carefully packed them back into their chests and then explored her husband's shelves, noting not only how many titles were unknown to her, but how many books lay strewn about the room, as if his library were well used. She found a page open to a poem and stopped to read.

The Garden of Love

I went to the Garden of Love,
And saw what I never had seen:
A Chapel was built in the midst,
Where I used to play on the green.

And the gates of this Chapel were shut,
And 'Thou shalt not' writ over the door;
So I turn'd to the Garden of Love,
That so many sweet flowers bore.

And I saw it was filled with graves,
And tomb-stones where flowers should be:
And Priests in black gowns, were walking their rounds,
And binding with briars, my joys & desires.

"Give me that," Milton barked, snatching the book right from under her gaze.

She retreated at once, confused by his censure. "I did not mean to spy, sir. I am a fan of William Blake, both his painting and his poetry. Have you seen his artwork in *Urizen*?" She desperately wished to return to their ease of conversation, to what had felt like budding friendship. What had upset him so?

"I've work to do, Elizabeth. Poetry, like fiction, is an indulgence."

Perhaps she'd chosen poorly by handing him *Ethelinde*. "Surely poems are a balm to the soul, sir, not luxury alone."

"Poetry is for romantics." Already he made to leave. "If you enjoy that sort of rot, you'll find Lord Byron's claptrap all over these shelves; I'll not touch his shite."

"And Blake?" she called after him, wishing he'd turn back. She yearned to know what words, fair or foul, moved his heart. For a heart existed in her husband's breast. It must, to own a library like this.

Had she not heard it beating loudly just last night?

Milton paused, his back still turned. "At least Blake, unlike Byron, knows experience corrupts."

***

He left her in his library, to do whatever she damn well pleased. He needed to escape his blasted wife, for she'd nearly put a spell on him, handing him that Smith book, precisely the sort of wild, fantastic fiction that sucked him in and did his brain no drop of good. Nothing useful to be gleaned from a book like that. *Hmph.*

Milton marched to his office to clear his head and pour himself a drink. He gazed out the window to the empty street below, the echo of hooves on cobblestone clattering as a lone hansom rumbled by. Nothing like the streets he'd grown up in. His children would never know the stench, nor weight, of poverty. His wealth would spare them that. He'd show his rotten sire that a bastard firstborn could not only achieve a ridiculous level of wealth, but form a dynasty all his own, a new bloodline to inherit the title and lands he'd amassed in Scotland, just like a bloody goddamned duke.

Milton's thoughts turned to the future mother of his children. Would Elizabeth read them stories at bedtime? Shower them with kisses while she did? She knew Blake, but did she read the poet's verse as Milton did? He doubted it. Magic lay in the alchemy between reader and book. He'd discovered this as soon as he had taught himself to read. It wasn't the author's words that mattered so much as the reader's mind feasting on them. Inside his head, his breast, his gut, words lived and breathed meaning—*his* meaning, and his alone—no longer the blasted author's.

The soul of any man was built upon his word.

He recalled the poem he'd read just last night in Blake's *Proverbs of Hell*:

Prisons are built with stones of Law,
Brothels with bricks of Religion.
The pride of the peacock is the glory of God.
The lust of the goat is the bounty of God.
The wrath of the lion is the wisdom of God.
The nakedness of woman is the work of God.

God yes, woman's nakedness… Milton closed his eyes and pictured his wife in all her God-given glory. There was poetry in a woman's flesh. Art in sex.

This much, he knew.

CHAPTER SIXTEEN

"Must we truly unwrap each blasted gift?" Milton tossed another useless parcel aside as his wife jotted another name to her list. "Murdoch is perfectly capable of—"

"It is not your housekeeper's duty to catalog wedding gifts, sir. It is our duty, as recipients, to thank our guests for their generosity."

"Such the proper wife, Lizzie. You've taken nicely to your role."

"I told you I should make you a good wife." She glanced up from her task. "I need neither Lady Stanton's lessons nor your instruction."

He frowned at her opinionated tone. What's more, he was still irked she'd discovered that poem by Blake. He'd hate to think she would 'discover his joys & desires,' only to 'bind him with briars.'

"You must open gifts too. Here"—he grabbed another from the pile—"this one has your name on it, and this has mine."

Elizabeth put down her pen to slowly untie the ribbon, revealing a book. She read its dedication, "A gift from the

Duchess of Allendale," then smiled at the title. "*Il merito delle donne*, or *The Worth of Women: Wherein is Clearly Revealed Their Nobility and Their Superiority to Men* by Moderata Fonte."

"Moderata who? Never heard of her. And I am not the least impressed by that title." He snorted. "Leave it to some Italian *donna* to declare her superiority over men."

"Are you familiar with our own English luminary, Mary Wollstonecraft? *A Vindication of the Rights of Woman* is a book you, sir, ought to memorize."

Had his wife just teased or scolded?

"Is that so?"

"Yes," she told him primly. "You may borrow my copy."

"Why Elizabeth, how very generous of you. I've a few books I might recommend you read, too."

"Oh?"

"Yes." His frown deepened, for she clearly thought him a bumpkin, despite his vast collection of tomes. He opened the box on his lap and pulled out a pair of red stockings and a note of—

A chuckle escaped his chest; he knew this gift giver's scrawl.

"Milton?" Lizzie quizzed him through her spectacles. "What have you received, please, and from whom?"

"The Duke of Allendale has given me a pair of red silk stockings with matching red ribbons." He suppressed a grin.

"Stockings?" Her brow furrowed. "Is this a joke, sir?"

"I do not don women's garments, Lizzie, if that is what you think. Though I know men who—" He checked himself. "It is a jest between friends."

The cheek of Wellesley!

She handed him another package, and while he opened it, she furtively pulled the Duke's note from the box, reading the same words he just had.

For Lord Redstocking, with gratitude for past services rendered. May your marriage be as happy as mine, old friend. —Wells

❧

That night Elizabeth was told to await her husband in his bedchamber, though the instruction had come from Gerald this time, rather than Milton himself.

Ginny's compassionate look told Elizabeth not to test the Baron's direct order.

She tamped down the excited panic in her breast, wrapped her banyan about her nakedness, and opened the door to her husband's chamber.

For a moment she stared at his room, because she'd been unable to observe anything but the plush carpet and firm mattress up to now. Tonight she noted the plain, dark drapes and simple wallpaper, his only two paintings those of a stormy landscape and a pompous Mutton in canine pose. Books were piled haphazardly on end tables and dressers amid decanters of liquor and snuff boxes, or were they boxes of pipe tobacco instead? It was every bit a masculine room, yet wholly unlike the rest of the house. Milton's bedroom was stark in comparison—and not a little out of order.

She longed to rifle through his books but did not dare.

The space surprised her, given how neat he kept his person and his dress. Yet the man also chose to dine alongside his staff; she'd been shocked to take dinner with her husband downstairs at the servants' table, rather than in the formal dining room. She'd sat beside Milton while Gerald had sat opposite, dishes passed hand to hand amidst pleasant household chatter.

An' Mutton approves o' the missus, Jasp? She'd overheard her husband's groom, two seats down, conversing with the Baron. The fact that every servant called Milton by his Christian name still boggled Elizabeth's mind.

Her husband's laugh had been so warm, so different in response. *I'll say he did! Ignored me through breakfast, th' cheeky mutt, an' wouldn't leave 'er side! I've a mind t' give t' beast a drubbin' fer it!* He'd been as crass as the rest, Cockney spilling from his lips, as if Milton were not at all whom he presented to the world outside his own home's walls. Perhaps here he was more his true self. Though not with her. With his wife he remained an enigma, a taskmaster, a…

Footsteps approached from the hall and Elizabeth quickly threw off her robe to assume the position he'd insisted she display. Such 'marital duty' made her feel apprehensive and exposed. It also made her—

Two raps to door. "Elizabeth?"

"Yes," she answered.

He entered quickly, turning the lock behind him, before he stopped dead in his tracks, making every inch of her flush hot.

He slowly walked about her, inspecting every angle. "I am pleased you now follow my orders without prompting, wife." He slipped her spectacles off her nose. "We wouldn't want these damaged during our … endeavors."

"I will remember to remove them next time. *Sir,*" she added softly.

He inhaled, as if about to speak, but then walked to his dresser and opened a drawer. "It is good you address me as sir in the bedroom, Lizzie, though I'd be even more gratified if you addressed me as master."

She choked on a cough, to imagine herself as willing as that. Yet Elizabeth remained deferential. She'd not push him this night. She wished to discover how he behaved if *she* behaved.

He approached her from behind to sweep aside her braid and clasp something weighty about her neck. Though she longed to touch it, she kept her gaze down and her palms pressed into the carpet.

"This necklace belonged to my mother and is by rights now yours, Baroness. Someday, you will pass it down to our daughter."

He wanted daughters, too, not just male heirs?

"I will give you more jewels, of course, but these will be the first our Barony holds."

There was that need of his again, to claim all he'd been denied. It was admirable, his desire to grow a dynasty, to protect what he built.

But only jewels could be owned, not people.

Milton traced the gemstones at her neck, his touch deliberate yet light. She shivered when his finger landed between her breasts, where the heaviest stone nestled. He traced the slope between both swells, then rolled one nipple into a knot. He palmed her breast lovingly, his other hand resting at her shoulder before his knuckles slowly stroked up and down her neck, achingly soft. In all her life, Elizabeth had never felt so … worshipped.

Milton whispered, "Come to bed, wife, and let us make a family."

❧

She was awakened by a warm, wet pull. Something was pulling at Elizabeth's left breast, sending sparks straight to her gut, where a fire simmered low in her belly. She was beginning to spark all over in short bursts of…

Her eyes flew open to her husband's head at her breast, his lips enveloping an entire areola, suckling and laving as if he wished to milk her dry. "Milton!" she gasped. "What are you —? *Why* are you—?" She looked down at his tousled dark hair in shock.

He released her orb only to blow across the glistening tip, sending a fresh jolt to her loins. "I can't wait to drink my fill."

He looked up at her, propped on one elbow, his muscular, scarred chest staring her full in the face.

Elizabeth flushed only more.

"It is sweet, you know, mother's milk." His fingertip traced the same throbbing nipple, making her loins tense with ache. "I was allowed a taste once." He smiled at the memory. "And I never forgot, always wanted more." His finger slipped to her other, unattended breast. "Like liquid sugar, Lizzie. Oh, to be a babe!" He laughed. "Here in this bed, you will feed our child and feed me, your husband. I'll stroke my heir's soft head"—he stroked her breast—"as you stroke mine."

Presuming those words permission, Elizabeth cautiously touched his locks, unbearably soft. How often did her husband bathe that his hair should feel so silken?

He straddled her torso to give both orbs his undivided attention while she squirmed beneath his bulk, her hands releasing his hair. She remembered his rule. "Permission to touch you more, sir, please?"

Milton's voice purred like a contented beast. "My back, woman. That is all you may touch. Only my back."

Elizabeth's hands scored the length of his flesh, feeling him shudder in response.

He roughly spread her legs and impaled her with one swift thrust.

She welcomed the rough ride.

❧

After, she lay on her side and watched her husband's chest rise and fall, his eyes closed to the sun's bright rays, a grin dimpling his mouth. She wanted to kiss that mouth but wasn't sure she was allowed.

She wanted to ask him a hundred questions, too, not least of which was *how* he knew how to render her … speechless.

She let her eyes traverse the litany of scars that riddled his chest since her fingertips could not. Some were superficial, but some cut very deep. One long, nasty tear went clear from rib to abdomen, as though he'd been sliced wide. She shivered to imagine it.

"Are you staring at me, wife?" Milton's dimples deepened, though he kept his eyes closed.

"I am enjoying the view," she boldly answered.

"Marred flesh does not offend the lady?"

"Milton," she ventured, "may I touch your scars? Do they hurt you still?"

His eyes flew open. "You may not, and they don't."

Elizabeth quickly looked away.

"They are not marks I like reminding of." He turned her chin back to face him. "It is not your touch I fear, but memories better left buried."

"Then may I hold you instead?" She did not understand this sudden urge she had, when she barely knew, let alone respected, this man. "I wish to…" Yet she couldn't say 'comfort,' for it made her sound as if she thought him weak.

"What do you wish, wife?" His dimples winked at her again.

"I wish to please you." She surprised herself. "And I don't know how, when so many others have pleased you so well before."

He roughly pulled her to him, molding her to his form. "Christ, Lizzie, you please me immensely. Just look how my prick leaps to your touch."

His manhood did indeed press hard against her belly, though she mumbled into his chest, "That is not what I meant, sir."

"Then what did you mean, wife?"

"I don't know!" She pulled from him, but he would not let go.

"Lizzie." Milton's voice turned stern. "Do not overthink this, or overthink me. 'Tisn't wise. You let that head of yours run away from you too often."

"Milton, I could no more stop thinking than I could stop breathing."

"Oi. An' don't I know it." His finger traced her nose before he reached for her spectacles on the nightstand, placing these squarely on her face. "But too much thought in a woman's head only leads a lady astray. I prefer my wife remain—"

"Ignorant? Passive? Doltish?" Elizabeth's hackles rose. "Milton, you do not speak so dismissively of Miss Li, who is also a woman—an accomplished businesswoman, I might add."

His eyes flashed.

"You'd not dismiss your own mother in such a condescending manner either, and she is an equally accomplished woman of business."

His dimples vanished.

"I deserve the chance to prove myself of equal worth. A woman as capable as both Li and—"

"Lizzie," he uttered sharply, "you are immensely fortunate not to have led the lives my mother and Li were forced to endure before either found success in bloody *business*."

"I do not question their pasts," she defended. "I question your dismissal of my person, your wife, as an equally capable, rational woman—circumstance notwithstanding."

He removed himself from the bed, allowing her a clear view of his fine backside.

"You are adorable when arguing a point, wife, but I am spent from a night of lovemaking and therefore in need of more sustenance than words. We can continue this discussion later, when I've a full belly and you are less hysterical."

Which was the worst thing he could have said, pummeling her pride only more. Elizabeth leapt out of bed, donned her banyan, and stormed back to her room, determined to spend the rest of the day *away* from her belittling toad of a husband.

She didn't care how well the bastard fucked, or how generous his mood might sometimes be. His comment had stung worse than the spankings he'd given, far worse than she wished to admit.

He'd wounded her intellect.

For the rest of the day, she remained locked in her room, skewering a certain brooding baron with her scraping, racing quill.

ACT II

RECKLESSNESS

I hate to hear you talk about all women as if they were fine ladies instead of rational creatures. None of us want to be in calm waters all our lives.

Jane Austen, from *Persuasion*, 1818

CHAPTER SEVENTEEN

Annabelle Winthrop prayed her sister fared well in her marriage to the Baron, because Elizabeth's hastily penned letter had revealed altogether little of her new life. Lizzie had sacrificed enough on Annabelle's account, certainly enough to not be burdened more. Which was why Annabelle had written back expressing the usual worries only—Papa's spending and Cook's health—not the worry that now plagued her every waking thought.

That plague was a certain Mr. Finch, who'd shown up three days after Elizabeth's marriage and now called on Annabelle every day since.

She more than disliked her new admirer; in truth, the man repulsed. He looked as old as Papa, with an unkempt, squat form and wheezing, lowly speech. What's more, he had a rotten tooth at the bottom of his mouth that he plied with his tongue, clicking it back and forth in the most revolting, obnoxious manner.

There was something off about the way Papa tolerated Mr. Finch, not to mention the way the man's eyes perused her person. And unlike Lizzie's Baron, Mr. Finch did not send tokens of affection or bouquets to the house. Apparently, he knew Papa too well to need to court her properly.

He was also her sole caller.

Annabelle feared what Finch's visits foretold, but she was old enough to solve her own problems rather than run to her sister for help. She would shortly come of age, even if Papa continued to lie about that all-important fact. She could be just as strong as Elizabeth. She simply needed to muster her courage and don thick armor. *Very* thick.

She pulled Mr. Harris's card from her pocket and traced the raised lettering with her finger.

Arthur Harris, proprietor
The Gilded Leaf
16 Surrey Lane, London

She would ask this gentleman for help, for if he knew a thing or two about her father's situation, he might be understanding of her own. And if Mr. Harris truly did own a gaming house, Annabelle might turn the tables for once and win her freedom from both Papa *and* Mr. Finch.

She knew better, of course, than to blindly trust a stranger, but compared to Finch, Mr. Harris was a veritable pillar of propriety who had comported himself at Lizzie's wedding most honorably.

She'd take her chances with him, rather than with Papa's odious new acquaintance.

❧

"A lady, Arty, brunette with sweet thrupney bits. Says y' gave 'er yer card?"

Harris frowned at his man. He hated the fact his childhood moniker had stuck with staff. Moreover, it was a quarter to one, *The Leaf* wouldn't open till eight, and he had a mountain of accounts to run through with his bookkeeper who was, as usual, late. He didn't need some buxom chit interrupting.

"*Fuck*," he muttered. "Fine, show her in, but be ready t' show her out, Tom. I've enough girls workin' me floor; we're not in need o' more."

"Right-o, Arty."

Two minutes later, Tom opened the door to a young woman who … *Double fuck*!

"Miss Winthrop." Harris immediately stood. "To what do I owe this great pleasure?" He shot Tom a *get-the-hell-out* glance, and his man did. Fast.

Harris rounded his desk and pulled out a chair for the lady, who blushed a becoming pink. She began to pluck at her gloves, then removed them entirely, only to place them awkwardly upon his desk.

She needed steadying. As did he.

He poured her a brandy, though the sap was strong, but he didn't have a bloody tea service waiting. He'd not seen hide nor tail of her father at his club since Jasper's wedding, and for Miss Winthrop to have kept his card rather than toss it surprised him not a little.

He placed the drink before her, which she downed in one gulp, surprising him only more. She boldly looked him in the eye. "May I have another, sir?"

Arthur was rattled, for her eyes, the color of lit amber, matched her auburn hair so perfectly she looked more fawn than human: a gorgeous, woodland creature.

"Of course, Miss Winthrop." He poured them each a second healthy portion, and this time she sipped more delicately.

"Mr. Harris, I must apologize for visiting you unannounced." Her gaze fell to the receipts strewn across his desk. "Have I interrupted your accounting?"

Jasper had dubbed his new sister-in-law an innocent, but the girl held her liquor and knew a ledger from a shopping list.

"I'm afraid my bookkeeper fails again to show, Miss Winthrop."

"I keep my father's books," she stated calmly, "and would be happy to assist, sir."

She was too much. "I rather doubt your bookkeeping is on the level required of a business like mine, miss." He tried not to stare at her bodice.

Her brow creased.

"But I appreciate the offer." He topped off his glass once more, taking another swig. "Now, how may I be of service to you?" He made a point to meet her ridiculously soft, doe eyes. "You do realize, that should anyone see you entering or leaving my establishment your reputation would be—"

"Ruined, yes. I'm aware." Her hand shook slightly as she stared down into her drink. "Mr. Harris, I seek assistance in a matter regarding my father's finances and thus my very future." Her hand steadied. "Now that my sister is newly married, my father is—for the moment, at least—flush with cash." She made a face. "But as you may surmise, sir, those funds will not last. Already there is a man my father entertains whom I…"

Harris leaned forward as her voice faltered.

"I fear expresses an interest in my person which I do not at all reciprocate."

Ah, he thought, the very thing Jasp feared would happen had, and soon. *Damnation.*

"I shall reach majority in but a month's time, sir, and should very much like to avoid being sold off before I am of age to reject this unwelcome marriage suit."

Harris admired the lady's pluck; she was also older than Jasp thought.

"In fact, I should like to amass enough cash of my own to secure my future without the need to marry at all."

He leaned back in his chair. Not nearly so meek, either. "And just how might *I* assist in this, miss? If you are not asking me to marry you myself, I don't see how I am to thwart your repugnant suitor."

Her face bloomed scarlet, but she held her ground. "Sir, you run a gaming house. I should like to place bets at your establishment to acquire enough funds to buy my way out of any marriage my father pressures me to accept."

Buy her way out o' marriage by gamblin' like her pot an' pan? Insane.

"Miss Winthrop." He resisted the urge to shake sense into her bouncing, brown curls. "That is a *very* bad idea."

Her lips pursed with displeasure.

"I am frankly surprised you'd wish to engage in the very same activity that keeps your father in waters so perilously deep."

She tipped back the rest of her glass and clanked it on his desk. "Mr. Harris, with all due respect, I am no fool."

The chit may as well have slapped him with her words.

"My sense of numbers is astute." Her eyes were now sharp as glass.

Crikey, Harris thought. "Shall we play a round of *vingt-et-un* then, miss?" He pulled out a deck from his top desk drawer, sliding it across to her.

"Yes, let's, Mr. Harris."

He won the first round neatly, as expected. But Miss Winthrop won the second and third, and every round thereafter. He did not need to test her further; she possessed the same uncanny knack for counting that Jasper Audrey did.

Harris swore under his breath. "You did not jest when you offered to help reckon my accounts, Miss Winthrop."

"I did not, sir."

He considered the lady anew. She must be desperate to come here on her own, to a gaming hell owner little better than a stranger, all to ask if she might cheat at cards to buy herself out of marriage.

"You *do* realize what you are asking, miss." He met her gaze.

Miss Winthrop's grip on her empty brandy fumbled so that the glass rolled clear across his desktop. He righted it.

"Mr. Harris, were women not barred from entering establishments such as your own, I would have gambled my family out of misfortune years ago."

"No doubt you would have." He poured her a spot more drink and shoved the glass back. "Tell me how you learned to play."

"Papa dealt me cards when I was a child; he called me his lucky little girl."

"And your sister? Is she aware of your … gift?"

"Lizzie has no interest in games of chance, sir. She remains our resident playwright, writing dramas we perform to amuse Papa. Her head remains buried squarely in her books, though she knows that I excel with numbers." A shadow crossed the lady's face. "My sister and I have managed our father's moods and finances without his knowledge our entire lives, Mr. Harris."

These Winthrop girls were no lightweights.

"But alas, as man of the house he somehow manages to squander every farthing we so diligently save."

Sharp words coming from such tempting lips… Harris leaned back in his seat. "It is indeed unfortunate to—"

"Be born a woman, sir?" Her doe eyes sparked. "Yet I can

remedy this, you see, by earning enough at your establishment to free myself from Papa for good. And I can do this without involving my sister, who has sacrificed enough on my behalf."

A single, sparkling tear tumbled down her flawless cheek, making Harris's bloody loins ache. "Miss Winthrop..." he began.

"Sir." She leaned forward, tear brushed aside and bosom all too deliciously close. "You are a man of business, of course. I am prepared to split my earnings with you, sixty-forty."

"But Miss Winthrop you're a—"

"I am aware I am a woman," she snapped. "But if I dress as a young man, and you introduce me as your cousin, or some lord's ward even, I might play without danger of discovery."

Harris violently shook his head.

"Fifty-fifty then."

"And just how much do you have to start, eh?" He scowled as the minx reached into her bodice—*Lord have mercy!*—to pull out a pouch of coin, emptying this upon his desk.

He snorted at the pathetic heap. "You'd need more'n that to even enter me establishment."

"How much?" She remained undeterred. "How much, at minimum, is required for entry?"

"Fifty pounds, miss."

She looked crestfallen.

"But even with that much coin, I'd not grant yer entry. I don't allow no inexperienced, unchaperoned ladies into *The Leaf*, for their own good, much as mine."

"Then I shall have to take my offer elsewhere." She stuck out her chin. "And you will lose out on my substantial profits."

Damn blast her!

"No, Miss Winthrop." Harris came to his senses fast. "You'll desist with yer mad plan an' instead seek yer brother-in-law's assistance." He was done with this conversation. "I'll drive yer to the Baron meself, right now in fact." He rose from his desk. "I'm sure he can resolve this in—"

"You will not, sir." She stood from her seat, shaking with visible anger. "I was quite clear I do not wish to involve my sister in this, and as a gentleman you will respect my wishes."

Lord help her, she thought him honorable.

"I'm sorry t' disappoint, luv, but as I own a gamin' hell, I'd hardly call meself a gentleman."

"But you were so gallant at the wedding! You gave me your card. You said you'd assist me."

She was again the chit Jasp had described.

"Well sure, miss, I can be charmin' when it suits." He crassly allowed his eyes to peruse her person, leaving no doubt as to why he'd behaved so politely before.

"Why, you are as insufferable as the Baron!" She scraped back her chair. "I am sorry I kept your card." She reached into her pocket to toss it on his desk. "Good day, sir."

Harris was pleased with himself until he—

"Wait!" He caught her about the waist just as she was about to exit. "You'll not endanger yerself by now visitin' some other gamin' den."

"Unhand me." Her eyes skewered him. "I may do as I wish."

She struggled in his grip but was unable to dislodge him. Harris had half a mind to throw her over his shoulder and deliver her to Jasper direct, *pain-in-the-arse miss.*

And then it hit him.

"O' course I can't keep you." He released her waist and took her hand, pretending again to 'gentleman.' "But I can, perhaps, offer a solution to your lack of funds."

"Oh?" Tiny freckles dotted the bridge of her nose. How'd he missed those?

He shook off her spell. "I am in need of a bookkeeper, it seems, and as you're in need of cash, why don't we discuss employment instead, over a glass of port perhaps?" He prayed she would accept; Jasp would flay him alive if she came to harm visiting some other den.

"Very well," she answered. "But no port, Mr. Harris. I've had enough to drink today."

With relief, Harris watched the lady sit back down. He allowed his eyes to devour her.

CHAPTER EIGHTEEN

"She *what?*" Milton could not believe his ears. "Annabelle Winthrop, pretty little milksop, proposed sharing her earnings with you, provided you let her game your patrons at *vingt-et-un?*" He remained incredulous. "Please tell me she's not—"

"Yer equal?" Arty appeared to be enjoying this. "Sure is, Jasp. In fact, I replaced me bookkeeper with 'er."

"You *what?*" Milton's incredulity doubled.

"I said, I hired Miss Winthrop as bookkeeper, t' keep 'er from runnin' to an even worse gamin' hell, which is what th' minx threatened t' do."

"Good God." Milton shook his head. "Lizzie's goddamn little sister…"

"Yes, yer wife's bloody sister, who *you* said needed protectin'."

"Well it is apparent I underestimated her." *Like I underestimated my wife.* "I'm sorry I got you into this, Arty, but it is clear we have a situation that needs immediate solving."

"Nope." Arty shook his head. "Already solved, Jasp. Did y' not hear me? I hired the chit. Fine bookkeeper too."

"Arty, that does not solve whoever this revolting suitor of hers is, nor how quickly her monster of a father will sell her off."

The two stared in silence at one another in Milton's smoking room.

"You should tell yer wife," Arty stated.

"Absolutely not."

"Are things not well in th' land o' matrimony, Jasp?"

"Arty, I do not wish to discuss my marriage. What I wish to discuss is how to keep Annabelle Winthrop from—"

"And just why're you so concerned with this miss?"

"Because she's my sister-in-law!" Milton erupted. "She is family now, and it is my duty to ensure she does not fall into—"

"Well you've a strange way o' showin' duty, Jasp, considerin' y' neatly swindled Lord Winthrop fer his eldest with nary a qualm fer that."

"Are you deliberately trying to vex me?" Milton rose to his feet. "Because if you are, I've a mind to wipe that bloody smirk from your face with my fist." He could, and would.

"Jasp, I ain't tryin' t' goad, guv, I'm simply pointin' out th' obvious. Y' pressured Winthrop, an' now another's doin' the same, like you expected might happen once word o' yer marriage got out. I don't want Miss Winthrop sold off neither, not when the girl's closin' me books at half price. But the fact o' the matter is—"

"The fact is, you will court her instead," Milton decided. "You will pose as a respectable suitor"—he amended his words at the look on Arty's face—"fine, *alternative* suitor, to create competition for her hand and drive this other fellow off. And as she'll need an excuse to leave her father's house to keep your books, you can court her in public and in private set her to work in your office. Done."

Arty's jaw slacked.

"Why are you looking at me like that?" Milton scowled. "It is the most obvious way to—"

"An' what if I'm courtin' someone else?"

Milton scoffed. "Arty, you plow through stage girls like other men plow through drink. You are not seriously courting any woman."

His friend flinched. "I may not officially be courtin', but there's a—"

"It is hardly a *lady* you woo. Just tell your latest infatuation that your courtship of Miss Winthrop is but for show, and then seduce the dancer or actress back into your bed. I don't see what the problem is."

"The problem, Jasp, is that you're callin' in a favor greater than what was asked at yer weddin'." Arty grimaced.

Milton almost felt bad. "I am, friend, and I am sorry for it. I did not intend for you to do more than keep an eye on Winthrop's gambling at *The Leaf*. I am doing my best to find his younger daughter some suitably bland nob from the *Ton*, but I've still too little influence with these dullards."

"Then why not talk t' yer wife?" Arty bit back. "'Tis the reason y' married her, right? Let 'er match make for her own sister. Hell, mayhap the girl's got eyes fer some gentleman what needs but a financial push. She's a sweet enough morsel to turn any chap's—"

"Sweet enough morsel?" Milton's lips curled. "Have a care, Arty, that you not court fair Miss Annabelle too far yourself."

Arthur harrumphed. "An' I'd warn you, Jasp, that if yer wife finds out you're scheming t' marry 'er sister off, she'll be none too pleased she weren't informed."

"Lizzie!" Milton bellowed from the hall. "Where the devil is my wife?" Having just sent Arty packing, he was in a foul mood following their discussion.

Murdoch hastened toward him. "Lady Milton's taken the phaeton to pay the Duchess of Allendale a visit, Jasp."

"Come again?" He felt gut punched.

"Lady Milton's taken the new phaeton and—"

"She is driving *my* phaeton? Alone? To visit Wellesley's wife?"

"Now Jasper," Murdoch began, "don't get yer knickers in a twist, lad."

"Fuck!"

"Jasp!" Her tone lashed. "We warned 'er not t' go without first askin' yer permission, but now she's mistress o' this house, we can't—"

"*I* am master of this house, Murdoch, and you lot take orders from me, not her."

Murdoch shot him a scathing look. "Boy, if you don't reign in yer temper, you're in fer a world o' married hurt." She crossed her arms and stared him down.

Only Milton wasn't listening; he'd known his housekeeper too long to let her shame him. "Murdoch," he said succinctly, "see that my horse is saddled. At once."

❧

Taking tea with the Duchess of Allendale was not only a joy, it was a balm. Elizabeth relished the freedom to make calls now on her own, as a married woman might. It made her soul feel light.

"Lizzie, pleasantries aside, you must tell me about your marriage." The Duchess set down her cup. "I admit your note concerned me."

Elizabeth recalled the haste with which she'd penned her post-wedding missive to the Duchess. She swallowed her nerves. "I fear the Baron's reasons for marrying me are not—"

"Above reproof?" The Duchess poured them each more tea. "I expect not. But you knew he was no gentleman when you married him."

"Yes." Elizabeth frowned into her cup. "Only I was not given a choice, Your Grace."

The Duchess rested her cup atop her swollen midriff. "Call me Charles in private, Lizzie," she reminded. "And no woman should be forced to wed a man she barely knows, let alone—"

"Then you were not … forced?" Elizabeth asked. "That is, you mentioned before the word coercion."

"I was coerced into becoming Lord Wellesley's mistress, Lizzie, not his wife." The Duchess did not blink stating this.

"Then why did you wed His Grace?" Elizabeth asked. "And why do you now seem happy?"

"Because I fell in love with the rake." She sighed. "He proved himself not only adroit in bed"—Elizabeth flushed at this—"but adroit in heart and spirit. By the time Roland Wellesley figured out he loved me too I made certain that man *earned* my hand in marriage."

Elizabeth's eyes widened. "You mean you—"

"Oh yes, turned the tables on him neatly." She grinned.

"You astound me, Charles. To think you went from—"

"Reluctant mistress to respectful wife? Humble housekeeper to haughty duchess?"

Her Grace was remarkably blunt.

"It was no easy journey." The Duchess looked wistful. "And you, my dear, are going about things quite opposite to me, for you have married first, and must now endeavor to fall in love."

"Love." Elizabeth harrumphed. "Love will never enter into my marriage."

"Is he good in bed, Lizzie?"

Elizabeth was unable to speak.

"Let us assume from the color of your face that he is. And let us admit you are not the only woman to assess Baron of Milton's abilities thus." Her eyes twinkled.

Elizabeth grimaced. "He has slept with half of London, yes."

"Then you have one point in favor of love, Lizzie, because carnal pleasure can lead to intimacy, which in turn can lead to trust."

Elizabeth shook her head. "I cannot trust him. He has proven himself so oft—"

"Is he capable of tenderness?" the Duchess interrupted.

Elizabeth paused. "It has felt so, on occasion, which confuses me only more, because his tenderness is fleeting, and he quickly reverts to being unnecessarily domineering."

"Hmm," the Duchess mused. "Tenderness and generosity. These, too, can lead to love. Point two falls in his favor."

"Does punishment point to love as well?" Elizabeth was unable to stop the words that tripped off her tongue. "For when I disobey him, he punishes me in the most egregious way. And if I—"

"Do not relinquish your soul to any man, Lizzie." The Duchess's tone sobered. "Only in love does one relinquish oneself and even then…" She shook her head, changing course. "Yet what of passion, dear? Is your husband passionate toward you?"

"Oh, he is passionate enough when he—" She flushed only more.

The Duchess studied her. "Then point three also falls to love's favor, because passion is as strong an emotion as anger and hate. Passion is not love's opposite. Indifference is."

Elizabeth was stunned. "You mean—"

"Does he punish with passion when you disobey him? Does he respond with passion when you irk or goad him?"

"He is a *beast* when I displease him. He is only tender when I—"

"When you submit or comply?"

Elizabeth nodded.

"Then he is not indifferent to you, which points toward either love or hate."

Elizabeth slumped against the settee. "Hate. He hates me."

"Or its opposite," the Duchess said softly. "My own husband, too, hid his heart behind his brash manner."

"I do not think my husband has a heart."

"That is not what Miss Li tells me, nor any whore in London."

"And do you often speak to London's whores?" Elizabeth forgot herself.

The Duchess laughed. "Oh, Lizzie, I have—never mind. This much I can tell you of your husband: He is a good man in some way, else my Roland would not consider him his friend. My husband never, ever wished to become Duke. He fought in vain to escape his birthright. Your husband, in contrast, has only ever wished to be a duke, yet never can, being but a duke's illegitimate firstborn."

Milton's father was no mere lord, he was a duke! Shock sank in.

"Both yearn for what they cannot have and forget, constantly, what they do have. Foolishly, they take their frustrations out on those they trust will hurt them least—and who deserve their wrath least too. None of which makes sense, but which is why, Elizabeth, I counsel patience in your marriage. Embrace the tenderness your husband grants and guard your soul against his need to control. But do not, my dear, give up on him entirely. Not until you've uncovered what drives the hurt he nurses." The Duchess gripped her belly as if she'd felt a kick. "You must unearth the man behind the baron."

Elizabeth pondered her Grace's words. Why was the Duchess's husband, a bona fide duke, friends with *her* husband, by-blow of some other duke? And which blasted duke? Or were the two half-brothers? More importantly, why did she feel like she was being punished for grievances Milton held which had nothing to do with her own family?

An image of her husband's scar-pocked flesh flashed through her head. Harm lay at the heart of Milton's hurt. It must, else he'd not shy so from her touch.

"Elizabeth." The Duchess interrupted her thoughts. "My cousin's coming out ball is this weekend, and it is time Baron of Milton and his new bride were seen in society. I'll ensure formal invitations get sent so both you and your sister may attend. It will be awkward, no doubt, but it's best you—"

"Where is she?" A voice boomed from the hall. "I know damn well she's here. Wellesley!" the voice shouted. "If you are harboring my wife, by God I'll—"

A second, lowered voice was heard to soothe the first.

The Duchess sighed. "Did you not tell your husband you planned to call on me today?"

Elizabeth shook her head.

"Well then, best get this over with."

Elizabeth knew she had but a minute to thank her new friend. "Your Grace, I—"

"*Charles*, Lizzie, please," the Duchess insisted. "You can 'Your Grace' me all you like at my cousin's ball, but in private I—"

"I am grateful for your counsel, Charles." She squeezed the Duchess's hand in her own. "I shall take your advice to heart."

And in Milton strode, the Duke of Allendale close at his heels. "Elizabeth, we are leaving. *Now*." Her husband's ice-blue eyes were storm clouds in the making.

"Of course." She curtsied, murmuring, "Your Grace" to both the Duchess and Duke, before she followed her husband out and into his phaeton.

❧

Milton sat stiff as a board beside Elizabeth, his thigh burning taut against her leg. She was both afraid and aroused—a state by now familiar. He'd hitched his mount to the back of the phaeton and kept the vehicle's gelding at a very brisk trot.

She steeled herself for punishment.

"You have disappointed me greatly, wife."

She worried her lip. "I did not think I'd broken any edicts by accepting the Duchess's invitation, sir. After all," she wagered, "to refuse would offend the Duchy, which I would never dream of doing, given your friendship with the Duke."

He looked like he wished to wring her neck. "You step on thin ice, Elizabeth. *Most* thin."

"Are you angry that I drove your phaeton?" As usual, her own temper rose in response to his. "I thought you wished it paraded about town."

A growl emanated from deep within his throat, yet Elizabeth could not seem to stop. He was being utterly unreasonable; her visit was entirely within normal social bounds.

"Or are you angry I left your bed this morning to breakfast alone in my room? I did so out of respect for your mood, sir, presuming you did not wish to—"

Milton shoved his tongue down her throat so fast she fell breathlessly silent. When he was done ravishing her mouth—not once breaking the horse's trot—he savagely hissed in her ear, "Shut. Up."

Elizabeth kept her mouth closed for the remainder of their drive back. Yet the moment they alighted from the phaeton, he marched her straight into his office, a room she'd yet to see. He locked the door behind them, and she feared at once he'd be a brute.

Sure enough, he pushed her to her knees and unbuttoned

his fall. "You will service me with your mouth, so that your lips rouse only my desire, rather than my continued ire."

Milton shoved his fully aroused cock down her throat.

It happened so fast, Elizabeth choked on her husband's thick member, her soul separating from her body, her mind scrambling to comprehend this attack. He was forcing her to acquiesce, and she tried valiantly to withstand him, please him even in order to bring an end to her torment, but his thrusts were relentless.

Until she peered up into his face and saw therein a look of utter desperation.

So. He was not immune to her, after all. The Duchess's words returned, making Elizabeth realize she might wrest back control, make him spill when *she* determined, not when he felt ready. The memory of Evie controlling that man's pleasure at *LeBrecht's* gave Elizabeth the nudge needed to use lips and tongue to full advantage.

And she did. She was soon relishing the tortured look on her husband's face as she worked him more lasciviously, enjoying her labor now as she moaned against his swollen, dripping rod, gripping his buttocks with both hands to take him ever deeper. She could sense him battling for control, struggling against her efforts—until he pushed her off and stumbled back, gasping for air.

"Fuck!" He yanked her to her feet and spun her up against his desk to lift her skirts and tear her offending drawers in two. Elizabeth welcomed his swift, harsh entry. She did not fear this. She felt empowered. Triumphant, even.

"You'll pay for that, harlot." He pumped hard and fast. "For I'll not spend down your throat till you're round with my child. My seed will not be wasted, Lizzie, not when it is your duty to give me heirs."

He shuddered inside her, without care for her pleasure this time, then gripped the nape of her neck to bend her over so that her forehead touched the wood of his desk. "You will remain in this position, arse up, to let my seed take root." He pulled out slowly, as if careful not to spill.

She heard drink poured at the sideboard while her body quaked over his desk. The bastard had left her in this degrading position because he could. She knew what he'd do next.

He softly stroked her buttocks while he sipped his blasted drink. "You will count aloud each strike I wield, as reminder of why I punish you today."

Only his words did not reduce her, they spurred her to revolt, fueled her competitive streak. She'd count until *he* gave up. Gave in.

"You will be given five strokes for wearing drawers again. Another five for attempting to control my pleasure, and ten for visiting the Duchess without my permission only to goad me on our drive back. All of which are rules, Elizabeth, you know full well you must obey."

"To hell with your rules," she muttered into his desk.

"What was that, love?" He put his drink down right beside her.

She wished to strike it to the floor, smash the glass to bits.

"Beat me all you like." She spoke through gritted teeth. "But to use the word *love* in jest is an insult I'll not take." A bonfire rose in Elizabeth's chest. "Love does not dominate, it cultivates, Jasper Audrey. Or have you never read Goethe?"

***

"*Love*, Lizzie," Milton hissed into her ear, "inflames."

His palm cracked her backside so hard she jerked, shouting "One!" in brash defiance.

"Two!" came out in willful disrespect, subsequent strikes met with only more perverse, adverse counts spilling from his wife's lips. She'd insulted his intelligence, his birth, and his position as her husband—and now the wench had the gall to reach ten with nary a tear.

By fifteen, Milton's breaths were ragged, his anger spinning out of reach. "Do you wish to continue, Elizabeth?" He squeezed her nape. "I did not plan to go this far with you," he threatened, "but if you continue to resist my orders, I will. Cease this mad defiance, woman, cede to me this instant."

"Do your worst," she spat as Milton stepped back, stunned.

Why would she not—break?

Without thinking, he strode to his desk, reached for his ruler, and then raised his arm, heart pounding, to silence her for good. Only she lost it on the third strike, puddling into tear-filled pleading, the slim wooden tool too harsh for her high-born flesh. He let it drop to the floor in disgust at himself.

Screams, smells.

Crushing weight pressed his chest, smothered all air, as a voice laughed low in his head: *There 'tis, Jasp. I taught yer well, didn't I, lad?*

He couldn't breathe, could barely see.

Milton fled the room. Reeling.

CHAPTER NINETEEN

Her husband had been too cruel; Elizabeth's life would nevermore be hers. Week two of her ill-begotten marriage and already all hope dashed. Destroyed.

Yet she'd weep no more, because Baron of Milton did not matter anymore. Nothing he could do or say to her would matter, for she was done trying. *Done.*

She rolled over in her bed to ease her aching buttocks. The Duchess of Allendale had been absurd to think love might ever enter into such a union as was hers, for her husband was beyond redemption. He'd beaten her with the same implement he used to underscore his sums, as if she were but another line in his accounts. Which she undeniably was.

There was no coming back from such an act. She had to find another way to exist in this world—*his* world. A way which excluded him from her day-to-day life as much as humanly possible.

Yet what world was that?

She pondered her predicament while she shifted her sore bottom once again. Her writing—books—might offer her salvation. They had with Papa. She might escape her rotten husband not in defiance of his orders but by escaping into worlds he could not touch, stories he could not bend to his will. Journeys she, alone, might travel in her mind, where the awful Baron could not follow.

Elizabeth willed herself to get out of bed and start the day. Before breakfast even arrived she stood—rather than sat—at her escritoire to write. She must find a way to withstand the brute, because she was too weak to withstand his beatings.

Milton owned her flesh, but he would never own her soul.

She focused on her story, making the brooding villain pay for his evil ways. She tortured him with ink, the only weapon she might wield. He would pay for his transgressions, suffer for all his sins, before he died an ignoble death mourned by none. He'd not harm the heroine again, because in the end, she would save herself, brilliantly.

As she scrawled words across the parchment a fat tear smudged her ink. Elizabeth blotted it with a curse, but then another fell, *plop*.

She used her kerchief to wipe her eyes, then sniffed and squared her shoulders. Once the page dried, she would simply write over the stains.

"Jasper, you are a blighter and a cad." Li glared at him, her ink-black eyes matching her indigo-black hair. "You cannot take a ruler to a blueblood's backside and think she will forgive you."

"Now that is not entirely true, Li," Milton answered. "I've taken a cane to many a—"

"Jasper, I am talking about an innocent young woman, not those depraved sods from the *Ton* who beg you to beat them so they feel something again. Your wife feels in abundance, all the time, in ways you clearly found appealing until you had the terrific bad sense to beat all feeling out of her."

Milton winced.

"This will require a deal more groveling than gifts. Frankly, she may never come back to you after such mistreatment. I warned you not to marry the eldest. I told you to—"

"Yes, *yes!* Li, I married the wrong goddamn girl and now I've injured the wrong goddamn girl too. That is not why I am here, and it is not the first I've had to eat humble pie before your royal highness."

Her frown became a scowl, because very few people on this continent would dare call her that, and he was unfortunate enough to be one of them.

"I will admit you are a loyal idiot, else I would not tolerate you at all." Li's mouth pinched. "I will speak with her, as should you."

"And say what? That I am sorry I beat her like I'd not beat my own dog? That I can't promise it won't happen again?" He snorted his disgust. "That I am a man so broken and despicable I cannot bear to tolerate the very spirit of defiance which draws me to her like a moth to flame?"

Li coolly stared him in the eye. "Yes, to start, you might say exactly that. And a good many other things. You married her, after all, so you are stuck with her. And if you'd rather not spend the rest of your life in icy détente with a wife you *chose*, Jasper, then revealing something of yourself, your past, is the only way she might begin to thaw."

Milton shut his eyes, in pain.

"I have known women like Elizabeth Winthrop, and they cannot be bought with expensive, pretty baubles. Woo her with depth, with the language of the books you say she admires. You may have mastered her flesh, but to master her soul requires more nuanced work."

"I do not want a wife to be *work*, Li." He ground his teeth.

"Then you chose unwisely, natterhead." She smacked him hard with her fan.

"Ow!"

"Go home, Jasper, and determine your own way out of this mess. I've my own messes to deal with. I don't need you complicating my life."

"Li, surely I do not complicate. Surely I do but—"

"Amuse, sir?" She smiled so coquettishly, so like the Li he'd known once long ago, that for an instant memories flooded back.

"No, *mon cher*," she told him, the moment dissolving like mist. "You no longer amuse, you abuse my counsel. Now get out of my shop and see that your wife grows to love you as I do." She cracked her ivory fan across his nose once more, sashaying from the room in her long red skirts, just like a princess would.

Milton sat a moment longer on the mat in Li's tea room. Never had he wished to cause his wife such misery and pain. He'd spanked her before as a means of control—his own and hers. But this last punishment had felt different. *He'd* lost control, an unforgivable lapse. Elizabeth had brought out the very worst in him, and he hated her for it, though he hated himself even more. She'd goaded him into breaking his own blasted code of honor—and now he'd pay for marrying the wrong woman for the rest of his godforsaken life.

Yet he wanted her, his longing for Elizabeth most bizarre. He didn't know why he wanted his wife's affection when he knew such weakness was at worst a liability, at best a futile hope. His past would forever haunt and taunt him. And Elizabeth would now submit to him for fear alone.

Fuck! He did not wish to be cruel. He simply wished to bring his wife in line.

To hell with Li's advice, Milton thought. He knew what he must do.

❧

"They all know, don't they?" Elizabeth asked Ginny as she soaked for the second time that day in a bath. Her bottom still ached, despite the arnica and witch hazel liniment her maid had liberally applied. The ruler had left raised welts; it would take time for her skin to heal.

"Well now…" Across the room Ginny fussed with Elizabeth's dress.

Of course they all knew. The servants had been too kind: a posy at her bedside and chocolate for breakfast. A croissant with a yellow pansy tucked beside it on the plate. Gerald had even complimented her green frock. It was mortifying one's household knew so much, humiliating to endure their pity.

"It doesn't matter," Elizabeth muttered to herself for the hundredth time that day. "It doesn't matter what they think of me now."

"Think o' you, ma'am!" Ginny's words exploded. "'Tis what they think o' *him*. In t' doghouse, he is! Burnt toast fer breakfast an' salt in 'is coffee. Jack even told 'im t' saddle 'is own mount when he made off in a huff this morn. An' deserves it, he do, every bit of our—"

Elizabeth interrupted. "Where did the Baron go, Ginny, do you know? I should like to avoid him if I can."

"Dunno, ma'am. A ride t' burn things off, I s'pose. He does that when he gets in one of his moods. Or went t' see Miss Li, mayhap. Depends right much on 'er counsel if y' ask me."

Miss Li, Elizabeth realized, had not replied to the letter she'd sent. Perhaps she should call on the lady herself, provided her beast of a husband would allow it. And her mother-in-law, Madam Audrey, had not replied either, hmm. No doubt Milton's closest confidantes wished nothing more to do with her now that she was his property.

They were not property. He respected their ability and intelligence, if not her own.

Elizabeth tamped down her infernal anger. She'd sworn off all emotion; she was turning over a new leaf in her marriage, one which focused inward, not outward or back. One which required as little contact with her bastard of a husband as possible.

That night, Milton slipped into his wife's chamber to deliver her a bedside note, presuming she slept. Instead, he found her submerged in a bath, eyes closed, dark hair floating like the Lady of the Lake. Her nipples peeked above in rosy decadence, her legs bent at angles so that her knees poked out. He was stricken by her beauty, and by how wretched her beauty made him feel.

He crept back to his room before she could catch him spying, yet sleep refused to come. He tossed and turned, imagining a way to right this sinking ship and amend his rotten ways. He imagined becoming the man he wished to be, rather than the man he seemed destined to remain.

She could hardly remain angry at him forever, could she?

Yet a voice inside Milton whispered that his wife could, and would stay angry. Because a woman forged like Elizabeth—fierce and smart and proud—might hold a grudge for a very long time. Li had. Years ago, Li had been so furious at both himself and Wells it had taken no small degree of groveling on both their parts for her to come around.

Not even Mutton could ease Milton's misery. The wolfhound slept at the foot of his master's bed, in reproach of all Milton was—and would never become.

***

Elizabeth sank deeper into the deliciously hot water, submerging herself in silence. She knew she'd taxed staff with a third bath as well as by taking dinner in her room. She'd managed all day to avoid her miserable husband but was sure she'd be forced to do her duty by him again this night, slave to his conjugal rights.

How she hated Mother England, whose women had no rights!

She willed herself not to fear her husband's touch, for she'd enjoyed their congress before. Only now she felt deceived—had allowed herself to *be* deceived—by imagining emotion ever entered the Baron's twisted mind. She'd confused bodily pleasure with sentiment, letting herself foolishly feel for the man when she was but a vessel for his offspring, nothing more.

Elizabeth broke the bath's surface and stepped out to don her banyan, having long dismissed Ginny. She reached for the salve beside her bed and saw a note laid across its lid.

> *Elizabeth, I will not ask you to visit my chamber this night. You are hurting, and I am unable to speak, let alone write, words to relieve your pain. There are no words to undo what I have done. I can only beg your forgiveness. —Milton*

Surprise, irritation, and a million other feelings flooded her mind. She stuffed his note into her drawer. He'd not said that he was sorry, he'd merely begged for *her* forgiveness. And why should she now shoulder his guilt? He was not, at heart, repentant. He was like a surly, sullen child. Perhaps staff had made him write it. Yes, Gerald had told him to apologize. Or Murdoch. Milton had acted sorry before and not meant it; let him lie in the bed he'd made and stew.

She applied more salve to her posterior, pulled on her night-rail, and laid herself upon her stomach, willing sleep to come.

When it did, her devil of a husband entered her dreams with singular insistence, until she awoke and poured her dreams onto pages lit by the faint light of dawn. Elizabeth covered one blank canvas after another in sprawling, curling script, her tale unfurling with fantastical reach into ever darker realms.

At times she did not recognize the words she wrote—as if they were not hers, but his.

CHAPTER TWENTY

Trapped in the drawing room with her father and Mr. Finch, Annabelle bit her tongue so that she would not weep. Scarcely two weeks since Lizzie had left and already, Papa looked to marry her off too. Though if she earned enough balancing Mr. Harris's books while pawning more trinkets from the house, perhaps she'd reach the fifty pounds she needed to play his tables.

Not perhaps, *must*. She would amass that coin, by hook or crook, because Mr. Harris had, in his own way, bolstered her hope. Rude at points, especially when he'd escorted her that first day out of *The Gilded Leaf* straight into a waiting hansom, but at least he employed her now for pay.

Besides, his all-too-wanton perusal of her person had felt quite different from Mr. Finch's rank stares. In truth, Mr. Harris's twinkling eyes had made Annabelle's insides flip. His hair was mostly flaxen, his skin a soft-bronzed hue, and his lips terribly inviting—not to mention the way his long legs had leaned rakishly against his desk.

Annabelle curbed her unwholesome thoughts. Mr. Harris was her employer, not some dandy to swoon over. He'd been thrilled she'd reconciled his books in half the time his usual bookkeeper took. He'd soon see she was a 'boon to business,' and then he might let her gamble at his tables and split the profits like she'd offered. With just a bit more effort, Annabelle was certain she could win Mr. Harris over.

The problem was, time was not on her side.

"You've a letter, miss." Papa's ill-mannered footman barged in, rudely shoving the note at Annabelle in front of her father and Mr. Finch. The two looked expectantly at her as she cracked open the thick seal.

The Earl and Countess of Denbigh cordially request the honor of your company at a ball in celebration of the coming out of their granddaughter, Miss Mercy Pendrake, this Sunday, nine o'clock, 8 Coventry Street.

"Bella, do not keep us in suspense," her father urged.

Suspense. As if he hadn't kept her and Lizzie in suspense all their lives…

"We have been invited to the Denbigh ball this Sunday, Papa." She was thrilled she might attend a ball, at last! "It is surely Lizzie's doing, as the Duchess of Allendale is the Earl of Denbigh's granddaughter, whose husband, the Duke, is a friend to Lizzie's husband, the Baron. May we go, Papa, please?"

"Why, of course we must go." Her father beamed. "And Mr. Finch may escort you."

Annabelle froze. "Father," she dopped her voice, "his name is *not* on the invitation."

"Then we shall procure him one. Write to Lizzie to request she do so."

"But Father, one cannot simply demand an—"

"Nonsense." He glanced nervously at Finch, whose tongue

clicked that awful tooth back and forth between his hairy, hanging jowls.

Annabelle's hopes plummeted; she felt she might be sick.

"Miss, you've another caller." The incorrigible footman barged in again, this time with a vase of blooms.

"Bearing flowers?" Papa stood from his chair, demanding, "What card was left?"

The footman handed him the card—while slyly slipping Bella a separate note—all while Mr. Finch scowled at the vase of red ranunculus.

"Ah." Her father looked suddenly nervous. "Mr. Finch, good sir, I am afraid we must bid you farewell as I have, er, business to attend to." He began to show their visitor out. "I do hope you'll call again tomorrow, sir. Don't you, Bella?"

She quickly hid the note in her dress folds.

"*Bella*?" Papa insisted.

She looked up. "Oh, good day, Mr. Finch." But already the man pressed wet lips to her knuckles. The moment he turned she wiped them on her skirts and furtively read the note.

Follow my lead. I will explain my reasons. —A. Harris

Annabelle's heart soared. Was Mr. Harris as 'dazzled by her charms' as his bouquet announced? She crushed his note into her pocket while Papa ushered Mr. Finch out.

Seconds later, Mr. Harris walked in, both callers surely having passed one another in the hall.

In three strides, Mr. Harris warmly pressed his lips to her hand.

Dry lips, she thought. *Dry and firm and…*

"Mr. Harris." She dropped into a curtsy.

***

Harris adjusted his waistcoat, because Miss Winthrop's genuflect had just granted him direct view of the lady's cleavage. He quietly cursed her beauty. Again.

"Harris." Winthrop sounded put out. "To what do we owe this visit, sir?"

"Why, your daughter, milord. Since making her acquaintance at the Baron's wedding, I've been able to think of nothing and no one else. I intend to court her."

"C-court her?" Winthrop stuttered. "But she is not—Annabelle is not even—"

"Lord Winthrop, was that not Mr. Finch I just saw leave your house? Does he not court your daughter too?" It took everything in Harris's being not to cuff this fool. "I realize Miss Winthrop has not been formally presented in society, but good sir, a lady so charming, accomplished, and tenacious of spirit"—he winked at Annabelle, making her blush—"renders a man quite powerless to resist. I beg an audience with your daughter this very day."

Winthrop fell speechless, as expected, his face turning a mottled maroon, veins pulsing at his temples. "I … That is …"

"Perhaps you are overcome by such declaration of sentiment, but I do not jest, sir. I am utterly enamored of your daughter and aim to woo her until she accepts."

"Accepts?" Winthrop's face mottled a shade darker.

Harris pulled Annabelle from her seat and tucked her arm in his. "A walk about the neighborhood for some fresh air is just the thing, don't you agree, Miss Winthrop?" He prayed she'd play along.

"Oh yes, Mr. Harris. Indeed, I should love a walk." She'd regained her composure quickly. "We won't be long, Papa," she told her father, who remained standing in the parlor in stunned confusion.

Harris quit the room with her as fast as his legs could take him—and before any chaperone should show up to interfere.

The moment they were outdoors, the lady coughed, *ahem.* "An explanation, Mr. Harris, is in order I believe?"

"Of course, Miss Winthrop. But first I must confirm: This Mr. Finch I just saw quit your house, is he the man you described courting you?"

"He is the reason I sought your help, sir."

"Then I understand your situation, miss, and empathize all the more."

"You know him?"

"Miss Winthrop, I—" He halted on the street, overcome. "We must do everything in our power to ensure you do not marry him."

She stiffened on his arm. "Then he is worse than I imagine?"

"Annabelle, he is—" He swallowed. "Forgive me for being so familiar, miss, but Mr. Finch is—"

"Not at all, sir." Her smile was radiant. "And you may call me Bella, as both my employer and, I now presume, my suitor."

"And you may call me Arthur, Bella. But if your father is at all mixed up with Ronny Finch, his courtship does not bode well for you, or for your papa."

"Which is why you have decided to court me too?" She arched one elegant eyebrow, making his knees weak. *Damnation, Jasp!*

Harris gathered his wits, fast. "Yes. More suitors create more competition for your hand, thereby demonstrating your worth."

"But posing as my suitor does little to prevent my father marrying me off to someone else, someone worse, perhaps, than—"

"No one is worse than Finch, Bella. *No one.*" He prayed she wouldn't ask why, because he didn't want to have to tell her.

"Then I must win big, sir, at your tables, in order to free myself." She met his eyes with fresh determination.

Harris scowled back.

"Please, Arthur, let me disguise myself and—"

"No." He pulled her close, turning them about. "You will be that much more vulnerable."

"But I will not lose!" She halted them there upon the street, nearly stomping her dainty foot in dismay. "You know I won't lose, so why can't I—"

Without thinking, Harris drew her to a dark doorway and pressed Miss Winthrop into the fibers of his coat. "Forgive me, Bella." He spoke roughly into her hair. "But I'll not 'ave you jumpin' from fry pan into fire."

Nor would her brother-in-law allow it. Harris reminded himself he was protecting this young woman for Jasper's sake, not his own.

The moment Mr. Harris dropped her home, Papa interrogated Annabelle. She, of course, gave him only the vaguest answers, pretending to still be his foolish little girl. Because whatever her father's connection to Mr. Finch, she now knew matters were worse than she'd assumed. Mr. Harris had given her every reason to think that if Papa did not submit to Mr. Finch's wishes, he'd pay a price beyond the mere financial.

She did not wish to know what that price would be.

Annabelle feared she'd need her sister's help after all, just as soon as she determined *how*. Though she had Mr. Harris on her side at least. Well, almost. He still wouldn't let her play his tables, but he was a better man than most to offer her his help.

And handsome. Lord help her, Arthur Harris had looked fine flashing her his singularly crooked grin. He smiled with his eyes too, emerald gems beneath that mop of gold hair.

Papa droned on. She must *not* start mooning over Mr. Harris. She was a lady of high morals, lacking only in funds. Substantial funds. She would require a great deal more cash than Mr. Harris was paying her to bookkeep, if she wished to free herself from Finch and future suitors.

The only way to do this, Annabelle slowly realized, was to beat both men at their game. *Indeed,* she smiled to herself while Papa continued muttering and sputtering. Perhaps she didn't need Arthur Harris's permission to play his tables. Perhaps she merely needed fifty pounds to gain entry to his den. And this she might accomplish with the help of her dear sister.

Annabelle's smile spread. Tomorrow she'd pay Elizabeth a visit. She didn't need Mr. Harris's courtship or his wages. All she needed was collateral. Though when he'd held her in his arms in that secluded doorway, she'd not wanted the moment to end.

CHAPTER TWENTY-ONE

"Wollstonecraft, eh?" Milton's tutor looked surprised. "I didn't take you for the sort to open Pandora's box, Jasper, but I am happy to open it with you."

"Yes, well." Milton dismissed Kilpert's words with a wave of his hand. "My wife mentioned the author in passing, so I merely thought to—"

"Wife, right." Paul Kilpert had been one of a handful to miss Milton's wedding. "All the more reason to read *A Vindication of the Rights of Woman* then. It will give you plenty to chew on, and even more to discuss with your wife should she be inclined to—"

"I have *no* intention of discussing it with her," Milton bit back.

His tutor wisely shut his lips. "Transcendentalism then, for today."

"Transcend-what?" Milton frowned. "Paul, you know I've no patience for pseudo-science and attempts to speak with the dead."

Kilpert grinned. "I am speaking of transcendentalist philosophy, Jasp. The idea that both man and woman contain knowledge of themselves and the world which 'transcends' that which our five senses can perceive."

"Poppycock."

"I assumed you'd think as much. But transcendentalism proposes knowledge can arrive through intuition and imagination, rather than through physical senses, or human logic, alone. It argues we should trust our inner selves to be the authority on what is right and wrong."

"I trust only those who trust in my own—" He was about to say 'authority' when a knock interrupted.

"Enter," Milton barked, annoyed.

Elizabeth walked in, stiff as a board.

He was at once put on edge.

"Please forgive the interruption, sir. Permission to speak with you a moment?"

Milton stared at his wife who stared down at the floor in a manner most unlike her. He grimaced. "Granted."

"In private?" Her eyes flicked to his guest.

"Paul won't mind." He suddenly did not wish to speak to her alone. "Kilpert, my wife, Elizabeth Audrey, Baroness of Milton. Lizzie, Paul Kilpert, my tutor."

"Tutor?"

"Yes." Milton flinched. "Kilpert fills the gaps in my education. You may recall I was too busy amassing my fortune to comb the hallowed halls of Oxford or Eton."

"Lady Milton." Paul bent politely over Lizzie's hand. "It is an honor to meet you. I am one of your husband's greatest fans, as he is not only my best student, but also my benefactor."

"Benefactor?" Elizabeth seemed only more surprised. "How, sir?"

"In exchange for our scholarly sessions, your husband pays me a stipend to research and write books on—"

"Kilpert, I pay you to tutor *me*, not my wife." Paul had stared at Lizzie long enough. He was also undoubtedly the sort of erudite young man to appeal to a mind as curious as Elizabeth's. "And Lizzie, you've obviously come with a request, so ask it quick, before I lose patience with you as well."

She promptly changed tack. "I would like permission to redecorate my chamber, sir," she asked.

Milton scowled to himself, irritated that she should interrupt him for something so frivolous as this. "Of course you may redecorate. I don't care how you arrange your private chamber. Cost is no issue."

"Thank you." Elizabeth bent her head again in deference. "It was a pleasure to meet you, Mr. Kilpert." She paused. "And to learn my husband continues to improve himself with further study."

Milton stared after her as she exited. "Scratch transcendentalism," he told Kilpert. "I wish to tackle Wollstonecraft instead."

❧

Relieved her husband had granted her request, Elizabeth sought Gerald to discuss constructing bookshelves in her bedroom. She would ask Murdoch and Ginny to move her to a guest room in the interim, because she was determined to progress *toward* something now, rather than stagnate in the morass that was her marriage. Bookshelves might seem insignificant, a paltry endeavor even, but they were a change, and any change, however slight, would help improve her mood.

She'd been surprised her husband had a tutor, though, for what did this Mr. Kilpert talk to Milton about? What did they read together? And why could she not join in their discussions? It might have brought them closer, she and her husband, had he only allowed it. Instead, he'd flippantly given her leave to redecorate, no expense spared—as if that would shut her up.

Well it would. She'd barricade herself with books and tutor

herself. In fact, she'd *write* her own blasted books. She'd emerge only when duty—

A footman appeared. "You've a caller, ma'am. Madam LeBrecht."

"*Oh.*"

A minute later, Elizabeth greeted Miss Li in the parlor. "It is good of you to call, madam."

"Your note concerned me, Elizabeth." The lady stared back, unblinking.

"Yes, well, wedding jitters are long behind me." Elizabeth's own pulse raced. "I have no illusions anymore as to the man I married."

"My dear, you know next to nothing of the man you married."

"And you do?" Elizabeth despised Miss Li's impertinence.

"Yes. And I will share what I know about your husband, provided you will listen."

Elizabeth squared her shoulders just as tea was brought in. "I am all ears, madam."

Li's gaze flicked over her as if she did not believe Elizabeth. "I urged Jasper to tell you himself about his past, but he remains mulishly reticent."

"But why?" The question burst from Elizabeth's mouth. "Why not reveal things to one's own wife, for goodness' sake?"

Miss Li took up the teakettle just like in her shop, pouring them each a cup in that long, fluid motion she had. "Elizabeth, you've been a wife for less than a month, knowing Jasper at most a week longer. That is reason enough, I daresay, as to why he won't reveal more."

Elizabeth tried not to scowl at the lady.

"If you had an unsavory past, would you wish to confide its sordid details to a mere stranger?"

"But I am not a stranger, I am his—"

"For all intents and purposes, Elizabeth, you are as much a stranger to him as he is to you."

Elizabeth's retort died on her lips.

"I am not here to defend your husband's behavior," Miss Li continued, "which is reprehensible, to say the least."

So Li also knew Milton had beaten his wife? Had he told her himself? Or did the lady have spies amongst the servants? Perhaps all of London knew.

"But I *am* here to explain, in part, why Jasper does what he does. I do not condone his actions, Lizzie, let us be very clear on this. But I should like you to consider, at least, that the man you married is perhaps not so terrible as you think."

Elizabeth's hackles rose. "And how is it you know him so well, madam?"

Her smile turned rueful. "Jasper and Roland—the Duke of Allendale, that is—saved my life. I am not a native of your land, as I am sure you have guessed. They found me on their travels to East Asia, where I was shackled, you might say, to a deeply undesirable fate."

Elizabeth's thoughts flew in a million directions, but she knew better than to interrupt and give Miss Li a reason to tell her less.

"I was grateful enough for their help that I rewarded both men in the only manner I knew how. And Jasper and Roland, being of youthful temper in those days, did not take kindly to being rewarded in like fashion." Li barely contained her smirk. "They thought themselves in love, but really they were but enraptured by my skill." She paused. "I know how to wrap a man about my finger, Elizabeth. I believe that is the expression here, yes?"

Elizabeth could not imagine her husband in love with anyone, not even Miss Li.

"When I let both men know I wanted neither of their hearts, they decided their friendship was worth more than a woman who did not return their affections. So they dumped me here in London and went about their—"

"They *dumped* you?" Elizabeth exclaimed. "After they'd used you so shamelessly?"

Li's eyes sparked. "Elizabeth, your outrage flatters, but I assure you it was *I* who used them. Back then, I trusted no man, none. I believed myself better off without them. Little did I know that London was not Kyoto. It was impossible to be as self-sufficient here as I'd been there..." She broke off, as if memories pained her.

"Suffice to say, I did not fare well in your fair city. Yet Roland and Jasper selflessly came to my rescue again, past grievances forgotten. They saved me not once, but twice, Elizabeth. Twice do I owe both men my life. And in return they asked for nothing."

The intensity of Li's expression nearly blinded Elizabeth.

"I do not think you realize what a gift that is to a woman with my past. They asked for nothing in return, Elizabeth. *Nothing*. And so I trust them like I trust no others. They are my family. And though I do not hesitate to call them out when they are being what you English call knuckleheads"—Elizabeth smiled at the lady's choice term—"at heart they are the most noble men I know. They are noble when it counts most, you see. When a person needs them most. I cannot call them good men, not the way you English define this word 'good.' But noble, honorable, these are words I understand. This is what allows me to trust them implicitly."

Elizabeth's tea had grown lukewarm. She recalled what the Duchess of Allendale had said of the Duke, and what all Miss Li's servants had told her of Jasper Audrey, friend to whores. Again and again they'd spoken of Milton's generosity. And yet with her, his own wife, the Baron remained callous and cruel.

Miss Li lifted the teapot as Elizabeth held out her cup for more. The liquid arced to the porcelain, not a drop spilled.

The lady swirled the dark brew in her cup before she inhaled its steam, bathing her face in mist.

"He beat you, I know," she told Elizabeth quietly. "He should not have."

Elizabeth could not respond to such a statement.

"He told me how much he regrets it, Elizabeth."

Her lips merely tightened.

"Jasper was beaten himself, often, as a boy. He was beaten to comply. And it was not his mother who beat him."

Elizabeth sucked in her next breath.

"When he was older, he beat others for their pleasure. It is a difficult concept to grasp, but for some, there is release in pain. And Jasper…" She sighed. "He was forced to do things to spare his mother, to defend those he'd sworn valiantly to protect."

Li's eyes met Elizabeth's with painful honesty—a look she imagined this woman showed few. "For a good part of his life, you see, Jasper had no control over his existence. He worked incredibly hard to regain that control, so when anything threatens to steal it, to upend the life he's so carefully built, I believe it robs him of his ability to think clearly. He reverts to old patterns, to instincts carved deep in his bones."

A chill crawled up Elizabeth's spine.

"And you, my dear, threaten Jasper in ways he's not been threatened before. Your very presence disrupts his life. With every attempt you make to understand him better, you force him to understand himself, to reconcile the present with the past—a task few willingly undertake. I do not think Jasper understood this when he married you. He did not realize that to open himself to feeling, he would also open himself to hurt. And so he fights this hurt, fights *you*, Elizabeth, with the only weapons he knows: punishment and pain. For that is how others hurt him."

Li took a long sip and leaned back against her seat. "I do

not tell you this to excuse his actions—please understand me." She looked at Elizabeth intently. "*Never* will I excuse a man who beats his wife, who beats any woman. But I do not believe it was Jasper's conscious intent to do you harm. And I stand by my knowledge of him as an honorable man."

Elizabeth remained silent, because Li's words made matters only more difficult; it was easier to hate her husband than to feel empathy for him.

"Tell me, Miss Li, do you know about his rules?"

"Rules?" The lady frowned.

"The Baron taught me six lessons the week we courted. Rules specific to his wife, apparently."

"Interesting," Li murmured.

"Do not cross him, do not insult by being late, do not goad him, do not touch without permission, do not try his patience, and do not disobey."

"*Hmm.*"

"You do not find this odd, madam?"

Miss Li regarded Elizabeth over her teacup. "If I know Jasper, he created those rules in order to protect you, Lizzie, from himself."

Elizabeth struggled to comprehend the lady's words.

Miss Li looked at her. "When it comes to Jasper Audrey, my dear, nothing is black and white."

The two fell silent, staring into their cups, until Elizabeth felt the need to ask one final question. "He also—" Her face heated. "He spanked me too, you see, and I did not—I did not find it unpleasant. It was not—" She struggled to explain. "It was more the release you mentioned before, when you said that some people seek…" She was too mortified to continue.

Li took Elizabeth's hand and squeezed. "My dear, what pleases two adults in the privacy of their bedchamber is no one's business but their own. What you enjoy and consent to is very different from that which is imposed on you." She tipped her head closer. "Should you *consent* to forms of punishment you find pleasurable, that is perfectly alright. It is only wrong when it is done against your will. Do you understand, Elizabeth?"

Pleasure in punishment?

"What you consent to accept from your husband is a matter between you and him alone. But you must consent to such obedience. You must desire it. Give it willingly, freely, and you may well derive pleasure from it, but if taken by force, against your will, you shall have no marriage." She set down her cup. "Jasper must understand this too. You must both find your way in this."

Li abruptly rose from the chaise as if she'd said too much.

Elizabeth let the lady go, her mind awash with thoughts too astonishing to contemplate.

CHAPTER TWENTY-TWO

That evening, staff welcomed Elizabeth to the dinner table and disregarded their master with blatant disrespect. Elizabeth, too, ignored her husband's presence, though he appeared to suffer the lack of conversation with surprising tolerance.

Afterward, she checked on her new bookshelves' progress, pleased to find her bedroom walls cleared and skeletal outlines already erected. She decided a hot toddy and book in bed were just what she needed to ease her overactive mind—along with a bit more salve to her bottom.

Miss Li's revelations had affected her more than she liked.

She was just settling in, backside nestled on an extra down pillow, when Ginny entered with the toddy.

"Milady."

"Ginny, you may as well call me Lizzie when everyone calls the Baron by his first name."

"Well sure, ma'am, but that's on account o' how you're an honest-to-God lady an' Jasp's just a—"

"Whoreson?" Elizabeth's wry tongue twitched. "Degenerate? Profligate? Pigsnout, perhaps?"

Ginny giggled. "Pigsnout, fer sure."

"Making me *Mrs.* Pigsnout." Elizabeth sighed. "I'd prefer you simply call me Lizzie."

"Right-o, Lizzie." Ginny grinned. "Though you'll 'ave trouble convincin' Gerald an' Murdoch t' call yer such."

"You must make them see reason." Elizabeth forced a smile. "And as I need no assistance tonight with my—"

"Ma'am." Ginny's face fell. "I'm afraid yer husband requests yer presence in his chamber this night."

Dread filled Elizabeth's limbs, though she straightened her spine. "Thank you, Ginny. I shall prepare myself."

Milton paced his study, debating what to say to his wife. He'd told Ginny to prepare her mistress for a visit to his bedroom, but he wasn't sure what sort of visit this ought to be. He swallowed his apprehension, for it was all too blasted complicated, and not at all how he'd envisioned marriage to be: a straightforward trade. He'd keep his wife in finery, she'd give him heirs. They'd both enjoy the bedchamber, and when they tired of one another, each might take a lover. Isn't that what men of the *Ton* did?

When he'd paced enough and imagined her prepared enough, he made his way to his chamber. He rapped twice, calling "Elizabeth?" before he heard her soft "yes."

The jolt to his loins the moment he entered was intense.

She was the picture of submission in naught but her stockings, their dark blue accentuating the paleness of her skin. Palms to floor and breasts thrust forward, her chin was bent in deference, just as he had taught her.

He walked a circle to survey the damage he'd done, appalled at the marks yet on her backside which were now a cluster of bruised hues. Shame washed over his soul as he reached inside his pocket and laid the diamonds he had bought that day about her slender neck. "I am sorry I hurt you, Elizabeth. I hope you can find it in your heart to forgive me." He clasped the brilliant stones at her nape, yet she remained in position, unresponsive.

"Lizzie..." He let one finger trail the slope of her shoulder and felt her shudder to his touch. "Say something," he added. "Please."

"I do not require gifts to do my duty by you, sir." She kept her head bent. "Take me to bed and do what you must."

Hurt surged in his breast.

"I am prepared to give you an heir. I ask only that you be quick about it."

Her words roused his ire, but the punishment was just. With a quick scoop he lifted her onto his bed and laid her on her belly to spare her more pain, then began to kiss her marred buttocks with reverence.

Still, she did not react.

Milton slid his hand between her legs but found her unresponsive. He tried to coax her into pleasure, but she neither moaned nor sighed to his softest touch. She did not so much as twitch, a stone beneath him. Lifeless.

In frustration he pulled her to her knees, on all fours now, but she was so terribly, terribly cold, he found no spark, no heat. And only monsters forced themselves on women.

Milton pulled away, appalled and enraged. He'd never raped a woman and he would not start now. Elizabeth was his wife and legally this was his right, but the act felt suddenly wrong. Criminal.

"Go to your room." His heart beat madly in his chest. "Get out. Now!"

Elizabeth threw her robe about her and exited so fast she nearly tripped.

Milton wanted to punch something, *needed* to punch something, because he was not some beast who would force his wife to beget himself heirs. Is that what she'd now make him do? Was that what she wished to turn him into?

By God, this was not how he'd dreamed of starting a family!

He raked his hair with both hands, fingers digging into his skull. She was punishing them both, denying him enjoyment but denying herself pleasure too, for he knew full well she'd enjoyed him before.

A cold and nasty thought slithered into Milton's pounding head, for he'd taken her against her will before. He'd been precisely such a beast when he'd struck her with his ruler.

He dropped to his knees in an avalanche of self-loathing, guilt roiling his gut and falling like lead upon his shoulders. Elizabeth hated him enough to forgo her own pleasure, her own happiness, just to punish him. *That* was how much he'd hurt her.

He knew the impulse intimately. How oft had he been willing to inflict pain and misery on himself to enact revenge upon his tormentor, to punish the devil in return? And now he'd done the same to this beautiful, bright creature. This innocent young woman.

He'd done his wife a terrible wrong.

But how in God's name did one right such a wrong? How to prove one was willing to do and *be* better? He couldn't go crawling on all fours, begging like a wolfhound.

Or could he?

By morning, a chocolate croissant rested on Elizabeth's breakfast tray, a fresh vase of flowers perfuming her bedside. The Baron's servants were wonderful, even if *he* was not.

Still, her husband could have taken her last night, as was

his right, yet he hadn't. He'd seemed unduly angry when he'd sent her away, for wounded pride or wounded ego, she wasn't sure. But those awful diamonds he'd given her—such glittering, hard stones, so cold and bright—had felt more like a yoke about her neck than an attempt at true apology.

She'd stuffed them in the box with his other necklace, though she didn't know what stones those were. Lapis lazuli, perhaps, given their mottled blue. She knew little about gemstones, having been forced early on to pawn all her mother and stepmother owned. She was herself not much for ornament either; her spectacles drew the eye no matter what dangled at her breast.

No wonder Milton wished to outfit her with jewels that sparkled, since she did not.

Elizabeth brushed tears from her eyes, realizing, oddly, that she wept. She was twenty-four today. Such a solid number, really. Was her life truly already over before it had even begun? Was a bedroom lined with books all she could look forward to while she birthed this man his heirs? Yesterday she'd felt more hopeful, but this day dawned fresh with despair.

Until Bella arrived, that is.

"Well go on, open it!" Annabelle sat on the edge of her seat, Elizabeth's snail-like approach to unwrapping gifts annoying her sister to no end. She cruelly unspooled ribbons an inch at a time, whereas Bella tore into all packages with gusto.

"Oh, you torture me on purpose!"

"Why, sister," Elizabeth teased, "I do no such thing." She dropped the ribbon and made an elaborate show of retrieving it from the floor only to smooth it flat so she might slowly roll it into a—

"*Lizzie*," Bella groaned. "Open it!"

With one quick tear she put Annabelle out of her misery, then hugged the slim volume tightly to her chest. "Bella, it is perfect! How did you know I've been looking for just this book?"

"You've only mentioned it a dozen times this past year." Annabelle rolled her eyes. "Now, at least, I can stop listening to you go on about how you've read all her novels but this one."

Elizabeth grabbed her sister's hand and squeezed. "Thank you, dear. You've made my birthday joyous, after all. I cannot wait to start Miss Austen's *Persuasion.*"

"I am certain the Baron will surprise you with a far better gift." Annabelle's eyes lit with anticipation. "Why, just imagine what his wealth might—"

Sorrow overwhelmed Elizabeth.

"Lizzie…"

"Don't." She turned away; Elizabeth did not want her sister to read her thoughts. "I do not wish to speak of him. Another time, I promise." She simply wished to enjoy Annabelle's visit. "Now tell me news of you, and of Papa. Has he—?"

"Run through the Baron's money yet?" Annabelle's sigh was sufficient answer. "Not quite, but he will, and Lizzie, I must ask you…" It was Bella's turn to look pained. "I'm afraid I—"

"How much do you need?" *Some* good ought to come of her union to a scoundrel.

"More than you'd expect. There is a matter that's come up, you see, which—"

"Say no more, Bella. You need never explain, as I can well imagine." Elizabeth paused. "Trouble is, I've yet to receive pin money from my husband. We've been married such a short while I've not even discussed this with him yet." She could have kicked herself for neglecting such a key marital conversation. "But I can give you a necklace to pawn, and once I've funds in hand, you may retrieve it for me. Will that do?"

Annabelle seemed relieved. "Yes of course, Lizzie, you know I hate to—"

"*Never* be ashamed to ask me for anything, Bella. It is why I married the Baron." She steadied herself. "And the man can continue to pay for the pleasure of my hand."

❧

"Miss Winthrop!" Milton was shocked to discover his sister-in-law in his foyer just as he was about to leave his house. "What brings you here today?"

"Why, I should think you know what, sir." Her brow creased.

"I am sure I do not."

"I came to congratulate my sister."

"My dear, our wedding was some while ago."

She looked at him most queerly. "You don't know, do you?"

"Know what?"

"That it is her birthday, oaf!" Annabelle instantly clapped a hand to her mouth. "Oh dear I—forgive me, Baron." She looked terribly contrite. "I did not mean to call you an—"

"Oaf?" He sighed. "But I am, Miss Winthrop, and worse. Only more vulgar terms are not fit for ladies' ears."

"Did Lizzie fail to tell you today is her birthday, sir?"

"She did." Could his day get any worse? "Which does not mean I haven't time, yet, to rectify the matter." He'd kill two birds instead of one. "Might you be willing to accompany me on a short shopping trip, miss, and assist me in procuring your sister a gift?"

"I—"

He'd not let her wriggle out. "As your brother-in-law, I am the ideal chaperone to lead you about town. What's more, I am in desperate need of your help, lest I buy Elizabeth a gift she hates, making her hate me only—" He stopped himself.

"You've had a row, haven't you?" Annabelle peered at him.

"I suspected as much, because she would not speak of you just now, and we do not keep secrets from one another."

Milton suspected this minx was keeping plenty from his wife. "Miss Winthrop, I do not doubt you and your sister are indeed very close. But I've not a clue what Elizabeth might like, so…" He leveled his blue eyes at her soft brown irises. "Help your new brother repair a marital spat?"

"Very well." Her lips pursed. "For Lizzie's sake, mind. Because she is the very best person in the world, and you don't deserve her in the least."

"And don't I know it," he muttered as he grabbed his hat and cane to lead his sister-in-law down his front steps straight into his waiting carriage.

CHAPTER TWENTY-THREE

Milton quietly delighted in his sister-in-law's ebullient company, for Annabelle Winthrop was not the cowering miss he remembered. In fact, she was the opposite of meek, though she was still no Elizabeth.

As they perused London's bookshops, she chatted amicably about which novels Lizzie had loved growing up and which books her sister had yet to read. Books Elizabeth had written in her youth (so she *was* a secret novelist) and which books her sister felt should never have seen light of day, making him laugh at quite a few Annabelle mentioned.

Milton began to think his wife had lived her entire life in books, and if he let her, she would in all likelihood continue to.

"Jasper." Bella interrupted his thoughts, and not because she'd addressed him by his first name—he'd invited her to do so the moment they'd settled into his carriage. "How do you know Mr. Harris, the gentleman I met at your wedding luncheon?"

Milton was instantly all ears.

"We grew up together," he told her. "Arthur's like a brother to me."

"But you are not … actual brothers?"

"No. My actual half-brothers would prefer I not exist. Arty is more brother to me than either of them will ever be."

"And you've no other siblings?"

"I have a half-sister I have never met."

She looked surprised. "Why?"

"Because I am illegitimate, Bella, by-blow."

She sucked in her breath.

"For all I know, my father left me even more siblings sprinkled about London."

She remained quiet after his pronouncement, slowly sipping her chocolate. Milton had brought her to the same locale he'd taken Lizzie, though Bella had not blinked when he'd ordered for her.

He watched her savor her drink, the mug cradled in her hands, and recalled whom else he knew had a sweet tooth: Arty.

"Jasper, is Mr. Harris's gaming hall—I believe he called it *The Gilded Leaf*—a reputable one?"

And there it was.

"Why do you ask, Bella?"

She avoided his stare. "He knew my father at your wedding, and as Papa is known to frequent such places, I thought it prudent to ask if—

"Mr. Harris runs one of the more respectable gaming hells in our fair city, miss, and tolerates no funny business. In fact, he's known to sniff out cheats."

"Oh, Papa never cheats," the lady neatly deflected. "It is why he loses so abysmally. Or rather, why he sadly suffers such bad luck."

His new sister was up to something. And given what Harris had said of her abilities…

"So if *The Gilded Leaf* is more reputable than other establishments, I assume a gentleman like Papa would require more funds to enter than he would at other halls, correct?"

"Miss Winthrop, titled gentlemen like your father rightfully forgo the poor man's gaming den, for not only are the fees and stakes less high in such hells, but the clientele decidedly less savory. Rarely is a man gutted like a fish and left to carry his own entrails out the door at Arthur Harris's fine establishment."

She blenched.

"Arty runs a safe business. And debts accrued are settled honorably, in private, rather than with fisticuffs."

He watched her swallow, then extend her chin. "And what of ladies, sir? Are there no comparable halls for their amusement?"

This chit was altogether too obvious. "Ladies, Bella, only play games of chance in the safe confines of their drawing rooms, or at house parties. Pin money rarely pays enough to play the tables at *The Leaf*."

Her lips pinched before she opened her mouth to—

"The only ladies you will find at Arthur Harris's house, dear Bella, are the very *willing* sort."

Her cheeks pinked.

Milton leaned back in his chair, pleased he'd dealt a blow to her none-too-clever plan. Though he'd best warn Arty the lady was not above scheming her way to his tables. And he'd best marry this girl off to some dull fellow fast.

"Had lunch with 'er, didya?"

Milton watched his friend's lips thin; Arty looked displeased.

"An' here I thought *I* were the man s'posed t' court her."

"Who the hell was that lout I just saw leave, Arty?" Milton

had knocked shoulders with a rough fellow exiting *The Leaf's* office.

"None o' yer beeswax, Jasp." Arty grimaced. "Now, why're you here—other than t' vex me?"

Unlike Arthur Harris, Milton chose not to converse in the language of their youth except when necessary—or when his emotions got the better of him. Which they did not. Arty, on the other hand, only spoke like a toff when he had to.

"Miss Winthrop is up to new tricks. She asked one too many questions of you over lunch."

"Well, well." Arty propped his feet on his desk. "The miss done likes me after all."

"Don't flatter yourself, man. She was asking about *The Leaf* and about other gaming hells where ladies might play. She also had me drop her near a pawnshop owned by a ruthless fence. If that's the Lombard the Winthrop girls have been using all these years, no wonder they—"

"Fuck," Arty ground out. "I thought I warned 'er off that scheme."

"The lady appears impatient." Milton was himself impatient to get home. "I need to step up my search for an appropriate suitor, Arty. The Denbigh ball this weekend should be an ideal excuse to parade her about."

"Aren't the Denbighs—?"

"Wellesley's in-laws, yes. I'll get you an invitation."

"Jasper, why the devil would I want to—?"

"You will attend, Arty, and fawn all over Miss Winthrop so that other men take notice. A woman pursued is a woman desirous. You know how things work."

Arty scowled. "Y' ask much, Jasp."

"You owe me much, and it's not as if I require you to seduce the chit, not that she isn't pretty enough to turn your voracious head."

"She's *too* pretty…" he grumbled.

"Then it should be no feat of heroism on your part to charm her. You've danced and flirted with enough women to—"

"But them twists an' twirls weren't ladies."

Milton took pause. "Arty, you are not falling for Miss Annabelle, are you?"

"God no!"

"Good." Milton grabbed his hat and cane. "I'll clue Wells in. He might even know an earl or viscount eager to wed. I'll need names and information if I'm to have influence. And Arty…" He halted at the door. "Pay attention to which fools are getting fleeced at your tables, ones that might be nudged. Annabelle Winthrop would make any man an agreeable wife."

"Jasp, wait."

Milton stopped.

"We've trouble."

"Oh?"

Arty looked nervous. Arty rarely looked nervous. Milton was now nervous himself.

"I know whose suit she's so eager t' escape."

Milton met his gaze. "Whose?"

"Ronny Finch."

His gut wrenched before it began its familiar, curling squeeze. "Tell me you did not just utter that man's name."

"Jasp, I'll not lie. We crossed paths this morn at 'er house, and th' girl confirmed it. Finch is courtin' her, 'tis why she's so desperate."

Milton's heart began to pound in his ears. "And you were going to tell me this *when*?"

"Today, guv, soon as I'd concluded business with yon lout y' saw leave."

It was taking everything in Milton's willpower to keep from throwing a chair across the room. "*Fuck,*" he spat.

Arty met his gaze. "Complicates matters, don't it?"

Milton would not crack. He could not.

"How much time do we have, Arty?"

"A bit, I think."

"Be at the Denbigh ball. Until then, do whatever you must to protect her. As will I."

❧

That evening Milton readied himself for battle. He'd relegated all thought of Finch to the dark dungeon of his soul where he kept his horrors chained. He'd let the beast out tomorrow, but not today.

Today he'd eschewed dinner to prepare for the apology he must offer his wife. But not before he'd tipped off staff to Elizabeth's birthday. If she was angry with him for spilling the news, he could always blame her sister. Besides, his cook baked delicious cakes. Lizzie could hardly be upset by that.

Already, sounds of merriment came from below stairs; he hoped they were fêting his wife well and good. He grabbed the gift he'd purchased and the other item he'd need, then headed to his bedchamber, to ready himself.

Because Li, blast her, had been right. He did not wish to spend his married life in misery. Détente must be reached—peaceful coexistence a requirement for the rearing of children at least.

Elizabeth needn't grow to love or even like him, but he needed her respect. And she clearly needed to feel respected by him in order for their marriage to work. That much he aimed to give her this night.

CHAPTER TWENTY-FOUR

Annabelle waited until the house was quiet before she pulled the hidden bundle out from under her bed. She removed her night-rail to don the breeches and boots she'd procured, then bound her breasts as flat as possible and pulled on the bulky shirt and jacket, tying a cravat as neatly as she knew to tie Papa's. She pinned her braids tight to her head, leaving side strands she'd trimmed to pull back into a short sort of tail, then donned a cap to hide the rest. In the mirror, she rubbed ash on her chin and upper lip, for just a shade of manliness.

She surveyed her appearance. Not quite apprentice and not quite titled young man, she looked somewhere in between. So long as she kept her head down, her speech to a minimum, and her gait a loose swagger, she'd pass.

And pass she did, for a mere two hours later, Annabelle could not believe her good fortune. Or rather, Bartholomew Brown's fortune. Her alter ego was winning big at *vingt-et-un* just like she'd known he would. Oh, she let him lose a few rounds to throw the other players off his scent, but Bart was a cool cucumber—even the ladies liked him. One in particular kept blowing kisses over his cards for luck.

Pride filled Annabelle's chest. If this was how Papa had felt the times he'd won she understood what drove him back, because the rush was incredible. Intoxicating! And she, as dashing Bart Brown, was invincible.

"Ooh, Mr. Brown," an admirer cooed at Annabelle's ear. "Steady now, lad, you've got 'im by the bollocks, reel 'im in." The lady's tongue shockingly caressed Bart's lobe.

Annabelle shivered; this was a bit much. It was also distracting her from counting. Moreover, the lady wore far too much perfume. Yet before she could politely ask the miss to step back, another voice hissed low in her other ear, sending a different shiver down her spine.

"Finish it," Arthur Harris ordered. "And then you walk—no fuss, no scene." His bruising grip on Annabelle's arm left no room for disagreement.

"A lucky young man indeed this night," he loudly announced above her head. "Though we've a matter t' discuss in private, regarding accounts. If you'll excuse us, gentlemen."

Annabelle didn't dare attempt to shake Mr. Harris off. Instead, she swept her earnings into a pile, met her opponent's eye with a nod, and pocketed her winnings.

"Aw, Mr. Brown, do stay, luv!" pleaded the perfumed lady.

"Next time, Lottie." Harris brushed the woman off. "Find another guest to entertain." He prodded Annabelle to start moving, which she did, her head held high.

The moment they left the hall, however, he marched her straight into his office and shut the door behind him, making Annabelle flinch. Only she was not Bella, she was Bart. And Bartholomew Brown feared no one.

She kept her voice gruff. "What seems to be the matter with my account, sir?"

"Drop the act, Bella."

"My name, sir, is Bartholomew—"

***

Harris yanked the cap from her head and pulled her by the scruff of her cravat to within an inch of his face, dangling her another inch off the floor.

She let out a most unmasculine squeak.

"Soot, Bella, really?" His lips twitched. "In a dim lit hall, mayhap, but woman, no amount of ash t' yer fair face will evoke a man's shadow." He broke into a grin before he laughed outright, relaxing somewhat his grip.

She squirmed to escape him but he tightened his hold. "I had the rest convinced." She met his eyes. "Your ladies even favored me."

Harris pulled her so close her nose brushed his chest. "I *pay* them to favor winners, Bella. Who do you think alerted me to your table?" The chit really didn't know a damned thing, he thought, realizing he was gripping an innocent miss rather harshly by her throat. He eased up.

"I did no one harm," she defended herself. "I let others win too. I played a fair game, so you've no right to—"

"Y' counted yer way to yer wins, miss, which in my book ain't fair, 'tis called cheatin'. Moreover, I don't allow women in me hall."

"I saw plenty of women in your hall!"

"Like to be one of *them* women, miss? Whores who service me tables and then service men upstairs, in bed, fer coin?

Her face bloomed scarlet but he didn't care. She needed scaring.

"D'you know what might've happened had you been found out, Bella dear? *All* chance at marriage to any one o' them gentlemen out there ruined the moment someone pulled yer cap from yer head."

"I've no wish to marry." She reminded him with force. "I wish to be *free*."

"Your freedom is only gained through marriage," he countered. "It's either that or sell yer body."

Her face fell precipitously before it darkened ominously. "Why are you so interested in my well-being, Mr. Harris?" She pinned him with fresh, determined eyes.

"I believe *you* approached me, miss, with yer proposition."

"Why did you give me your card at my sister's wedding?"

Harris's thoughts scrambled.

"Did my brother-in-law put you up to this, sir?"

Fuck.

"Does my sister know about this?"

"Listen, miss, I know nothing at all about yer—"

"Blast." She stomped her foot.

"Did you just swear, Miss Winthrop?" He stifled a smirk.

"Bartholomew Brown does indeed swear and gamble and flirt with ladies, Mr. Harris. And if you'd let well enough alone out there he would have—"

"Cleaned me out o' house an' home, I'm sure." Harris was amused, aroused, and now all sorts of entertained. "Damnation, Bella, you are one—"

He stopped himself.

"One what?" She glared back, hands on hips outlined so perfectly in those snug breeches Harris had to shake himself straight. "I am goin' to take yer home now an'—"

***

"No." Annabelle stood her ground. She'd not come this far for nothing.

"What do you mean, *no*?" Mr. Harris crossed his arms, cutting a most fine figure, blast him.

"You will do nothing, sir. For you are not my keeper,

regardless of what brother Jasper says. I will see myself home, and you will not breathe a word of this to anyone or so help me I will … I'll …"

She could not come up with a single executable threat, *damnation.*

Harris stepped close enough to scald her with his gaze. "You will do exactly as *I* say, miss." His lips brushed her jawline as he spoke low into her ear. "And not because your brother-in-law asked me to deal with you, but because you entered *my* place of business, flouted *my* rules at cards, and then cheated shamelessly at *my* bloody tables. Do you know what I do with guests who disrespect my house, Bella, hmm?"

His breath was hot on her cheek, his hands hot at her waist now too.

"If they are gentlemen, I settle it as gentlemen do, at dawn with pistols, or I tip them off to the coppers and land them a while in gaol. But a girl as fetching as you, well…" She heard him lick his lips. "I put her to work t' pay off her debt. Would you like that, pretty Bella? To pay off yer debt in service t' me?"

She gasped, panic flooding her chest along with something else she could not name.

"Annabelle," he whispered seductively into her ear, "answer me."

"No," she got out weakly, her legs beginning to fail as he steadied her waist, his hands slipping lower than they ought.

She froze, and he swiftly stepped back.

"Good," he told her brusquely. "I'll find you more respectable clothing before I drive you home and inform your father of your—"

"Arthur, please." Her heart galloped in her breast. "Deliver me home only do not tell Papa. He mustn't know. I'll make it up to you, I swear. I'll do your books for free, only please do not tell him." If her father knew of this, he'd marry her to

Finch tomorrow. "Baron of Milton need never know either, I'll do anything to—"

"*Anything*, Bella?" He harshly cut her off. "Take care what you offer, miss, for a man less than myself might turn such offer into somethin' else."

She backed away. "I didn't mean … That is, I didn't think you'd …"

"That's just it." His eyes bored into hers. "Y' didn't think *at all* this night. For this is not the *Ton*, miss. Men here'll treat a girl like dirt if she's not protected by family, money, or a husband. Imagine yerself in just this situation, in a different gamin' hell, locked in a room, defenseless and alone, beggin' on yer knees an' me a different man."

Annabelle pulled a knife from her pocket. "I am not defenseless." She waved it wildly at him. "And I am not a—"

In a flash he grabbed her wrist and squeezed until she yelped and dropped the knife. Then he bent back her arm to roughly pin her to his body.

"*This* is what I meant." He tightened his grip until she winced. "Don't ever show yer hand in battle, woman. Like in cards, always keep yer cool. Had you let me approach, had you softened t' me and then, when I were close enough to touch, used yer knife t' gut me, thrustin' in an' up, you'd've had a chance in hell."

He pushed her away, his boot landing neatly over the knife as he bent to pick it off the floor and slide it into his pocket.

"Fine." Annabelle exhaled a shaky breath, forced to concede defeat. "I am clearly not your match, sir. Only if you've any decency at all, Mr. Harris, you will escort me to my father's house in secret. I give you my word I'll not gamble at *The Leaf* again."

Mr. Harris nicked his head in a sour grimace as relief flooded Annabelle's breast.

CHAPTER TWENTY-FIVE

Elizabeth sat tucked in bed, reading Austen's *Persuasion*. The servants' loud revelry still filtered through the house as they continued her birthday celebration with bottles from her husband's cellar.

She'd insisted on it.

Annabelle must have spilled the beans, for Elizabeth had told no one it was her birthday. Still, cake and champagne and a table full of foot-stomping well-wishers was not a bad way to end the day, especially when birthdays were usually disasters. Father forever gave gifts too expensive to keep, forcing her and Bella to pawn them back. And if he gave no gift at all, it sent him spiraling with guilt so that his daughters spent their fêted day striving to improve *his* blasted mood.

This birthday, however, had felt different.

As to where her husband was, Elizabeth did not care. Perhaps he'd left the house to avoid the hubbub. Perhaps he was visiting Miss Li again this night. Given all she now knew, why shouldn't he choose Li over her, his wife? It didn't bother Elizabeth in the least whom her husband now spent his nights with, so long as he did not spend them with her.

She brushed back a tear, irked by her annoying emotion. Equally irked when Gerald, not Ginny, poked his head in.

"Ma'am." He refused to meet Elizabeth's eye. "The Baron asks that you attend him in his chamber."

She wanted to howl her fury at the moon. Had the man no soul? And on her birthday no less? To send Gerald to deliver such edict too, rather than her maid, felt all the more debasing. Why was Milton so unfeeling? What had made him into such a beast? Her thoughts brought little comfort as she flung off the bedclothes and pushed her night-rail to the floor, slipping on her stockings before she threw her banyan about her naked limbs. She'd lie there like a lump again, an unresponsive wife, and see how well he liked *that*.

She stomped down the hall in her stockinged feet to her bedroom, pausing to steal a look at the nearly-completed shelves lining two walls. Elizabeth steadied her pounding heart, entered her husband's chamber, and gasped.

Milton knelt at the foot of his bed, naked, in the same position he'd taught her to assume. His head was bent and his palms lay flat at his sides behind him, every sinewed muscle in his bearing bulging and straining, his jaw clamped rigidly shut.

She stared at him. "Is this some joke, sir, meant to mock me?" Her eyes flitted to the object lying prone beside him on the floor: a ruler. "Do you find this humorous? Piquant? To present yourself to *me* now for punishment?" Her ire rose. "Or is this meant instead to goad me into action so you might turn on me more savagely than before?"

"For God's sake, Lizzie, just take the bloody ruler and beat me with it!"

His anguish made her freeze, his voice unrecognizable. For one terribly long breath she contemplated his very real words before she hefted the vile implement in her hand and tested its feel, tipping it for balance before she poked him with it.

He did not flinch.

"You do not jest," she said in shock.

"No."

"You wish me to strike you as you struck me."

"Yes," he hissed.

"You are insane."

"No, Elizabeth." He ground out her name through clenched teeth. "I have given this great thought."

"Great thought?" She felt insane herself. "You have given it *great thought*?"

"I wish us to start over. This … evens the score."

"My God, you are a fool or fiend—nay, both, to imagine this might even the score." She shook her head. "What does that even mean, Milton, what score? Are we keeping points as to who's been beaten more, who's the greater cad, the lesser whore? What the devil do you mean, to present yourself so … so …" She was suffused with rage and sorrow and such wretched, awful confusion, she couldn't finish.

"Elizabeth, take the ruler and beat me, woman, you know you want to. Do it, blast it. Just *do it*!" His gaze was so intense she had to tear her eyes away.

She picked up the tool and braced herself to perform as her husband demanded. She stared at his naked back, at the scars riddling his flesh, and dropped the ruler to the floor, sinking to her knees beside him as her lungs gulped air.

She was better than this. Elizabeth would not strike a fellow human, even if that human ordered it.

Her next breath caught on a cry she did not utter. And then she fisted his hair, to hell with his rules. She forced him to look at her. "I will not."

He seemed stunned.

"This does not even the score, it only makes me into you, as someone surely made you into them." She was shaking so hard her teeth rattled in her head. "I will not beat you or any person. I'd rather you beat me yourself than be forced to mark you now." She trembled with the truth of it, even as she let his head drop to his chest.

He choked back a sound and Elizabeth drew him to her without thinking. She cradled him to her breast and stroked his silken curls, feeling his chest heave with effort. His weight sank deeper against her until she enveloped him in her arms. And then she pulled him across her lap as if he were a boy and not a man.

In that moment a strange calm overtook her, for she recognized the gift she'd just received. Her husband had opened himself to her in the only way he knew how—through pain. She might not agree with his approach, but shockingly he had tried.

"Jasper." She rocked his body there upon the floor the way one rocked a child to sleep. She did not know where the instinct came from. "Take me to bed, husband. Regain yourself."

***

Had he heard her right? Had his wife just offered herself after all he'd done and said?

Had Elizabeth called him by his true name?

Milton's howling, inner demon retreated to its cave, allowing his breath to flow and his flesh to feel the rise and fall of her soft breast against his cheek—soothing, pillowy. Her words rang so earnest, so honest, something splintered in his soul.

"Lizzie, I'll not take you against your will. I would never—"

"I know this," she told him softly. "You did not take me last night."

He lifted his head. "You hate me." He was convinced.

She exhaled. "I do not hate you, husband. I do not *understand* you."

"There is nothing to understand." He slumped again.

"Oh, I beg to differ." She did not smile; the moment was too solemn. "I think, sometimes, 'tis you who hates me. Sometimes I think you should have … It no longer matters." She sounded sad. "We are stuck with one another, so we must make the best of it." Her eyes blinked back tears as she shifted, straightening her body. "I am willing to try to improve things between us, Milton, if you will also try."

This was too much, when he'd expected so much less. His arms slipped about her as he reversed their positions. "I am willing to try, too, Elizabeth. I mean that, but you were correct, before, when you said that someone had—"

"Did they beat you when you were young?" she asked. "Is that how you got your scars?"

"Were I to tell you every evil I have witnessed, experienced, or myself inflicted, Lizzie, it would only scar *you*."

"Tell me!" she implored. "Scar me with words so that you are not *my* devil but instead caught in some other devil's path, the recipient of a different devil's wrath. Jasper, if you keep me at bay I will insist only more. It is my nature to seek answers."

Lord was that ever true.

"Lizzie, I've made a mess of things."

"Yes," she declared, "you have. But I have too. Another woman would have better accommodated your wishes and followed your six rules. Not to mention cost you a great deal less in broken spectacles."

"And bored me to no end." Milton was amazed he could smile. It felt good to smile. "You challenge me at every turn and please me very much in bed, Lizzie."

"Nonsense," she mumbled.

"'Tis true. You, wife, have the most gorgeous derriere, and the most pleasing breasts to ever fit my palms." He slid his hands inside her robe.

She let out a sound like a kitten's faint mewl, melting him

into a puddle. He pulled her up with him. "Come, I've a gift for you on your twenty-fourth birthday." He led her to his dresser, where he handed her a package.

Elizabeth slowly unwrapped it, her face alighting with pleasure. "How did you—?"

"Annabelle took me shopping this afternoon and informed me not only of your true age, but of my being a true arse. Why did you not tell me it was your birthday, Lizzie?"

"Birthdays are fraught," she admitted. "But your gift…" She looked longingly at the book. "To receive a first edition with the author's signature is…" She smiled up at him. "Thank you, Milton."

His body bloomed as if fed by warm, summer rain. The sensation made him bold. "I thought, perhaps, we might read it together evenings in bed."

"I should like that very much, Milton."

Had his wife's heart just opened a crack?

"Shall we start tonight?" She surprised him more.

"It is your birthday, Elizabeth, you may do as you like."

"As I like, eh?" She grinned. "Now *here* is a side of my husband I very much enjoy seeing."

"At last, a bit of me she likes!" He plopped his naked self upon the bed and patted his side for her to join him. "Shall I read first, or would you like the honor?"

"Oh, I think you should begin." Her eyes perused his person before they landed at his groin, his blasted cock at half-mast already. She handed him Shelley's *Frankenstein* as she eased in beside him. "I should like to hear you read the story. You've a lovely, deep voice, Milton. It is most melodious."

"You joke."

"I do not." Though her eyes laughed back at him. "I paid you an honest compliment; be so good as to accept it."

Milton cleared his throat and opened the book to read.

To Mrs. Saville, England.
St. Petersburgh, Dec. 11th, 17--
You will rejoice to hear that no disaster has accompanied the commencement of an enterprise which you have regarded with such evil forebodings. I arrived here yesterday; and my first task is to assure my dear sister of my welfare, and increasing confidence in the success of my undertaking…

Elizabeth snuggled closer, soon resting her head on his chest. He liked how she felt. How *this* felt. He read on, content.

❧

Milton turned pages as quietly as he could, the sun boldly peeking in through curtain cracks as his wife stirred beside him. He'd been unable to sleep. Too restless from conversation, love-making, from *all* that had changed between them, he'd taken up the book again to read. He found he could not stop.

She stretched and yawned before *scratch*, a page scraped, and her eyes flew open.

"Milton, are you—?"

"Reading, darling." He gave her nose a quick peck before he turned another page.

"If you are reading ahead, sir, that defeats entirely the purpose of our reading the book together."

He planted a warm, wet kiss to her forehead next.

"How long have you been awake? And just how far ahead have you—?"

"Shh, Lizzie." He placed a finger to her lips, eyes not leaving the page. "I am just at the part where Dr. Frankenstein's creature has found his creator, listen."

Life, though it may only be an accumulation of anguish, is dear to me, and I will defend it. Remember, thou hast made me more

> *powerful than thyself; my height is superior to thine; my joints more supple. But I will not be tempted to set myself in opposition to thee. I am thy creature, and I will be even mild and docile to my natural lord and king, if thou wilt also perform thy part, that which thou owest me.*

Elizabeth cleared her throat.

"What?" Milton frowned. "Do you not like my monster voice?"

"Oh, your monster is even better than your Victor Frankenstein." Her lips twitched. "No, it was the last line you read which, er, resonated." Her eyes glowed.

Milton looked back at the text. "Why, Lizzie," he smiled, "do you mean to say you will be *mild and docile to your natural lord and king*?"

She poked him beneath the covers. "Not unless you *perform your part* and give *that which thou owest me.*"

"And just what doth your lord king owe you, woman?"

"Respect!" Her grey eyes flashed. "And freedom and—"

He hushed her with his lips, letting the book fall to the floor. He kissed her silent, then kissed her silly, kissing her into submission as he kissed his way to her core, to make up for past wrongs and past hurts, for birthdays gone awry.

Milton worked very hard that morning to be the *lord and king* his wife deserved. The sort of man he felt Elizabeth was owed.

CHAPTER TWENTY-SIX

Annabelle slept like the dead following her visit to *The Leaf*, but by morning her spirits were at an all-time low. When she counted the money Mr. Harris had graciously returned her—minus his house cut, of course—she'd enough to buy back Lizzie's necklace from the Lombard but not nearly enough to play tables anywhere else.

And then her father made matters worse. "*Bella*," he belted from the stairs. "Mr. Finch is here to call on you. Annabelle!"

Her heart sank more. How was she to escape marriage to that awful man when she earned but pennies closing Mr. Harris's books? She'd felt invincible last night as Bartholomew Brown, because *he* was capable of anything. Yet here at home, in her everyday drab dress, she felt utterly unable to affect her future.

She stared at the flamboyant gown Mr. Harris had made her wear home, no doubt borrowed from one of his 'working' ladies. It lay draped over her chair in reproof, needing to be pressed. She ought to be grateful Arthur had dropped her off a few houses down so she could slip inside last night unseen. She should be grateful more had not gone awry, given what he'd demonstrated *could.*

She hid the dress deep in her garderobe, then made her way downstairs where she coolly greeted Mr. Finch. Annabelle looked askance at the vase of inappropriate red roses the man had brought. He did not 'love passionately' nor 'desire her romantically.' She kept her hands in her lap, wishing to tear her skirt fabric into bits, while her father fawned, as usual, all over Mr. Finch.

"Is that not delightful, Bella?" Papa nudged her with his foot.

"Quite," she answered without hearing a word.

"Then I looks forward t' accompanyin' yer t'night, Miss Winthrop."

"Accompanying?" she blurted, realizing she ought to have been paying closer attention to their conversation.

"T' the Denbigh ball, m'dear. You've not forgotten, 'ave you?"

The lecherous man's eyes perused her so liberally he made her shudder.

"When last I were here, y' could talk o' nothin' else, miss."

"Oh yes, the ball, of course. Forgive me, Mr. Finch, I feel rather poorly today. Perhaps I am coming down with something." She pretended to sniffle. She would not accompany this man anywhere tonight or any other day. How had he possibly wrangled an invitation?

"Milord." Papa's coarse footman tromped in. "Mr. Harris is 'ere fer Miss Winthrop. Says he's to take 'er fer a drive."

Papa paled a shade more white as his guest's face glowered red. Annabelle took the opportunity to rise swiftly from her seat. "Goodness, I'd quite forgotten Mr. Harris invited me. I shouldn't like to keep him waiting." She scurried out without a glance back, forgoing spencer and parasol while her father's voice boomed from the parlor. "Annabelle Winthrop! You have not taken leave of Mr.—!"

But already she was out the door, on the front step, and grabbing hold of Mr. Harris, who'd been waylaid over the hedge by Lady Stanton. He tipped his hat to both lady and pug as Annabelle hurried him toward his curricle. As he helped her up she urged, "Drive quick, I beg, sir. Before Papa can snatch me back."

Harris snapped the reins, his curricle tossing Annabelle directly into his lap. She righted herself by way of his thigh, which was embarrassing enough, until the weight of his palm steadied her own leg.

She stared at his hand in brief panic. "Must you … grip my skirts so?"

He squeezed her through her dress. "Oh I must. It is so very high up we sit, and the road so treacherously bumpy." The devil curved his fingers slightly in, making Annabelle push him off.

His hand reappeared at her waist. "This better, miss?" He dug his thumb into the back of her stays, right where her laces ended.

"Mr. Harris," she declared, "I did not leave the company of one man's untoward advances only to be accosted by another's!"

"Well, if we're courtin', 'tis me job to tease an' flirt." He threw her such a roguish grin she stuck out her tongue at him without thinking.

"Lord, but you are easily riled!" His laugh made him only more handsome.

"A gentleman flirts in a wholesome, not vulgar, manner, Mr. Harris."

He removed his palm from her waist to take her hand in his lap instead. "This more proper? Whatever man marries you, miss, will have a devil of a time behavin' himself."

"And just what is that supposed to mean?"

"It means, Bella dear, the man you marry'll struggle not to ravish you silly whenever and wherever he can."

She gaped at him in shock.

"An' if y' keep lookin' at me like that I'm liable to kiss yer."

She shut her mouth and trained her gaze forward, her hand in his palm suddenly sweating.

Two hours later Miss Winthrop had neatly reconciled Harris's books; he had to admit, this arrangement was suiting him nicely.

"Is it true, sir?" she asked in the quiet of their drive back.

"Is what true?" Harris trained his eyes on the road, rather than stare at her too much.

"That you always … bed a girl before you hire her?"

Blood rushed to his face. "Where the devil'd you hear that, miss?"

"From one of your … staff." She blushed crimson.

"Which staff?" He lashed back. "Were it Tom? Or bloody Janie, me house madam?"

"J-Janie."

"The nerve o' that woman," he muttered, shaking his head.

Miss Winthrop remained silent and Harris began to feel like a lout, even though bedding girls was anything *but* awful. Hell, it was the opposite of awful.

"I do it t' make sure they suit," he finally told her.

She shifted in her seat. "I'm afraid I do not understand, sir."

Harris wasn't sure she could handle the truth, but he didn't want her thinking worse of him than she already did, *thank you very much, Janie*. He cleared his throat. "Me mum were a harlot, Miss Winthrop, same as Jasper's. We grew up as brothers, though we're not blood. But without no dad, raised only by whores, well, I understand women differently than most men."

"I make no assumptions of you, Arthur," she told him. "You are an enigma to me."

He snorted, debating his next words. "Not all women can prostitute themselves, miss. Nor should any woman be forced to." He might as well tell all. "When a girl approaches me t' work at *The Leaf,* I'll not hire her if she's not able t' sell her body t' men. And there's only one way t' know if she can. So I sleep with her once, as test. An' if she don't suit, I find 'er employment elsewhere."

"Elsewhere?" She sounded shocked. "You mean you—?"

"I don't send her t' no poorhouse, if that's what you think."

"No, Arthur, I only … I am surprised you'd take such interest in—"

"I ain't Finch, miss," he bit back. "What *he* does t' girls is beyond…" But he wouldn't go there. "I find 'em positions, most often in service, in houses like yer own, or Jasper's."

"Oh." She again fell quiet. "I take it you have slept with a great many women then."

"You askin' me t' supply you with a number?"

"No." She again blushed prettily. Ridiculous, how pretty. "I meant only that you must be quite experienced."

Harris kept his mouth shut.

"Arthur…" She hesitated. "Is bodily congress truly all that terrible for women and all that wonderful for men? Because if this is true, then marriage is a fate more cruel than I—"

Harris could contain himself no longer. He cupped her cheek in his gloved hand and kissed her full, sweet lips so urgently her amber eyes flew open.

"I can assure you, Bella"—for necessity, he adjusted his seat —"if done right, the act is just as wonderful fer woman as it is fer man, as God intended it. An' anyone what tells you otherwise knows *nothin'* o' lovemakin'."

For the remainder of their ride, Miss Winthrop perched stock-still beside Harris, while he sat atop his curricle thoroughly inflamed. She was a great many things, this lady, but a fool she was not. He'd put nothing past her anymore. Nothing.

Stealthy as a cat and sleek as a kitten, he thought as he pulled up to her address and watched her enter her father's house. She was unskilled and untrained, but Annabelle Winthrop had courage in abundance.

Which in his world, was no small thing.

❧

"Down, boy!"

Mutton promptly sat, something Milton's wife had been trying to get the wolfhound to do for the past half hour. He was enjoying Elizabeth's attempts.

"Why does he listen to you and not me?" She pouted, looking every bit a baron's wife in her red ball gown, his diamond necklace matching her wedding spectacles. Milton was eager to show off his Baroness tonight at the Denbigh ball and further his social goals.

"You've not mastered the right tone," he told her. "*Come!*" Milton ordered, and the dog trotted right over. "Now call him to you."

"Come!" she said sharply, but the dog laid his head on his paws, dropping to his haunches. "Mutton, *come*!" She stomped her foot, but the hound only looked at Milton as if to ask if he should humor the lady?

She sighed. "Oh, I give up, you lump." She scratched Mutton behind his ears. "You love your master, don't you? You love *only* him, I know, you dear, sweet lummox."

Milton jealously wished his wife would scratch *his* ears with such affection. Though she'd warmed to him again. In bed, at least.

Elizabeth straightened her shoulders. "I suppose it is time we present ourselves to the world, sir."

He laid her wrap about her shoulders. "You're not anxious, are you, Lizzie? Your sister will be there, and the Duchess, of course, as well as Lady Stanton and any number of distinguished guests you've met before at these affairs.

"I shall be fine, Milton, except that I shall be scrutinized now as wife, rather than be allowed to fade into the background as mere wallflower."

"I doubt you were ever a wallflower, Elizabeth."

"How little you know, sir," she grumbled.

"I know you've been an obedient wife and left your drawers in your room as instructed, haven't you, Lizzie?"

She blushed. "I have followed my husband's wishes, yes."

"I am glad to hear it." He spoke low into her ear. "Because I intend to put you at ease on our journey there."

By the time he bundled her into his carriage, her blush had spread deliciously to her slender neck, a sight he appreciated for a moment before he embarked on full seduction.

Milton patted his lap in invitation, "Come, Lizzie, let me prepare you for the ball. But draw the curtains first. I do not wish to share you with half of London. I want my wife all to myself."

As she loosely pulled them shut he admired her equally slender wrist. He admired everything about her since she'd refused to beat him with his ruler. Elizabeth's strength of will amazed him, though it was her surrender he wanted right now. Her diamonds caught slivers of light from the now muted streetlamps the carriage passed, while that tiny crease of ever-present consternation he adored marred her lovely brow.

"Are you playing coy, dear? I promise a most satisfying ride."

Leaning back against her seat, Elizabeth shyly shook her head. The world was shut out, the carriage lulling them like a cradle. Milton savored this reprieve, just the two of them alone, before society should wreak its havoc, as it always did.

"You will disturb my coiffure Ginny worked so hard to achieve, sir." She worried her lips with her teeth.

Nervous. That's what's amiss.

"Elizabeth." He tried the same tone he used on Mutton. "*Come.*"

Her breath hitched, but she obediently settled atop his lap, wreaking an altogether different sort of havoc on his loins.

He raised her skirts, lifting her to straddle him. "Better," he murmured into the valley of her breasts, adjusting her knees so that her legs more comfortably parted. Her bosom rose rapidly, breaths fluttering in her chest like some bright, exotic bird, poised for flight.

"Milton, you mustn't rumple my dress, not on a night as important as—"

"Lizzie, luv," he purred low in his throat, "I'll not mess a hair on yer head."

She tried to say more but he stopped her with his finger. And then he pushed that finger slowly into her mouth.

"Undo my fall," he ordered, and she did, even as he slid his finger lasciviously between her rosy lips. His other hand slipped below her skirts to her hot, ready center, where he dipped into her heat, mirroring the motion at her mouth, stroking her at the same steady pace.

Elizabeth whimpered as she palmed his stiffening cock. His hands now shifted her hips, positioning her over his hardened prick, then seated her onto his length. Her breath stuttered as he leaned forward to gently steal a kiss. He pulled her lip with his teeth, then licked her cheek.

"God, Lizzie." Milton groaned his pleasure. "Ride as slow or fast as you like. Drain me of all seed. I wish to feel every squeeze, feel your lovely cunny milk my prick dry."

He slipped the finger he'd had between her legs between

her lips, and she suckled so eagerly, so sincerely, he nearly came right then and there.

Milton controlled himself, letting her guide their sensual, slow ride.

He leaned his head against the seat as she consumed both his finger and cock, finger and cock, undulating and alternating her body between the two motions as the carriage rocked across the cobblestones. Until he was not sure where flesh ended and heaven began.

CHAPTER TWENTY-SEVEN

Attached to her husband's warm, supportive arm, Elizabeth entered the Denbigh residence both flushed and bothered. Flushed because her body was still reeling from the intense sensations she'd just been granted, and bothered because it had not bothered her nearly enough to be ravished en route to this ball.

The practicality of going without drawers had been made abundantly clear the instant that earth-shattering, final arse slap to her bare bottom had made impact.

As Milton led her inside, his seed still sticky between her thighs, Elizabeth surveyed the scene. This home was not as grand as her husband's, but clearly no expense had been spared. From plentiful punch bowls to gleaming candelabras and artfully arranged bouquets, the Earl of Denbigh's granddaughter was a fortunate debutante indeed.

Elizabeth also surveyed her husband, who looked resplendent in a dark grey evening suit and indigo cravat. The ensemble turned his eyes a darker blue than usual, eyes which had shone brighter ever since the night of her birthday when he had offered her a ruler in place of an olive branch. Elizabeth's flush spread as she recalled their amorous endeavors that night and the morning after, as well as every night and morning since.

And now, God help her, a carriage.

He was growing on her, her husband, and not just his skills in bed. He'd shockingly read Wollstonecraft's *Vindication* with his tutor, Mr. Kilpert, and had even deigned to discuss the work with her one evening after dinner. Of course their debate had devolved into debauchery, but for once Milton had worked her mind, not just her body.

Elizabeth shook off her distracting thoughts. She must steel herself for the *Ton's* inevitable verbal attacks. She loathed social affairs like this one, except, of course, to dance. Dancing with an adroit partner made up for all the rest.

"Your card, Lizzie."

"My card?" She'd barely heard her husband. "Oh yes, you must take the first dance, Milton." She smiled warmly at him, only to be met by a deep frown.

"I do not dance, Elizabeth, but will ensure you do not lack for partners." And the audacious man began to fill her card with names.

"Milton, you cannot—"

He continued, heedless.

"Sir, do you not know how a dance works? You cannot randomly fill a lady's card with names! And what do you mean, you do not dance? You danced at our wedding for goodness' sake."

"I know how a dance works, Elizabeth." Pain marred his handsome face. "But I'll not have strangers dancing with my wife. You may dance with any name upon this card but no one else."

There it was again: his incessant need to control. Though

he'd allowed his entire wedding party to manhandle her during *that* dance.

"Milton." She sweetened her tone. "You cannot expect me to behave properly in society yet curtail me in such unseemly manner. I cannot turn down requests to dance simply because you have not written a gentleman's name upon my card. I shall insult half the *Ton* if I do."

***

She had a point. *Blast.*

"Furthermore, it is a husband's duty to dance the first minuet with his wife."

Double blast.

"I don't know these sorts of dances, Lizzie." Milton dropped his voice. "I know only jigs and reels and sailor's—"

"Husband," she smoothed, "trust me to judge whom I dance with tonight. If the gentleman is an ogre I'll feign a headache or request a glass of punch. There are ways to avoid distasteful partners. Believe me, I know every trick."

And he did believe her. What he couldn't believe was how neatly she'd argued her point. She was too clever, his wife. Too clever by far.

A vision of her in his carriage made him roughly inhale his next breath, because he'd tupped her good and well astride his lap, gripping her lush backside by the end, fingers digging into plush arse cheeks, her neckline bedecked in his diamonds. The more he learned her body's desires the better he might guide her toward his own—and the sooner he might master her soul.

"Very well, Lizzie, I will allow you to choose your dance partners tonight, but this evening shall be a test, like the tests I set you during courtship. And if you do not—"

"If I do not pass this latest test, *sir*"—she coquettishly batted her lashes—"you may punish me as you did that first time in the park, and afterward I promise to be most … contrite." She licked her lips, making Milton's breeches tighten again uncomfortably. *Vixen!*

❧

Half an hour later, Elizabeth took the cup of punch her husband brought her and made herself drink. "Milton, they are staring."

"Of course they are, darling, you look radiant." He flashed an overly bright smile at an elderly lady fanning herself; she threw him a nasty glance back.

"No, that is not why they are staring." Elizabeth knew a withering glare when she saw one.

Milton downed his own punch. "I warned you our marriage would cause a stir." He set his glass upon a nearby table just as a stiff-necked couple approached.

"Milton." The gentleman nodded while the man's wife failed to acknowledge Elizabeth at all.

"Stevens." Milton drew himself tall. "My wife, Baroness of Milton," he introduced. "Elizabeth, may I present Lord and Lady Stevens, of Cavendish Hall."

"My pleasure." Elizabeth gave the lord her hand while the man's wife eyed her with open hostility. "Lady Stevens." Elizabeth forced herself to smile. "It is an honor. Are you well acquainted with the Denbighs?"

"Why, I should think." The lady sniffed. "I have known their granddaughter since birth. She is *most* impressive."

"Undeniably, madam." Elizabeth wracked her brain for conversation. "Though I've yet to have the honor of—"

"And such promising prospects. I imagine a *marquess* may even be within Miss Pendrake's reach," she gloated.

Elizabeth tightened her grip on her husband's arm. "Or perhaps a *duke*, Lady Stevens, is not out of the question? My husband is good friends with His Grace, the Duke of Allendale, whose wife, as you know, is Miss Pendrake's cousin. Why, just the other day the Duchess and I took tea together. Such a lovely woman, the Duchess."

Milton squeezed Elizabeth's waist as the lady's scowl deepened.

"To be sure, Miss Pendrake could well achieve marriage to a duke, what with her superior *breeding*," the lady intoned. "Certainly better than a mere baron."

Elizabeth stiffened. "Oh, I should never disparage a baron, Lady Stevens." She let her eyes disparage Lord Stevens before pressing her body closer into Milton's. "A baron's ability to so wholly devote himself to his wife's every pleasure is a benefit of marriage I cannot recommend enough."

Lord Stevens' jaw dropped while his wife turned red with indignation.

Elizabeth pinched her lips into a smile. "Milton, darling, shall we?"

"Of course, dear. If you'll excuse us, Stevens, my lady."

He led Elizabeth away, but not before she felt his hand drop and pat her bottom, in plain view of both snobs.

The moment they were out of sight, however, she slumped against his arm. "Did I offend, husband?" Milton's face held the oddest expression. "I admit, my tongue can run away with me, but I could not stand the manner in which that woman—"

He swept her into a dimly lit corner to steal a most improper, passionate kiss, hiding her behind his tall frame. "You were thrilling, Lady Milton." He pressed his bulging waist into her hips. "A perfect foil to those nasty fobs. And if we weren't at a blasted ball right now, I'd show my gratitude by lifting your skirts and pleasuring you till you screamed my name."

Elizabeth nearly puddled to the floor.

"But alas, such pleasure must wait." His face dimpled.

"We've rounds of conversation to get through yet." He led her back out of the shadows. "I'll fetch you something stronger than punch to resettle you, dear."

Elizabeth needed that drink. She needed *something* to take her mind off the man who'd just stolen all air from her lungs. Again.

CHAPTER TWENTY-EIGHT

Annabelle anxiously scanned the Denbigh ballroom for her sister, whom she'd yet to see. Worse still, she was forced to dance another round with Mr. Finch, who stood just short enough the fellow's noxious breath fell hot upon her décolletage. Bad enough the message this second dance sent, but the man also barely knew his steps, forcing her to back-lead him.

Pure torture.

She envied every other lady at this ball, but most especially the lady at its center: Miss Mercy Pendrake. *She* danced with one fine gentleman after another, the flowers woven into her hair winking as she twirled past, her face lit with joy. She burned so bright with promise Annabelle felt certain the young lady would wed by season's end. Whereas if Annabelle did not find a way out of Mr. Finch's odious arms, she'd be wed to *him*.

Disapproving stares continued their way; it was obvious to all Mr. Finch did not belong at this affair. Even ladies she'd been introduced to hid their faces behind their fans when she chanced to meet their eyes. Gentlemen looked right through her, as if she were tainted by association. Which she was, for

Mr. Finch would never have been granted entry to this ball were it not for her father's embarrassing groveling at the door. Or perhaps it was news of her sister's scandalous marriage that had the *Ton* all staring at her so? Annabelle searched again for Lizzie. Had the Baron not come? She needed a friend, someone, to save her from her misery, to rescue her from the repulsive Mr. Finch.

***

From clear across the ballroom, Milton scowled at the man currently dancing with Elizabeth. He didn't like what he saw, nor did he enjoy the Duke of Allendale's sharp elbow to his ribs.

"What?" he snapped.

"Staring daggers at your wife is not going to change the fact *you* still don't know your steps," Wellesley remarked. "Besides, is that not Kilpert, your protégé of a tutor, leading your wife about the floor? I assume he's on your 'acceptable' list."

"He will be stricken from said list for this display," Milton ground out.

"In that case, mind if I ask your Baroness next?"

Milton finally tore his eyes away. "Yes, go rescue Lizzie from Kilpert." He hated how Wells always cut to the chase. "He's filled her head with enough literary claptrap for one night, I'm sure."

"You might whisper similar claptrap, friend, if your wife is a true bluestocking." He paused. "Oh ho, make that a *red*stocking instead!" Wells was positively jolly. "I say, Jasper, is Lady Milton wearing my wedding gift to you?"

Milton caught the color of Elizabeth's ankle at her hem. "Wells…" he growled.

The Duke was still chuckling when their former shipmate

Banks, now Captain Banks, ambled up, stuffed into an unbecoming suit.

"This is the last goddamned fancy dance I attend with you dandies." He yanked the cravat at his neck before his eyes chanced upon the belle of the ball. "And who, lads, is that fine morsel?"

"My wife's cousin." Wellesley's tone bit. "You may dance with anyone but Miss Pendrake, Banks."

"Christ, Wells, I merely looked…"

"In fact, go dance with Jasper's wife." The Duke caught Milton's eye. "Since he cannot *satisfy* his lady in this regard."

Banks grinned his pearly whites in his rotten, thieving face. "I'm off to seduce your wife then, Jasp."

Ingrates. Milton wished to throttle both his so-called friends when Wellesley stiffened noticeably beside him.

"Is that…?" The Duke's face crumpled. "Jasper, tell me Hieronymus bloody Finch is not at this bloody ball."

Milton tore his eyes from his wife to follow Wellesley's gaze squarely to Ronny Finch, holding Annabelle Winthrop in his greedy, meaty paws.

"How the deuce did he get in?" Wells blurted.

Rage, swift and bitter, filled Milton's veins, but before he could yank Bella from that vile man's clutches, Arty swooped in.

***

Harris spotted Finch with Miss Winthrop just as their dance wound down. Too angry for words, he made straight for Annabelle, snatched her from Finch's grasp, and promptly dragged her off, leaving the cur to fume and sputter upon the floor.

Harris swore under his breath as the music forced his feet into triplets. He waltzed Bella into the swirling fray, grateful to past lovers who'd taught him how to dance; actresses always knew the latest steps.

"Miss," he hissed, "did Finch say or do anything this night to indicate he might—"

The pain in her eyes almost made him miss his step; he kept them in ever closer, tight formations. "Bella, did he—"

"Forgive me." She blinked back tears. "His hands, Arthur…" The poor girl shivered in his arms. "He took such liberties while dancing that I—"

And that did it. Harris harshly stepped on her hem, neatly tearing her dress before he tripped her straight into his arms and swept her off the floor to announce to all and sundry that Miss Winthrop had twisted her ankle, he'd see her to safety, no need to halt the dance.

And indeed the waltz carried on with barely a hiccough, the musicians not missing a beat, couples' footwork unimpeded. Harris carried Annabelle out of the ballroom into a nearby parlor where he settled her onto a chaise and swiftly shut the door.

"Mr. Harris!" The lady's outrage rattled. "We must leave at once! At once, I say!"

He approached her panic with calm. *Best do this quick.*

"Now, miss—"

"You cannot bring me unchaperoned to an empty room, sir. Why, you tripped me quite on purpose!"

"O' course I tripped you, woman. How else was I t' bloody ferret you out o' that blasted ballroom an' away from Finch's grasping hands?"

She stared at him in shock. "But that does not condone your behavior. Sir, I must insist you…"

He ignored her lengthy protest to push up her skirts, pull off her shoe, and roll one pretty stocking off her all-too-shapely leg to wrap about her 'twisted' ankle. He worked so fast she'd barely time to beat his head with her fan before he heard the doorknob turn.

Harris laid himself atop Miss Winthrop just as gasps erupted from the threshold. He was too busy probing Annabelle's delicious mouth with his tongue to pay their audience much bother. Why the hell hadn't he kissed her like this sooner?

A shriek interrupted his ardor such that he reluctantly pulled away, Bella panting beneath him.

"*What* is the meaning of this, sir?" The Countess of Denbigh trembled with indignation, propped between two ladies keeping the ball's hostess upright.

He tipped her his best rogue's wink. "Forgive the impropriety, milady, but I could not wait to kiss my betrothed. Miss Winthrop has just made me the happiest man alive."

Annabelle sat bolt upright and opened her mouth to—

Harris kissed her silent again.

They caught Finch scuttling toward an exit, Milton grabbing the rat by his scruff to propel him into a room Wellesley tore open.

"I will have your sorry arse for breaking into a private home, Finch," the Duke snarled.

But the devil merely laughed. "Yer pretty Duchess let me in, Wells. Seems she didn't know our history. Quite th' golden dish," he jeered.

"Why are you here, scum?" Wellesley's self-control impressed.

"*He* knows." Finch nicked his head at Milton, whose hand fast slipped about the blackguard's neck as his own temples throbbed viciously. Everything in his being longed to howl and kick and scream.

Yet he did not.

"I'm engaged to 'is sister-in-law. Soon t' be part o' th' family, ain't that right, boy?" His vile grin sickened. "Such a delectable morsel, Miss Bella. So deliciously ripe fer—"

Milton cut off the man's air, turning Finch's face a nasty blue.

"Jasper," Wells barked, making him only slightly relax his grip. The Duke turned his ire back to Finch. "I highly doubt Lord Winthrop would allow his daughter to marry your foul self, Ronny."

"Oh he has, an' he will." Finch's grin widened until Milton again cut off all air, wishing to squeeze the man dead. And he would. This time he'd—

"Damn it, Jasp, don't choke him until *after* we've made him talk."

Milton dropped Finch, who stumbled to regain his feet.

"And why in damnation did you not tell me Finch was after your sister-in-law?"

"Because, *Your Grace*"—Milton's hands suddenly, almost violently, trembled—"I'd no intention of allowing the man anywhere near her."

Hieronymus Finch's laugh echoed in Milton's head. "Still championin' poor defenseless lasses, eh Jasp?" He was positively merry in his malice. "I danced with dear Bella this whole night, lad, right under yer nose, an' not once did y' notice, not once. I've wooed 'er fer weeks with flowers an' fine words, same as you courted 'er sister. Y' showed me how t' purchase me way into society by purchasin' meself a respectable wife. An' what better wife t' purchase than sister t' yer own." His face gleamed in triumph. "T' bring us close again, boy. For y' are still me boy, Jasp. Me sweet, whippin'—"

Milton threw Finch against the wall and began to beat the living breath out of him, the Duke's voice faintly shouting amid the hum in his head, until Wells hauled Milton off Finch to keep him from killing the man.

Because he would. He'd kill him this time.

Milton chafed in his friend's hold, panting and snarling as Wells muttered, "Not here, Jasp. Not at the blasted Denbighs. Later. But *not* here."

Milton swallowed his rage and steadied his hand. He stared fiercely into Ronny's already swelling, bloodshot eyes. "You harm a hair on that girl's head and God help me, I will murder you in cold blood."

With a sick crunch, Finch readjusted his nose. "No doubt y' would, Jasp." He spat blood on the Denbigh's carpet. "But once that girl's me wife, ain't nothin' you nor anyone else can do t' keep 'er from me. An' I *will* wed sweet Bella. I'll get exactly what I wants and what I deserves."

Wells twisted the rat's arms behind his back and shoved him into the hands of two footmen who'd arrived unannounced; they must have heard the hubbub.

As the servants escorted Finch out, Milton continued to see red.

The Duke poured him a drink. "Jasper, you will tell me now what in bloody hell is—"

Milton downed the glass and wiped sweat off his upper lip. "It'll have to wait, Wells, before Arty does something rash."

"Such as?"

"Create the sort of ruckus he's known for." Milton poured himself another drink to steady his still shaking hands. "He's separated Miss Winthrop from Finch, but the ensuing rumors will no doubt ruin her." Milton set his glass down. "I urgently need to speak with Arty, and then I've a score to settle with that weasel Winthrop."

Wellesley met Milton's eyes. "You *will* tell me all before you leave this house tonight," he ordered.

"Oi, Capt'n. You've me word."

CHAPTER TWENTY-NINE

The gentleman Elizabeth now danced with reminded, oddly, of her husband. He was as tall and lean, and exuded a similar predatory stance. He had the same coloring, same build somehow, as Milton. The resemblance was so uncanny she began to suspect them somehow—

"Lady Milton, I hope you've not suffered too much at the hands of your husband this night."

She stiffened in his arms. "I suffer only your comment, sir."

His lips curled. "I am referring to the slight paid you by Lord and Lady Stevens." His words sank in. "The *Ton* do not look favorably upon a purchased Scottish Barony."

"And who are you, sir"—Elizabeth's eyes blazed up at him—"to question my husband's title?"

His laugh made her skin prickle. "But I introduced myself to you already, *miss*." He demeaned her further. "I am Lord Mathers, the Duke of Lennox's heir."

"My lord, I must insist you call me by my—"

"I beg your pardon, Lady Milton, for the slip," Mathers murmured, though his face began to frown, and not unlike her husband when he looked displeased. “I say, madam, is that not your sister being carried off?”

Elizabeth turned, gasped, and immediately fled Lord Mathers to follow a tidy crowd down the hall. She could not believe Annabelle was here after all. Not once had she laid eyes on Bella or Papa; she’d assumed they’d forgone their invitation altogether.

The scene she stumbled onto, however, left little doubt her sister was in great distress.

Annabelle reclined upon a chaise, looking both disheveled and flushed, her ankle bandaged with her stocking while a fair-haired gentleman spoke in measured tones to Papa, whose face shone bright with disagreement. Two ladies, meanwhile, fanned the Countess of Denbigh in rapid flutter as onlookers whispered words Elizabeth only thinly caught: *disgraceful — just like the sister — utterly ruined — shameless!*

She pushed her way through the crowd toward Annabelle before—

“*Ooh* Lizzie, is it not romantic?” gushed Lady Stanton.

Elizabeth gaped at her former neighbor. “I … beg your pardon?”

“Why, Mr. Harris has just proposed and been accepted by your sister! Such a handsome young man too, as handsome as your own charming husband. You Winthrop girls *do* know how to catch them.” She stifled a giggle.

Elizabeth was beyond all patience for this lady. She shoved past her to envelop Annabelle in a protective embrace. “Bella, dearest, what has happened?” she whispered into her sister’s ear.

Annabelle sank her head to Elizabeth’s breast. “I am ruined, Lizzie.” Her voice caught. “Mr. Harris has ruined me.”

Elizabeth righted herself. “Out, everyone,” she commanded as multiple heads swiveled. “This is a family matter requiring great delicacy, so I beg you, please, return to the dance. Lord Winthrop and I will see to my sister's wellbeing."

The Countess of Denbigh pursed her lips in clear disapproval but allowed herself to be led from the room by her entourage. The remaining gawkers followed suit, including Lady Stanton, who blew Elizabeth a parting kiss.

She ignored the impossible woman's cheek and turned her attention to her father and the man she presumed was Mr. Harris. "I will hear from each of you now as to what has occurred." She fixed her gaze on Harris first. "Starting with you, sir."

"Lady Milton, I have been courting your sister ever since the happy occasion of your wedding, being so enamored of her that I—"

"Lizzie, do not listen to a word this man says!" Papa cut in. "Why, he is the very cheat who forced my hand the night I lost you to the Baron! It was in *his* gaming den."

Annabelle's face drained of color.

"Gaming den? Which?" Though recognition slowly dawned as Elizabeth looked from Harris's hangdog expression to her father's blustery denial to Bella's awkward demeanor.

All three knew something she did not.

"Annabelle." She shifted her focus. "What have you been keeping from me, sister? Is it true Mr. Harris has been courting you? Is it true you just accepted his suit?"

But before Bella could answer, the Duke of Allendale strode in with Elizabeth's husband two steps behind him. Milton looked alarmingly unkempt.

Her husband immediately addressed Mr. Harris. "Arty, you will escort Miss Winthrop and my wife home in your carriage. Wells," he caught the Duke's eye, "you will make excuses to the Earl and Countess of Denbigh for our hasty departure and the other mess we left. I trust any circulating rumors can be dealt with by yourself and the Duchess?"

"You may depend on our discretion, Jasp," the Duke replied.

"Elizabeth, we will discuss all once I am home. Winthrop, you are coming with me, *now*." And without a look back, Milton hauled Papa away.

Elizabeth was unsurprised her husband should command matters thus, but it insulted her no less. She was about to protest both his interference and indifference when the Duke himself turned to both her and Annabelle.

"Lady Milton, Miss Winthrop, the Duchess and I will do everything in our power to dispel all scandal. You are in the safest of hands with Mr. Harris to see you both home. Now, if you would be so good as to follow me discreetly, I shall arrange for Arthur's carriage to be fetched and your wraps collected before you set off."

Elizabeth stared at the Duke; what the devil was going on?

"Lady Milton." He took her arm to lead her away, Mr. Harris following with Annabelle. "Your husband has everything in hand. He will ensure this entire misunderstanding blows over and is no doubt arranging matters with your father as we speak."

Likely true, but Elizabeth chafed to have been the last to know anything. It was a truth that burned.

"Have you *no* idea who that man is?" Milton snarled at Winthrop, who cowered and sniveled before him. "And have you no shame? To sell your daughter so soon after I'd given you a small fortune for Elizabeth?" He was beside himself. "What is wrong with you, to have so little honor, so little control!"

"It is *you* who have no honor." Winthrop whimpered his defense. "You stole Lizzie from me, you and Harris. You rigged that game at *The Leaf*, I know you did. And Finch confirmed it. Said you were a cheat, said you'd counted your way to duping me. So when he offered to—"

"How much do you owe him," Milton cut Winthrop off.

"It is not a matter of owing; it is a matter of—"

"How much, damnation."

"That's just it!" Winthrop cried. "It is a matter of-of having already … *given*." He barely exhaled the word.

"What did you say?" Something nasty slithered down Milton's spine.

"She…" The man began to tremble.

"What. Have. You. Done?" Milton's fists began to tingle.

"Bella was…" The old man lost it; he began to cry.

"You didn't." Milton seethed.

"I'd no choice! He'd cleaned me out entirely! All the money you gave me…" Winthrop continued an inchoate litany of excuses, while Milton breathed in and out, in and out, to keep from strangling the wretch.

It took every ounce of his self-control.

When he had steadied himself, he told the idiot in as calm a tone as possible, "You mean that in place of cash you wagered your daughter to Hieronymus Finch? To *Finch*?" He began to spiral into anger so black it—

"Fuck!" He hurled a decanter against the wall, shattering it into shards.

Winthrop cowered in full now, blubbering that he hadn't meant to, he'd not known what kind of man Finch was, he'd thought Harris far worse. Even Milton had tricked him that night his luck had failed…

Milton knew his own actions had steered Finch to do exactly what he himself had done. From Winthrop's perspective, Milton's actions *were* deplorable, even if he'd merely asked for Lizzie's hand after cleaning the man out. Finch, however, had played the table for Annabelle outright: to own her, married or not.

Milton felt physically sick.

"Listen to me, Winthrop, you will not allow Finch near your daughter again, do you understand? Stall him when he visits; say she's fallen ill. I don't care how you do it, but you *must not* allow that man to claim her. He is the foulest devil to walk this earth, and he will destroy Annabelle, married or not. I shall find a way to clear your debt, but if you so much as—"

"Baron." The simpering lord groveled. "I'll do whatever you ask, I swear it, only why did Mr. Harris now—?"

"Harris is doing his bloody best to outwit Finch, you fool, at *my* behest. He'll not harm your daughter, and we can only hope his actions this evening have thrown Finch off his game."

Milton shuddered at just how far this situation had gotten out of hand.

"Pull yourself together, man. Go home and keep your daughter under lock and key. From now on, you let *me* deal with Finch."

CHAPTER THIRTY

When their carriage pulled up before Jasper's posh diggings, Lady Milton's words did not surprise Harris in the least.

"I shall see my sister home first, sir," she insisted.

"Ma'am, I have every intention of—"

"No." Her lips set. "You have damaged my sister's reputation and schemed behind my back with my husband this entire night."

"Lady Milton." Harris was too tired for this fight. "I urged your husband to inform you of your sister's situation and, I might add, I counseled your sister to do the same." He shot Annabelle a look. "But neither listened, forcing me to take matters into my own hands tonight."

The lady took pause. "I'll grant they are equally pigheaded."

From the corner of his eye, Harris saw Miss Winthrop flinch.

"But you deliberately compromised Annabelle this evening and that alone—"

"Lizzie, please," Bella interrupted. "I should like to speak with Mr. Harris in private. I promise to call tomorrow and explain all, I swear, only give me this time with him, I beg."

Well done, miss, Harris thought, for he doubted anyone else could have convinced Milton's wife otherwise.

The lady did indeed capitulate. "Very well, Bella. But if I do not receive word from you by noon tomorrow, you can expect me on your doorstep." She skewered them both with sharp glares before she disembarked from the carriage.

The driver drove on with the crack of his whip while Miss Winthrop wasted no time to launch her attack. "Arthur, why did you lie? Why tell everyone I'd accepted your proposal?"

"Why, t' spare you more shame, miss. Turn ruination into celebration." *Obvious, weren't it?*

"No one was fooled, sir." She seemed only more peeved. "In fact, that performance of yours made it all the less believable or honorable." Her hands fidgeted in her lap like moths dusting cloth.

"Ah." He cleared his throat. "Y' didn't like me kiss."

"It was most improper."

"The best kisses always are, miss."

Her hands began to bunch and knead her skirts. "You have placed me in an untenable position, sir, one which—"

"And I apologize for it, truly." He donned, again, the guise of gentleman. "Annabelle, I'm afraid the only way forward now is for you to marry me, and fast. Because the jig is up. Finch is on to us. He'll stop at nothing till he has you for himself."

Miss Winthrop's eyes widened, as if gears slowly turned in her head. A minute later, however, the lady had found her nerve again. "I am certain there is another way forward, Mr. Harris. Now that my sister and the Baron are aware of my situation, I've no doubt they will—"

"Bella, luv, I'm takin' yer t' Gretna, and that's th' end of it."

Her mouth fell open.

"I am sorry it's come to this." He dropped the Cockney to ease her shock. "It was never my intent. Had you not—" He stopped himself, for it mattered little what might have been. All that mattered now was keeping her from Finch. "Had things gone as I'd wished, we'd not now find ourselves in this predicament. But the only way to keep you safe from Finch is to marry you myself. Which is why I compromised you so thoroughly."

"You are mad." She shook her head. "*Mad* to think I will marry you! I will find another way. I will—"

"Annabelle…"

"No, this is absurd." She grew more agitated. "Utterly absurd. You will deliver me to my father's house this instant, and tomorrow I will visit Lizzie and the Baron, and together we will—"

"Bella, I'm afraid there's no other solution."

"There is always another solution!"

He leaned across the carriage to take her hand. "It won't be real, th' marriage. I'm not that sort o' man. We'll have it annulled once Finch is dealt with."

"Annulled? One does not simply annul a legal marriage with vows that bind unto death!"

"If the marriage is never consummated and one can prove coercion, then—"

Her doe eyes were large as an owl's. "You do not wish to marry me at all."

"'Course not." He frowned. "I were simply doin' Jasp a favor by—"

"Doing him a favor?" she burst out. "So *he* told you to give me your card at Lizzie's wedding, did he? Told you to court me, told you to-to *ruin* me?"

"Well, no," Harris admitted. "That last bit were my idea."

"Let me out," she ordered. "You let me out this instant. I shall find my own way home."

"Bella, luv, now don't be difficult. We'll sort things out once we're married."

"There will be no marriage!" She wrenched open the carriage door, the night air hitting with surprising cold.

"Christ, woman, shut the bloody door!"

She moved to fling herself from the vehicle, but Harris hauled her to his seat, where she rained fists and words upon his person, demanding her release.

"Stop this carriage!" she screamed. "Let me go!"

Using torso and leg to pin her down so that he nearly sat astride her, Harris managed to free his hands to douse his kerchief with the small bottle he kept for just such purpose, shoving the fabric roughly over her nose.

He palmed her face with the cloth until she fell limp beneath him, cursing her for making him do precisely what he hadn't wished.

❧

Milton arrived home late wanting only his bed. He handed his hat and cane to a footman and wearily climbed his all-too-grand staircase. Tiresome enough to attend a coming out ball, but to deal with Finch of all evils—his gut did another nasty flip—not to mention Harris compromising Annabelle, and the pissant father, Winthrop...

He was exhausted.

But he'd find no rest with a wife such as his, oh no, for there she sat, propped atop *his* bloody bed with a book. Mutton warmed her toes, sprawled across the bedclothes where the blasted hound knew he shouldn't be.

"Off!" Milton barked.

The beast slunk away, looking guilty as sin.

Elizabeth peered at him over her spectacles. "What took you so long?"

"Why are you in my bed, woman?"

"I am reading," she answered pertly, "and waiting for you, of course."

"Well in future you are to wait in your own damn chamber." He unknotted his cravat. "You enter this room at my request only, as it is my private space."

"I beg your pardon, sir, for assuming a wife, of all persons, is allowed entry to her husband's bedchamber."

He ignored her jab and began to remove his clothes, which felt stiff and sweaty from the evening's upset. Elizabeth watched him undress, her dark braid draped to one side of her neck which nestled nicely against his pillow, making him forget, for an instant, his irritation—until she opened her mouth again.

"What did you say to my father, sir?"

"That he is not fit to walk the earth for what he's done to your sister." Milton sat at the bed's edge to pull off his hessians.

"And just *what*, exactly, has Papa done to Bella?"

"Traded her like chattel to the vilest man in London." He dropped his boot. "And it is by the Grace of God, in the form of one Arty Harris, that she's been spared that heinous fate."

Her shock was great. So great, in fact, that she remained blessedly silent.

Milton stepped out of his breeches.

"You mean Mr. Harris deliberately compromised Bella in order to—"

"Arty contrived tonight's scandal to keep her from Hieronymus Finch, yes."

He pulled his shirt over his head, till he was clad only in smalls. He hoped his fine physique might distract her from more questions.

It did not.

"And just who is this Mr. Finch, Milton?"

"Lizzie, darling," he drawled, "I have dealt this night with the taunts of society, the simpering of your father, the profound endangerment of your sister, and the one man in London who strikes fear in my breast. I should like to go to bed."

"But Milton, you have yet to explain who this—"

"As I said, wife, I should like to go to bed." He crawled in beside her. "And since you are here, you may as well ease my troubles." He removed her spectacles from her face, snatched the book from her hands, and turned down the oil lamp.

"Milton," her voice rose, "you cannot—"

"Be a good wife for once, Lizzie, and let me fuck you, please."

"Of all the—!"

She silenced nicely, not only by his kiss but by his hand sliding the length of her night-rail to untie the silly ribbon at her neck. "Mmm, better." He broke from her lips to nuzzle her neck, pushing the material off her shoulders to expose her breasts.

"Milton, I cannot forget my sister is in danger simply because you now choose to—"

"Mmm, yes, wife." His hand pushed her night-rail to her waist, tugging it off her hips. "We shall discuss everything come morning, I promise." He peppered light kisses across her belly.

"This cannot wait until—"

He swallowed her words once more with his lips, before he yanked the obnoxious gown free, leaving her bare atop the bedclothes.

"I'll take care of everything tomorrow, luv. I promise to keep Annabelle safe. Now stop talking and"—his knee pushed her legs apart—"grant me this reprieve." He entered her so swiftly all thought fled at how heavenly she felt, cocooning him in heat.

"Good girl," he groaned into her bosom, beginning to

gently rock and thrust against her womb. "You are so lovely, Lizzie, when you obey me."

At last, all troubles eased, his head relaxed. Milton felt nothing but his wife's sweet largesse.

❧

Come morning, however, his oh-so-willing Baroness had become an all-too-intent bulldog who poked him beneath the covers. "Milton, I insist you now tell me—"

"Woman, can you not wait until after I've had my coffee?" He groaned into his pillow and draped his arm over his head.

"No, I cannot, because you distracted me from all discussion last night, and I must know how best to handle my sister's situation."

"*You* are not handling anything." He rolled over to face her. "You will stay out of matters so that *I* may do my job."

"Your job?" She appeared thoroughly put out. "Is Annabelle not my sister, sir? And should not any actions taken therefore include, nay, require my full participation?"

Milton wished to God he were still asleep.

"Annabelle is now my family too, Elizabeth, and therefore my responsibility. And my job, wife, is to protect my family, which I fully intend to do." He rolled over again, thinking that ought to end it.

Apparently not.

"How can you claim to protect your family by keeping them—me—in the dark? Milton, it is not fair. I am not some ignorant miss. I am wise in ways you—"

"Wise, Lizzie, really?" He locked her in his gaze. "You have no idea what kind of man Finch is, nor what fate lies in store for your sister should he—"

"Yes, and how *should* I know this, Milton, when you deliberately keep it from me?" She was in a state alright, though her lovely tresses trailed her breasts in alluring, dark lines that made his blood flow straight to his groin.

He forced himself to focus. "Elizabeth, trust me to know what is best. I've a long and nasty history with Finch, and I will deal with the man in—"

"History, I see," she fumed. "Yet another piece of your past you are unwilling to divulge, even when that past clearly informs my sister's present danger. Do you think me so naïve, sir? Do you think me not apprised of my father's own checkered dealings? Think I haven't spent my life negotiating payment of his debts with men who threatened and—?"

Milton roughly grabbed her arm. "What men, Lizzie? Who threatened you?"

"Debt collectors, Milton! Tradesmen! You met that nasty butcher the first day you called at our house. I have spurned, stalled, and sweet talked my entire life to protect my sister, or do you forget I agreed to this marriage to protect her from *you*?"

Milton wanted to simultaneously throttle and devour her, for she crackled and sparked just like the day they'd first met. He knew it would be a grave mistake, however, to distract her again with the persuasion of flesh.

"Tradesmen and debt collectors, Elizabeth, are not Hieronymus Finch." He tamped down his disgust at even uttering the fiend's full name. "They are angels in comparison."

"Then who in hell's name is he, Milton, and why is Mr. Harris mixed up in all of this?"

"Cursing now, Lizzie? Did I marry a hoyden, perhaps?"

She folded her arms, hiding her lovely bosom; he wholeheartedly disapproved.

"Do not tease me, sir, not in such serious matter as this. Who are these two men who vie for my sister's hand? I will have answers."

Milton rose from his bed, making an effort not to stare at his wife's naked glory lest he fall to ravishing her again. "When we married, Lizzie, I knew the funds I gave your father would not last. More than this, I feared the very manner in which I'd won your hand would serve as a model for your father to marry off your sister in similar lucrative manner."

***

She'd had the very same thought, making Elizabeth's insides churn with only greater worry, but she would first hear him out. She listened closely while Milton dressed.

"Arthur Harris owns a gaming den—one I invest in myself. It is a hall your father frequents, and where I played him at cards the night I gained your hand. Arty is also my most trusted friend. I asked that he introduce himself to your sister the day we married, so that he'd know who Annabelle was. I also asked him to keep an eye on your father and report to me his losses and wins. Arty did me a favor in this, Lizzie, nothing more."

His story made sense, but events still did not add up.

"What I had *not* counted on was Finch, of all men, pursuing Annabelle." Milton grimaced. "The moment Arty discovered Finch was courting your sister, I made Arty court her too. To show your father—and Finch—that more reputable gentlemen might compete for her hand."

"Reputable, sir? The owner of a gaming den is a reputable choice of suitor for my sister?"

"Elizabeth, I'd begun soliciting more respectable options for Annabelle, but your father's ability to run through cash is" —his face soured—"remarkable. Finch's suit came along faster than I could drum up serious interest for Bella amongst the gentlemen of the *Ton.* Nor did I have time to consult my own solicitor as to the legality of providing her with a dowry your father could not steal."

"I see." She chewed her lip. "So without consulting me, or consulting Annabelle, you decided to wed her off to a gentleman of your own choosing."

"Yes." He buttoned his fall. "The sooner she is married the sooner she is safe from predators."

"Like you," Elizabeth stated.

"Come again?"

"Like you, the predator who snatched me."

"Elizabeth, I am a far cry from—"

"Are you, Milton?" She let out her hurt. "Is that why you chose not to marry Annabelle yourself, because you saw in her a woman of greater worth? Is it why you now go out of your way, behind my back, to secure her an honorable marriage, while you had no qualms—no qualms at all, sir—taking me to altar against my will?"

"Have a care, Lizzie." His gaze darkened. "Because by the time we'd finished courting, I recall you were not as unwilling as you claim."

"You seduced me, sir." She grabbed her night-rail from the floor. "And I am appalled to discover how underhanded you have been with my sister too." She threw the billowy gown over her head. "Not once did you apprise me of matters, or share with me your concerns for Bella's future."

Tears began to well in her eyes, and Elizabeth did not know why. She knew only that for Milton to have deemed her opinion, her assistance, irrelevant—unnecessary, even, in steering Annabelle toward a happy match—hurt.

"All my life," she told him, "I have shielded my sister from men's baser natures, hoping she might marry a gentleman more worthy than our father. So for you to disregard, nay, discard my help, as if I were an annoyance, an impediment to your plans"—she aggressively brushed back tears—"makes me all the more disappointed in you, sir. Deeply so."

"Then I am sorry I fail you yet again, wife."

So now *his* pride was wounded?

"But I maintain my intent was and remains honorable in regards to both your sister and yourself."

"Honorable!" she exploded. "In no way was the manner in which you gained my hand in marriage honorable, Jasper Audrey, and well you know it."

Their eyes locked as Elizabeth's pulse hammered in her chest, "*Milton!*" being bellowed from the bowels of the house, followed by a sudden, shuddering slam and "*No, I will see the bastard now!*"

Hushed, low voices commenced before heavy steps thudded in approach. "I demand an audience. At once!"

Elizabeth and Milton froze, both straining to discern the ruckus in the hallway.

"Papa?" She ventured toward the door before fists pounded, "Let me in, damn you!" and she jumped back, colliding into Milton's hard frame directly behind her.

Her husband turned the key and her father tumbled inside, scowling.

"*You* let this happen!" He pointed his finger at the Baron, who took a step back. "Where is she, blast you? Where has Harris taken my daughter?"

Her father's words chilled Elizabeth's heart.

CHAPTER THIRTY-ONE

Annabelle awoke with a head of lead. She groaned into the warmth that surrounded her, until that warmth stirred.

"Rest, miss. We'll stop soon for food."

"Food?" She could barely form the word, her tongue as thick as cotton. "Drink. I need—"

A flask was placed to her lips, making her splutter at the liquid's harsh burn. She tried to push it away yet discovered her wrists bound. She opened her mouth to speak but *mmph* was all that came out.

"My ears still ring from your screams, my person still bruised by your fists, miss."

She blinked into a blurry face: Arthur Harris. The blasted man smothered her voice with his palm.

"*Mmph*!" She blinked again at his blond, handsome self—collar creased below the fresh shadow at his chin—then narrowed her eyes at him.

"But if you are ready to behave like a sane creature and discuss matters civilly with me, I will remove my hand and release you from your restraints."

She nodded, wary.

His knuckles grazed her jawbone as he let go his hold, allowing Annabelle to find her tongue again.

"Mr. Harris, you will untie me. Now."

And he did, though the rake seemed to savor the act. He rubbed her wrists back to life, sparking fresh friction, until she pulled them free and roundly slapped his face.

"*Ow!*" He touched his cheek in shock. "What the devil was that for?"

"For abducting me! Ruining me! For trussing me up like some … some …" She could not find the word, which only frustrated her more, making her slap him across the other cheek instead.

"Damn blast it!" He quickly bound her wrists again. "I thought you'd be more rational, woman, but clearly you are—"

"Rational?" Annabelle's rage reached new peaks. "I'll tell you what is rational, sir. *Rational* would be delivering me to my father's house. *Rational* would be dancing like a gentleman, rather than tripping and kissing me so shamelessly I—"

His whiskey-flavored tongue invaded her mouth as Arthur Harris took full advantage of her restrained state. He plundered her lips with abandon, stroking and teasing so thoroughly she relived last night's kiss all over again.

When he was done, he met her eyes with thinly veiled desire, and she felt it too: a shameless hunger.

"Slap me again and I'll do more than steal a kiss, Bella." He panted, out of breath.

"You wouldn't … dare." She panted back.

"Wouldn't I?" He crushed her to his chest, his waistcoat rough against her bodice.

Annabelle struggled to think straight. "I require you to stop the carriage, sir."

He was not the least bit swayed.

"I must … I am in need of …" Her cheeks flushed. "I must

relieve myself, and if you do not wish me to do so here upon the carriage seat, you will stop this coach at once and let me out."

The blasted man laughed.

"I mean it, Mr. Harris. I will—"

"Piss yerself, Bella? Very well, miss." He rapped the carriage roof until the wheels jolted to a stop. "Out y' go." He opened the door for her.

She looked from him, to her bound wrists, and scowled.

"Y' wish me t' untie yer first?" He smirked. "Oh no, dearie, you've proven yerself too reckless fer that." He jumped out and neatly lifted her down, then nudged her toward the wooded roadside. "Be a minute, Fred," he told the driver, who hopped down to check his team.

"Mr. Harris, you will untie me this instant and allow me the dignity I am afforded as a woman of—"

"Genteel birth? Esteemed society?" He somehow managed to make those words sound coarse. "Miss, you're but a bird in need o' pissin', who'll squat an' do her business whether I hold yer upright or not."

Her jaw dropped.

"And if you think I'd be so foolish as to bloody let you loose, Bella darlin', you don't know the half of me."

He pushed her forward, and Annabelle, unable to delay nature's call a moment longer, blushed five shades of red behind the copse of bush where he assisted her in her bodily function.

❧

Elizabeth looked from her father's scowling visage to her husband's furious face and fast regained her wits. "Milton, please pour my father a stiff drink. And Papa, you will explain to us, calmly, I beg, precisely what has happened to Annabelle."

Her father frowned at Elizabeth's half-dressed state a second longer before he downed the brandy Milton handed him. "That swine Harris did not deliver Annabelle home last night." His tone was bitter. "I took early to bed, in quite the state"—he glared again at Milton—"unaware she'd not returned. A maid discovered her bed unslept in this morning, and when we scoured the house, she was nowhere to be found."

Elizabeth's right leg seized into a painful cramp; she hadn't realized she'd been tapping her foot this entire time. What father does not wait up for his daughter's return after such ruinous night as was Bella's?

She began to tap her left foot instead, grumbling, "I should never have left them alone. Never. Why did I let her convince me otherwise?"

"You left them alone?" Papa's eyes flashed. "After that man—"

"Well, *you* did not check to see that she had returned safely!"

"Listen, both of you." Milton paused to swig brandy straight from the bottle, wiping his mouth with the back of his hand. He looked equal parts disgusted and exhausted. "If I know Harris, he's either hidden Annabelle away at *The Leaf*, or he's ferreted her to Gretna, both of which—"

"*Gretna*?" Papa's face turned purple.

"*To marry*?" Elizabeth's own voice squeaked.

Her husband's jaw twitched. "Would both of you just *sit*!" he ordered.

As one, Elizabeth and Papa sat.

"I trust Harris with my life, so I trust him with Annabelle's life too. She will not be harmed. She may be ruined in the eyes of society, but she'll not be *harmed*. So you will calm your overwrought selves and listen to me."

He rang the bell, no doubt in need of coffee rather than more spirits this early in the day. "Neither of you understand whom we're dealing with. Finch hurts women and derives pleasure from hurting children. Not only does he run a nasty gaming den and bawdy house, but he also deals in flesh. Human flesh."

"You mean he … sells people?" Elizabeth asked.

"Yes."

"But slavery is illegal." Papa pushed back. "Mr. Finch never once gave the impression he—"

"There are many ways to enslave a person, Winthrop, but once one human has bought another, for service of any sort, that relationship, the person purchased, it is a form of slavery." Milton's tone was laced with bitterness, and Elizabeth felt a sudden, sharp chill. Had he not purchased her, too, in marriage?

"No, I cannot believe this." Her father shook his head. "Not in London, not Mr. Finch. Not once did he allude to such dealings. Why, upon first meeting the man he struck me as—"

"He reels people in till they dangle from his hook, with no choice but to do his bidding." Milton's face hardened.

"And you believe he wishes to wed Annabelle because…?" Elizabeth drilled deeper. She'd not waste time on Papa's circuitous thinking.

"*Because he can.*" Milton slammed the brandy bottle down so hard upon the bedstand she jumped. "Because he has a grudge against me and knows that by taking your sister as wife he can insinuate himself into *my* life, forcing me to acquiesce again, as if I were his bloody—" He inhaled a shaky breath, not finishing his sentence.

"So it is because of you that Bella is now in danger." Fresh anger surfaced, bubbling in Elizabeth's breast.

"No," Milton fired back. "It is because of your father that Finch now has the means by which to *take* Bella. I merely paved a path the day I married you." He slumped against his bedpost, as if to prop himself up.

Elizabeth stared at the floor. She would not explode with fury, nor would she let her fear for Bella get the better of her now. She mustn't. "Then what do you propose we do, sir?" She stared Milton squarely in his face. "Or are we to rely solely on Mr. Harris to keep Annabelle from Mr. Finch's clutches?"

***

Elizabeth's words, her tone, hurt; Milton blamed himself enough for this mess.

"Harris will keep Bella safe. My faith in him is absolute. Whatever Arty does, he does for good reason. As for Hieronymus Finch, I'll make sure that man does not lift a finger against anyone in my family again."

"But if he's taken her to Gretna…" Winthrop sniveled.

"And would that be such a terrible thing?" Milton snarled, taking two steps closer to tower over his father-in-law. "Would you rather she be married to Finch? Abused? Shared? Pawned to other men for use?" He would not spare this worthless coward the truth. "If Arthur Harris deems it necessary to marry your daughter to keep her safe from Ronny Finch then you should thank God he is so willing."

Winthrop cowered in his seat.

Lizzie placed a hand on her father's shoulder. "You needn't be so harsh, sir."

"Oh I think I must," he bit back. "Neither of you can fathom what it is to be *owned* by that man."

Silence draped the room until Milton cleared his throat—and mind. "I will make inquiries today, to determine where Arty has taken Annabelle. You, Elizabeth, will accompany your father home and pretend to visit your ailing sister. Take Ginny as your companion, then stash her in Bella's bedchamber. She is roughly your sister's size and coloring and can play the role of a young lady taken to her bed."

"And you, sir." Milton turned to Winthrop. "*You* must stall Finch for all you're worth, because he will demand Annabelle's hand in immediate marriage now. Tell him she is overcome by the incident at the ball, that she is distraught. Tell him she requires time yet to recover. Do everything in your power to make him believe she resides within your house, because if Finch gets word that Harris has her, he will pursue them, ruthlessly."

"But how can I prohibit him from—?"

"Good God, man, it is your house! And she is your daughter!" Milton had long lost all respect for his father-in-law. "It is within your right to demand Finch leave your property."

Winthrop looked like he would fold to a flea.

"Do you trust your servants?" Milton asked.

"Well, I … That is …" The fool faltered so long Milton turned to Lizzie.

"Some are trustworthy," she told him bluntly, "some not."

"I'll install a man to keep an eye on things and ingratiate himself with staff. He'll soon know what's what."

Elizabeth straightened her posture. "Very well. That is our plan for the moment."

Thank heavens she was the opposite of Winthrop. Milton didn't want his wife controlling *him*, of course, but her decisiveness was in other ways a gift.

"And *we*, sir, shall continue this conversation in more detail once I return." She briefly met his eyes before she addressed her old man. "Come, Papa, let me show you to the drawing room. I will dress quickly. We can discuss Annabelle on the drive home."

She led her father out, without a backward glance at Milton.

CHAPTER THIRTY-TWO

"Forgive me, Papa," Elizabeth loudly announced, "I should have sent word last night, only Bella's ankle remained too weak." She hurried Ginny, head bent beneath a wrap, up the stairs of her father's house, the maid pretending to limp. "Come, sister, let us get you settled. All will be forgotten in a few days, I am certain."

And Ginny, bless her, let out a well-timed sniffle.

Elizabeth had discussed their ruse with Papa and her maid on the carriage ride back. Only Cook, their most trusted servant, would know it was not Bella in her bedroom, and only Cook would be allowed entry inside. No one was to disturb Miss Annabelle until she regained both her nerves and the use of her ankle.

Once inside Bella's bedroom, Ginny quickly changed into one of Annabelle's night-rails and climbed into the bed. Elizabeth locked her sister's room from the outside and went in search of Cook, who quickly grasped the situation—and pocketed the key to Bella's room even quicker.

Next Elizabeth sought Papa. He sat slumped at his desk,

head folded in his hands, and for a moment she almost pitied the man. Until she thought of Annabelle.

"What would your wives think now, Father, were they alive to witness your present state?"

He remained silent, then looked up and gnashed his teeth. "Would that I had died alongside them, Lizzie! Would I were long buried too!" Tears welled at his eyes. "I was a wretch to both, and now to my poor Annabelle. God help me, I am a wretch…"

Loud pounding made Elizabeth grip her father's hand; she hadn't time to indulge his sorry self. "Follow my lead, whoever now knocks. Be *now* the father Bella needs. Protect her, though you did not protect me."

A moment later, a man stepped into her father's office who looked the very description of Hieronymus Finch. Elizabeth swallowed her fear and began to spin a tale worthy of her sister's unwell state, and her own storytelling talents.

Alas, the man's beady-eyed expression told her he'd not bought a word she'd said.

"Grieves me t' hear yer sister is so poorly, milady, though a moment with meself, her betrothed, is sure t' cheer the lady's spirits."

Elizabeth shuddered at his repulsive sneer.

"I might deliver her me flowers in person, just a brief hullo." His gaze lit upon the nosegay he held, a bundle of 'everlasting love' or baby's breath.

She shuddered only more.

Elizabeth's lips felt parched. "That is most kind of you to offer, Mr. Finch, but I think it best we let Annabelle rest. Perhaps in a day or two you may wish her well in person."

"Oh I'll be back t'morrow, ma'am." His eyes glittered. "Y' can depend on it." Those eyes landed next on her father. "A promise is a promise, after all." He grinned again, one tooth dangling on a thread.

Elizabeth's stomach flipped. "Ah yes, promises." She swallowed her nerves. "I believe my husband, the Baron, promised me just this morning that he would pay you a visit." She remembered to smile while speaking.

"That so?" Finch's eyes gleamed. "Always a pleasure t' deal with Jasper."

"Such a shame I did not see you at our wedding, Mr. Finch. I hope it was not an oversight on my husband's part to have forgotten to invite you."

His face clouded over. "Not at all, Lady Milton. Jasp an' I go way back, see. *So* far back, seems we've known each other a lifetime."

"Strange, then, that he should not mention you, Mr. Finch, given all my husband shares with me."

"Shares, eh?" His eyes lewdly swept her form. "I imagine he's had 'is fun with you." He laughed, low and nasty.

"Now look here, sir." Papa finally came to Elizabeth's defense. "I do not take kindly to—"

"No, you listen t' *me*, old man." Finch's tone turned dangerously ugly, dangerously fast. "I gets what I am promised, or I takes what is mine." His eyes turned to slits. "So you tell that sweet daughter o' yers I'll be back t'morrow, expectin' she greet me nice an' pretty. Fer if she don't"—his eyes glinted maliciously—"I'll make sure both you an' she knows it."

He turned to Elizabeth. "An' you tell yer fine husband t' come visit anytime, *Lizzie*, now that we're nearly family."

Elizabeth took great offense but bit her tongue.

"Tell Jasp he's had his run, but Finch is back fer good." He bored his eyes into hers. "You tell 'im exactly this, sweet Elizabeth: Tell 'im Master Finch done returned t' punish his boy."

The man's nasty, rasping cackle followed him out and down the hall as Papa's entire body trembled, glued to his seat. Elizabeth, too, sank into the nearest chair, her thoughts awhirl, churning with assumptions more awful than the next. Was this the man who'd scarred her husband, abused him as a child? And if he was, what horrors might he inflict on Annabelle? She desperately needed to speak with Milton, though she dreaded relaying Mr. Finch's words.

❧

Harris had secured them lodgings, meal, and stable, for the horses needed rest. Hell, *he* needed rest. They'd made good progress on the road and had not been followed, a miracle he attributed to Jasper likely reading Winthrop the riot act. All of which left Harris feeling a measure of relief—except that Annabelle might still steal off if he let the chit out of his sight. Though if he seduced the miss instead…

He disgusted himself. She was not some doxy seeking employment at *The Leaf*. She was a respectable young lady—too respectable for the likes of him.

He watched her polish off her meal, the abrasions on her wrists filling him with guilt. He'd undone her restraints after ensuring their room's sole window was high enough the minx wouldn't jump.

She began to undo her hair, piling pins upon a small table before she shook her chestnut locks free. "I should like a bath," she announced, dropping the last pin to her pile.

"Darlin'," he drawled, "this ain't the sort o' place as even *has* baths fer guests. You may wash with yon pitcher." He motioned to the room's washstand as she wrinkled her nose. "Well, go on then." He leaned back in his chair. "I'll just sit 'ere an' stare."

"You will turn around and afford me privacy, sir."

"I think not." He knew better. "Yer wrists are unbound an' me wits are not lulled. If y' wish t' wash, do, but I'll not fall into no trap. Whatever skin y' show, dearie, I've seen before in abundance." He looked her over in a crass caress.

The lady deliberated, no doubt desperate to wash the grime from their journey. She squared her shoulders and pushed her chair back from the table. "You won't mind helping me out of my dress then, will you, Arthur?" She turned her back, lifted her hair from the nape of her shapely neck, and let her hips swing.

Temptress.

In two strides Harris began to unhook her, pushing her dress roughly from her shoulders, and then, though she'd not asked him to, he began to unlace her stays.

He peeled them from her midriff and gripped her hips.

She froze.

"Better, miss?" he hissed low in her ear. "Or have you let a man undress you before, let him touch those parts of you"—his hands slid up her hips to brush the undersides of her breasts—"most tender of feeling?" He lingered there a minute too long as she stiffened.

"Or maybe, miss"—his lips nearly nibbled the lobe of her ear—"I'm the first and only man to touch you so." She shuddered. "Maybe, vixen, you even *want* me to." His lips hit her cheekbone and traced a line to her mouth as he leaned her back, kissing her until she melted into his arms and pressed her body into his own.

Harris broke free and yanked her dress to the floor, leaving her in naught but her shift. "I'll be neither fooled nor bewitched." His heart beat loud in his chest. "Wash up before y' take yerself to bed."

His hands shook as he shed clothes on the other side of the room. Yes, she'd tried to seduce him—and had bloody well almost succeeded—but that was not how this would work. *He* was the seducer and *she* the innocent, and a rotten corner of his soul whispered that if he took her maidenhead tonight all difficulties would cease, for then she'd have to marry him. Meekly.

It would solve everything. Only he'd promised her, and Jasp, no lasting harm, and if he was one thing, Harris was a man of his word.

Fuck! All thought ceased the moment Miss Winthrop turned about. Titillating enough to watch her wash from behind, but to see her blot dry her damp shift, nipples mocking him like two winking darts…

He wrenched his gaze away and adjusted his straining breeches, then grabbed a blanket from the bed to thrust at her chest. "You'll take chill. Warm yerself by the fire." He gruffly guided her to a chair he yanked closer to the flames. Then he walked over to the washbowl, pulled his shirt over his head, and scrubbed his skin until he shivered.

Hell's bells, what had he gotten himself into?

***

Warm at last beneath a blanket before the fire, Annabelle wondered why she'd ever thought she could seduce a man like Arthur Harris into letting down his guard. Of course he'd seen right through her utterly unschooled attempt. He was a man of the world while she was but a flibbertigibbet, an annoyance foisted on him by her brother-in-law. Besides which, how was she to make her way back to London on her own, in the dead of night, without a penny to her person?

She'd been a fool to even try.

Annabelle left her seat to crawl under rough bedclothes. She again pondered escape, refusing to accept her fate, turning ever more elaborate plans over in her head as if she were a character in one of Lizzie's dramas. It mortified her to imagine the Baron might even be *paying* Mr. Harris to abscond with her. And where would her blasted kidnapper sleep now that she rested upon the room's sole bed?

A minute later he snatched her pillow and curled up like a

dog on the floor by her side. She heard him stir, wood boards creaking softly, then still, as if he were asleep.

Annabelle blew out the remaining bedside candle while her body pulsed and hummed. A vision of Arthur Harris's broad shoulders glistening with water in the glow of firelight came unbidden to mind, making her toss and turn and sigh.

"Woman, stop yer thrashing," he grumped from the floor. "Fer such a fine-bred lady, you're as dainty as a sow in labor, gnashin' and grindin' yer teeth."

"I am not a sow in labor, swine," she pushed back. "It is *your* fault I cannot sleep, stuck in a carriage a night and a day and now locked in this room with you, forced to—"

"Forced t' what, princess? Sleep in a soft bed, after a hot meal an' clean wash? Lord, that this should be so awful." He snorted.

"Oh, go to hell, you cretin!" She flung herself to the other side of the bed, as far from him as she could possibly get.

It felt like forever before she slept.

CHAPTER THIRTY-THREE

Milton had stopped by *The Leaf* to learn Harris was indeed en route to the border. He did not relish telling his wife this news.

In fact, he cursed his lot as he searched for Elizabeth first in the drawing room, and then the library. He swore altogether much these days, which was unbecoming of a baron, though lately he felt less the titled gentleman and more the lowly whoreson from the East End. It was Finch, worming his way back into Milton's life again. For years he'd been focused on his devil of a sire instead of his childhood demon, but now the two merged into a single, solitary evil in his head.

He loathed that his wife's sister was mixed up in all of this. It was the last thing he'd wanted, and it complicated his plans. What he wanted was to start a family of his own, to enjoy the wealth he'd amassed, and of course to make his father pay.

Hardly asking much, given the hand he'd been dealt.

He'd always desired more from life than he'd been given, and why shouldn't his dreams be bold? Milton had a blood right to riches. His mum had regaled him with stories of life beneath his father's roof, of the sumptuous meals and glittering rooms the man enjoyed. Horses, hounds, and hijinks of all sorts had been music to Milton's young ears—he didn't blame her for indulging his childhood fantasies. Lord knew she'd needed fantasies, too, to keep herself from going mad.

Hunger was a funny thing though. It never left, even when one's belly was full.

And his *was* full. His house was more opulent than his father's, his silly phaeton the most expensive for miles. Yet the more he gained, the less sure he felt, as if he lived some sodding parable of conceit in which the rest of the bloody world still didn't see him for who he was: a man of worth.

"Lizzie." He stopped in his tracks, frowning, for there she stood on a small step stool, painting bookshelves alongside staff.

His butler would get an earful.

She turned, brush in hand, a smudge of paint on her cheek. He shoved down a vision of his wife in that smock on her knees, pleasuring him.

"Why in God's name are you … painting?"

"I wished to speed completion," she answered, as if her statement were not utterly absurd.

He shook his head at her. "When you are done, I'd like a word."

"Have you news?" She looked so eager, so filled with hope, he hated that he must disappoint her.

"Yes."

"Then I shall come at once."

***

Elizabeth put down her brush, wiped her hands on her smock, and followed her husband down the hall. Since meeting Hieronymus Finch this morning, she'd felt thoroughly unsettled, restless almost with worry. Painting shelves distracted only so much.

Clearly, Milton's past with Finch fueled the awful man's desire to snare Annabelle, meaning blame rested not just with Papa this time, but also with her husband. Who *was* the Baron, that he should be mixed up with such a scoundrel? Miss Li's words repeated in her head: *Milton is the man he is because of his past.* And that past was key to understanding the present—key, she felt, to ensuring Annabelle's future.

Elizabeth was determined to uncover her husband's past if she had to wrest the answers from Finch himself.

"Drink?" Milton offered the moment they entered his office.

"No, thank you." She took a seat before his desk, recalling what had transpired here once before. She shivered.

He brought bottle and glass from the sideboard to pour himself a brandy, and Elizabeth felt like she'd arrived for an interview, an awkward one at that. For to expose oneself so nakedly in body to another person, yet remain inwardly so guarded, hiding one's thoughts and feelings even as one bared one's flesh, continued to split her psyche in two.

"I have news of Harris and your sister, but first tell me of your visit with your father. Is Ginny installed?"

Surely news of Bella superseded all else! Yet if she wished to gain answers, she must gain her husband's good graces first.

"She is, sir. Cook alone is aware of our ruse."

"Good." He downed his drink. "And your father knows I am sending a man over?"

"He is apprised."

Milton poured himself another. "Had he word yet from Finch?"

She hesitated. "Mr. Finch called while I was there, yes."

Her husband gripped his drink so tightly the veins on his hand bulged. "And you choose to tell me this only *now,* Lizzie?"

"I … Forgive me, Milton. I did not mean to keep this from you, I merely—"

"*Any* news, Elizabeth, any hint of information you have concerning Hieronymus Finch is to come to me at once. Do I make myself clear? At once!"

She shrank in her seat as he violently pushed back his chair to pace the carpet. "What did he say, how did he conduct himself? Tell me what you know."

Milton was upset beyond reason; she must tread softly, lightly now. "Mr. Finch wished to speak with Bella, but Papa and I put him off. He said he'd call again tomorrow; it was more a threat than a request." Elizabeth followed her husband's long strides about the room. "He said he always gets what he is promised, even if he has to take it for himself."

***

Milton stopped to stare at his wife. He wanted to crush her to him knowing she'd been in the same room with Finch, let alone exchanged words with the fiend. "Lizzie, what else did that cur say to you?"

"He … had a message he asked me to give you."

Milton's heart hammered a slow, sluggish thump in his head. For a second, he could hear only its painful beating. "Out with it, woman."

"He said: *Master Finch has returned to punish his boy*. He said it twice, Milton. Every word that man said struck fear into my breast."

He turned away; he could not bear for her to see his anguish. The devil had returned to ride him like before. Only this time Milton was older, wiser. Harder. This time he would rise like a phoenix from the ashes of his youth, and strike his demon down.

If he didn't, he was doomed.

"Milton…"

He continued to pace.

"You have yet to tell me news of my sister."

Muscles screaming from the message she'd just delivered, he clenched his fists, his mind oceans, leagues away.

"Milton," she snapped. "Tell me what news of Annabelle. Where has Harris taken her?

"En route to Gretna as we speak."

"No." Her face drained color. "No, Bella would never agree to that. You are mistaken. Harris has hidden her somewhere safe, somewhere—"

"There is no place 'safe' from Finch, Lizzie," he snarled. "Arty's done what he must. Marrying Bella is the safest course of action."

"Marriage is hardly safe." Elizabeth's lenses flashed at him, catching light. "She barely knows Harris."

"He is better than Finch; it is that simple."

"Marriage is not simple," she fired back. "There must be another—" She abruptly ceased. "Why, to think I spared Annabelle marriage to you, only to let her fall into Harris's hands is detestable."

"And do you regret that choice? Were it better she'd married me so that *you* fell prey to Finch instead?"

She scowled. "Neither option is tenable, sir. And you should have told me this news at once, rather than ask me to—"

"And what difference would that have made, Lizzie, eh? Tell me how that would have changed a goddamned, blasted thing." It took all his willpower not to suddenly weep.

"If we leave for Gretna right now and spare no haste—"

"They are at least a full day's journey underway, two if they drove through the night. We'd never catch them, it is futile."

"You say that just to dissuade me," she accused. "You *mean* for him to marry her. You planned this all along! Keeping me in the dark on purpose, telling me nothing of your past with Finch. You trust me even less than Bella and Papa do. And what have I done to warrant such treatment? Not *one* of you has seen fit to tell me anything at all, and I'll be damned if—"

He shut her up the only way he knew how, with a brutal kiss, though she fought his lips as much as she fought his grip, pushing him off.

"I will not be silenced in such base manner! I will bloody ride to Scotland myself to stop them!"

Milton steadied his emotions in order to objectively assess his wife, all fire and brimstone yet again, wild eyes shooting daggers at him. She was just mad enough to saddle a horse and take off, which was the last thing in the world he needed when she might very well be—

The image of her round with child momentarily terrified him.

He swallowed his fear fast. "Elizabeth, nothing we do now will stop Arthur Harris from marrying your sister, but it is not so awful a fate."

"Don't tell me what is not awful," she fumed. "I know what it is to be at the mercy of a man, at *your* mercy. That, sir, is married woman's fate. Why, you treat the servants better than you treat me! You speak to them as equals, allow them familiar use of your name. You behave toward them in every way as friend and family, whereas me you treat like—"

He physically shook sense into her. "Woman, stop behaving like a hellcat and start acting like an adult."

"Hellcat?" Her voice pitched higher. "Oh I'll give you a hellcat, Baron. I'll make you rue the day we married. Rue the day you stole me from my home, stole my sister from me, stole *all* that I hold dear!"

She was spinning out of reach, trapped in a spiral she could neither quell nor contain. He knew that maelstrom well.

"Give me your glasses," he ordered.

"No! I shall not be—"

"Now, Lizzie," he repeated. "No argument. Give them to me or I shall take them from you."

"Rot in hell, Jasper." She spat his name like it was poison.

And rot in hell he likely would, he thought, plucking her spectacles from her face to slip into his breast pocket, then spinning her around to secure her hands behind her back. He marched her to a footstool, where he sat himself down and deposited her over his lap.

The moment he lifted her skirts she opened her mouth to protest. "You cannot—!"

"Elizabeth, I do this for your own good."

"It is abuse of power! You wish to humiliate me, degrade me!"

Down came the first crack, knocking the wind from her lungs. "Count for me, Lizzie."

"No!" she howled. "I will not do your—"

"Two." He laid into her other cheek.

"—bidding, blast you!"

"Count, woman," he urged more sternly.

"No, you filthy, sodding—" Her words were swallowed short by his fourth wallop.

"Elizabeth." His tone brooked no argument. "*Count.*"

She gasped, "Five," as he dropped another smack.

"Six." Her voice grew stronger.

"Seven." Control slowly returned.

"Eight!" she cried, triumphant.

And on he slapped, till she'd counted to sanity and collapsed, in exhaustion, across his lap.

Milton rocked his wife in his arms and pressed a kiss to the top of her head. Her rage, thank God, had passed.

CHAPTER THIRTY-FOUR

"Milton." Elizabeth stirred on his lap. "How did you … *know*?

"Know what, luv?"

"Know to … do what you just did?"

"Because I've needed it meself. We're not so different, y' know."

She paused. "I do not understand, sir."

He pulled her closer, stroking her hair. "When I were…" He corrected his speech. "There was a time, Elizabeth, when I was younger, that I lost control all too easily, my temper too readily riled. Li helped me find an outlet for that anger, a means of controlling my emotions by letting go the impulse to control."

"You mean you allowed others to do to you what you just did to me?"

He hesitated to reveal more, yet he needed her to trust him in this business with Finch, with her sister and Arty. "Yes, only I did not just allow it, I welcomed it, as, I sense, you welcomed your own release just now. That does not mean I continue to need it. I am better at controlling my impulses. But I have sensed in you a similar need since that day in the park. What I did just now, Lizzie, was not done in anger, it was done to assist. It can be done even upon request."

She pulled her tear-streaked face from his waistcoat, making his heart constrict.

"You mean to say that if I asked you to … spank me you would … indulge it?"

"Of course. I enjoy it, Lizzie. Not to cause you pain—though pain is involved, that is not the point—but to help you gain peace. It is not unlike the release found in bedsport, is it not? One can give and receive pleasure in this manner, too." He feared he'd said too much.

"And if you needed such release yourself, would you ask me to aid you too?"

"Hmm."

"Well," she pressed, "would you?"

"If you were able, yes. Only you were not able before, if you recall, when I offered retribution." He did not wish to remind her of his awful, past transgression.

"But that was different, Milton, you were asking me to—"

"How was it any different?"

"That was not spanking, sir, that was flogging with a ruler."

"Hmm."

"Surely there is great difference between—"

"Is there?"

She frowned, her face, however, now curious.

"Elizabeth, whether one uses ruler, hand, switch, or whip matters little, in the end, so long as the desired result is achieved, the outcome willingly agreed upon by both parties. What I did to you that time was—"

"No, it cannot be the same." She shook her head. "The pain of one is so much worse than—"

"Some find release only in pain." He looked away, to hide

his own. "Some gladly suffer pain, while others can barely tolerate a splinter or a scratch. It varies."

"But—"

"Lizzie, what I inflicted on you that day was wrong not because I used a ruler instead of my hand, but because I forced you to bend to my will when you did not consent to it."

"But I did not consent that first time either, nor did I consent to—"

"Yes, and I am not proud of those moments." He inhaled a breath, unsure how to explain his twisted logic to her. "I was training you, teaching you how to be my wife." He paused. "It was also because I sensed in you a need."

***

Elizabeth was awed by her husband's sudden honesty. She wanted more, wanted to keep him talking now that he at last shared something of himself with her.

"And just why must I be *trained*?"

"Because of who I am, Lizzie, because of my past! Because there is great evil in this world, men like Hieronymus Finch, who now threaten the very family I wish to create with you!"

"So all you've just revealed, actions reprehensible in nature, *all* of it you claim to have done solely to protect your future family, to protect me?"

"Yes." He traced her cheekbone with his knuckles in such a gentle, loving manner, she shivered to his touch, incredulous.

He made no sense.

"Milton, will our children also suffer at your hand? Would you—"

He reacted so violently she nearly tumbled from his lap. "I do not strike children." His pain was so raw, so tightly coiled, brutal understanding flooded her core.

"Finch's message … Your scars …"

He looked away.

"Milton, let me touch you, please." The urge to comfort overwhelmed her.

He dropped his head and she cautiously tilted his chin. She traced his Grecian nose and beautiful, full lips with her fingers, before she placed both hands to his cheeks and drew him in for a gentle kiss. She rained tender kisses across his brow and temples, along his nose to chin and neck, returning again to his lips as she whispered into his mouth, "I do not wish to hurt you, husband, I wish only to understand you."

He groaned as if in pain.

"Will you let me? Do you trust me enough?"

He buried his face in her neck. "I am not worthy of the effort, Elizabeth."

She fisted his hair as she pressed him to her breast. "*I* shall be the judge of that," she told him gruffly. "If you would but open yourself to me, I would fill you with worth, smother you with it. I'd sink my greedy hands into your flesh and ply you with—"

"Greedy hands, eh?" His own elicited a soft *oh* from her mouth. "And what might I, in turn, sink into your flesh, wife?"

His lips caught her neck's tender skin and suckled there until she moaned. He'd leave another mark, but she didn't care. Elizabeth welcomed his possession.

"Mmm." He moved on to a different, more sensitive sliver of skin.

"Milton…"

"Call me Jasper, Lizzie."

"*Jasper*." She closed her eyes in rapture. "Take me to bed, please."

"Now, wife?" he teased. "'Tis midday, madam."

"Now," she repeated. "For if I am to give you that family you crave, we'd best get to it."

He laughed, warmly, from his gut. "Purely for reasons of procreation the lady wishes to bed her husband, eh?"

"Jasper, I am not—"

"You are no simpleton, Lizzie, no demurring wife." His lips curved. "No, you are a hoyden who must be fucked, well and often, only not always in bed." He began to untie her painting smock.

"Jasper, we cannot—"

"You are to call me master or sir when we play, woman, and right now I wish very much to play." His hands continued their work as his normally blue eyes smoldered grey.

Elizabeth thrilled with anticipation.

He yanked her dress to her waist. "Be a good wife and go lock the door. Then stand before me and strip."

She flushed to her roots. "Here?" she asked. "In your office?"

"Yes, here." His eyes flashed. "Over the footstool. Many a night I've dreamt of such a moment and now that you are willing, I'll not deny myself the pleasure."

Elizabeth hurried to do as bid. When she returned she stood before him and stepped out of her dress.

He stared at her as if he wished to tear the remaining garments from her himself. Instead, he pushed her to her knees, a sly grin upon his lips. "Does it thrill you to acquiesce, Elizabeth?"

The moment demanded honesty. "Sometimes," she whispered.

"Does it arouse you to obey me?"

"Yes, *sir*," she hissed as his hand encircled her neck. Desire pooled in her gut.

"Then I was right about you, sweetheart." He spoke softly. "There is no shame in submission, Lizzie, there is instead great strength. It pleases me to command you, it pleases you to obey, and our pleasure need be that simple. This, too, a form of release."

Elizabeth's longing for this man was so counter to all she thought of herself that she puddled right there on the floor.

"Touch yerself, luv," he ordered wickedly. "Strip bare fer me an' touch yourself. I want t' watch you spend afore I fuck yer t' within an inch o' yer life."

Elizabeth died and went to heaven. Or perhaps, she went to hell and back with this man. She didn't care. She'd take communion with her devil of a husband if it meant learning, knowing his soul.

The more he revealed, the more she understood. And wanted.

"Bella!" His wife startled upright, naked on his lap.

Blast. Milton was sure he'd made her woes disappear by sating her completely. But no.

"Lizzie, there is nothing we can—"

"Jasper, my spectacles."

He pulled them from his pocket and placed them on her nose, only to suffer the full force of her frown.

"You must tell me why you trust this man Harris, why *I* should entrust my sister to his care. I shall not rest until I know all, sir. You shall not distract me again."

He wanted to kiss away her crease of consternation but knew this conversation was inevitable. The day was rife with talk.

"Arthur Harris is like a brother to me, Lizzie. His mum was a whore, same as mine. We grew up together, looked out for each other."

"So he is family, like Miss Li?"

"Yes, though being older I took Arty under my wing, at

first." She snuggled deliciously back into his arms. "That's what we call him, though he hates the name." He suppressed a grin. "But Arty's treatment of women has always been impeccable."

"He employs whores at his gaming den, does he not?"

"He does." Milton paused. "And *his* whores, Lizzie, are treated even better than Li's."

She snorted. "One's treatment of women cannot be impeccable, Jasper, when one employs them as prostitutes."

"It can when it's their choice." He reminded himself he'd married a lady. "You do not understand, Elizabeth, you cannot fathom how—" He shook his head. "There will always be a market where men, even women, pay for sex. What matters is not if it happens, but how."

Her brow creased even more.

"Arthur Harris is no more a gentleman than I am, not as the *Ton* defines the word. But he forces no woman into employment, and if a girl comes to him in need yet is unable to sell her body, he finds her another position, often in service, here in my house."

Elizabeth's eyes grew wide as saucers.

"Arty pays his girls well and protects them even better."

"And his father?" she asked. "Is Harris, like you, a bastard?"

The thought of Arty's father raised the specter of Milton's own. "Unknown, nor do Arty much care. He were a happy mistake, one his mum failed t'—"

One look at her face made Milton get hold of himself fast. "Lizzie, for me to detail the life Arty and I led would only cause you—"

"It causes me far greater distress when you withhold things from me." She looked hurt. "Jasper, I am not so sheltered that I do not comprehend the lengths women will go to protect, or prevent, children." She peered at him over her spectacles. "Tell me the truth, from now on."

"Harris will not harm your sister. He'll marry her in word only, not in deed."

"So he'll not—"

"Consummate the marriage, no, which will allow for an annulment once all threat of Finch is gone. Your sister will be socially ruined, Lizzie, but Annabelle's innocence not stolen from her."

She stiffened on his lap. "I do not think that possible."

"I told you, Arty would never—"

"Annulment." Her voice was flat. "Annulment is nigh impossible under the law. Once Annabelle marries Mr. Harris, it will be legally binding. The law does not allow—"

"We'll find a way," he told her, though he'd need to consult his solicitor. "Regardless of law, Lizzie, 'twere better yer sister be bound to bonny Arty Harris, than be destroyed by Ronny fuckin' Finch."

Milton wrapped his arms more tightly about his wife, disturbed by how his speech had slipped again. She snuggled deeper into his arms with a small, soft sigh and he let his fingers dimple her delicious thigh. She didn't remark on his speech, nor press him for more of his past. She was pliant and pleasant, though that head of hers still churned atop her lovely, lithe neck. She'd submitted her body to him, but still not her mind.

Would she ever? Perhaps not, but he was secretly thrilled she'd warmed to him this much. He hated that Finch had reentered his life, but Elizabeth, in her way, made Finch bearable.

Much was bearable when one had a willing wife, God bless.

By morning, as light streamed in through her husband's bedroom windows, Elizabeth boldly traced a scar at Milton's temple which disappeared into his thick shock of hair. She studied his features, peaceful yet in sleep, and wondered how he'd come by the many marks that riddled his body. Though she had an inkling now: Finch.

She recalled rule number four and withdrew her hand with a sigh. Why could he not tolerate her touch, yet hand her a ruler with which to beat him? She had so many questions still.

He stirred, grabbed her to him, and nuzzled her neck. "I've a confession to make, wife."

"Oh?"

"I finished the book."

Elizabeth stiffened. "The book you promised we'd read together?"

"Yes. Couldn't stop. Read the rest in one sitting, that time you were angry with me."

"*Which* time, Jasper?"

His hands began to roam. "I do not recall precisely when, Elizabeth, only that you were angry, and I felt I'd been a monster like Victor Frankenstein himself. He deserved his own Elizabeth even less than I deserve you." His hands slid up to cup her breasts. "Is that why you like the book so?"

"I read that novel long before I met you, sir, so no, that is not why I like it, though the parallel is apt." She bit back her laugh. "Your tutor, Mr. Kilpert's, assessment of you is also apt."

"Which is?"

Elizabeth chose her next words carefully, rule three uppermost in mind: goading was never wise.

"When I danced with Mr. Kilpert, he praised both your intellect and desire for self-improvement. He holds you in great esteem."

"And is that all you discussed with him?"

"I told him that should you allow it, I would be pleased to join your sessions with him, as there is much I could also stand to—"

"You wish for him to teach you too, hmm." He seemed to chew on this a minute. "I shall have to hire a far older, uglier tutor for you than Kilpert."

"Older and uglier! Jasper, do you think me so shallow that I should—"

"I think you a very bright, attractive woman, Lizzie, just the type to turn a young scholar's head. And unlike Dr. Frankenstein, I'd rather not experiment with the union of two minds as brilliant as yours and Paul's. In fact, I'd be a fool to throw temptation at—"

"Temptation! But Jasper, that is utterly—"

"I'll allow a tutor, Lizzie, but not Kilpert."

He was being ridiculous, and she told him so with a line from the book: "*There is love in me the likes of which you've never seen. There is rage in me the likes of which should never escape. If I am not satisfied in the one, I will indulge the other.*"

"Are you quoting Mary Shelley, Lizzie, or telling me your lust for Kilpert is such that you would—"

She walloped him with her pillow. "I have such *rage* against my husband that I would—"

He pinned her to the bed, his eyes blue-black. "Take care how far you push me, wife."

"And I'd warn you, Jasper, not to—"

He stilled her with a kiss so intense she was momentarily stunned.

"You were saying, Lizzie?" His arms still refused her the slightest motion.

Elizabeth gathered her wits; the blasted man knew just how to upend her thinking brain. "If you will not let me join your academic discussions, at the very least I insist Mr. Kilpert embark upon a course of dance instruction with you. If we are to be seen again in public, you must learn to lead me about the dance floor." She held her ground. "It is your duty as my husband. And it will further the *Ton's* esteem if you dance not only with your wife, but with the likes of Lady Stanton."

His smirk became a scowl.

"You cannot argue my logic." She knew she had the upper hand. "And Mr. Kilpert is undoubtedly a more spry dancer than any fuddy-duddy you find to tutor me. We three might work together to instruct you in formal dance. That is, after all, why you married me rather than one of Miss Li's whores, is it not?"

"Infernal woman," he muttered, rolling himself off both her and the bed.

"Shall we start today, husband? I am happy to write to Mr. Kilpert of your desire to—"

Milton grabbed a pillow and walloped the word 'dance' right off her lips.

Elizabeth grinned. She snatched the closest cushion and walloped him back, reminded of someone else she knew who loved a good pillow fight.

Bella!

Her smile vanished, replaced by that singular, gnawing worry she could not seem to shake.

Without a word, Milton put down his weapon and folded her back into his arms. "No harm'll come t' yer sister, Lizzie. I swear it."

She closed her eyes against his chest and breathed.

ACT III

RAGE & REDEMPTION

Doubt thou the stars are fire; Doubt that the sun doth move; Doubt truth to be a liar; But never doubt I love.

William Shakespeare from *The Tragedy of Hamlet, Prince of Denmark* (1599-1601)

CHAPTER THIRTY-FIVE

"You've a caller, ma'am."

Elizabeth looked up from her plate, breakfast still settling in her stomach along with more worrisome thoughts. Milton had left to pay his man Marty, and her father, a visit, because just yesterday he'd sent his loyal footman to Papa's house to keep an eye on Ginny.

Her husband did not trust Papa or Finch; Elizabeth did not trust them either.

Gerald coughed. "'Tis Madam Audrey, ma'am."

Oh. "Show her to the drawing room, Gerald. I'll be down presently."

She took a final bite of toast and adjusted her hair in her dressing mirror, nervous to greet her mother-in-law. When she arrived, she found Murdoch already doing that honor.

"Why, Mary Audrey, fancy seein' you here this hour o' day!"

"All well then, Martha? My son treatin' staff as he ought?"

"As well as he were taught, Mary." The housekeeper winked.

Their familiarity reminded Elizabeth she was still the outsider in this house, still not 'family.'

"Madam Audrey, it is a pleasure to see you again, ma'am."

"Call me Mary, dear." The lady settled herself on her son's settee. "I received your letter, Elizabeth, and apologize for not calling sooner. Matters of business delayed my visit."

"Marital matters have improved considerably since I penned you that missive, Mary."

"I am glad to hear it, dear, but that is not why I've come."

Elizabeth tensed.

"Li informed me of your sister, how Finch pursues her." Her lips thinned. "I am deeply sorry for it."

"Thank you for your concern, madam."

"You must call me *Mary*, Lizzie, not madam."

"Forgive me, Mary, I am not used to—"

She brushed Elizabeth off. "I suspect Jasper has not apprised you in full of Hieronymus Finch, but your sister is in grave danger, and you deserve to know the truth of that man, of what he did to your husband, my son."

Elizabeth was suddenly all ears.

"You see, I failed as a mother. I failed to protect Jasper from Finch when my son was young and it—" She stilled. "It is painful for me to recount."

"Madam. *Mary*." Elizabeth impulsively took the woman's hand in her own. "You needn't—"

"I must." Her eyes flashed. "You must be told what Jasper will not say."

Elizabeth steeled herself as a cloud passed over Mary's face.

"When Jasp was born, his father insisted I give the babe up, told me he'd pay for a baby farm." She inhaled a breath. "But I refused to relinquish my child to such a place, and so the Duke abandoned us, cut off all funds and contact."

Which duke? Elizabeth thought. There weren't that many…

"I'd been a servant in the Duke's house, I was not a—" Her gaze pierced Elizabeth. "I was not a loose woman before his Grace fancied me, and it was flattering to be fancied, nor had I much choice in the matter." Her hands plucked at her dress. "But he did not fancy an illegitimate child, especially as he was about to marry and produce legitimate heirs." She continued. "The Duke would not employ me in his house or give me a letter of reference after our falling out, so without his help I was destitute."

Elizabeth's heart cracked.

"I sold what I could, at first, and then I sold myself, but it was dangerous to earn on my own. By the time Jasper toddled on two feet I found Finch. He kept a house, you see, where I'd heard women were well fed. He promised I could keep Jasper even, promised a decent cut of pay." She swallowed. "But he lied. All my earnings went toward our keep, leaving me nothing to save, to build on. He took Jasper too, the moment my boy was old enough. At five years only he was farmed to chimney, then mill, and when I protested he—"

Elizabeth could barely stand to hear more.

"—punished me severely. He punished any woman who defied him. And the worst was, I'd nowhere else to go. No family to turn to. Without means I was trapped in Finch's hellhole."

Elizabeth brushed back tears as Mary Audrey smoothed her skirts.

"Elizabeth, I do not wish to cause you grief by—"

"Grief!" she exclaimed. "Mary, I am affected by your *own* grief, that you should relive such horrors in recounting them to me."

"It is my past. My son's past too. Only now that Finch has returned…" She stared hard at Elizabeth. "If *I* struggle to revisit memories, it must drive Jasper to extremes."

Elizabeth's gut wrenched imagining the horrors her husband had endured at such a tender age.

"He was a sensitive lad, too, when young. But he soon hardened. Like too many children he learned to survive. And yet we were together at least, in our misery, and comforted one another as best we could." She looked almost wistful. "By the time Jasp was ten or so he'd grown tall and strong for his age. Stubborn like his father." Her face pinched. "My son grew up too fast, saw too much of life inside a brothel. He witnessed how Finch treated women, how the ogre treated me."

Elizabeth's hand shook as she reached for her tea, then promptly set the cup back down.

"Jasper was very brave but foolish to try to protect me. He stood up to Finch one day, challenged him in a way he should not have." Mary's voice choked. "I didn't know until much later because he didn't tell me. For *years*, Lizzie, my boy did not tell me what that man did."

Elizabeth reached for her mother-in-law's hand.

"Finch put my poor son in his place, showed him who was master over us all." Her next breath stuttered. "He made Jasper into his literal whipping boy, Lizzie, our punishments suddenly ceased." Her face was awash with pain. "Finch no longer laid a hand on his whores, but every infraction, any cause for discipline, was meted out, instead, on my darling boy."

Elizabeth could stand no more. She rose from her seat to embrace her mother-in-law and simply held her, without speaking.

When Mary Audrey pulled away the lady wiped tears from her eyes. "He withstood that torture for too many years. You must understand I did not … Jasper hid it from me, and Finch only marked him where it would not show. By the time I suspected, realized what he'd endured…" She cleared her throat. "There were rumors, of course, but Finch was so feared no one dared speak the truth. And I—" Her voice caught. "I failed my boy, Elizabeth. You do not understand what it means to be a mother and fail to protect your own child."

Elizabeth again gripped Mary's hand. "You did everything in your power to keep him with you, alive. It is his father, the Duke, who failed him. Not you."

Mary dried her eyes with the handkerchief Elizabeth gave her, then straightened her spine. "Thank you, dear, I am not—I have made peace with matters, as has Jasper, to some extent. He never blamed me, only surely you understand, now, his desire to prove himself the son his father should have wanted, rather than discarded."

Elizabeth did.

"And yet in place of any real father Jasp had only Finch." Mary's tone turned grim. "At fifteen my boy had grown into a man. He towered over Finch, and he'd take the beatings no more. He must have realized his own strength, or perhaps he simply snapped that day, I don't know, because he ripped the whip from that ogre's hand and beat Finch with his own instrument of torture. Beat him bloody and left him for dead."

Elizabeth gasped.

"Jasper came for me then. Like a grown man, my boy came and took me away from Finch's house—we simply walked out. No one stopped us. It was as if every soul there had been under a spell, men and women alike, because everyone stood back and let us walk. It was unreal."

Elizabeth tried to picture that moment, picture her husband, still a boy, forced to rescue his own mother.

"Jasper found work then, at the docks. Earned pennies at first but enough to keep us from starving. And I worked too, of course. With my son for protection it was easier. I found others like me, women who'd escaped worse, and we joined together, formed a collective to look after one another, including our children. And Jasper, he..." She hesitated. "I don't know how much he's told you, but he was part of our collective too, helped me train new girls and later took wealthy patrons himself. Our group became a business, eventually Miss Li's business, and to this day every working woman there owns shares in it."

Elizabeth was stunned.

"It also allowed Jasper to heal, something my son desperately needed. For once, *he* was in control. Finch didn't try to find us either, kept a low profile for a very long time. I think it wounded his pride, that he'd been bested by a boy. But his hatred for Jasper grew in quiet, because later, when Jasp and Wells brought Li back from their travels, he—"

"Finch took Li, didn't he?"

"Yes." Mary met Elizabeth's gaze. "She ended up in his clutches, as payment, I suspect, for what Finch felt Jasp had stolen from him. And she was enslaved in ways worse, even, than I'd been."

Bits clicked in Elizabeth's head. "Milton stole Li away again, just like he'd stolen you from Finch. Only your son was in love with Li, so Finch—"

"Love? No." Mary shook her head. "Jasper was *livid* at Li. He and Lord Wellesley, now the Duke of Allendale, thought her the most frustrating woman on earth." Levity returned to the lady's face. "Li exists in a league above the rest of us mortals."

Elizabeth longed to know more, but it was her husband's story his mother now told, not Li's.

"Jasp and Wells have the utmost respect for Li, and she for them. It is why, once Li was safe from Finch, they proposed the idea for her business, why I help her run our brothel. She is extremely savvy, even in a culture foreign to her. And she's family now, though you already know this."

Elizabeth nodded. "Your story explains much, Mary. It also explains why—"

"Finch now comes for your sister."

They both fell silent.

"There is some sick paternal bond between Finch and my son that goes beyond that man's rage at Wells and Jasper stealing Li. Because to marry your sister is to tie himself to Jasper for good, force him into a relationship again. As if Jasp were the son Finch never had, or the heir he hoped to raise. But you mustn't let Finch take your sister, Elizabeth. He will do unspeakable things to her. Unspeakable."

Elizabeth believed her mother-in-law, and finally believed her husband did have Annabelle's welfare uppermost in mind. His intentions had been noble from the start: to protect Bella from Finch. And by not revealing more, to protect her, his wife, from Finch too.

"Thank you for confiding in me, Mary, for your trust."

"Be patient with him, Elizabeth. Jasper's borne much and done much to protect others. Too often he fails to protect himself." Her smile was sad. "I imagine he's not been easy on you, dear, but what you do not realize is—"

"He has a heart." Elizabeth's own ached with this new knowledge. "I am beginning to understand him better, Mary, though he remains at times most frustrating." She gripped her mother-in-law's hand once more. "I will try to be a better wife to your son."

"You've been exceptional thus far." Mary patted Elizabeth's hand. "My boy can be a domineering arse. But he's loyal, Lizzie, and he chose *you* for his wife. It may seem his choice was arbitrary, but do not be fooled. He cares for you, else he'd not have tested you as he did, nor try to protect you and your sister as he now does."

Did she care for him too? Elizabeth buried the idea, to be explored later. She was not done seeking answers. "Mary, is Milton's father the Duke of Lennox? Because I danced with the Duke's heir, Lord Mathers, at a ball just last week, and he looked remarkably like—"

Her mother-in-law's face pinched. "Jasper asked me never to reveal his sire, dear, but your assumption is not without grounds."

Elizabeth had her answer. Still, a thought niggled.

"After all you've endured, all you've just told me of your past, Mary, why do you continue to work with Miss Li? Why not live with your son instead? Surely he would welcome the chance to keep you in comfort now that he—"

"Can?" Mary Audrey's eyes were startlingly bright. "I'm sure he would, dear, but I swore long ago never to be dependent on any man, and that includes my son." Her face hardened. "If I can keep other women safe from demons like Finch, improve their circumstance—"

There will always be a market for sex, Milton's words whispered in Elizabeth's mind.

"—I will continue to support them and their children as best I can." She stared at Elizabeth. "For too long I had no freedom. It is more dear to me than life. Freedom *is* life."

Milton surely felt the same. His need to free himself from Finch—and his father, the Duke's, shadow—must have driven him to amass his wealth, to wish to build a dynasty of his own. But where did she, Elizabeth, fit into her husband's plans? Not as a means to *his* ends but as means to her own? What of her own need for freedom?

As if reading Elizabeth's thoughts, Mary Audrey rose from her seat. "You'll find your way yet with Jasp, dear. His priority now is to keep your sister from Finch, but once that threat is gone, you must earn Jasper's trust. And you will. You must both learn to trust. Insist he see you, Elizabeth, and he will. He found in Li his equal, and will find it in you too."

The lady let herself out, leaving Elizabeth to sit a while longer in her husband's drawing room. She was as worthy of respect and freedom as Miss Li. She must simply prove this to her husband. Love was not an option, but she could gain his trust. She could become his family in more than name alone, and Elizabeth realized she wanted this.

No, she needed it.

She made her way back to her chamber, mulling over Mary Audrey's words, her steps echoing through the halls. When she closed the door behind her, she stared a moment at her collection of books now lining one wall. Her beloved volumes looked lonesome next to the surrounding bare shelves. Perhaps she should have added them to her husband's library, but here they welcomed her like old friends.

She pulled her manuscript from a drawer and decided to read over her unfinished work, from the story's very beginning. For too long, she'd let it languish, but now she made notes in the margins as she read, recognizing her characters' motives had since changed.

Elizabeth pulled a blank sheet from her stack and dipped her quill in ink. The brooding baron remained a scoundrel and a villain, but he must be recast. This time he would entrap the lady in his snare yet be cloaked in mystery and intrigue. And in the end he'd save her from an evil greater than himself.

The heroine, however, must see through his dastardly disguise. If she did not, they both would perish. If she did…

Elizabeth was not sure how her story would end. She knew only that her words, this time, flowed with hope.

CHAPTER THIRTY-SIX

When Milton arrived at the Winthrop residence, no footman greeted his knock. In fact, the front door was slightly ajar, which set his hackles up and his hand to his hip, where he always kept a blade. He slipped this to his palm and pushed the door in with a faint groan, his senses on high alert.

The house was eerily silent, enough to prickle his skin. He should return with more men, yet return to what? If trouble had come, his servant Marty would have sent word. Unless Marty were in trouble, in which case Milton would not leave his loyal footman here alone. Or Ginny. *Christ.*

She'd be in Annabelle's room, upstairs.

He trod the carpeted staircase light as a cat, steps faintly creaking under his weight. He scanned the empty hallway on the landing, his nerves increasingly on edge. No house should be this quiet so close to midday's chime. He should turn back; he was no fool. Or had he grown soft in wealth?

He'd faced worse with less; he'd not leave now.

Methodically, Milton pushed open each door he passed, knife drawn as he peered inside for signs of life. Door after door he opened in slow succession, revealing nothing but empty rooms, until the last one opened to Ginny, bound and gagged in the bed, shaking her wide-eyed head in a warning that came two seconds too late.

❧

The ceremony at Gretna passed: Annabelle had become Mrs. Arthur Harris with hammer to anvil, *bang*. Her new husband left her standing before the forge, staring blankly into the hot coals, as he signed the blacksmith's book, then bid her do the same.

She did so in a daze, whereas Mr. Harris looked altogether relieved. He declared her now safe and announced he would find them lodgings for the night, trade their team for fresh horseflesh.

She blankly followed him from stable to inn, where she finally took note of her surroundings, of how pleased Arthur seemed, arms crossed, as he surveyed the room he had just procured them for the night.

Her wedding night.

Annabelle gulped, the boisterous, bawdy noises filtering up from the downstairs tavern dragging her back to the dilemma she now faced. Though she was too exhausted to care where she slept. She dismissed the room's solitary bed frame with barely a blink and greedily eyed the bath being filled instead.

While maids continued to haul in buckets of steaming water, their driver appeared, handing Mr. Harris something.

"Come, wife, I've a gift for you." Arthur played groom and Annabelle played along, though her situation was no game. She was good and truly married, she realized with shock, her shock greater still when Mr. Harris slipped a gold band onto her ring finger.

"A goldsmith melted me coin t' forge this." He cocked her a

smile, an errant blond lock falling over one eye. "I hope it'll do."

Annabelle's heart inexplicably ached. "I—thank you." She hiccoughed back tears. *Ridiculous.*

"Sit with me a moment, luv. It's been a rough journey, I know." He led her to the room's bed and pulled her to his lap, where tears suddenly streamed unbidden down her cheeks.

"Better, miss?"

"Yes." She gulped. "I don't know what's come over me."

His thumb traced soothing circles at the back of her neck. "Yer nerves're wrought, no shame admittin' that."

She loved his drawling accent, so different from her own, the vowels more melodic, the consonants dropped. "You are kind to indulge me, Mr. Harris."

***

"'Tis but common courtesy." Harris buried his nose in Bella's neck, not caring he took that liberty now she was, in name at least, his wife. The minx snuggled closer on his lap, making one part of his anatomy painfully aware of the lady's plump posterior.

She adjusted her seat and looked down in dismay. "Have I hurt you, Arthur?"

"No." He winced. "'Tis not hurt, exactly."

"You mean I—" She shifted again. *"Oh!"*

Harris braced himself. "Don't move." He was desperate to keep her from brushing his poor rod more.

She pursed her lips. "Arthur Harris, as I am now your wife, I wish to know."

"Know what?" He refused her any more wiggle room on his lap—for her own good.

"I wish to know what it is like, one's wedding night."

"No, you don't."

"Arthur, I merely wish to *know*, I do not wish to endeavor."

"You wish me to describe to you, in detail, how a man deflowers his bride?" His prick was even more aroused.

"Yes. It is not fair ladies are kept in the dark while gentlemen know all, and given that I am now legally married, I feel entitled to educate myself. You are clearly experienced, so—"

"Woman, do you honestly wish to kill me?"

She chose that moment to shift her seat again, making him curse anew. "Damn blast it, Bella, stop movin'!"

"But why, Arthur?" Her innocence was stunning. "This is precisely what I mean. You order me about because of your, well, *manhood*, yet I've not the faintest idea why it hardens so in my presence."

"Lord have mercy," he muttered as he physically removed her from his person and scrambled off the bed.

She stared directly at the bulge at his crotch, making him curse her only more in his head.

He turned from her sightline. "Take yer bath, woman, whilst I exit this room fast. I'll not be teased nor tempted into seducin' you, wife or not. I'll return in half an hour, an' you'll bolt this door while I am gone. We clear?"

"Yes, Arthur."

He was already halfway out.

"Only Arthur…"

He stopped.

"I did not intend to tease. I am in earnest. I respect your efforts to protect me from Mr. Finch."

He refused to look at her.

"Which is why I trust you, of all men, might be willing to share with me what others deny in explanation."

He groaned, letting his forehead sink to the doorframe. "Annabelle, I beg you, stop talkin'." And with that he hastened downstairs for a pint or ten to clear his head and loins of the lust she'd just unleashed.

❧

Tucked in bed, Elizabeth tossed and turned, unable to sleep. Milton had not returned home for dinner, and though she knew he was a man of business, she did not know exactly what that business was. In fact, she'd never asked how he'd amassed his fortune, though she assumed it was through dubious means: gambling, investments, backroom deals. She accepted this about her husband—she accepted a great many things, it seemed—but at no point in their brief marriage had he disappeared without word of his return.

She'd spent the afternoon at her desk continuing her brooding story, so engrossed in writing the dinner hour had snuck up fast. Afterward, she had answered correspondence and even penned Mr. Kilpert that letter requesting the tutor educate her husband in the art of formal dance. Gerald had not known the master's whereabouts, telling her only that Jasp was known to take off when in a mood. Only her husband had been in a fine mood this morning, one more elevated than usual, jocular even. Their congress last night had felt like more than mere procreating too, leaving her miffed Milton might seek comfort in another woman's arms.

Li's arms.

Though Mary Audrey's words assuaged her some. Li was Milton's family, not his lover anymore. Yet she had been, once. Elizabeth was tempted to await Milton's return in his bed again but recalled his displeasure the last time she'd been so bold. *Blasted man*, she thought. Just when she was warming to him, he had to go and disappoint. Disappear.

She grabbed Miss Austen's *Persuasion*, said a silent prayer that Annabelle, *please God,* remain safe with Mr. Harris, then settled into bed. She read how bitterly Anne Elliot regretted her decision to decline Captain Wentworth's hand.

Foolish woman.

❧

When Harris returned, his wife unbolted the door and stomped off to curl herself into a ball beneath the bed's thick coverlet. Three pints downstairs had done him good, and the bath was warm enough he decided to slip his body in. Soon, splashing water and spitting logs were the only sounds disturbing his thoughts. That and bursts of laughter from the tavern below.

He soaked until the water grew cold, then shook himself dry, donned his smalls and shirt, and settled in beside the new Mrs. Harris. As a married man he had a right to soft ticking; no more floorboards for him, not this night.

"Arthur." Annabelle's soft voice surprised him. Why the hell was she not asleep?

"I wish to know." She turned to face him beneath the bedclothes, an inch now from his nose.

"Leave be, Bella."

"Please. I trust you to tell me."

He rolled onto his back, groaning, as he willed his raging cock into obedience, an order his prick refused outright. She'd not relent till he supplied her with an answer, and the trouble was, a man did not describe such things, a man simply *did* them.

He ought to have ravished her the first night he'd spirited her away, for then he'd not now find himself in the unbearable position of being married to a temptress, legally entitled to a temptress, yet honor bound not to enjoy said temptress.

He cursed Jasper Audrey as he tried to wriggle his way out of this godforsaken moment. For if there were a God, the Rotten Bugger was testing Harris's willpower like never before.

"Arthur." Bella's fingers lightly brushed his chest, then immediately withdrew. "Why won't you tell me?"

"You want *this,* miss?" He roughly placed her hand at his groin, that she might know what she did to him and understand how unbearable it was.

"Oh..." She slowly exhaled, her hand frozen upon his poor cock, which twitched enthusiastically beneath her touch.

And then the witch began to pet him.

Harris choked, unable to speak.

"Please, Arthur, I shan't do more. I wish only to explore."

So he let her, sight unseen, fondle him through his smalls. Only his wretched body responded with need so intense, he died without the least bit of warning, shuddering his release.

She froze; Harris sighed with abject disgust.

"Goodness, I—" She removed her hand from the situation, but he trapped it atop his poor prick, insisting she witness its diminishment.

"Y' wished to know what it's like." He remained cross. "Well, now y' do."

"Mr. Harris, I hope you do not think me—"

"I think you nothing short of remarkable, miss." He meant it. "Y' made me spill in me smalls like some virgin yob. Quite the feat."

"Like a virgin?" She stilled. "Do you mean the first time you laid with a woman you also—?"

"Spent too fast?" His laugh hurt. "Somethin' I've not done in years. That's how little I can control myself with yer ladyship, which is why I begged you not to tease me with yer—"

"But Arthur, I never meant—that is, I did not always mean to flirt. I did not realize it might be difficult for a man to—"

"Withstand a woman's charms? Well, 'tis. Damned difficult."

Silence ensued. Something profound had changed between them.

"Arthur, I am sorry I frustrate, but I am not sorry for what just occurred."

Not sorry? Harris was further stunned, for the only sort of educating a lady of her breeding ought to get was from her—

He groaned, for he now *was* her husband. Who better to show her what she could expect in marriage, nay, demand of her true husband one day?

Suddenly the situation took on an all new cast, because Mrs. Harris might benefit from a partial education in carnal relations. As, he realized, might he.

"Then you'll not be sorry for what I teach you next, Bella." He slid his hand up her leg as the whites of her eyes flashed at him in the dark.

Harris grinned. Mayhap he was just the man to shed light.

Elizabeth slept fitfully, but when there was still no word from Milton by morning, no indication that he'd returned at all last night, anger spiked her breast. She wasn't jealous, for how could she be when her husband had bedded half of London already? Yet he'd bedded those women *before* he'd married her, not since. Had he sought one of Li's girls last night? Or Miss Li herself?

She stewed through breakfast, Mutton's head heavy on her lap. The dear fellow would not quit her side. His behavior was as out of character as her husband's, especially with Annabelle absconded and the threat of Finch still looming large. Especially after they'd made peace of sorts with one another. Milton had revealed more of himself to Elizabeth in the last two days than he had in their week of stormy courtship, or in the weeks since they had wed. Why vanish now?

Something was off.

She'd visit *LeBrecht's* and demand answers. Because if anyone knew where Milton was, Miss Li did.

CHAPTER THIRTY-SEVEN

Back in the rumbling carriage, Annabelle snuck looks at her new husband as he stole brief glances back. They had a long journey home, even with a fresh team of horses. And this time Annabelle traveled as a married woman, no longer the naïve maid she'd been.

Though technically she remained a virgin. Last night, Arthur Harris had illuminated her delightfully in certain regards yet kept her woefully in the dark about the rest, leaving her longing for more knowledge of the marriage bed.

She trained her eyes out the carriage window, fingers knotting her skirts. Her new husband was far too compelling, and she'd been very bad indeed last night. He'd allowed her to explore much of his intriguing, masculine form. If Lizzie were to discover what Annabelle had done with Arthur Harris, husband or not, her sister would surely die of shame.

"Shall I teach you a game, Bella?"

"Game?" She blinked. "Er, yes. I suppose I could use the … distraction."

"I thought, perhaps, t' continue yer education from last night."

"In a *carriage*, Mr. Harris?"

He laughed. "I do not mean to ravish you."

Heat rose to her cheeks.

"Though a well-timed wheel rut while makin' love only—"

"Mr. Harris!" she admonished.

He grinned. "I meant a friendly game o' questions, Bella, whereby high card asks an' low card answers, else players pay a forfeit."

"What kind of forfeit?"

"What odds would y' like t' play for, wife?"

She liked how he'd started calling her his wife. "What does one usually forfeit?"

"Clothing, ma'am. Till not a stitch is left."

Annabelle began to sweat beneath her dress.

"However, a kiss might do instead." His grin broadened.

"Oh" was all she could muster.

"And only if low card should refuse t' answer, o' course. All questions, see, might further yer education."

Safer play than in a shared bed. Perhaps she'd even learn a thing or two about Mr. Harris besides his uncanny ability to card trick and love make.

"Very well, Arthur, I agree to your game. What do you call it?"

"Y' might know it as 'Questions an' Commands,' but I prefer 'Truth or Dare.'"

Elizabeth loudly rapped Li's knocker, *LeBrecht's* sign creaking stiffly in the wind above her head. She'd wanted to take her husband's phaeton on her own again, but Milton's stable master had refused, telling her *master's orders.* Thus, she had been driven.

The door opened to Li herself wrapped in a burgundy

banyan, her dark hair hanging like drapes about her shoulders. "Lady Milton, I should hope you have good reason to—"

"Is he here?" Elizabeth demanded.

"Who, madam?"

"My husband."

A man's voice called from inside, "Li?"

"A minute, darling. Stay put."

Not Milton. Elizabeth exhaled. "Miss Li, forgive me, I must—"

"Apologize, yes, but let us move this conversation indoors rather than continue it on my front step."

"Is Mr. Damon your guest?" Elizabeth's curiosity got the better of her as she followed Li inside.

"No." Li remained brusque. "Though clearly, the man left an impression on you."

Elizabeth's cheeks flamed.

"And as I should like to return to the gentleman currently warming my sheets…" She arched one elegant eyebrow.

"Jasper did not return home last night." Elizabeth stopped there, embarrassed.

"Lady Milton, my caller does not enjoy interruptions. Explain yourself. Quickly now."

"Forgive me, Miss Li. I am simply concerned that Jasper did not send word. Our relations have improved, you see, such that I thought he would not seek the company of—"

"Whores?" Li's brow arched skyward.

"Yes." Elizabeth's face heated only more. "I assumed in marriage he would not stray. At least, not until heirs were born."

"Of course he's not strayed. It is not in Jasper's nature. He would have told you he wished to sleep with other women, allowed you, as well, to sleep with other men. Elizabeth, wherever your husband may be, I assure you he is not in another woman's arms."

Relief flooded Elizabeth's body even as Li regarded her with impatience. "I cannot speak to Jasper's whereabouts, Lady Milton, only to his impeccable character."

Elizabeth scrunched her lips.

"Well, perhaps *impeccable* is not the correct English word, but his intentions are mostly honorable. I am sure he has good reason to be gone and will explain himself when he returns."

"And if he doesn't?" Elizabeth's inner fear found voice. "His absence makes me uneasy given all that has occurred between my sister and Mr. Finch."

Li's head snapped up. "Hieronymus Finch?"

"Yes. You see my father—"

"Elizabeth, you must tell me everything. At once." Li's entire bearing stiffened. "But first I must inform my guest I shall be longer than he likes."

Li took off, leaving Elizabeth alone, her thoughts skittering like pins into the dark corners of the lady's dress shop, fear winding its way up her spine.

Harris sat across from his wife—*wife!*—and watched her worry her bottom lip. He wished to bite it. In truth, he wished to do worse. He didn't know if he'd been foolish or wise to indulge this genteel lady. He knew only that he'd relished educating Mrs. Harris on her wedding night.

He willed his raging cockstand back into submission. All morning long in this blasted, swaying carriage his prick had threatened mutiny, because his bloody wife was the worst temptation ever. He would return her to her family intact, damnation, *intact*! Though at the rate they were playing, it would be her body alone that remained intact. He'd already corrupted her mind; one had only to look at her now to know it.

"Dare," Harris grumbled, having drawn a low card. He'd no desire to tell Bella how many women he'd bedded in his thirty years on earth, because that number was likely both more and less than she expected, and he'd a reputation to uphold.

"Dare?" Her fetching lips twitched. "Oh, I shall have to think a moment." Her eyes fell to his waist.

"Bella, we forfeit kisses only, so I expect you to—"

"Remain the lady I was yesterday, when you have enlightened me in so many ways? I think not, husband." The minx grinned. "I think I shall ask you to kiss me where I like or"—her look turned even more wicked—"dare you to let me kiss you where *I'd* like."

Harris instinctively crossed his legs. "Annabelle…"

"Unbutton your fall, sir."

"*Woman*," he pleaded.

"Unbutton your fall, else answer the question truthfully. That *is* how this game works, is it not?"

Harris stared at the jezebel he'd wrought by his own perverse making and swore effusively in his head. Alas, neither pride nor prick would grant him leeway. He unbuttoned his fall, revealing just how much her words aroused him.

❧

Miss Li had listened intently to Elizabeth's tale before she offered her sober advice. "If you've still no word of Jasper once you return home, Elizabeth, you must immediately take action. Do not underestimate Finch. Start your search where you believe your husband last went, at your father's house, not here with me. But take men with you for protection. Do not travel unaccompanied. The bitterness between Jasper and Finch runs deep. That man will use whatever means he has to strike not only at your husband and your sister, but at you too."

Elizabeth's hopes sank.

"And if Jasper has not returned"—Li gripped Elizabeth's hand—"send word to me at once. The Duke of Allendale has left for Cumberland, but there are others here in London, friends to both myself and your husband, who will help."

Elizabeth suddenly wished it were some rival whore she needed to battle for her husband's attention, rather than this dastardly villain Finch. She squeezed Li's hand, then nearly ran to the phaeton, driving straight to her father's house.

There disaster greeted her: Furniture was overturned and papers scattered all about. Shattered china littered the floor alongside drapes ripped from windows. The house had been shabby for years, but carnage such as this violated all that was decent.

Elizabeth's blood ran cold.

Milton's man, Marty, approached her in the foyer, but before he could utter a word, her father appeared, wringing his hands. "Oh, Lizzie, it is just terrible! Terrible, what has happened!"

"Papa—"

"Just *look* what they have done to our home! Everything my wives treasured, all shattered, destroyed!"

Elizabeth's irritation mounted. "Papa, it is terrible, yes, but tell me—"

"Every treasured wedding gift now—"

"Father!" Elizabeth barked. "Tell me what, exactly, has happened."

He continued his lament. "Unthinkable that someone should be so—"

"Who?" She gripped his shoulders to shake sense into him. "*Who* is responsible for this?"

He stared blankly at her. "Why, that's just it, Lizzie. I've no idea why anyone should wish to do this."

She gave up and searched for Marty. What she found,

instead, was a household huddled inside the kitchen, Cook attempting to hush her scullery's soft weeping. Staff rose as one, chairs scraping the floor, the instant they saw Elizabeth.

"Miss Lizzie!" Cook discarded the maid to press Elizabeth to her breast. "Thank heavens you've come."

"Tell me what has happened. Papa is incoherent."

Marty stepped forward, looking grim. "A word in private first, ma'am?"

Elizabeth nicked her head. "Cook, put the kettle on. I'll be but a minute." She followed Marty out into the same courtyard where her husband had once neatly tossed a butcher—a lifetime ago.

"Ma'am." Marty lowered his voice. "Finch sent men t' rough up the place, lookin' fer somethin' or someone, an' I fear they may've found 'im."

"What do you mean, found him? Found whom?"

"Master Milton, ma'am."

She shook her head. Impossible.

"Took Ginny too, ma'am."

"Took?" Elizabeth did not believe his words. "Took Ginny where? Where is the Baron?"

"Dunno, ma'am. We were locked up all night, only managed t' break down the cellar door an hour ago. I were about t' run an' fetch yer, ma'am. No idea where Ginny were took, nor Jasp. Know only as I heard yer lady's maid tryin' to sweet talk 'im before she fell silent."

"Sweet talk whom, Marty? *Who*?"

"Finch, ma'am. Didn't yer ol' man tell yer Finch himself paid his lordship another call?"

"No." Elizabeth's heart raced. "My father made no sense at all." She inhaled a steadying breath. "Details, Marty. Now."

"Right. Only…" The blasted man looked embarrassed.

"Do not spare me, sir. I promise I'll not faint." Though Elizabeth did indeed pale with every shocking word Milton's servant spoke. By the end, she gripped the footman's arm to keep herself upright.

Back in the carriage, her alarm only grew. Ginny had been taken by Finch, only where Marty did not know, and Elizabeth had no idea what to do about it either. Her husband's man believed Milton had also been taken, yet he wasn't wholly sure; he'd been in the cellar with the rest of staff. Nor did Papa's addled brain equate Finch's earlier house call with the ensuing ransacking of his home. Only the cautious tread Marty had heard ascend the stairs after the house had fallen quiet made him believe Milton had come. He knew his master's gait.

Li's words returned to Elizabeth: *If Jasper is not back, send word to me at once.*

She rapped the carriage roof, urging the driver faster while reminding herself her husband had friends. Marty would keep watch over Papa, and Cook would restore order to Father's house.

Elizabeth simply prayed both her husband and lady's maid awaited her at home.

Yet the moment she walked in, Gerald's face said otherwise. She handed her pelisse to a footman as Gerald silently followed her into the parlor, Murdoch right behind him.

Elizabeth told them all she knew, imploring, "We must act quickly to find both Ginny and Milton. Moreover, we do not know for certain the Baron was taken by Finch, for Marty could not confirm—"

"Oh, he has 'im." Murdoch shook her head, tears starting in her eyes. "That connivin', schemin' lout has our Jasp. I feel it in me gut. He's never let 'im go, poor lad. Haunted that sweet boy his entire—"

"Will you be quiet!" Gerald's voice cracked. "Did y' not hear th' mistress, woman? We're t' remain rational an' composed."

Elizabeth had never witnessed her husband's two most

dependable servants in such distress. She'd been counting on them to keep *her* calm.

"An' how's a body t' stay sane when our lad's been snatched an' poor Ginny's also gone missin'?" Murdoch lashed back. "An' Miss Winthrop as like married t' Arty by now, if she's not been—"

God. Elizabeth's panic reached new heights. *Annabelle.*

"An' what good's it alarmin' th' mistress with such talk, eh?" Gerald's face shone red. "You've a job t' uphold, Martha, an' from where I stands y' best—"

"From where *you* stands, John Gerald, you'd best watch yer tongue, lest I toss both you an' yer ring!"

"Both of you, stop." Elizabeth's pitched tone matched the fury on Murdoch's face. "Are you two married?" She looked from one to the other.

"Betrothed," Murdoch muttered. "Nigh five years, though he's taken liberties."

Gerald bristled. "I've done naught but what you wanted, woman."

"Enough." Elizabeth cut them off. "I do not care what squabbles you have, married or not. I must know whom to trust and whom to beware. I will send a message forthwith to Miss Li, but I should like to hear from each of you, calmly and coherently, what you believe to be our best course of action."

Neither would look at her.

"I am inclined to report the ransacking of my father's house to the authorities, for start, though we cannot—"

"*Don't!*" the two cried in unison, startling Elizabeth.

"Ma'am, you tell th' bobbies an' it'll be that much worse," Gerald explained. "Finch's got th' peelers in 'is pockets, an' Jasp an' Arty done run afoul of 'em too oft in their youth. Ain't no love there, ma'am, only trouble."

There seemed no end to trouble, Elizabeth thought. No end!

"Then please," she implored, "what *do* you suggest?"

This seemed to jolt them finally, for both proceeded to tell Elizabeth all they knew of Finch, and all they feared. By the end of their recounting, Murdoch announced the best anyone could do was pray Ginny and Jasper would both be found alive.

Nerves utterly frayed, Elizabeth broke down and wept.

His wife sighed in the crook of Harris's arm, a bundle of worry. Nothing seemed to ease her trepidation on this, the final leg of their journey. Neither games nor kisses did the trick as their carriage rolled toward London.

"I know you're not asleep," he grumbled.

"You cannot know if I am sleeping or—"

"You're stewin'. So out with it then." He poked her midriff.

She huffed. "I am afraid what people will think when we return, what Papa will say."

"Bella, once your old man's apprised in full of Finch, he'll thank his lucky stars I made off with yer when I did."

"Oh I doubt that very much, Arthur."

Harris felt kicked. He'd saved her from a hideous fate, at no small cost to himself. Winthrop better be bloody grateful.

"You see, it is not…" She looked embarrassed. "It was my mother's dying wish that I should marry well, to make up for her own failed union with Papa."

"So yer mum weren't happy. Sounds like most married ladies I know."

Bella began to pluck lint off his waistcoat this time, not her skirts. "She felt degraded by Father's gambling. At least, Lizzie has always implied as much. I was so young when my mother passed, I hardly remember her."

"Well I don't see how marriage t' *me* should reflect poorly on *you* when yer father betrothed yer t' Finch," he ground out. "He'd no concern fer yer honor, yer future, let alone yer well-being when he gambled you to that man, Bella. Not gambled, sold. So if you think fer an instant that my marryin' you is less honorable than yer father's dishonorable—"

"Arthur, society will look unfavorably upon you not because you own a gaming hall, but because you are not titled. They would have looked just as unfavorably on Mr. Finch had I married him."

"Yet Jasper's respectable because he bought himself a bleedin' Scottish Barony? A blasted title makes all th' difference, do it?" He was angrier than he liked, and he didn't know why.

"It is not what *I* think, Arthur, it is—"

"What th' rest o' them bloody toffs'll say, I see."

She looked like she wished to take back her words, but she couldn't. It was all true.

He cut to the quick. "Well y' can rest pretty, wife, as I'm deliverin' you t' the Baron and Lady Milton first, before we see yer dear papa." He scowled. "I've a might many things t' discuss now with Jasp, not least o' which is whether he's dealt with yer former beau yet."

He knew his tone was ugly, but Harris didn't care.

"An' when we *do* visit yer fine father, you'll breathe not a word of annullin' our marriage, Bella, not a word." He pierced her with his gaze. "Fer appearance's sake, you'll live with me at *The Leaf* until Finch is no longer a threat. You'll share me bed so it appears we're truly wed and no gossip spreads." He stared hard at her. "Do I make myself clear?"

She lowered her gaze. "Yes, Arthur."

He glared out the carriage window, his mood sullen as hell as they entered London's outskirts.

CHAPTER THIRTY-EIGHT

Elizabeth paced the floor in Milton's office while Mutton's eyes followed her every step, tail barely thumping. The wolfhound missed his master. *She* missed his master too. Her emotion surprised her, but there was no denying how she felt. "Where are you, Jasper?" she muttered as her mind raced from one scenario to the next, with the next always worse than the first.

"Ginny's returned, ma'am." Gerald appeared, sounding out of breath.

"Thank heavens!" She rushed after him down the stairs into the parlor, where she found not only Ginny but Murdoch and Miss Li, who must have left *LeBrecht's* the minute she received Elizabeth's note.

Ginny regaled them of her travails while Elizabeth took stock of her maid's alarming appearance. The girl's dress was in shambles, her skin bruised purple in spots. She'd been roughed up but naught worse—or so she claimed.

"I don't know more, ma'am, honest I don't." Miss Li had unleashed a flurry of questions at Elizabeth's poor lady's maid. "I've wracked me brains tryin' t' remember more."

"But you are certain they have Jasper," Li pressed.

"Yes'm." Ginny met Elizabeth's eyes across the room. "I've no doubt."

"Kusottare!" Li swore in a language Elizabeth did not recognize.

Murdoch intervened. "I ought t' run Ginny a bath an' feed her a bite, ma'am."

"Of course." Elizabeth forced herself to smile at her maid. "We've kept you long enough, Ginny, forgive us. Your description of events has been invaluable. We are very relieved you have returned."

The girl bobbed a curtsy. "Be right as rain soon, ma'am. Happy to—"

A commotion in the foyer stopped Ginny midsentence, however, as unintelligible shouting punctuated the silence. Before Elizabeth could blink, a bearded man burst inside, dragging Annabelle behind him.

Harris.

Elizabeth rushed to crush her sister to her while Mr. Harris insisted, "Jasper. Now."

Without letting go of Bella, Elizabeth told him to take a seat, though the man refused her order and remained standing, scowling. She sent Gerald for sandwiches and tea, Murdoch having already left with Ginny, and then Elizabeth sat as close as humanly possible to Annabelle on the settee.

Miss Li proceeded to bluntly summarize the situation for Mr. Harris, who looked bewildered by the news. He also looked older than Elizabeth remembered, or perhaps it was the beard. The man began to mutter expletives as he paced the parlor floor, grumbling, "What a bloody goddamned disaster…"

Annabelle sent him furtive looks, twisting her skirts. Perhaps her sister had succumbed to Mr. Harris's charms, though that was the least of Elizabeth's concerns.

"Arty." Li checked his nervous pacing. "You know as much as we do now, and you also know Finch. We are certain Jasper's being held in the cellars of *The Canary's Lair*, where Finch kept me. It matches the maid's description too well. The question remains, how do we get him out?"

Elizabeth looked from Li to Harris. Both cared deeply for her husband, but they were also known to Finch, and likely known to Finch's associates too. Li, especially, stood out.

"I'll go." Annabelle stunned them all.

"Are you mad?" Elizabeth blurted.

"Out of 'er mind, more like." Harris's face blazed. "You'll do no such thing, wife."

Which was the wrong thing to say to Annabelle; Elizabeth could have told him that.

Bella held firm. "I shall go as Bartholomew Brown, my alter ego. He is unknown to Finch and skilled with cards. In fact, he is adept enough he shall easily infiltrate *The Canary*'s tables to determine where the Baron is being—"

"No." Harris yanked Bella from her seat. "I forbid it."

"You cannot." Annabelle tried, but failed, to free herself from his grip while Elizabeth, incensed, grabbed Bella's other arm.

"Lady Milton," Harris started, "yer sister's under the mistaken premise that—"

"You will release her at once," Elizabeth demanded. "You will release my sister into my custody forthwith." She attempted to pry Annabelle from his grasp. "She shall remain with me now until—"

"Hell no," Harris growled, holding fast. "As me wife, I've more claim t' Bella than you, Lady Milton."

Elizabeth's own grip tightened, until Bella kicked Harris's shin and promptly freed herself.

***

"I will not be treated like a child." Annabelle extricated herself from Lizzie's grasp. "Nor will I be treated like property, sir." She glared at Arthur. "I will make my own decision in this and future matters."

Both stared at her like she'd grown horns.

"Neither of you see my plan for what it is: sound. I have passed before as Bart Brown, at Mr. Harris's own gaming house, where none but he guessed my sex and only because he'd been tipped off." Her eyes flicked to Arthur, who was still scowling. "I am the perfect foil, because I am the person Finch least expects to rescue Milton."

One could have heard a mouse sneeze, the room was so quiet.

"She has a point, you know." Miss Li came to Annabelle's defense. "Miss Winthrop as Mr. Brown will be the last person Finch suspects foolhardy enough to steal Jasper from him. But Bart will need help. Finch keeps the key to all shackles on his person, so even if you gain entry to his dungeon, miss—*Mrs.* Harris," she corrected, "you will be unable to release Jasper without—"

"Dungeon? Shackles?" Lizzie's voice cracked with pain. "Do not tell me that man has Jasper chained like an animal."

"Elizabeth, you must prepare yourself for the worst," Li gravely intoned.

Lizzie clapped a hand to her mouth, stifling a cry.

"I can do this, sister." Annabelle knew she must. It was because of her the Baron had been taken. It was because of her that Lizzie had married the Baron in the first place. "I am not afraid of Finch. I—"

Arthur roughly hauled her to him. "You'd best fear Finch, Bella. You'd best be deathly afraid o' that man."

"Yes," Li interjected, placing an arm about Elizabeth's quaking shoulders. "We would all be wise to fear him."

The room stilled once more, as if every head silently churned.

Li broke the quiet. "Any rescue we attempt shall require careful, detailed thought. Let us now calmly work out a plan."

Annabelle stared deep into Arthur's eyes, willing him to trust her, before she turned to her sister. "I am indebted to Mr. Harris for saving me from Finch, Lizzie. And as I am now his wife, I will remain with my husband. It is my choice."

Elizabeth looked exhausted, but she was not without words. "You will not go into *The Canary's Lair* alone, Annabelle. I will accompany you."

"What?" Arthur exploded. "Hell no. Why, in two shakes you'd give Bella away with those bloody spectacles, woman."

"I shall go without, Mr. Harris, and you will refrain from—"

"Écoutez!" Li's voice cut like ice. "We must reach Jasper soon." She crossed her arms. "Time is of the essence, friends; let us not waste it bickering." Her lips made a *moue.* "And our plan must be sound."

CHAPTER THIRTY-NINE

Harris felt a poke.

"Arthur, wake up."

He groaned into his pillow. "Blast it, woman, I were finally asleep." He was exhausted from a night of restless tossing, thoughts of Jasper again being tortured at Finch's hand making him sick to his gills. "Why pester me now, when—"

"Arthur, I do not wish to wait."

He cracked open an eye. "Wait t' rescue Jasp?"

"To … *you* know." She poked him again.

"Stop pokin'!" He felt cross. "An' tell me straight what you're so eager to—"

She met his eyes with determination.

"Oh no." He shook his head, furious she was still worrying this bone. "Nope, I won't. I gave me word, Bella. And naught will make me—"

Only her hand landed where it shouldn't, where it gripped his morning arousal.

"I'm yer husband in name only, miss." He leapt from the bed to hastily don his clothes. "An' of all times t' ask…" He shook his head at her, disgusted.

Annabelle's demeanor and tone shifted fast. "Forgive me, Mr. Harris. I did not mean to offend." She, too, slipped from the bed, turning her back to him to dress.

"Y' didn't offend, 'tis only—"

"No, I offended your honor and must beg your apology. I am clearly not myself." He thought he heard her sniff. "It shan't happen again."

"Sweetheart." He reached to touch her shoulder.

"Don't!" She pulled away. "Please do not pretend affection. You are right, of course. I should never have asked, not with all that has happened."

"Bella, luv…"

But she rushed from his room, making Harris wish to punch something, hard. He should have handled her better, but his nerves were as taut as gut strings on a fiddle.

And why ask *now* to be debauched? Did their scheme scare her too? Bella was right to fear Finch, and fear the role she'd offered to play. Which is why he wouldn't let her. He'd take a small band of men straight into Finch's hell and wage battle instead, rather than send his wife into that snake pit with her sister. He was still angry at Li for encouraging Annabelle's half-baked idea.

Nor would Jasp stand for such madness either.

No matter how convincing Bella was as Bartholomew Brown, she was but a slip of a girl beneath men's clothes, with not nearly the brawn needed to throw a fellow should she get jumped. Both she and her sister would be quickly overpowered if it came to a brawl, which it likely would. They'd have only their wits, and he'd lived enough to know wits were never enough.

Instead, Harris would strike early. Having grown his beard on the journey to Gretna, he was now grateful he'd kept it. That and a bit of dye to darken the blond should prove disguise enough. *His* plan removed Annabelle and Lady Milton from the equation entirely. And he'd put that plan in motion this very night while Bella paid her father a long-overdue visit.

Perhaps it was best they'd quarreled. He'd get Janie to color his hair right now.

❧

Elizabeth paced her husband's study and fretted, because there was the plot hatched in her husband's parlor—with Gerald, Harris, and Li—and there was the plot she'd hatched in private, after, with Annabelle. She and Bella would implement their plan a full day prior. Namely, tonight. They would not wait for Harris to 'gather more men' or for Li to 'send a girl in to spy.' Time was of the essence.

Elizabeth knew their plan might not work, but the other plan might not work either. Surprise was their best weapon; every story she'd ever read confirmed this. Odysseus, after all, had conquered an entire city with his Trojan horse. Instinct told her Finch's greed was the proper bait—greed for power and wealth. And the fewer known actors the better, lest God forbid the fiend sniff out a rat.

The sole other person Elizabeth would apprise was her husband's man, Marty, whom she'd see when they dined this evening with Papa. Harris could not forbid Annabelle from visiting Father now that she was back in London, and Marty should know their scheme in the event things went terribly awry. Which they wouldn't, Elizabeth told her worried self, because she could not bear the thought of Jasper suffering a second longer in that evil man's grasp.

She gulped, knowing full well the danger she and Bella faced, yet Finch could not marry Annabelle now that she was legally wed to Harris. And Elizabeth was a lady, after all, not a foreigner like Li or a servant like Ginny. Surely, if discovered, Finch would treat her differently.

Mutton's thumping tail beat in time to her nervous pacing. Heartsick for his master, the hound now followed her everywhere about the house. Elizabeth, too, felt sick at heart. She'd taken to sleeping nights in Jasper's bed, Mutton curled at her feet, because the sheets still smelled faintly of her husband.

She rued that day she'd made light with Bella and envisioned herself a widow enjoying the Baron's riches, for here she was, on the brink of just such future, wishing the very opposite. She longed for Milton to be home. Or was it but concern for his well-being? Oh, she no longer knew what she felt for Jasper Audrey!

"Ma'am?" Gerald appeared from out of nowhere. "Mary Audrey's takin' tea with Murdoch in the kitchen, should y' wish t' join 'em."

"Is she? Thank you, Gerald. I shall."

He turned to leave.

"Gerald?"

"Ma'am?"

"Do you think our plan will work?" Elizabeth did not know why she asked. It was a futile question when the plan the butler knew was not the plan she and Annabelle would follow.

"I should hope." He met her gaze. "But only God knows fer certain. Though if anyone can bring Jasp home, 'tis you, ma'am. He misses you somethin' fierce, I'm sure."

"I cannot tell, Gerald, if the Baron loves or loathes me."

"I've known Jasp fer years, ma'am, an' what that man loathes more'n anythin' is weakness in his self. And *you* are Jasp's great weakness, along with Mutton here." He bent to scratch the wolfhound's head.

Elizabeth did not believe the butler, because her husband did not allow himself to be weak. He may be as vulnerable as the next, but he did not show it. Ever.

She followed Gerald out, Mutton close on her heels, and forced a smile as she entered the kitchen. "Madam Audrey, it is so good of you to—" Yet one look at her mother-in-law's distraught face made Elizabeth cross the room and envelop her in an embrace.

"I am so sorry," Elizabeth whispered into Mary's ear. "I am doing everything in my power to secure Jasper's safe return."

Mary brushed tears aside as she pulled away. "I've no doubt you are, Elizabeth, but this plan of yours, as Li tells it, is sheer insanity."

Elizabeth's hopes plummeted. She crumpled into the nearest seat as Murdoch quietly left the kitchen.

"I lived under Finch's thumb, Elizabeth, and if he truly does have Jasper, he will use him to extort both favors and funds from you. And that will only be the beginning."

Elizabeth willed herself to have faith. "With all due respect, Mary, no plan is foolproof. We've no choice but to try." She steadied her shaking hands. "Jasper would do as much for any of us; you will not scare me off."

A faint smile crossed Mary Audrey's face. "Indeed, Lizzie. You make your husband proud." Her smile grew. "I did not come to warn you *off* your scheme, dear, merely to warn you of the holes in that scheme."

Relief washed over Elizabeth.

"Listen to what I share, then bring my boy back to me."

And Elizabeth did listen, intently, even as she quietly turned her and Annabelle's plan over in her mind. Finch was less protected than assumed; he kept but one man at his side, meaning Annabelle's retrieval of a few choice ingredients from Mr. Harris's larder might just do the trick.

Her sister had learned a thing or two on her journey to Gretna which should prove useful to them now. At least, Elizabeth prayed it would.

❧

Hours later, however, she was not thinking of their plan, Elizabeth was contemplating wringing her father's neck.

"Lizzie." Annabelle shot her a warning glance. "Do not berate Papa so. It is Mr. Finch who deserves our wrath, not Father."

They were sitting in their father's drawing room, visiting with him, only Elizabeth had failed, again, to temper her anger —anger which felt more justified than ever. Her husband's very life was threatened, for God's sake, while Papa remained insufferably unaffected by anything but his own blasted concerns. Cook had reported she'd heard him weeping nights, the recent upset with the house too much for him to bear. Not Annabelle's kidnapping to Gretna, mind. Not the Baron's disappearance. The man's blasted *house*.

Or perhaps Father worried his debt to Finch would not get settled now that Milton was missing? Well he ought to worry. He ought to—

Papa dramatically dabbed a kerchief to his brow. "If your dear, sweet mothers could only see the two of you, married." He loudly blew his nose.

"You leave our mothers out of this," Elizabeth's ire only increased. "For you to invoke their names, after such shabby treatment of both—"

"*Lizzie*," Annabelle hissed. "We did not come to rile Papa, but to show him we are well, to ensure he is well, and to get on with our lives, forgiving and forgetting." She pinned Elizabeth with her gaze. "We mustn't let *other* frustrations affect current feelings."

Elizabeth slowed her breathing. Annabelle was right, of course. Fear was getting the better of her. She yearned for her husband's firm presence—and even firmer hand. His palm on her backside would have helped clear her head. A quick spanking, absurd as that thought was, had curative properties she desperately now craved.

"Forgive me, Father. My nerves are overwrought." She inhaled a breath. "And you are right, Bella, the past matters little anymore. In fact, we shall stay the night, for old times' sake, and join you for dinner. What say you, Papa?

Winthrop looked from one daughter to the next. "'Tis true I am so lonesome of late I don't know what to do with myself. The house is much too quiet with the two of you now gone. Do you think I ought to marry again? I hear one is never too old to take a wife. After all, a kind and loving widow with means may just put my heart to ease again."

Elizabeth resisted the overwhelming urge to throttle him. Instead, she placed a hand on his arm. "I should like nothing better than to discuss the idea over dinner, Papa. I'll have Cook set the table for three. Bella, why don't you peek at Father's accounts before we dine. To make sure all is in order."

No doubt he was up to his tricks. Again.

Once the house fell silent, they slipped out, Elizabeth in half-blind state led by Bartholomew Brown's steadying arm. She'd stashed her spectacles in her skirt pocket rather than risk being found out, for she could see enough to get by; the world would simply blur.

Annabelle had given Elizabeth a dress gaudy enough to look the part. She'd also dusted off an old powdered wig to hide Elizabeth's black hair, turning her into a painted *catin de la révolution* named Babette. Bette would hang on Bart's arm—both trollop and good luck piece to his card sharp.

Elizabeth prayed their ruse would hold, for tonight all childhood playacting skills would be put to test. Annabelle, at least, was a good actress.

She gripped her sister's hand inside the hansom Bart had

hailed. "Bella, I must thank you for coming to Milton's aid. I did not think I'd grow to care for him, yet—"

"You have," Bella finished. "And he for you, Lizzie. My day spent shopping with your husband proved he cares for you a great deal. You could have done worse than marry Baron of Milton."

"Like marry Arthur Harris?"

"Well, t' be sure, he's less catch than yer fine Baron." Bella slipped into character. "Though you're a sweet skirt, Bette." Bart coughed his voice lower. "I may just marry you meself!"

"Ooh, Monsieur Brown." Elizabeth played coy with an affected French accent. "You win well enough at zee tables, sir, and I may just accept."

"You'll bed me first, Bette." Bella's words shocked. "For only if y' please me twixt th' sheets will I—"

"Annabelle." Elizabeth fast dropped her act. "Wherever did you learn such coarse language?"

"Why, from my husband, sister. You should hear Arthur speak. More tricks up that man's sleeve than—"

"Bella." Elizabeth grew serious. "Have you developed feelings for Mr. Harris? Because the way you—"

"Don't be ridiculous." Bella's voice hardened once more into Bart's. "He's naught t' me but a means to an end, as is th' game we play t'night."

Elizabeth did not believe her.

"We must focus on finding Milton, Lizzie. On getting him out. I shan't allow distraction to cloud my mind, and neither should you."

Elizabeth hardened her resolve. "Agreed. Once we have Finch's attention—and gain his master key—we find and free Jasper."

Bella patted her suitcoat's breast pocket, making Elizabeth instinctively reach for the beribboned locket that collared her throat. Annabelle had prepped two handkerchiefs, and Elizabeth wore arsenic about her neck.

They were as ready as they'd ever be.

CHAPTER FORTY

"Another win fer th' young gentleman!" the dealer announced, reshuffling the deck while Bette squealed French delight and peppered Bart's cheek with kisses.

"There now." Bart peeled the lady off him. "Y' can show yer pleasure later in bed, woman, I've another round t' win." Annabelle made sure to grimace, because Bart looked older when he scowled. She'd practiced in the mirror.

The crowd gathered about their table laughed, making Bette pout, her hand lingering at Bart's arm. "Don't play too long, *mon amour.*" Lizzie smiled seductively. "A lady does not like to wait."

"Yer call, sir," barked the dealer.

Bart gave Bette a small nod. He had to win but a few more hands before his lucky streak was noticed and an audience with Finch all but guaranteed.

He inhaled a breath, pretending to scratch an itch as he felt for the knife he wore at his waist, hidden beneath his vest. Arthur had demonstrated how easily one could be unmasked; Annabelle as Bart would not make that mistake twice.

"An' t' whom do I owe this pleasure, good sir?" Finch sidled up behind Annabelle, making her insides briefly quake.

"Brown, sir. Bartholomew Brown, at yer service." Bart kept his head low, offering no hand to shake or hat to tip.

"Well, well, Mr. Brown. Fer a lad so young, y' play exceptionally well. An' a fair lady by yer side, my my." Squinting, Finch looked Bette over. "We ought t' ave ourselves a wee chat in me office t' discuss opportunities here at *The Canary* fer a talented lad like yerself."

"Why, I'd be delighted, Mister…?" Bart feigned ignorance.

"Finch, young sir. An' may I ask who this fetchin' creature is?" His gaze raked Elizabeth again, settling on the fake mole at her cheek.

"Mademoiselle Babette," Bart introduced. "Me very own Lady Luck." He gave a healthy swat to Lizzie's posterior.

"Why, Monsieur Brown, you naughty *garçon*!" Bette chirped, leaning into Bart's arm to afford Finch a better view of her French bosom. "I am not yours alone, sir."

It was Lizzie's job to locate the key kept on Finch's body; she'd need to get close, repulsive though that task may be.

She threw Finch a wink. "I can be any man's *bonne chance*, for a price."

"Knows 'er worth." Finch's hand clapped heavily to Bart's back, jolting Annabelle. "You'll have t' earn big t' keep her." His nasty laugh sent chills up her spine. "Let's talk in private o'er a glass o' port, lad." Finch guided Bart by the nape of his neck from the table. "You too, miss." His beady eyes flashed at Bette. "We'll make a party of it."

❧

Harris scanned the room, cap low and head down, pretending to focus on his game. He didn't care that his hair was carrot red, didn't care if he won or lost this hand. He cared only for finding Jasper alive and getting his men safely out of this rat hole, for the place was crawling with lowlifes, though as yet still no bloody sign of Finch. The devil would walk the floor at some point, though. An owner always showed his face at least once in the course of a night.

And this night was ripe for surprise. Harris's army of yobs from the docks and men from *The Leaf* had discreetly trickled in with coin aplenty to play the tables—and promise of more should the job go as planned. The moment he gave the signal, they'd storm the hall and cellars to spring Jasp free. A better plan by far than that poison nonsense cooked up by Bella and her sister; no way in hell would he let his bloody wife into Finch's lair. He hadn't needlessly tortured himself marrying Miss Winthrop for her to end up in the devil's maw.

"Well hullo, handsome." A painted lady sidled up to watch him play.

"Miss." Harris tipped his cap. "You're a sight fer sore eyes, but I aim t' earn more'n I spend this night."

"Pity." Her hand trailed his arm with a pout.

He merely smirked in response, following her swinging hips until his eyes hit upon a different backside whose crooked gait he knew. Harris watched Finch lead a young man and wench away from the tables. He didn't like the grip Ronny had on the boy, and he didn't like the look of that boy's own hips either. His hackles rose with infuriating alarm, for the wench beside the young man's shapely arse had Lady Milton's blasted stature. And from behind, that lad looked suspiciously like one Bartholomew Brown.

Finch brought them to the bowels of *The Canary*, to an office decorated with brocade tapestries and dark, velvet drapes, all blood red in color, next to gold-gilt sconces reeking of gaudy taste. It was just as Li had described it, which meant Finch's dungeons must also be close. Caverns, Li had called them, or underground caves hollowed out. A single burly guard stood watch at Finch's door just like Mary Audrey had foretold.

The man's brawn made Elizabeth anxious, though everything now made her insides flip, most especially the fact Finch had not let *her* fetch his port, but had poured himself and Annabelle two glasses instead. Arsenic foiled, damnation!

He looked like Midas himself seated behind his massive desk as he clicked his dangling tooth back and forth, back and forth. Bella as Bart simply sipped her drink, leaning back in her chair the way a man would—a man who did as he pleased and knew what he wanted.

Her sister was shockingly good at being that man.

"Now Mr. Brown, might I call yer Bart, sir?" Finch stared hard at Bella.

"Mr. Brown'll do."

"So that's how 'tis, eh?" He leaned forward, stare narrowing. "A man o' business, same as me. Good, good." His head flicked to Elizabeth, who stood just behind Bart's chair. "Y' won't mind if th' lady sits with me then, while we chat?"

In the distant recesses of this foul man's lair, Elizabeth thought she heard metal scrape, chain on stone.

"She's a mind of her own," Bart nodded at Bette, "an' can do as she likes."

Elizabeth took the opportunity to sidle over to Finch and boldly seat herself on his lap, placing her arms about the foul man's neck. He immediately slid his arm about her waist and squeezed.

"Now here's a lass what knows her place." He pinched her roundly, making her wince, though she began to twine her fingers into the greasy curls at his neck, searching for a chain between skin folds—in vain.

Bart kept his cool. "I'd remind you th' lady came with me, sir, an' she'll leave with me too."

"That so?" Finch leveled. "Why don't we play for her then?" He pinched Elizabeth hard enough this time she yelped. "She understands th' stakes, an' you've a clear talent, boy." He reached into his desk and pulled out a deck. "My win takes th' lady, and yer win takes her back."

Bart remained shockingly calm. "Yer game don't favor me no gain, sir."

"Right-o, *Bella*." Finch lurched forward, violently knocking Elizabeth from his lap. He planted both hands atop his desk and loomed across the surface. "But it sure do even th' score."

Elizabeth's heart leapt as Annabelle thrust her own chair away from the desk, refusing to back down.

"You just call me some girlie name?" Bart puffed himself up as much as he possibly could, making Elizabeth both proud and terrified for her sister. When and where had Bella found such courage?

Finch coughed a sick snort while the scrape of metal grew more audible from the dark. Someone was here. Could it be Jasper? Or was it a different, sad soul in chains? Elizabeth's skin tingled as she peered into the dark, far arches of this cavernous vault. Her eyesight was too poor to make out more than shadows, but her hands now roamed Finch's body from behind. She patted his pockets in tease, pretending to stroke his upper arms, his chest, his waist. She felt something hard through the lining of his waistcoat as hope leapt.

"Annabelle, darlin'," the devil drawled at Bart, "y' make a handsome lad, but them hips swing too well on yer fine, heart-shaped arse. An' yer eyes, me sweet"—he leaned closer across the desk—"are too rare a color t' mistake."

Elizabeth froze.

"Wondered how soon I'd get a visit after yer sister's maid delivered me message." He laughed, and Elizabeth's hand scrambled for the key, but his own gripped hers in a twist so vicious he made her cry out.

"An' as fer *you*, Lady Milton..." He wrenched Elizabeth to his side, painfully pinning her arms behind her back. "Though I've enjoyed having yer French self on me lap, dearie, 'tain't no place fer a married lady, now is it?" His voice slid malevolently into her ear. "Did y' wish t' pay yer husband a visit, ma'am?" He snickered. "He's here in me lair, trussed an' waitin'. Go on then—go an' give yer man a kiss." He pushed her so roughly, Elizabeth landed hard on the floor, her hidden spectacles biting into her thigh with a *crunch*.

She scrambled to her feet, shaking with rage. "You've no right to hold my husband hostage, sir, just as you'd no right to swindle my father for Annabelle's hand!"

"Quite th' spitfire." His laugh was pure wickedness. "Only I've had enough o' yer type assumin' I'll do yer biddin'." His laugh all but died. "Because this here's *my* turf, Baroness, so you'll do as I say now, yer bonny sister too—if y' know what's good for yer." He reached across his desk and dragged Bella clear across the surface.

"Please!" Elizabeth cried. "Let her go or—"

"What?" Finch snorted. "Y' think a few screams down here'll disturb my sorts o' guests? Think me guard'll come runnin' t' yer rescue? I've men crawlin' this den, ready t' pounce at a word, nay, a blink from me." He hauled Bella off the desk, planting her body flush against his own, his hand gripping her neck.

"I'm sure you do." Elizabeth's resolve only grew, for if Jasper were here she *would* get him out. This wretch needed a lesson in decency. She had a perverse desire to provoke him as much as she humanly could. So she did.

"Only I wonder, sir." Elizabeth trained her eyes on the squat blur before her. "Why should a man as successful as you need to entrap an innocent young woman like my sister, or kidnap an honorable man like my husband? Is it that you recognize you will never be accepted by society, no matter how great your wealth, how pure your bride? That no man or woman of class would ever stoop so low as to admire you, but will only ever revile you? That not even the lowest of scum, your army of degenerates, serve you with true fealty, their loyalty needing to be bought with blackmail and coin?" Both Li and Mary Audrey had explained how Finch gained, and wielded, power.

"What a lonely life you must lead, Mr. Finch. How sad you require both my husband and my sister to rouse anyone's attention. What else are you unable to *rouse*, I wonder?" Somewhere in that small, mean heart of his she hoped she poked his Achilles. "No matter whom you use, or how often you cheat and steal, you will never receive the respect you crave from those who are your betters. You are pathetic." She shook her head at him in disgust. "Society does not even deem you a *man*."

Bella let out a short, choked gasp. Did Finch now squeeze her sister's very breath? Elizabeth heard Annabelle wheeze and flail, then watched her claw at the hand encircling her throat.

"Fine speech, miss," Finch hissed at Elizabeth. "But if you'd rather not see th' life squeezed out o' yer bonny sister, you'll apologize on yer knees t' me, *now*."

Elizabeth instantly dropped. Head bent and chest thrust forward, without thinking she assumed the position she'd been trained to perform for her husband.

Because nothing mattered but Bella now. Nothing.

"Lovely," he crooned in his sick, rasping voice. "Just lovely, Lizzie. That's how I likes yer, yes."

Elizabeth heard her sister gulp air, but all hope had vanished, the stakes turned perilous.

"I see Jasp taught yer ladyship well. A right nice addition t' me house you'd make. Tell me, Lizzie, did he tan yer bottom too? Show yer all the delights I taught 'im as me whippin' boy?"

That noise again, iron scraping stone, and Elizabeth knew, she simply *knew* Jasper was in this cavernous hellhole with them. He must be.

She would not let her panic overcome her, though her heart galloped in her chest. She must do something, say something, and say it fast.

"Please. I'll show you all I know, perform however you wish. I know how to give a man pleasure, only I beg you, let Annabelle go." Her thoughts, and breaths, grew frantic, for Finch seemed to suck the very air from this gold-gilt cave, making her lungs struggle almost as much as Annabelle's.

"Pleases me t' hear yer beg, comin' as it does from yer ladyship's fine-bred lips." He laughed. "An' yer offer's mighty temptin'. I'd be a fool not t' sample yer wares, an' yet…"

In horror Elizabeth watched Finch slide his remaining free hand beneath Bella's vest, to where she'd bound her breasts.

"I'm partial t' yer wee sister, see, as she is, after all, me *affianced*."

Elizabeth's mouth went dry as a desert. He was going to take what he'd wanted all along: Annabelle.

"An' as I'll need yer on th' outside, t' funnel Jasper's funds t' me coffers an' gain me entry t' th' gentry's abundant plenty, well, I can't do that if you're tied up in me rooms here at *The Canary*." He chuckled. "Though it paints a pretty picture, don't it, Lizzie? Yer haughty self, bound t' me bed."

Mary Audrey had predicted Finch would wish to keep both Jasper and Bella here, his prisoners, and let Elizabeth go, forced to do his bidding out in the world, for however long he wished.

She must think her way out, fast, for she'd no weapon with which to strike, no hand with which to barter now that she'd already bartered her flesh. What else could she possibly offer? The arsenic hung useless about her neck.

"Mr. Finch, I beg you…"

"Beg louder, lass." His voice turned gravelly, more lascivious in tone, as Bella struggled in vain to ward off his roaming hand.

"I've a mind to take Miss Annabelle right here an' now to th' tune o' yer sweet beggin', Lady Milton. How's that fer compensation, eh? Yer sister's ripe flesh fer yer terribly smart words."

"Sir…" She was desperate to forestall him. "Annabelle is married to Mr. Harris. She can no longer wed you."

"Easily annulled," he said, tearing fabric as Bella's lungs again gasped air. "An' no doubt not married fer real, are yer, luv?" His hand slid inside her sister's breeches as a voice snarled low, "Paws off me wife, Ronny."

Harris!

But Finch cut off Bella's air, her sister's choked sob the only sound Elizabeth heard. She remained on her knees, Harris dead in his tracks at the threshold, where Finch's guard, behind Harris, lay sprawled across the floor.

Elizabeth did not think, she lunged for Finch's bollocks but met the man's thick thighs instead. She dug her nails into his trousers as Harris rushed him head on.

Metal glinted in the light as Elizabeth screamed and Harris froze, a blade pressed perilously to Annabelle's pale throat. The room took on an eerie glow as the hearth's blaze licked air in a burst of orange heat—just as Bella violently refilled her lungs with a stuttering gasp.

"Now that we're *agreed*, again," Finch rasped, his knife flush at Bella's throat, "'tis time I were more clear." He glared at Harris. "You'll return to *The Leaf*, Arty, an' annul yer sham marriage. And *you*"—he kicked Elizabeth with his boot, where she remained crouched upon the floor—"will go home an' await instruction."

Elizabeth did not move.

"As fer you, luv…"

Elizabeth shuddered for poor Annabelle, held hostage by Finch.

"You'll stay here as me betrothed, till we're wed nice'n proper."

"Finch." Harris's tone barely concealed his rage. "As businessmen, surely we can come to some—"

"No." Bella surprised them all, her voice faint but firm. "I'll not be bandied back and forth between you like some object. I shall decide my fate for myself."

***

Harris's knees nearly buckled under the weight of Bella's brave, clear voice. God help him, he was in awe of his wife. No, he was in love with this woman and also, madder than hell at her.

"You broke my betrothal to Mr. Finch." She trembled as she turned to Harris, her eyes flashing him a warning, or so he thought. "Which brought my sister this misfortune. I shall not be the cause of more misery, Arthur. I shall repair the harm done by remaining with Mr. Finch. You will indeed annul our marriage."

Harris ground his teeth. If she thought for one second that by sacrificing herself she'd save him or her sister—

"Bella!" Lady Milton implored from the floor. "Do not acquiesce! We can come to some agreement. Surely, as businessmen they must—"

"No," Annabelle repeated, and Harris now watched her like a hawk, saw her left hand creep to her hip. He slid his own hand to his belt, where he kept a second blade. "I will marry Mr. Finch, and he will release Baron of Milton. We shall be a family, Lizzie. Papa too. That is what I wish." She placed her shaking right hand right over Finch's knuckles, where he still held the knife to her throat. "Please, sir, put away your blade and treat me like the gentleman you were when we courted. I wish only to reconcile. You will release the Baron to my sister, will you not? For once we marry, he shall be a brother to you. He shall be your family too."

In the course of all her hogwash, Bella's eyes beseeched Harris to ... what? *Wait*? He didn't know what she planned, but she had something up her sleeve, or rather, at her hip.

He was terrified by what she might do next.

"Mr. Finch, you will honor your pledge if I now honor mine, will you not?"

And miraculously Finch lowered his blade, slipping it back up his sleeve, his other arm still wrapped firmly about Annabelle's waist. She flashed Harris another look; his every nerve was lit.

"The skirt's got more sense'n th' lot o' you." Finch looked smug. "You'll suit, Bella darlin', 'specially if y' continue in such docile manner as this."

The fiend loosened his grip, and Bella slowly turned about, allowing Harris a slim opening to lunge forward. Only Elizabeth lunged the very same instant for the man's short legs and tripped Harris in the process. He hit the floor hard and looked up just as Bella cupped Finch's cheek, diverting the man's gaze from Harris back to her.

"I promise to be a most dutiful wife, sir." She kissed the devil hard on the lips as she thrust her left fist deep into his gut, jerking up. Just like Harris had bloody taught her.

Surprise painted Finch's slack face, while Bella stared agape at the knife sticking out of the man's torso. Finch staggered back, grasping the handle, as Harris sprang into action.

He slit the devil's throat from behind, letting Finch slide to the ground with a sick thud backward.

The cur clutched his throat as blood slowly seeped out. Harris determined a second cut was not needed as already, a dark stain began to pool beneath Finch's head.

Elizabeth caught Annabelle just as she crumpled, but Harris wrenched her from her sister and crushed her to him. *Safe.*

The Baroness did not waste breath. "Milton is here, I know it." She shouted into the room's dark arches, "Make noise, Jasper, show us where you are!" Her voice bounced off the low stone ceiling as a clank of chain scraped for answer.

God's truth, Jasp *was* here. Harris knew he must act, but his wife trembled in his arms, teeth chattering for shock.

"Luv," he told her softly, "he can't hurt you no more."

"But I killed him, Arthur, I—"

"No, Bella, y' merely stuck 'im one. *I* killed Finch, hear? Y' did naught but wound 'im. I did th' deed, an' I'm not sorry I did. He were an evil man. Y' did no—"

She fell apart in his arms, heaving dry sobs as he simply held her, held on.

***

Elizabeth blinked from her brave, breaking sister to the dark spot spreading beneath Finch's stilled form. She would not faint. The man had deserved worse than the mercy he'd received in death.

She swallowed her revulsion and knelt in the sticky puddle of blood to search his still-warm body for his key. After a minute she held up a strange-shaped tool with a sharp, curved end to Harris, who simply nodded yes. She grabbed a candle from the wall and headed to the furthest end of the room, toward the lowest arch, and was immediately swallowed by darkness.

Elizabeth felt her way along a damp, stone wall, her sorry flame doing little to light her way. She knew she was descending because the air grew more dank with each step she trod, though she'd not gone very far. Her eyes strained in the feeble light, the corridor opening into a colder, more cavernous room. She raised her candle to peer into the space and could just make out a shape against the far wall.

"Jasper!" She stumbled forward, in her haste nearly extinguishing the flame's weak flicker.

Her hands met skin, the body familiar, heart beating strong. She could not see his face but felt a gag at his mouth. "*Harris*! *Bella*!" she yelled, her voice bouncing off stone.

Footsteps approached, yet in her rush to free her husband she dropped her candle with a hiss to the floor. Elizabeth cursed, struggling to undo the knot at the back of Jasper's head, thinking only, *He lives. Thank God, he lives.*

"Water…" he rasped the instant his lips were freed.

Her voice broke on a sob, for she had none to give. Elizabeth gave him her lips instead, sharing what moisture she had, not caring that his own cracked and bled, his mouth as coarse as dust.

She gave what she could until Harris arrived with more light, Bella gasping at the sight.

For once, Elizabeth was grateful she could see only dim, blurry shapes.

Harris turned Annabelle away. "Head down, luv. Don't look. Go find 'im some clothes, a blanket, anythin' t' cover 'im."

Bella hurried off as Elizabeth handed Harris the key. Her hands shook too much, her sight too poor. The moment Harris unlocked Jasper's shackles, her husband slumped into his friend's arms.

Together, they half carried, half dragged Jasper between them, blinking into the bright glow of Finch's gilded office. There, Annabelle wrapped a wall drape about him for modesty, as Elizabeth searched for water but found only spirits and port.

Jasper drank the port in fits and starts, hunched in Finch's large desk chair. Harris, meanwhile, pulled Annabelle's knife from Finch's body. He wiped the blade on the dead man's sleeve and handed it to her.

"I must return t' the tables—my men await me signal. Remain here with Jasp and trust only those who give my name if they approach."

Annabelle gripped the blade and nodded.

"And the bloke at the door's out cold, shouldn't stir, but if he—"

"Never mind him. Make haste," Annabelle told him.

Elizabeth barely registered the kiss Harris gave her sister. She stood behind Jasper, unsure if she might touch him. He continued to gulp port beneath the heavy drape, buried in its crimson folds.

She did not dare.

Annabelle fetched one of Finch's bottles and stood watch beside the guard's unconscious body. When the fellow groaned, she removed a kerchief from her pocket, doused it with drink, and smothered the man's face.

CHAPTER FORTY-ONE

In the end, escape was easier than Elizabeth expected, for Mr. Harris chose a thief's exit over a warrior's. He let his men play out their coin to keep Finch's dealers and thugs no wiser, taking but a handful with him to smuggle Elizabeth, Jasper, and Annabelle out.

They left Finch where he lay and his guard's unconscious body at the door in greeting. Harris thought it best the East End assume Jasper Audrey had slit Hieronymus Finch's throat. It wouldn't be the first time Jasp had escaped *The Canary's Lair.*

The hansom ride back was silent. Harris kept Bella close, and Elizabeth supported her husband's weight, his body still wrapped in Finch's thick drape. As her sister curled deeper into Harris's arms, Elizabeth listened to her husband's ragged, rapid breaths. He leaned so heavily against her shoulder it began to ache.

When the hansom pulled up to Milton's townhouse, Harris jumped from the carriage to run inside, bringing servants back with him to whisk Jasper from Elizabeth. Before she knew it, Gerald was helping her out and barking orders for the doctor to be fetched. Soon Murdoch was leading her upstairs to her room, where Ginny's voice soothed, *All will be well, ma'am. Leave it t' Murdoch an' Gerald. Some warm milk before bed.*

Elizabeth protested—she wished to see Jasper—but Murdoch insisted the doctor be allowed to do his job. Elizabeth might go later, after. Ginny's voice lulled her more as she was stripped of her wig and bawdy dress, then tucked into bed and plied with milk. Elizabeth's head sank into the softness of the pillow, eyes closing as Ginny smoothed her brow with a warm cloth.

Before she knew it, she'd drifted into a deep but troubled sleep, only to awake in a sweat, heart racing with visions of blood flowing from Jasper's split head, drowning them all in a wave of murky red that rushed like rapids through Finch's cavernous, glowing vault. Elizabeth leapt from her bed and flew to her husband's room to make sure he lived, breathed.

She was stopped dead in her tracks by the sight that met her.

Gerald sat slumped in a chair beside his master, snoring faintly, with Mutton sprawled at his master's bare feet. And Jasper, poor Jasper, lay on his chest, his back riddled with wounds, his flesh wickedly flayed. They'd washed and stitched his injuries, but the slicing cuts and striped lashings—

Elizabeth bit her knuckle to stem the cry about to burst from her pounding chest.

She forced herself to look, to burn her husband's wounds into her brain, while she quietly, bitterly wept. She knelt beside him, careful not to wake him, and though she knew she ought to ask permission, she brushed a curl from his pale forehead and traced the lines of his gaunt, exhausted face.

He was returned to her. That was all that mattered.

She remained on the floor beside him until her head fell to his bed, matching him breath for anguished breath.

"Lizzie." Milton's voice startled her awake. "Go."

For a moment she wasn't sure where she even was. Her

knees felt stiff and sore. "Jasper." She raised her head, confused. "I—"

"Go," he ordered more forcefully.

"But—"

"Leave!" His voice was harsh, his eyes fierce, burning.

She blinked back tears. "No, I'll not go! I've worried sick and will not now—"

"Gerald!" He barked, the butler snorting awake. "Take her away. I want her gone. *Now.*"

And Gerald, standing quickly, took Elizabeth in hand to drag her from the room.

"Why are you doing this? Gerald, let me go! Why do you not wish to see me? Jasper, I wish only to—"

But he averted his gaze, refusing even to look at her, as Gerald ushered her back to her chamber and locked the adjoining door behind him.

Elizabeth stood alone in the middle of her bedroom.

Her husband did not want her. Had he ever?

Naked and chained, like a dog on a leash. Worse. Treated worse than a bloody dog.

Milton brutally berated himself for walking straight into Finch's trap. He'd grown soft in wealth and foolish at that—a fool, as well, to think marriage to a blueblood might achieve a blasted thing. He'd endangered his wife, her sister, and Ginny. Three women at Finch's bleak mercy all because of him. Fuck!

He strained at his irons until the shackles bit his wrists.

"Feels like home, don't it, Jasp?" Finch's voice rang out in the cave's echoing darkness. "Like y' never left, eh? 'Cause y' ne'er did, boy. An' now, thanks t' you, I'll have meself a fine wife, with yer own fine missus to do me every biddin'."

His laugh sent a shudder down Milton's taut spine before that voice hissed sudden and low in Milton's left ear. "I couldn't ask fer a better whippin' boy, Jasp. Missed yer somethin' awful when y' left. Though y' didn't leave politely, didya, lad? Y' left me fer dead."

The slow drag of Finch's blade dripped blood down Milton's hip. He knew this course of torture, knew exactly how Finch toyed with flesh. He prayed for death. Harris would marry Bella, and Li would counsel Elizabeth as his widow, ensuring Ginny and the rest of staff remained employed, secure. He wasn't needed. He'd failed them enough.

"Jasper..." Finch's lips brushed his ear, the man's breath hot as hellfire. "Where'd y' go, boy? I want yer here, with me. 'Tis what makes this so delightful. Remember all the good times we two had? Remember how y' screamed so loud y' begged me fer a gag?"

Milton panicked like a child. Anything but—

Too late, a stale rag was shoved into his mouth and knotted tight behind his head. He thrashed and strained and—

"Jasp!" A hand shook Milton's arm, puncturing the scene. "Jasper, you're dreamin'. Wake!"

Milton's eyes flew open to Gerald's concerned face.

"'Twas but a dream. You're safe, lad. Safe."

Sweat poured down Milton's cheeks, or were they tears instead? He lifted his hands to his face and saw they shook.

"Rest now. Go on, sleep."

"Gerald, how long have I been sleeping?"

"Drink this."

Milton took one sip of the bittersweet liquid and thrust the glass back. "No laudanum, damn you! I do not wish to sleep!"

His butler frowned but set aside the glass.

"Don't let her see me like this."

Tears. Bloody tears streamed uncontrolled down his face.

"I couldn't bear it, do you hear me? Keep her away, Gerald. Whatever it takes, keep her out."

Death would be a better fate.

❧

Annabelle shivered beneath the bedclothes, terrified to be alone with her thoughts. Arthur had tucked her into bed at *The Leaf* after shooing Janie's curious self out—*You'll get yer missing frock back, woman, off with you now, 'tis late!*—but the specter of Finch, gutted by her own hand, ate at her conscience.

She could still feel the blade's resistance as she'd pressed hard through cloth and flesh, the shock on Finch's face, his sharp intake of—

Arthur brought her hand to his lips. "I've things t' attend to, luv. Get some rest."

"Arthur…"

"Hush now. We'll discuss all once you've slept."

"Arthur, stay with me, please?" She couldn't bear to be alone. Not yet.

He met her eyes with kindness, then slipped under the bedclothes and wrapped her in his warm, strong arms. Only then did she feel safe, burrowing into his comforting heat. And she must have drifted off, because the next thing she knew a hand stroked her awake, softly cupping her cheek. Annabelle pressed her face deeper into that hand to escape the light that pierced her eyelids.

"Mrs. Harris." Arthur spoke softly. "You are without doubt the bravest, most reckless woman to grace this earth. Why, I ought to turn you over my knee for the insanity of what you and your sister attempted last night on your own."

She opened her eyes to peer up at him. "Kiss me, Arthur."

And he did. He met her lips with pulls and nips as his hand crept softly up her leg.

"Should I discipline or reward you, wife?" he murmured at her neck.

"Arthur…"

"Yes, luv?" His tongue traced a path down her collarbone, his hand nearly at its destination.

"Arthur, I do not wish to wait," she whispered. For she

didn't. She'd nearly lost him, nearly *been lost* herself to Finch. Arthur Harris was all she wanted now and forever.

"Blast it, Bella!" His demeanor instantly changed. "I told you before I'll not—Christ, woman, why must you be so bloody insistent?"

Annabelle was aroused, embarrassed, and wounded, all at once. No, she was humiliated.

He must think her no better than a tease.

"I am sorry I displease you." She swallowed her hurt and grief. "You are right, of course. I am intolerable in a great many ways, but as your wife, I do not think I am being unreasonable in this." She willed her heart not to break. "Perhaps it were best we part beds, now that pretense is no longer needed."

"Bella…"

"This way you may get on with your business, and I with my life."

She threw off the bedclothes to vacate his chamber as fast as her legs would carry her. She was like any other woman with loose morals who offered herself at *The Leaf.* No, worse. Because *those* women Arthur had bedded, and he would not bed her.

From the hall she heard him loudly utter, "Fuck!"

CHAPTER FORTY-TWO

"Ma'am, y' mustn't take it personally. Jasper's had an awful time of it an' needs his space is all." Murdoch's attempt to soothe only irked Elizabeth more.

"But I am his *wife*." She remained ardent. "Who better to care for him, tend his needs, than myself?"

Murdoch plunked the breakfast tray across Elizabeth's lap, expelled a loud sigh, and sat on the edge of the bed. "Ma'am, yer husband don't wish fer yer company right now, an' you'd be wise t' heed him. What he don't need is more upset, so you can rant all you likes t' me an' staff, but you'll obey his wishes in this."

"I do not appreciate your tone, Murdoch."

"An' don't I know it." The housekeeper's lips thinned. "But me duty's t' Jasp; I'll not be swayed. You do yer job as mistress o' this house, an' I'll do mine. An' when Jasper's ready—when *he's* ready, mind—he'll be yer husband again."

Elizabeth huffed, for what more could she say? Her husband did not wish to see her, though she longed to see him. She must be patient. She must do her duty. She must obey his wishes. Even now, in this, she was forced to follow his bloody rules.

A week had passed since they'd brought Milton home, and by all accounts he was healing well. But she did not know this for herself, because he still refused to see her. He let only his most trusted servants into his room, along with his mother and Li, which made Elizabeth privately seethe. Miss Li had begged an audience with Lady Milton, as had Mary Audrey, but she'd refused both in a fit of pique. It hurt too much to know her husband trusted everyone but her, his wife.

She knew she should be patient—he'd suffered horrors she could not begin to comprehend. But she could not quell her overwhelming need to connect to him again. Nor did she understand why he rejected her so completely.

It just hurt, all of it, damnably much.

Elizabeth did her best to behave as a good wife should and must, but she was desperate for delivery from this impasse. She'd called twice on Annabelle already, but though Bella claimed all was fine, her sister did not seem happy in her marriage to Mr. Harris. Not that Elizabeth had strength to dwell on Annabelle; she could barely bring herself to read, let alone write—the two pursuits she had always depended on for comfort in bleak times.

She'd received a response from Milton's tutor, Mr. Kilpert, in the midst of her distress, though she'd nearly forgotten that she'd written to the man. He'd replied in such a perfectly polite manner, happy to instruct the Baron in dance, that she'd been taken aback by how normal his words read—in contrast to her husband's continued, confounding behavior.

She'd written back at once, explaining the Baron was presently unwell but would inform Mr. Kilpert himself when he wished to begin instruction. And then her mind had turned again to Milton. Would he deign to speak to her today, or invite her to his room, to his bed again? Perhaps he would shun her now indefinitely. She could not know, for she knew nothing of her husband anymore. Nothing!

She had only Gerald's words for comfort: *He's healin' fine, ma'am. He'll see yer when he's ready. Yes, he saw Miss Li again today. Don't worry yerself, Lady Milton.*

But of course she worried. At length.

Did Gerald think her so unfeeling? Did everyone think her immune to her husband's pain?

❧

He'd not face her. He couldn't.

Milton remained in a dark spiral of hurt, allowing only those who'd known him longest—known Finch themselves—entry to his chamber. He was desperate to avoid his wife, whose very presence brought on panic. The fact that she had witnessed him in such degraded state, chained naked like a beast—*that she and her goddamned sister had been the ones to rescue him for fuck's sake!*—filled him with such self-loathing, he could not bear to look at her, converse with her, let alone make love to her.

He was a shell of his former self. Unworthy of her respect.

Milton had warned Gerald that if Elizabeth were let into his room again he would dismiss the entire household. And he meant it. Both Li and his mother had pleaded otherwise, but theirs were the arguments of women; he could not forgive himself for needing saving. He'd not even been able to save his wife's sister, for God's sake, bloody Arty had. His thoughts spun in circles, his dreams, both waking and sleeping, wracked by tortures recent and those buried deep in his past. His body might well be healing, but his mind remained a wretched morass.

Again and again he returned to that moment in Finch's dungeon when Lizzie's voice had washed over him like a gentle spring rain—the smell of her, the heat of her soft, womanly self brushing his ravaged, flayed flesh…

It had been a punishment worse than death.

❧

When you hear men talking … all they ever do is speak ill of women. … And I don't quite know … who exactly it was who gave them a greater license to sin than is allowed to us; and if the fault is common to both sexes (as they can hardly deny), why should the blame not be as well? What makes them think they can boast of the same thing that in women brings only shame?

"Lady Milton, have you shared this passage with your husband?"

"I have not, Mr. Kilpert," she answered. "I doubt very much Fonte's work would interest the Baron."

"Oh I should think the very opposite, ma'am." Kilpert smiled. "Fonte is precisely the sort of writer Jasper likes to sink his teeth into. Your husband relishes thorny ideas. We do not always agree, of course, in our interpretations, but he is always open to debate. In fact, he consistently approaches our discussions with sound reason, rather than mount ineffectual, emotional arguments."

Mr. Kilpert could not possibly be describing Elizabeth's husband. Milton's tutor had unexpectedly stopped by to enquire after the Baron's health, and as Elizabeth had been reading the Duchess's book to distract herself from her woes, she'd taken the opportunity to ask his opinion on a passage.

Not only had the gentleman's answer not disappointed, he seemed to welcome, and even respect, her thoughts.

"Perhaps the Baron is open to masculine debate, sir, but I assure you any reasoning I, his wife, engage in is met with derision. I should never be so bold as to hand my husband this book."

"I am sorry to hear that, Lady Milton." Kilpert frowned. "I admit, I took you for more courageous."

Heat rose to Elizabeth's cheeks as she flipped to a different passage to hide her embarrassment. She cleared her throat:

> *And when it's said that women must be subject to men, the phrase should be understood in the same sense as when we say we are subject to natural disasters, diseases, and all the other accidents of this life: it's not a case of being subjected in the sense of obeying, but rather of suffering an imposition, not a case of serving them fearfully, but rather of tolerating them in a spirit of Christian charity, since they have been given to us by God as a spiritual trial.*

"Ah yes." Kilpert nodded enthusiastically. "I recall that passage well, Lady Milton, for its indictment not just of man but of God."

Elizabeth's heart beat faster. "I believe Fonte describes woman's plight with absolute precision, sir."

Kilpert leaned forward. "So you agree men are a spiritual trial? You do not think Fonte's words contain, perhaps, a hint of humor?"

"Mr. Kilpert, men are without doubt woman's greatest trial."

"Greater even than the perils of childbirth?"

"Are they not the same peril?" she countered. "Without man, woman does not suffer birth—neither its pain nor risk. Man subjugates woman physically by impregnating her, just as he subjugates her morally and intellectually by imposing his will upon her."

"And yet without both sexes humanity ceases to exist, their

joining required to perpetuate our species. Without man, woman, too, ceases to exist."

"But Fonte does not argue biology, Mr. Kilpert. She argues society, morality, history. It is in these realms men systematically subjugate women." Elizabeth warmed to their debate. "How different might society look were our roles reversed and women held power over their own bodies. Our species should continue even then, should it not?"

"May I?"

Elizabeth handed him her book. He flipped ahead and read:

> *Do you really believe ... that everything historians tell us about men—or about women—is actually true? You ought to consider the fact that these histories have been written by men, who never tell the truth except by accident.*

Elizabeth smiled as their eyes met. Mr. Kilpert was exceptional. A man unafraid to speak truth. She wished her husband had this scholar's moral fortitude.

***

Just outside the drawing room, Milton overheard all. He was, to put it mildly, livid.

He took off down the hall, emotions churning in his breast. Who the hell did Lizzie think she was, taking over *his* weekly sessions with Paul? He did not recall approving this—he recalled telling her she could hire herself a different tutor, anyone but Kilpert. Yet here she was, discussing radical ideas with his man.

Though what else should he expect? He'd lost command of her the moment she'd rescued him from Finch. And once obedience was lost, it was impossible to regain, let alone retain, control of one's wife.

Elizabeth was clearly enamored of his tutor, who was everything Milton was not: well-bred, erudite, and disgustingly polite. Paul Kilpert was not the sort of fellow who needed to purchase himself a high-born wife. He didn't need rules to protect his wife from himself, didn't need his wife to submit to him in bed for fear he'd lose control of himself. No, he was the ideal bloody gentleman for a lady like Elizabeth.

And Milton loathed him for it.

He hated Elizabeth too, for not wanting, not choosing *him*. He'd held hope before Finch, had sensed her warm to him, hell, begin to like him even. But he'd mistaken tolerance for affection. For *love*.

The rotten word popped unbidden to mind, a stab to his chest. Love did not enter into marriage, was not synonymous with a wife. A man loved his friends, his family. Milton would love his children someday. He prayed Elizabeth was with child already so he needn't make more visits to her bed. For if she wasn't…

He felt viscerally punched by the thought, forced to press his back against the wall to keep the world from spinning.

What if she was already pregnant? What if by entering *The Canary's Lair* she'd put not only herself but his heir at risk? Christ, what if both she and the babe had died? Panic so intense filled his breast he—

"Jasper?" Murdoch appeared at his side like a blessed vision. "You alright, boy? Y' look like you've seen a ghost. I'll have a cuppa brought t' yer room." She frowned with concern. "I've not seen you up an' roamin' th' halls, Jasp. 'Tis good t' have yer about again."

"Murdoch, please." He brushed her off as he gulped a lungful of air. "I've no wish for bloody *tea*."

"Shall I tell the mistress, then, that you're—?"

"No, you are not to tell your mistress you have seen me at all. Nor have I any desire to see her."

Murdoch's concern turned. "You're makin' a mistake, Jasp." She leveled her gaze at him. "You keep hidin' from yer wife like this and she'll start t' think y' care not a whit for her no more."

"And what if I don't?" he snarled, his insides roiling. "What if I married her for her title only, an' she fer me coin? What then do it matter if I hides or flees from 'er, eh? It don't! So leave me th' hell alone, Martha." His speech had disintegrated along with all shred of self-control. "An' mind you follow orders an' stop meddlin' in me affairs."

Milton leaned heavily against the wall to keep from falling as Martha Murdoch stomped off with a parting huff. Disgust filled his soul. For himself, for Elizabeth, and for blasted Paul Kilpert.

CHAPTER FORTY-THREE

No longer did the brooding baron eye his captive with a lecherous, bold gleam. He now abandoned her for days on

Elizabeth put down her quill and sighed. "Bella, what ails you?"

She tried to hide the fact she wished her husband, rather than her sister, had just interrupted her writing. Because she'd not had one word from Milton still, despite the stern talking-to she had delivered both Murdoch and Gerald regarding the Baron's untenable behavior.

They'd been unable to sway him either.

"It's gone, Lizzie." Bella tore off her gloves.

"What is, dear?"

"Your necklace. The one you gave me to pawn. The one I swore I'd return. *Gone.*"

"Are you certain? Did the Lombard say who bought it? And the terms of the loan…" She frowned. "Has it truly been so long since you—?"

"That's just it, Lizzie. I had enough to buy it back and had every intention of doing so, but then Arthur dragged me to

Gretna, and when we returned all thought was only for Milton, and now…" She looked distraught. "I am so sorry, sister, truly. I never meant to lose it."

Elizabeth sprinkled pounce on her page. "Given the Baron's present mood, Bella, I doubt very much he will inquire after some necklace."

In truth, the only business Milton inquired after anymore seemed to be business itself. He holed himself up in his office to pore over what? His overflowing coffers and the daily newspapers? She knew he took long walks with Mutton and even longer rides in Hyde Park, by all outward appearances healed from his ordeal. At least, the doctor no longer stopped by.

"Lizzie, is the Baron still unwell?"

Elizabeth hated when Annabelle read her thoughts. "I do not wish to speak of him. I wish to hear from you, sister."

Only Bella did not say more. Instead, she stood there and wrung her hands in the same annoying manner as Papa.

"Dear, in a week's time you will come of age. Have you discussed your future at all with Mr. Harris? Because I must be honest. The law makes it exceedingly difficult to—Bella, would you cease twitching!" Elizabeth could not take a second more.

Annabelle dropped with a thud into a chair.

"Please be frank with me about your feelings for Mr. Harris."

And Bella was. She declared herself utterly, miserably in love with Arthur Harris, who lamentably, regrettably did not love her back.

Elizabeth was not surprised by her sister's impassioned response, but it was hardly love Annabelle must feel for the man. Love existed in myth and story only, not in the misery of everyday life. Surely, Bella confused gratitude for affection when it came to Mr. Harris. Though gratitude was not the worst way to begin a marriage.

She feigned a headache so that her sister would leave, her

thoughts returning to her own cur of a husband who did not merit her concern in the least. She deplored how the entire household now tiptoed about the Baron as if he were a fragile vase, or worse, a box of lit tinder. She couldn't stand the fact she lay in bed nights debating going to his room, begging him to tell her all that plagued him.

Elizabeth knew what plagued him: demons neither she nor anyone in this house could vanquish. Instead, they all walked on eggshells about their master while he spurned every attempt at approach.

Her only comfort had been her brief conversation with Mr. Kilpert—and her writing, which she'd taken up with a vengeance. *The Brooding Baron* grew more dark with every page she penned, for the hero was no longer the lady's savior. He was a thorn in her side, his motives obscure.

She shook off the pounce and re-read the last line she'd just inked .

> *No longer did the brooding baron eye his captive with a lecherous, bold gleam. He now abandoned her for days on*

Elizabeth dipped her quill in ink.

> *end, locked in his rented room, to go where she did not know. The landlord alone delivered the lady sustenance, tasteless fare, but she ate it nonetheless. She was determined to survive.*
>
> *Only the landlord soon sent a servant in his stead, a lackey instructed to ignore her every plea, but she would not give up her attempts. The lady began to converse with the servant at mealtimes, using every feminine charm she possessed. And slowly the man spoke back, grunts only at first, until she'd gleaned he, too, was a prisoner in this house, beholden to the wicked baron.*
>
> *She must break not only her own chains now but help this poor*

servant break his. Perhaps in solidarity there was hope. Perhaps together they might defeat the baron.

The lady had no choice but to try.

❧

From outside, in the hall, Milton observed them hunched over a book, seated so close their foreheads almost touched.

Inside him, something snapped.

He stepped into his parlor. "Kilpert, I did not give you permission to tutor or seduce my wife." His snarl made the scholar jump and Elizabeth drop the book.

Kilpert instantly stood. "Jasper, I assure you, I have not—"

"You most certainly *have* been making love to my wife in a most egregious manner."

"Milton!" Lizzie's initial elated expression quickly turned to dismay. "Why, nothing could be further from the truth. Mr. Kilpert simply—"

"How dare you shamelessly cavort with another man under my roof, woman?"

"Jasper, please," Kilpert beseeched. "This is a simple misunderstanding which—"

"I gave neither of you permission to meet," Milton stated coldly. "Yet you have done so behind my back, and even now—"

"Milton," Elizabeth cut in, "for God's sake, listen to yourself." Her small frame shook. "Before you fell … ill, I wrote to Mr. Kilpert asking him to instruct you in dance, as you had agreed. When I replied to his response, I informed him you were unwell. He only stopped by to enquire after your health." She paused as if to steady herself—or embellish her tidy story. "Had you deigned to speak with me, I'd have discussed his letter with you, but instead you've spurned my every attempt to—"

"Instead, you thought only of your own interests."

"No! That is the—that is the very opposite of what I—"

"Elizabeth, you may cease with your excuses, and Kilpert, I no longer require your services."

"Jasper." The man tried again. "Lady Milton speaks the truth, for had I known you disapproved of our meeting, I should never have—"

"You've had your eye on her since the Denbigh ball, sir, don't try to deny it."

Kilpert's blush confirmed as much. "Baron." He defended himself. "I admit your wife is an exceptional woman, but I would never be so bold as to—"

"But you have, and you'd be bolder still, no doubt, with time. So let us do away with pretense and speed things to their natural completion. Lizzie, on your knees."

Her face blenched as Kilpert's eyes widened into saucers.

"Did you not hear me?" Milton's gaze pierced Elizabeth. "I have her trained, you see." He glanced at Kilpert's horrified face. "She obeys my every order."

His words were foul, but the beast inside him demanded to be fed. "I'll let her give you payment, as it were, for services rendered." He pushed Lizzie to her knees before Paul. "And since she remains my legal wife, it's best I watch the transaction, to ensure payment is received in full."

Elizabeth struggled to rise but Milton held her down, gripping her shoulders as he pushed her toward Kilpert's crotch.

"*Jasper*," Paul hissed, fists balled at his sides. "Do not do this. The man I know you to be, the man I admire, would never demean his wife in this manner."

But Milton's hands only tightened on Lizzie's frame, digging into her dress. "Elizabeth will service you in my presence, rather than do so behind my back."

With a look of pure disgust, Kilpert stormed from the room.

Elizabeth wrenched herself free. "Bastard," she hissed from the floor. "How could you be so cruel? To your own friend, to *me*!"

Her pain mirrored perfectly the ache in Milton's breast. He stared at her, at a loss for words.

"How could you treat me so abominably, when for weeks I have worried myself sick for you! When *all* I longed for was your safe return, your health and well-being." She backed away from him on the floor like a wounded, cornered animal. "You are despicable to treat me thus. You are the very worst of humans, Jasper Audrey, to turn the love and respect of marriage into something so hideously *ugly*!"

Elizabeth fled the room in tears.

Milton stood a moment longer in his parlor, frozen in place. Had she said *love* in regards to their marriage? Had she uttered the word *respect*?

He walked right out of his lavish townhouse. Not once did he look back.

❧

Elizabeth stumbled to her room, to her bed, tears stinging her eyes. She could neither forget nor forgive what Milton had just done, whoring her to another man on his parlor floor. She was not a wife, she was chattel.

And her husband was no better than Hieronymus Finch. Whatever tortures Milton had endured, whatever evils others had inflicted to make him into the monster he was, did not absolve him of this crime. She had obeyed him in marriage, denied her own needs, compromised her own morals and judgment as his wife, but this crossed a line.

Now, she could hope only for survival. She would wall herself into her room with her books and her writing and avoid him at all cost, simply suffering his existence. She would destroy all hint of feeling she'd ever held for Jasper Audrey and resign herself instead to the brute he'd just savagely shown himself to be.

Elizabeth physically recoiled from her thoughts, a wave of nausea overcoming her so fast she rushed to her bedroom washstand to lose the contents of her stomach, as if she purged her husband from her soul.

CHAPTER FORTY-FOUR

Milton wandered the streets, the park, the Thames all night. He walked the city he knew, where he'd lived all his life, in better or worse hellholes. Where he'd lied and cheated and thieved and yes, even killed. But never in all his years on London's streets had he felt so bereft as this.

He no longer knew why he'd done it. He'd been angry, of course. He'd wanted to punish both Lizzie and Paul but more, perhaps, he'd wished to punish himself. Because now she'd leave be. Surely now Elizabeth would cease her ridiculous attempts to reconcile, to make him into a respectable husband. What lady in her right mind would love a man like him? Li hadn't, and Elizabeth was even more righteous and principled. He'd been a fool to hope. Worse still, he'd let Lizzie down—he, who'd sworn to protect his family, had let them all down when he'd allowed Finch to snatch him from Winthrop's house as if he were a boy and not a grown, goddamned man.

The moment that devil had put him in irons, he'd been lost.

"D'you enjoy our play as much as I do?" Finch's knife twisted an

open wound, making Milton's nerves scream and his body shake, forcing his brain back.

"Stay with me, boy. Don't leave now. I need yer here, feelin' the fine flick o' me blade."

Milton's flesh was licked by fire, his insides ablaze.

"Count fer me, boy. Remember?"

As I was goin' to St. Ives,
Upon the road I met seven wives;
Every wife had seven sacks,
Every sack had seven cats,
Every cat had seven kits:
Kits, cats, sacks, an' wives,
How many were goin' to St. Ives?

God, not this wicked, evil game! Milton knew the bloody answer. He'd learned it the hard way, same way he'd learned to count every wound carved into his flesh. If all were bound for St. Ives—the narrator, the wives, the sacks and cats and kits—'twas 2,801.

Instead, he held up one shaking middle finger, because only one man in that trick rhyme traveled—the narrator was the correct answer.

Finch bent Milton's finger back until the bone nearly snapped. Nearly, because the fiend knew just how far to take a man to make him break. It's what the devil enjoyed most.

"Ain't no fun t' end so soon, boy. We'll have t' play a different game." And his grating, lazy voice began a new, twisted rhyme.

Sing a song of sixpence,
A bag full of rye,
Four and twenty naughty boys,
Baked in a pie.

When the pie was opened,
The birds began to sing.

Wasn't that a dandy dish
To set before the king?

"I were set t' make you me heir, Jasp—with your blue blood and my sharp brains, what all we could've accomplished… But y' ruined that." His face soured, the blade digging deep enough now Milton screamed.

In desperation he pictured Lizzie, willing his mind to hold fast to her sweet visage instead. He'd focus only on her innocence, her loveliness, as he took the twenty-four blows meant to filet his body—the pie's baked crust. For he was Finch's naughty boy, and clearly always would be. But if he held on to his wife's warm smile, her spectacles winking in sunlight, she might become his dish, and he her one true king. She'd give him four and twenty strapping sons, birds heralding each birth, singing of futures bright, so bright…

Blight. Milton viciously kicked a stone off the pier.

It was better Elizabeth hate him.

Is that why he'd done it? Why he'd treated her and Kilpert as he had? To spare her worse hurt? He gazed out at the water, moonlight sparkling across its grim depths. How many bodies lay at the bottom of the Thames, those drowned willingly, and those tossed in, their lives cut brutally short? At least now Lizzie would cease trying. It was astonishing, really, how valiantly she'd tried to make their doomed marriage work, tried to grow affection for him. But he was a worthless cause. He could be neither reformed nor remade—by her or anyone.

Once a whipping boy, always a whipping boy.

A day later, Milton braced himself for Dr. Hollingsforth's assessment, because Murdoch had called the doctor not for him this time, but for his Baroness, who apparently now cast up what little she managed to swallow. He'd not visited Lizzie's chamber nor spoken to her since the incident in his parlor. Nor had he heard from Kilpert, though he'd penned the man a short letter of apology. He had no proof the scholar had done anything worse than make eyes at his wife. And one couldn't call a man out for looking, no matter how much one wanted to.

"It appears your wife suffers two distinct conditions, Jasp."

"Are they curable?" Milton cut to the chase.

"One, yes, the other, I fear, less."

"Well, out with it, Doc."

"Jasper, are you feeling well yourself? After all you endured I suspect you—"

"I am healed." He was irritated this man had seen him at his lowest. Everyone bloody had.

"The good news is your wife is with child, and the bad news is she suffers a dark melancholy."

Shock, elation, terror—all at once—coursed through Milton's veins.

"It happens to some, this melancholy, though usually it comes after, not before, the birth."

"She is with child?" Milton repeated in a stupor.

"Yes, though it is early still."

"And her health otherwise? I was told she's not been eating."

"Normal for early pregnancy; in a few weeks she'll lose the nausea and gain back the weight. That is not what concerns me. What I worry about is her—"

"I'm to be a father, *Christ*." Terror, elation. Again.

"Jasper, Lady Milton is strong enough to physically bear your heir, but her humors remain unbalanced. She is listless and gloomy, with little regard for herself. And if the babe is to be born healthy, the mother must get fresh air and mild exercise in addition to eating well."

Milton barely listened. He was to be a father. *Fuck*.

"In my experience, a woman's emotional state can affect

the health of the developing child, not to mention her capacity to care for that child once born."

"I—forgive me, Doc, I am ... I did not expect such news so soon."

"Well, you've been married some while now, Jasp."

"Yes."

"You must ensure her mood improves, else the health of your heir may suffer."

Milton finally heard the man.

"I do not know the cause of your wife's melancholy, Jasper, but I suggest you uncover it."

Milton sucked in his next breath. *He* was the cause of Lizzie's unhappiness, but not a blasted thing would change that. She was stuck with him, God help her. As he was stuck with her.

"I shall do my best, sir."

"Good." Hollingsforth rose from his seat. "I'll check on her again next week, see if her nausea has abated. And Jasp"—he gave Milton a stern look—"take care of yourself too. Your wounds may be healed, but less visible scars remain."

"It is my wife you need worry about, sir. Not me." Milton ushered the man out, eager to avoid more scrutiny.

❧

Elizabeth did not believe the doctor's words. She was not with child; she was simply ill, in bed. Sick to her stomach, perhaps, but mainly sick at heart.

Not even her sister's joy upon learning she was to become an aunt cheered Elizabeth's spirits. She'd barely been able to stomach Annabelle's most recent visit, casting up her breakfast before her sister's very eyes.

She desperately did not wish to be pregnant. It bound her only more to the Baron when she'd begun to fantasize faking her death and changing her name, allowing Milton to marry again. Or had that been a chapter in her novel?

Some other woman could give her husband his coveted heirs, because he clearly did not want her for his wife. Elizabeth lay listless in bed and wished herself dead.

Only that wasn't true, damnation, because she didn't want to die, she wanted her rotten husband back! She wanted the man she'd begun to uncover, whom she'd quietly, secretly hoped had grown fond of her too. There'd been signs he cared, enjoyed her company beyond mere enjoyment of her flesh. Before Finch, she'd held hope.

Now no hint of the man she thought she'd known remained.

The Baron still did not deign to speak to her. Not once had he visited her sickbed, even knowing she now carried his long-sought heir. Though one night she'd dreamt he stood over her, staring down with tears in his eyes. A dream.

His disregard, his treatment of her was inhumane.

She crawled out from under the bedclothes to fetch a sheaf of paper and a heavy book. She laid the blank pages atop the book's hard cover, placed the inkwell within bedside reach, and began to write an entirely new story. The brooding baron would not brood. Instead, he'd be hell bent on the heroine's complete annihilation, though the lady would of course fight back.

In this story, Elizabeth would kill the antihero and resurrect him as an entirely new man. Failing that, she'd kill the heroine. Something, someone, had to die—or change.

CHAPTER FORTY-FIVE

It was a relief Mrs. Harris no longer slept in Mr. Harris's bed. She'd taken a room of her own, albeit not on the same floor with his working girls, and Harris once again kept her busy at his books. He, meanwhile, was doing his utmost to annul their blasted marriage, with progress slower than he wished due to one sticking point: his solicitor deemed the feat impossible.

Which is why Harris had spoken to Jasp, who'd sent him to *his* man instead. Jasper's solicitor thought there might be a way around matters, but he did not guarantee success, and Harris did not like the solution. Only it didn't matter what he liked, he had to try for Annabelle's sake. Thus, he had agreed to have the man draw up a damning document listing every rotten deed Harris had ever done, including quite a few he hadn't.

It was finished just in time for his wife's twenty-first birthday, though Harris gave it to her a day early.

"Arthur, what is this?"

"A gift."

"How did you know tomorrow is my—?"

"The girls all talk, Bella. Y' think I don't hear things?"

She blushed.

"I hope you're pleased."

She skimmed the contents, her face clouding over. "But Arthur, this is dreadful. It paints you in a terrible light. Why, to read it one would think you the most dishonorable, reprehensible rake in all of London!"

"Yup, added in the dastardly parts meself. Quite th' story, eh?" He was pleased with his work.

"But why do such a thing?" Her lovely face crumpled. "Why would you knowingly perjure yourself in such awful, unflattering terms?"

"T' make it legal." He frowned back at her. "The solicitor says there must be blame—irrevocable proof—t' achieve annulment. He insisted a doctor prove yer chastity too, but I paid the feller off so you needn't submit t' no exam."

"You mean a doctor would have—?" Her face turned scarlet.

"Bella, don't worry yer pretty head o'er aught what got written. Society deems me a lowlife as 'tis. Y' need only sign t'morrow in the presence o' me solicitor as witness, an' the matter'll be done." He did not understand why her entire body seemed to radiate displeasure. "Why the long face? I thought it were the perfect gift."

"Oh it is perfect, all right." Her eyes began to fill. "It is perfectly splendid. I don't mind in the least what you have allowed them to write about you, not in the *least*!"

And out she ran, tears spilling from her eyes and the document discarded on his desk, making Harris wonder what the hell he'd done this time to rile her.

Come morning Arthur's working ladies surprised Annabelle with a birthday tray, replete with chocolate and flowers.

She pulled the covers over her head and told them to go away.

Janie shooed the others out, threatening Annabelle, "Now that ain't no way to treat folks, Mrs. Harris, an' as I'm sure Arty'd like t' congratulate you too, you'd best—"

"He won't." Annabelle sniffed. "He doesn't want me, Janie. Never has."

Arthur's house madam yanked on the bedclothes, exposing Annabelle to the brisk morning air. "What's this now?"

"He's drawn up a document to annul our marriage." She yanked them back.

"Well o' course he has." Janie fisted her hips. "Arty always keeps his word." She took one look at Annabelle and pursed her lips. "Quite the pair you are." She tsked. "Looks like you've a choice t' make, Mrs. Harris, one yer husband'll not make for yer."

"But he already has." Annabelle roughly fluffed her pillow, then punched the thing outright. "I'm to sign his blasted document so he can send me away, so you and he and everyone here can go on living as though I never existed."

"You think he'd forget you that fast?" Janie's brow rose. "Why, he's been moonin' about th' place e'er since y' took yer own room. He's sweet on you, ma'am, only he knows he ain't good enough fer yer kind."

"Of course he is good enough!" Annabelle was outraged. "Arthur Harris is the most generous, kindhearted man I know."

"You talkin' 'bout the same man as dragged yer t' Gretna an' slit Finch's throat?"

"But that was—he did those things to protect me. Everything he did was—"

"I'm chaffin' yer." Janie grinned. "Arty's a gem."

"Then why say he is not good enough for me?"

"'Cause he's not titled—a whoreson same as Jasper. Only

Arty's no striver like yer sister's fancy Baron. He sticks to his own, meanin' he'll ne'er be yer equal in name."

"Well *I* am no striver either," Annabelle insisted.

Janie's lips twitched. "If y' want Arty as yer husband, ma'am, you'll have t' be more direct, 'cause he thinks he can't have you. Don't mean he don't want you."

"But I've *been* direct. I've—"

"Just bed the man, Bella, an' then he'll have t' stay married." She smirked. "An' do it afore them papers need signed. In fact, why not skip on o'er to 'is room right now?"

Annabelle thought Janie insane.

Until she did not.

Harris was roused by a tickle, as if a flea had got under his sheet. He reached to scratch the itch but was met with supple skin instead.

Had he been so rumdum last night he'd invited a chit to his bed? 'Twas true he'd tipped the brandy, but he'd stayed true to his bloody wedding vows this entire time.

He rolled and planted his face into a bosom that smelled divine. The plush, pillowy breasts reminded him of Bella the night he'd first educated the miss. Harris sampled one bud in his state of half-sleep and groaned. He climbed atop the inviting body, yet in place of give felt limbs stiffen, making him scramble off so fast he—

"Arthur, stop running from me, please! I wish to consummate our marriage, and I do not want to sign that awful document!"

Bella's face swam into focus as Harris froze, braced for flight beside his wife. He could not tear his eyes from her.

"I have tried to tell you, but you would not listen, or you chose not to hear, and I simply cannot bear the thought of never knowing your true feelings." She gulped. "If you do not want me for your wife, Arthur Harris, I will sign what I must and pester you no more. Only I think you the most wonderful, dear, generous man ever to—"

He kissed her in desperation, with a need so intense it overpowered his heart and loins. There'd be no leaving this bed or escaping his arms, not when body and brain had found union at last.

He'd make Mrs. Harris his wife for good this time. At last.

❧

"Jasp, y' ought t' speak with 'er."

Gerald's continued needling grated. It was late and Milton wanted his bed. His butler could go to hell.

"Gerald, if you continue to provoke me I'll—"

"What? Fire me an' half th' staff? Hire bloody strangers who'll care even less fer yer miserable self? Because I warn you, Jasper Audrey, our patience is growin' thin, an' yer wife sure as shite don't deserve such treatment either. If y' mean t' lose 'er fer good, boy, you're doin' a damn fine job of it."

Incensed by his butler's words, Milton reached for the nearest object to fling but instead crushed the thin glass in his grip. *"Fuck!"* He stared at the shattered mess of lamp dome on the floor, blood dripping from his hand.

Gerald snapped open a kerchief and neatly wrapped it around Milton's bleeding palm. "Soddin' idiot," he clucked like a surly hen. "You're an arse, Jasp, an' need more'n a few rounds in th' ring t' knock sense back into yer dull skull. Bustin' things like a boy…"

His butler pushed him toward another lamp and unwrapped Milton's bloody fist to begin plucking bits of glass from his flesh. He was still fussing when Elizabeth's billowy self rushed the room in her night-rail, spectacles askew. She looked from Milton, to the shattered oil lamp, to Gerald.

Too pale. Too thin. *Christ.*

"Forgive me," she said stiffly. "I heard something … break."

Her voice flayed his heart to ribbons.

"Lady Milton, will y' see t' Jasp a moment, please? I've an urgent matter downstairs." And out Gerald scurried, the bleeding opportunist.

Elizabeth cautiously approached.

Milton turned from her. "I can manage."

"Removing glass from one's dominant hand is no easy task."

His heart spasmed. "Someone else can—"

"Am I truly so abhorrent to you, sir, that you would spurn my offer to help?" Her words lashed. "I'll not speak, if my voice repulses. I will simply pluck out shards."

"Lizzie, that is not what I—"

"Don't speak to me either," she bit back. "Just allow me to assist." She took his hand in her palm.

He was both chastened and aroused by her presence, for it had been ages since they'd stood this close. The smell of her, her touch on his skin… The way her dark braid framed her neck, so elegantly elfin while the rest of her was so deliciously—

Milton forced himself not to think of his wife's anatomy. "I trust you are feeling better?"

She did not respond.

"I meant to offer my—"

"Congratulations?" The word puffed from her lips. "Are we at a house party, sir, that you only now acknowledge your wife is with child, with your precious heir?"

He deserved her ire. He deserved far worse. "I did not wish to upset you more during your convalescence."

"How considerate of you not to wish to *upset* me."

"Lizzie, I know I've been a—"

"Do not speak, sir. Your actions leave no doubt as to how little you regard me."

"Elizabeth, I cannot..." He was at a complete loss for words, while feeling miserably, abjectly sorry. To stand so near to her while she methodically pulled slivers from his hand was doing things to him which he'd tried desperately to avoid.

"I will remain your wife—I've no choice." Her tone stung. "And I will raise this child as best I am able, but I will engage in the bare minimum of necessary interaction with you, Baron. I have not forgotten your treatment of me or Mr. Kilpert."

Milton blinked as something wet fell to his hand.

"If you are in pain I will slow my efforts."

"It is nothing," he said stiffly.

The air between them blistered, yet when she finished, her words surprised. "Why did you crush the lamp?"

"Need you ask?" His voice cracked.

She rashly cupped his cheek. "Jasper, if you are hurting I will—"

"Damn it, woman, can you not see how painful tenderness is to me?" He violently withdrew, leaving her to stare back at him with such wide, wounded eyes he felt kicked.

"I do not know how else to be." She stepped further away. "I can no sooner deny tenderness of feeling than I can mete out revenge with a ruler. It is not in my nature to abuse, Jasper. I am not Finch, and so I cannot—" Her face paled even more. "Clearly, I cannot give you what you need."

She left. Elizabeth left him with his hand plucked clean and his heart splitting in two, tears falling like sparks from his eyes. He stood in his room wanting his wife more desperately than he'd ever wanted anything in the world.

That he could not have her—did not deserve her—was the greatest evil Finch had wrought.

CHAPTER FORTY-SIX

Elizabeth's nausea had abated enough that all desire to remain abed, in the prison of her husband's home, fled. She found every conceivable excuse now to escape, beginning with a visit to deliver Bella her belated birthday gift.

To her surprise, she discovered her sister in the lap of marital bliss. Arthur Harris was not the match Elizabeth had hoped for Annabelle, but if he made her happy and kept her safe, God bless.

She would have liked such happiness herself.

Papa and Cook also fared well enough now that Father's house was back in order. Already, a wealthy widow had appeared in his sights, but even this thought did not rankle. If the lady brought Papa happiness, so be it. If she brought him funds, all the better. For what did any of it matter anymore? Elizabeth's perspective had fundamentally changed, or perhaps her anger had simply receded. Bella didn't need her, and Papa would muddle on. She even paid a call to Lady Stanton and her pug, realizing she preferred the company of her odious former neighbor over the company of her own odious husband.

Though her visit with Lady Stanton was less odious than expected. In fact, the lady regaled her with such a healthy dollop of gossip, Elizabeth was reminded that a world existed beyond the confines of her own diminished life.

She must make an effort to venture out more often.

"Lizzie, dear, I daresay you neither look nor sound yourself this day. Is all still rosy in the land of matrimony?"

"Thorny as ever, Lady Stanton." She pasted on a smile.

"Come, come," the lady tutted. "Why, my own Lord Stanton, bless his dear, departed soul, was not nearly so thrilling as your Baron."

"Thrilling, madam, is overrated."

"So honeymoon ends, and ho hum sets in?" The lady peered closely at her.

"Not all marriages begin with honeymoons, I fear."

Lady Stanton pinched her lips as she stroked Sir Wigglebottom's head. "You are in a slump, I see, and the only way out of that, dear, is to remind yourself there are worse marriages than yours."

Elizabeth stifled her retort.

"Now don't grow angry with me just because you are angry with your husband," Lady Stanton chided. "I know that look."

Elizabeth bit her tongue. Barely.

"You need correcting, Lady Milton, and since your mother is no longer with us, I shall take it upon myself to—"

Elizabeth rose from her seat.

"Sit down, Baroness!" the lady barked. "You may leave as soon as I have finished, but you will do me the courtesy of listening to my words now as it was *you* who called on *me*."

Elizabeth could not argue with that pronouncement. She sank back into her seat.

"The Duke of Lennox is hosting his heir's engagement ball this Saturday. I shall procure you and the Baron an invitation and—"

Elizabeth tried, but failed, to interrupt the lady.

"As one does not refuse a duke, you will of course attend. And in attending, you will be reminded, I hope, of every match avoided when you accepted Baron of Milton's hand. Every sallow male face judging this season's debutantes will make you grateful for your husband, for you would have been miserable with their lot, Lizzie, admit it."

Would she though?

"They ignored you the moment you came out and spoke unkindly of your spectacles after. Yet now, as Lady Milton, you may enter any ballroom in London with your head held high."

Elizabeth was incredulous. Lady Stanton had not a clue as to what the *Ton* truly thought of her husband's purchased Barony or of her, his purchased bride. Milton had married Elizabeth to raise *his* standing in society, not the other way around. How was this lady so blind?

She clearly had no idea who the Duke of Lennox was to Baron of Milton.

Elizabeth rose. "Thank you for receiving me today, Lady Stanton, and for your attempt to cheer. I am afraid, however, that my husband is not accepting invitations at present, so please do not trouble yourself in this regard. I shall manage marriage one way or another, especially now that I—"

But the blasted woman had already guessed. "Why, what wonderful news, my dear! And never you mind your mood. It comes and goes in your condition. It is quite normal to feel out of sorts when one finds oneself in such a blessed state. Oh, I am so very, very pleased! *Aren't we, sir?*" She jiggled Sir Wigglebottom on her lap, planting a kiss to his wrinkled head.

Elizabeth began to creep toward the door. She did not feel blessed, she felt cursed.

Lady Stanton vigorously caressed her pug. "Do call again, Lizzie, or I shall call on you. *We must check up on her, mustn't we?*" she crooned over her wriggling bundle.

❧

Elizabeth even stopped by *LeBrecht's* on the pretext of shopping, though she was promptly whisked off not for a new fitting but another brutal stripping.

"What took yer so long?" chided Rose as Miss Li's maids began to rid Elizabeth of all parts again grown hirsute.

"You've let yerself go," tsked Mae. "I'm surprised Jasp didn't send yer back sooner."

"Grown sloppy in matrimony." Evie tittered.

"Lord Milton has not been himself." Elizabeth sobered their mirth. She longed to tell them everything, to spill every wretched feeling she'd buried deep. Instead, she swallowed the lump in her throat. She would not cry. She'd cried enough to form a lake.

"You two quarrelin'?" Rose broke the silence.

"Yes." Elizabeth's resolve weakened. "And I do not think our disagreement can be mended." She yelped as Mae ripped off a patch and murmured, "Sorry, luv," before moving on to the next bit.

Elizabeth's eyes filled with tears from more than mere discomfort.

"He's not an easy man, is Jasper," Rose remarked, "but he's a good man, miss." There was an edge to her voice. "I'd remind yer ladyship that what Finch did t' Jasp ain't a thing a body can forget."

Elizabeth knew this, had known this for some time, but it did not change the fact her husband would not allow her to help ease the horrors he'd experienced.

"He is broken," she muttered. "He is broken, and he can't be fixed. He won't *let* me fix him." That idea only ever worked in fiction. No heroine in real life could 'fix' the hero. He must somehow fix himself.

"You love 'im though?" Evie asked her gently. "If y' love

'im, y' can't stop tryin', no matter how oft he spurns yer attempts. Y' must try till he tells yer t' stop."

"I think he has, Evie." Elizabeth was overcome by sudden grief. "He's put up a wall I can neither scale nor crack."

"Then more fool him," Mae got out. "He's an arse t' let a lady like you go, ma'am." Her eyes met Elizabeth's. "Mayhap y' ought to let 'im know it."

Milton was miserable, but it was a misery he knew, familiar.

There was comfort in such misery, perverse though that may be. He surveyed his desk: The week's papers were neatly stacked, his ledgers in a tidy state. A painting of Dover's white cliffs hung opposite his view. He'd always wanted to visit and perhaps now he would. His affairs were in order, his body mostly healed, and his house ran efficiently despite his servants' grumbling. He existed as before, only with a pregnant wife under his roof.

And Finch gone, for good.

Dover might help him put matters firmly behind him, do him good to breathe its fresh, salt air. Because the beast lived on in his head, in his dreams still. If he left, Elizabeth would be well cared for by a staff that doted on their mistress more than their master anyway. Nor would she lack for company; he knew she made visits about town without his permission because he had her tailed. Fortunately, reports confirmed she'd not gone to see Kilpert, though calling on Lady Stanton had raised a flag.

As for Arty, curse him, Milton's best mate had made things worse the day he'd stopped by to share that Mrs. Harris was, deed done, in truth made Arty's wife. The pride in his friend's voice, Arty's veritable glow, had moved Milton to do the unthinkable: attempt apology with his own 'trouble an' strife.'

But of course it had gone terribly. He could no more repair his broken marriage than he could repair his broken sodding soul.

He recalled the pages he'd read littering Elizabeth's desk when he'd not found her in her bedroom but instead found her writing laid out.

> *The lady was faint with hunger, but it was not food she craved. She hungered for knowledge, comprehension. She had succumbed to her base urges, to the mirroring call in her breast, yet though the beastly baron had seduced her, she'd forgiven the man his lust. She knew the fire of his loins, his rough, demonic touch. But she could not forgive how fast he'd cast her off once he'd learned she carried his child. Was he repulsed now by her person, or had he loathed her all along, duping her into submission while he'd toyed with her flesh?*

His wife's writing had smacked disturbingly of *him*, making Milton skim another page like some starved, greedy fool, only to discover the lady in Lizzie's story falling in love with a lowly servant. Only which servant, damnation? Was Kilpert not his rival after all?

"What are you doing?"

Milton had startled so much he'd dropped the page he'd been reading.

"I think it best you leave my room before I throw this book at your head." Elizabeth's sudden appearance had thoroughly unnerved him.

"Lizzie, I…"

"I mean it, sir." She'd had a thick volume tucked under her arm.

"I came to—"

The book had flown, and he'd ducked, just in time.

"Elizabeth, please let me—"

"Speak? *Now* you wish to speak?" She'd marched right up and poked his chest, making him step back.

"You did not let me speak." She'd poked again, harder. "While you convalesced, you let everyone but me, your wife, visit. Why?" Poke. "What did I do but try to comfort and support you? Why do you refuse me, Jasper? *Why*?" Her sharp, grey eyes had pleaded with such pain he'd stumbled from her chamber and slammed the adjoining door behind him, gasping against the wall like some goddamned gutted fish.

And now, seated at his neatly ordered desk, the memory of that moment made everything ache anew. He had no ardor left for life, let alone bodily congress. He'd not go near her till they must embark upon a second heir; he didn't trust himself. Should Elizabeth require servicing she could avail herself of one of Li's men. So long as she did *not* bed Kilpert.

Though why Lizzie bedding Paul should disturb him so bloody much made no bloody sense. He really shouldn't care. And why the devil did he sneak into her room nights while she slept, to stare at her face, which only in sleep looked peaceful anymore?

A footman entered and delivered the day's post, jarring Milton from his despair. He sorted the stack but stopped short at a letter embossed with the one seal in Christendom that had the power to strike dread in his heart: the Duke of Lennox.

Elizabeth stared into her dressing mirror, Ginny readying her for bed, when her husband, the bastard, barged in.

"Leave us," he ordered Ginny, who scurried off so fast Elizabeth hadn't even time to bid her maid good night.

He rudely tossed a letter at her, demanding, "What is the meaning of this?"

She glanced at the seal. "I assume we've been invited to a ball, sir."

"Did you orchestrate this?"

"And if I did?"

"Answer the question, Elizabeth."

"Goodness, my husband knows my name. How shocking."

"Blast it, Lizzie, did you or did you not secure us this invitation?" He stepped closer.

"I did not, sir. I presume Lady Stanton did, despite my protestations."

"So you admit you are behind this invitation."

"No, Lady Stanton offered to procure us an invitation, and I told her it would displease my husband if she did."

"But you visited her. You chose to call upon a lady you've made abundantly clear you despise."

"Oddly enough, I find her company now preferable to that of *others*."

He winced. "Elizabeth, I do not wish to curtail your freedom more, but if your calls elicit invitations like this, I will insist on approving all visits in advance, or accompanying you to them."

She lunged from her seat, stopping herself just in time. "Curtail me?" Her heart raced. "I am already your prisoner for life, so you will not order me about. You lost that right. And as for your six bloody rules, they are null and void. Do you hear me, sir? Null and void! I will not obey you. I will see whom I like and do as I please, and you will put up with it, because I am your wife in name only, sir, no longer in deed!"

Milton's face turned a shade so white he looked like he might faint. Or murder her.

"I am no longer your wife because you do not treat me like one," she raged on. "You share nothing with me anymore—I do not know where you go or whom you visit nights. Nor do I care. I will bear your heirs, but that is all you will get from me. Do you understand what I say, sir? I want nothing to do with you. *Nothing*."

Milton's face clouded ominously. "I'll show you a whole

new goddamn set of rules for provoking me, woman." He dragged her to a chair and flung her, head down, over his lap, where he proceeded to lift her shift and strike her bottom with such vehemence she gasped.

"You cannot treat me like this!" She squirmed to escape his blows. "You cannot, you bastard, you cannot!"

Yet her husband's heavy hand continued its unrelenting strikes. And despite her searing anger she was lulled, slowly and surely, as if his slaps grabbed and held her anguish, stilling both her heart and mind. Feelings unfurled which she'd been stifling for weeks, allowing emotion to overwhelm thought, to tear through her unimpeded. Soon he no longer held her in place, she lay limp across his lap, welcoming his blows. Elizabeth gripped the chair's wooden legs beneath her as the carpet below absorbed her tears.

When Milton stopped, his breaths ragged, she did not want him to.

He briefly held her in his arms, the moment bittersweet. Then, without a word, he laid her on her belly on her bed, and walked out.

Seconds later Ginny rushed in to administer care to Elizabeth's burning buttocks. The cool cloth the maid applied made Elizabeth suck in her breath. What had her husband achieved by thrashing her like this? Had he put her in her place and reestablished his control, or had he granted her relief, shown her he still cared?

It did not matter. Nothing did. He was her lord and master whether she wanted him or not. And she did not. Elizabeth realized in that moment that she did not want her husband because Jasper Audrey did not know how to love.

***

Mere steps away from his wife, Milton paced his chamber

with such intense longing he could not stand the coward he'd become. Again, he'd turned to punishment, for what else should he have done? He could not have told Elizabeth the truth: That he wanted her in his arms, his bed, his life. That he regretted past actions, current actions, hell even all future actions!

While Ginny's muted voice soothed her mistress through the adjoining wall, he wanted to break it down and beg his wife's forgiveness. Only he did not deserve her grace. He deserved only Elizabeth's loathing. And now she would be forced to attend his sire's awful ball with him, to play a role she'd all but screamed she would reject. For Elizabeth had made it very clear she would not be a dutiful, doting wife. She would not follow his six clear rules. He could spank her into a stupor, but he could not spank her soul into submission. Hell, soon he'd not be able to spank her at all.

And then a worse thought pressed: What if he had harmed the babe just now, jostled it in her womb somehow?

Milton beat his head against his wall in torment. He didn't want *this* kind of blasted marriage, he wanted so much bloody more! Yet this was all he'd ever get. All he bloody well deserved. And he, alone, had made it so.

He slumped against the wall and curled himself into a ball. He'd spared Lizzie his tears, at least. He'd mopped those up as fast as they had rolled down his cheeks, his face the mirror image of his wife's, weeping upside down across his knees.

In a corner of his mind he heard a nasty snicker. *Forever me boy, Jasp. Evermore.*

The brooding baron chuffed low, his voice so base and wicked, the lady cowered in the cave. Her love lay bleeding in her arms, barely

breathing from the bullet wound to his chest. She must do something to save him. She must…

"Pretty miss," the baron hissed, "come out and show yourself. No harm will come to you, dear. Leave the servant there to die. He does not deserve your sweet affection."

He is a better man than you! she wished to shout from the cave's dank depths. Only she knew better than to respond, for the baron always twisted what she said. Her love moaned in pain; if she did not get help soon, he'd perish in her arms. Could she barter with this devil? Could a man as dastardly as this baron be trusted to keep his word?

She had to try.

"I will come out if you swear you'll help him. Swear it, and I will give you what you want."

"What I want?" The baron's voice sounded closer, as if he had already entered the cave. "Tell me what that is, miss, and perhaps I will."

What he wanted? The lady's heart began to pound. She knew what the baron wanted, didn't she? Or did she not? He'd never expressly stated it, it had only ever been implied. He wanted her hand in marriage, her father's wealth, but more than this he…

Her palms began to sweat as her mind opened to the unthinkable.

The brooding baron wanted her love.

Could she give him this, in exchange for her true love's li

Elizabeth's quill broke. *Blast.*

She crumpled the page into a ball and launched it clear across the room. She could not even write anymore; her story made no sense. What the devil was her heroine thinking? The lady couldn't possibly love the villain, not when her true love lay bleeding in her arms. It was utter, abject nonsense. Drivel that no one would ever wish to read.

She would never be an author, never amount to more than

a broodmare for a husband who didn't love her and never would.

Elizabeth closed her eyes in pain, and then she swallowed her hurt. She fetched a fresh page. What was she if not persistent? She retrieved her broken quill and cut a new edge with her pen knife. So short now it cramped her hand, she could still write with it. Just.

She'd see where the story took her, because at least it took her away. Her writing remained the only thing she could control. It was escape from her existence.

Freedom from *him*.

CHAPTER FORTY-SEVEN

Two days later, Milton entered Elizabeth's room unannounced. "Why are you not dressed?"

She stared at him from her bed. "I do not feel well enough to attend tonight's ball, sir. Please extend my apologies to the Duke, who I am sure will understand once you inform him of my condition."

Milton scowled. "Get up."

She scowled back. "I do not feel well, sir."

"I don't care how you *claim* to feel, wife. This is one engagement we must both attend, nor will I make excuses when you are perfectly well. You will dress this instant."

She did not blink.

"Elizabeth, I will not hesitate to dress you myself, so I advise you—"

Up she got, striding to her wardrobe to grab the first gown she saw. His loathsome tone reminded her of when they'd first courted. When he would approach her like a wolf primed to strike.

Perhaps they'd come full circle.

Sure enough, her husband barked more orders. "Choose a gown that suits my mother's jewels."

"I have decided to wear the diamonds instead." She prayed he'd not react.

Milton grabbed her arm. "You will wear the stones I tell you to wear and you will match your dress accordingly, Elizabeth. Do not argue me this."

She swallowed her emotion, for she must be honest if she wished to survive his wrath. "Milton, I am sorry, but I no longer have your mother's gemstones."

He dropped her arm in shock. "How do you not have the blue jasper?"

Elizabeth's breath hitched. *Not lapis lazuli, jasper!*

"I let Bella pawn the necklace when she needed cash. You'd given me no pin money, and I thought the diamonds too valuable, so I—"

"You *what?*" His voice thundered.

"Milton, I am terribly sorry." His indigo eyes had turned to flint, his face shrouded in darkness. Still, she must come clean. "Annabelle promised its return, and as I had nothing else of value to offer her … She planned to buy the necklace back, but then Harris stole her to Gretna, and when they returned Finch had stolen you, so …"

His lips became a thin, taut line.

"By the time she could visit the Lombard again, the necklace was gone, and the man would not say who'd bought it."

Milton stared at the floor, inhaling so terribly slowly she feared he might cease altogether to breathe.

"Sir." She bowed her head. "Had I known the stones were dear to you I would never have given them to Bella. I am truly sorry."

He straightened his spine. "That was my mother's necklace, Elizabeth. You knew that. It was the sole gift my father gave her, the stones a very rare blue color. She sold it when he abandoned her, and I spent years tracking it down to gain it back. She gave me the necklace for you to wear as a family heirloom, to pass down someday to a daughter. It is no small thing you have lost."

"Forgive me, Milton." She meant it. "I never meant to—"

"See to it you dress," he told her coldly. "And do not wear the diamonds. If you cannot wear my mother's necklace, you shall wear no ornament at all."

His rebuke cut more than any rage he might have shown. She'd wounded him gravely, failed him by losing what she now understood was his very namesake.

Already, this night was a disaster.

Their carriage ride passed in stunning silence; the Baron did not so much as glance at Elizabeth, not once. Everything about his person exuded betrayal. Disgust.

Perhaps he'd hate her forever.

She did not want to attend this awful ball or meet Milton's awful sire, the Duke. She was certain Lennox was his father, though she was not about to ask.

When they arrived at the Duke's impressive residence, Milton stiffly took her arm. The entrance hall embodied old-world charm—the very opposite of her husband's modern townhouse. Its dark, oak paneling and ornately carved flourishes breathed of history, legacy, and power. Elizabeth imagined it the very house young Mary Audrey had scrubbed and polished as a maid. Of course Milton would insist she attend; she'd been a coward to make excuses. It must be brutal for him to stand in his father's home as guest only, never family.

She vowed to play her role as best she could to support Milton, for his mother's sake. When this ball was over, she would allow her anger full force again, but tonight she would perform with grace.

Elizabeth exchanged vague pleasantries with whomever approached, while inwardly upbraiding herself for the loss of the jasper gemstones. How had she not realized their significance? Nor recognized the Duke's invitation for what it was: an abject insult. Although if Lady Stanton had been the one to—

"Lady Milton, may I have this dance?"

Elizabeth looked into a face oddly familiar.

"Lord Marley, madam," the gentleman introduced himself. "I believe you met my brother, this evening's man of honor, at the Denbigh ball."

Ah, Lord Mathers, Milton's half-brother and her own all-too-rude dance partner that night.

Meaning Lord Marley was her husband's other—

They were interrupted by Milton himself, who pulled Elizabeth away without a backward glance at his half-sibling.

"Why were you speaking with that man?" His fingers dug into her arm.

"Because he spoke to me, sir. Should I behave instead as ill-tempered as you?"

He tightened his grip and dragged her to a row of side tables. "You will stand here"—he positioned her beside a potted palm—"and drink punch with all the other married ladies while I speak to men of business." Milton's face remained inscrutable. "You are to dance with no one."

Elizabeth reined in her pique; she'd not make matters worse for her husband. Not this night. "Whatever you desire, Baron."

"Do not test me, wife."

"I do not, sir." He'd misread her. "There is no need."

He looked queerly at her a moment before she disengaged from his grasp and headed for the punch bowl, her heart and stomach heavy.

"Lady Milton!" A voice rang out behind her.

The Duke of Allendale.

Elizabeth forced herself to swallow a sip of the overly sweet drink.

"Madam, are you quite well? You look uncommonly pale."

"Your Grace." She bobbed a curtsy. "I believed you to be in Cumberland with the Duchess. Is she well? Has she—?"

"Charles is fantastic." He beamed with pride. "Gave me a blonde angel this time. We named her Addie after her grandmother, though I think she's more a *Maddie* the way she howls for her mother's teat."

Elizabeth smiled at the Duke's unseemly description.

"Now where's that bastard husband of yours? Hiding, no doubt. I can't believe Lennox had the gall to invite him. How's Jasp handling it? Skulking in a corner I imagine."

The Duke took one look at Elizabeth's face and fast led her from the punch bowl to a corner enclave. "Lady Milton, you look decidedly unwell. I'll fetch Jasper."

"No, I am fine. Please do not … Please, *do not* fetch him."

He stopped short, frowning. "Madam, I am entirely at your disposal tonight, should you wish to leave the ball early. Or should you wish me to thrash your husband instead."

Elizabeth hastened to amend his opinion. "Your Grace, I am—" She resorted to honesty. "You see, I now find myself in that state your wife most recently—"

The Duke's entire bearing shifted. "Why Lady Milton, that is great cause for celebration! And explains much. I must congratulate Jasper, and you'll write to Charles, of course. I am only here on my wife's orders, you see, to interfere on behalf of her…"

Only Elizabeth stopped listening. She felt nauseous again. She longed for a dark corner in which to hide, or an empty room to lie down in.

"Again, my congratulations, Lady Milton." The Duke

bowed low over her hand just as Elizabeth looked up into the face of the one person she might rightfully blame for tonight's disaster: Sir Wigglebottom's mistress.

She nearly lost her punch right then and there.

***

From clear across the ballroom, Milton watched the insufferable Lady Stanton take Wellesley's place. Lizzie would survive the dull sycophant, same as he'd survived the boring swell he'd just sent packing. Milton could talk business with toffs, but he didn't know how to make idle chit chat. That's what a wife was for: to ward off the nobs who forever made him feel ten inches tall. He both longed to be these preening peacocks and simultaneously murder them.

Meanwhile, his sire's weighty presence cast a heady glow the Duke's guests were drawn to like moths to a flame. They'd come to curry favor, to be seen and heard and acknowledged. Milton had come because he'd had no choice. To refuse such an invitation was social suicide—to accept was his own private hell.

He knew where the Duke of Lennox sat, but he refused to look the man's way. He'd not acknowledge a father who did not acknowledge his own son. Two could play that game, though he wondered again why his invitation had been sent. He doubted very much Lady Stanton had swayed Lennox. At most, she'd simply planted the idea.

He was envious of his friend, Wellesley, for having not only a dukedom to his name but a loving duchess for his wife. His own Baroness was more enemy than ally now; Elizabeth would sooner help a louse than assist him this night.

They'd made their appearance. Could they not already leave? How long must one stay at these affairs before one was permitted to vanish? Perhaps he could use his wife's condition as an excuse. God knew she employed it often enough. He was about to go and fetch Lizzie when Lady Stanton handed his wife off to his bloody half-brother, heir to all that should rightfully have been his.

***

Elizabeth had no desire to dance again with the unpleasant Lord Mathers, yet she'd no choice but to accept his arm, foisted on her by Lady Stanton. Had the woman no tact? Milton would be livid; she sensed her husband's fierce frown from clear across the room.

"I am so pleased you chose to attend tonight's ball, Lady Milton." Lord Mathers embodied that particular style of 'slippery polite' Elizabeth loathed about the *Ton*. "What do you think of my betrothed? Is she not exquisite?"

Extremely accomplished … impeccable bloodline … a perfect duchess … He droned on about his fiancée's attributes, though Elizabeth did not, in all honesty, know which attending lady even was this man's intended.

She wanted rid of him. Fast.

"May I ask, Lord Mathers, why you do not dance with your bride-to-be?" Their eyes met. "It must be a chore to suffer my person, sir, when you might instead enjoy the charms of your affianced."

"Oh, it is no chore at all, Lady Milton." His tone turned canny. "Quite the contrary, dancing with you brings me great joy, for it allows me to present you to my father, who has long wished to assess your own fine *attributes*." And the obnoxious man turn-twirled her into an audience with the Duke of Lennox, seated like royalty at one end of the dance floor.

Elizabeth dug in her heels, but Mathers urged her forward.

"Your Grace." He spoke loud enough that nearby heads

turned. “I present to you Lady Milton, the Earl of Winthrop’s daughter.”

Lennox’s eyes met Elizabeth’s with cold appraisal. She knew their ice-blue color. They were her husband’s eyes, precisely.

“Lady Milton, I am delighted we meet, at last.”

“Your Grace.” She dipped into a genuflect.

“You are enjoying the evening.” It was less question, more command.

“Very much, Your Grace. Congratulations on your son’s engagement,” she murmured.

“I have not seen you dance yet with your husband, Lady Milton. Did he not accompany you?”

How she hated this man in this moment. “My husband does not enjoy dancing, Your Grace, though I assure you he is in attendance.”

“I am glad to hear it, Lady Milton, though a man should never leave his wife alone too long upon a dance floor.”

His insinuation stole her breath.

“Happily, my husband does not suffer your concern, Your Grace.” She would not let this duke insult her or her husband.

“I find that most surprising, Lady Milton, for Baron of Milton seems most keen on propriety, given his rather *humble* origin.”

She wanted to punch His Grace for such thinly veiled insult, yet Lord Mathers’s grip on her arm held fast. Elizabeth prayed Milton remained too far removed—or far too occupied—to hear a word of this exchange.

“Your Grace, I believe you do not know my husband in the least.”

“I know he married a spitfire.” The Duke’s eyes raked her person, lingering at her spectacles. “An ill-bred wife who’s altogether lacking. But then, Baron of Milton’s own breeding lacks class.”

A hush fell over those close enough to hear.

Elizabeth did not think; she reacted. "The only ill-bred individual I see here, Your Grace, is the one seated right before me."

***

From afar, Milton watched his bloody half-brother present Lizzie to their bloody sire for no other reason than to humiliate her, he was sure. He pressed his way through the crowd to try and reach her, but it was difficult to push through the throng.

He'd been set up; he felt it in his bones. The invitation to this ball was but a ruse to give him a public drubbing, a stern ducal set-down. His old man reveled in demeaning others, which was why Milton had worked so damned hard to prove his worth in wealth, title, and influence. Yet here he was—amidst a slew of blood relatives, no doubt—trapped beneath his father's roof, prey to the Duke's power.

He clenched his fists, desperate to snatch Lizzie from his sire's clutches and protect her from that man's ugliness, yet he failed her even in this. Again, he could but impotently stand by and watch his wife take the brunt of his father's cruelty. For Lennox was as brutal as Finch. He used words instead of knives, cut-downs and social jabs instead of beatings and gouged flesh. But the effect remained the same: to bend one to his will.

***

The Duke looked livid.

"Turn around," he barked, and Elizabeth's body obeyed as if Milton himself had ordered Mutton *sit*. She obeyed without thought, facing the ballroom now instead of the Duke, her mind a sudden blank.

A weight fell to her chest as His Grace clasped something cold about her neck. She shivered.

"This belonged to an old acquaintance of mine, Elizabeth, a person close to your husband."

Her wits returned; he'd not only demeaned Milton's mother, but used Elizabeth's given name.

"It seems they were misplaced."

He had purchased the necklace from the Lombard! Only how had he known?

"It is only fitting, I think, that I should be the one to place these stones about your neck." He tugged the clasp, and then his finger traced her breastbone in a manner so intimate and degrading, a vision of Finch with Jasper flashed through Elizabeth's mind.

She twisted about and slapped the Duke of Lennox flat across his face, the crack of her palm ringing in the hall. "Bastard," Elizabeth hissed at the Duke's disbelieving face. "You are a bastard of the worst degree. A true bastard, sir, not one born, but one made. And I do not care who hears me say it." Her voice grew louder still, for Elizabeth had entered a state from which there was no turning back.

"You would treat you firstborn with such contempt as this, and publicly no less? What man *does* such a thing?" She wished to slap him again. "What man deliberately, cowardly shames another by so vilely abusing his wife? What man disavows his own flesh and blood?"

Her rage only rose. "You are no Duke, sir, for you have no honor. My husband is a far better man than you, and should have made a better duke. He may be but the fruit of your base actions, but to those who love and serve him, he is more worthy of fealty and affection than you will ever be."

And Elizabeth, without thinking, spat at the Duke of Lennox's feet.

Outrage ensued, voices shouting, talking over one another,

as spittle trickled down the Duke's immaculate black boot. He remained still as a statue, his face turning purple, while his heir, Lord Mathers, crept slowly backward.

Elizabeth's heart beat with righteous contempt. *This man* stood between her and Milton's happiness. Not Finch.

"Husband," she announced at the top of her voice, "if you can hear me, take me home. I do not wish to lay eyes upon your rotten sire ever again."

Within seconds Milton was beside her, leading Elizabeth through the crowd of dumbstruck onlookers who stared as if the pair were ghosts, the throng parting for them like water.

As if they were untouchable.

CHAPTER FORTY-EIGHT

Mind in a blur, Milton hauled Lizzie past footmen lining hallways, past statuary and vases overflowing with blooms. The bouquets brushed his body as he dragged her at a terribly fast clip, her anger continuing to pulsate, vibrate between them.

He was in awe of this woman who'd just spat like a common fishmonger's wife upon the Duke of Lennox's feet.

"Milton." His wife's voice remained clipped. "I will apologize for my public display just now, but I will *not* apologize for my words to that man. Because he is the most wretched, abominable, most—"

Milton pressed her up against the wall in a kiss so urgent, he paid no heed to the stony footmen and marble busts that stared their fill. "Don't you dare apologize, woman." He dipped his lips for another wild kiss, his heart pounding madly in his breast. "It is *I* who must apologize, *I* who am speechless before your bravery. I am more humbled, more proud, more—"

She looked back at him, thoroughly confused. "Milton, I just destroyed all chance of you ever—"

"Elizabeth, you just restored my very faith in humanity. And I love you for it, woman. I love you with all my wretched, unworthy heart."

Her eyes were moons of shock; Milton swallowed his nerves and tried again.

"Luv, I don't know when, or if I always…" He was bungling this, damnation, when it was imperative he get it right. "I need you," he blurted. "Not your breeding, not your education, not even your womb. I need *you*, Lizzie, because I love you. And I've been an arse not to say it sooner, not to admit it even to myself. But I am telling you now how blessed I am to be your husband, how desperately I wish to undo every injury I ever caused you, every time my miserable, deplorable self failed to protect and uphold you, to love, cherish, and honor you."

Her brow furrowed, for why should she trust his words? Why trust a blackguard at all?

"Lizzie." He gripped her hands, his body trapping her against the wall. "I achieved all I ever wanted, but it was nothing next to you, nothing I truly needed. No blueblood ever stood up for me like you did, defended me before your kind." And it was true. It was suddenly the greatest truth he knew. "No one ever spoke so strongly on my behalf." His eyes misted as he swallowed and blinked.

She gripped his hands back. "I've failed you too, Jasper."

She took him utterly by surprise.

"I misjudged your motives and intentions, forever assuming the worst. I was rash to enter Finch's lair alone with Annabelle, and impatient when you needed time and space to heal. I should never have given Bella your mother's necklace, should never have entertained Paul Kilpert behind your back. I have disobeyed every one of your six rules so often I—"

"No." He shook his head. "You were never in the wrong, Elizabeth. I alone—"

She held his hands, his eyes captive. "If you love me as you say, you must accept my apology, Jasper, because that is how love works. You must love me without bluster, without beating yourself to bits."

Who *was* this woman?

"I am your wife, sir. And as your wife I will speak my mind."

More like she read his mind.

"You will take my apology with grace," she ordered.

She—ordered—*him*?

Milton bowed his head. Her forgiveness was too much.

"Permission to touch you, sir?" she asked.

"Christ, Lizzie, I was a beast! A cad! As evil as Finch or my father to order you and Paul to—"

His heart hammered so hard his chest physically hurt. "I regret that day more than any other. It will always be a stain, a blight upon my soul."

"Jasper, I do not excuse your actions, but I forgive you for them. As, I am sure, will Mr. Kilpert."

She wasn't real. And he sure as shite wasn't worthy. He wasn't—

"You must also forgive yourself."

"Never." He vehemently shook his head. "But I'll make it up t' you. I'll be the man y' deserve, no more bloody rules. And none of society's damn rules either. To hell with the *Ton*, Lizzie, I'm done." He didn't care his speech slipped. He'd be himself, for fuck's sake. "Y' freed me, woman. Rescued me not just from Finch but from years o' being slave t' me own desire fer revenge." His thoughts raced faster than he could form the words. "One slap, luv, one sweet, hard slap laid low me rotten sire an' proved me worth t' every nob in London, to th' very world that bloody Duke upholds. An' y' did it better'n I ever could've, Lizzie, fer which I am more grateful than you will ever know."

"Jasper—"

"I want naught more than t' return all I stole from yer, wife. I'll give it all back, pay yer father a thousand times over if you'd but—"

Her lips locked on his with a passion he was overjoyed to discover. Elizabeth kissed him with such relish that when she finally tore free, her eyes demanded answer.

"I don't think I can wait, luv."

"Nor I, husband," her lips quirked.

Milton kicked open the door beside them and hauled his wife into the room. They'd consummate their marriage for real this time, in his father's bloody house. *Fuck him.*

***

Whatever was now happening—happening *to* Jasper Audrey—Elizabeth grabbed hold and held tight. This was her chance. At him.

She kissed him, giddy with hope. She didn't care that they behaved like naughty children atop the Duke of Lennox's escritoire. Items fell to floor, ink spilled to rug, as Jasper rucked up her skirts, heedless of papers, quills, or finely wrought inkwells. For the first time ever, Elizabeth did not just rut atop a desk, she *made love* to her whoreson husband, his every thrust a proclamation, her hips an arching, reaching promise of her own.

She wrapped her legs about his waist to draw him deeper in, to call forth his tenderness and turmoil, his longing and his lust—a man who straddled both worlds in any bed, on any desk, against a wall, in a swaying carriage. She loved his surly swagger and his not-so-subtle jests. His intensity had inflamed her from the moment they'd first met.

It still did.

When they collapsed, spent and silly with joy, Jasper

beamed, his face pure light. He was the handsomest man alive. Whereas she—

"You look a mess, wife, a gorgeous mess, but a mess nonetheless." His lips twitched, breaking into a bold smile. "And what the devil were you thinking, attending a ball without your smalls?"

"I was but following my husband's orders, sir."

He laughed before he breathed the words "*Good girl*" directly into her ear.

Elizabeth thrilled to his praise. "Besides, you gave me no time to dress. Why, I'd barely laced my stays before you bundled me into your carriage." She pursed her lips. "You'd best straighten that necktie and button your fall before some esteemed member of the *Ton* walks in on us, Baron."

"Let them," he proclaimed. "Let the world see my love for you, Lizzie, I will hide it no more." He palmed her cheek. "You are exquisite, inside and out." His other hand fell to her belly, to cradle the life that grew there, waiting.

She placed her hand over his. "I love you, too, Jasper Audrey." She said it so softly she wasn't sure he'd heard. They remained hand over hand, in easy stillness, until she, too, cupped his cheek. "You are not an easy man to love." She gazed into his face. "But I am not easy to love either. Let us do better than we have, Jasper. Let us do our damnedest from this day forward."

He pressed his forehead to hers and answered, "Yes."

❧

Later that night, Elizabeth wriggled her naked body deeper into her husband's. She was content. No, smitten.

The Baron of Milton had spent an inordinate amount of time seeming to memorize every curve, crease, mole and freckle on her body after they'd made love again, this time in the comfort of her husband's welcoming bed. The moment they'd returned from the Duke's ball, Jasper had ignored Murdoch and Gerald's inquisitive faces and dismissed Ginny outright.

He'd also kicked poor Mutton out before he'd undressed Elizabeth himself, praising her for going back to *LeBrecht's* until she was sure she'd blushed five shades of red.

"Jasper, I hope our newfound understanding doesn't mean you'll stop … you know."

"Stop what, love?" He bent to suckle her breast with such fervor she was reminded she'd soon nurse a babe, no longer just a husband.

"Stop, well…" She squirmed beneath his onslaught.

"Stop *spanking*?" He rolled her to her side and gave her rump a playful swat.

She squirmed more. "Yes."

"Hmm." He paused to lavish his attention on her right nipple next. "Perhaps we ought to come up with a fresh set of rules then, wife. Rules which might account for your clear need for discipline." He began to pet her backside in anticipation of another slap, making Elizabeth shiver with anticipation.

"And what rules do you propose, husband?" She could not believe she now wanted to follow this man's rules. Provided they were, of course, agreeable.

"I thought simply to amend the ones you broke so oft." He spanked her again, sending tremors up her spine.

"Amend how, sir?"

"I like it when you call me *sir* in bed, Lizzie." He began to nibble her ear. "And I should like it even more if you continue to obey me in the bedroom, continue to assume the position I showed you on our wedding night."

Heat pooled between Elizabeth's thighs. He was still the man she'd married. He would still warm her bottom when she needed it most. She gave up a small prayer of thanks and then gasped at an invasion she'd never felt before.

"And I should like entry *here* someday, Elizabeth, to every inch of you." His finger slowly probed her rear, engendering there sensations she'd not dreamed possible.

"Will you allow it, love?" he whispered. "I promise you great pleasure, if you trust me to give it."

"Please," she begged too quickly. "Jasper, don't—!"

He did not stop but probed her more, invading her quim next with his other finger. His hand now worked both entries, building in Elizabeth pressure and pleasure that was achingly intense.

"I'll not stop unless you speak a word only you and I will know. What word shall it be, sweetheart? Something you'll not forget. Give me a word, darling, that will always make me stop."

"*Watercress*," Elizabeth gasped, then nearly wept when his hand abruptly ceased.

He laughed. "Watercress is perfect, Lizzie."

"Jasper?"

"Yes, love?"

"*Please*," she urged, greedy now that she had him. Greedy for so much more.

"New rules, Lizzie." His voice grew stern. "And you will count them for me, loud and proud."

"Yes, sir, only—"

"On hands and knees, Elizabeth."

She scrambled to obey.

"And when we reach the end you'll shatter." His voice was thick with promise, or did she only dream it?

"Can you do that, love, can you come on my command?"

Desire fast threatened she'd do just that.

"I'll try, sir," she murmured, head down in position.

Her husband's hand cracked across her backside as Elizabeth gasped for air. "One!" she announced, awaiting his first rule.

"Do not cross me when I am right," he ordered. "But if I am wrong, Lizzie, I shall admit as much and beg your forgiveness."

She tingled with warmth.

"Do not delay my gratification!" His voice rang as loud as Elizabeth's resounding "Two!"

"Though I promise to gratify you always, wife, with equal pleasure."

He made her gush all the more.

"Do not goad me into spankings; I alone determine punishment."

"Three!" She nearly wept her relief when he added, "That rule is non-negotiable, Lizzie."

"Do not touch without permission," Milton uttered next, then paused before amending, "but touch frequently with my blessing," making Elizabeth declare "four" with a soft smile.

"I will get better at this, Lizzie. For you, I will try."

Tears welled in her eyes before he announced, "And do not knee me in the bollocks, woman, else you will not sit for weeks."

"Five!" Elizabeth laughed out loud.

"Find that funny, do you?" He gave her bottom an extra wallop.

"No, sir." She stifled her grin.

"Lastly, do not disobey me in the bedroom, Lizzie. Anywhere else I shall tolerate your temper, but here..." He slipped his hand between her legs to stroke her where she teetered on the edge of impending, building—

"Here in bed, love, you must do as I command, so come for me now, Lizzie. Come on my order." Jasper's hand came down in a rush of cool air just as Elizabeth screamed "Six!" and pleasure rocked her world, filling her body, her soul with bliss.

Light and heat suffused her, sparking to the tips of every limb. Seen and loved like never before, she was his and he was hers. She knew this as surely as she knew he'd make love to her again, taking her to new heights of freedom from all her fears and inhibitions.

She reveled in the life—the family—they might create here in her whoreson husband's bedroom, and in the world at large.

Free to be their honest selves, they were worthy of one another's love, at last.

EPILOGUE

1840, ONE YEAR LATER

All morning long Milton's wife had fussed and flitted about the house like a gnat on fruit or a fly on shite. In fact, nothing Murdoch or Ginny or anyone said seemed to have any effect, though the servants tried their best to slow their mistress. Lady Milton, however, would not be deterred. She appeared hell bent on ensuring every last detail was in place.

Perhaps 'bee on clover' was a kinder analogy?

Milton loudly cleared his throat, *ahem*, three times while his wife remained oblivious, bent over a list with Gerald. Only when he barked, "Lizzie!" did her head snap up, at last.

He flicked his eyes to her dress, making her look down, with a gasp, at the two damp spots on her chest. She sheepishly took their daughter from his arms. "Forgive me, Jasper." She settled on the settee and began to loosen her smock as Gerald and the others slipped out.

"I told you this was too much, too soon." Milton frowned.

Their daughter latched and began to suck emphatically.

"Only it's not. We've hidden ourselves too long. It's time we show the world—"

"*You* are my world," he told her. "I don't give a tinker's curse about anyone else." Especially when he watched Elizabeth nurse Gemma. There was no more perfect sight in all the world than his two gorgeous girls, together.

Lizzie pursed her lips. "But it will matter to *her*." She looked down at their daughter. "And to future children. We do them no favors by—"

"Elizabeth, I've enough blunt to leave a whole brood of children the kind of inheritance that should last for generations. I don't know why you insist on throwing a formal ball so soon after giving birth."

"Gemma is nearly six months, Jasper; I should hardly call half a year too soon. Moreover, Annabelle has been of great assistance, as have your mother and Li, and Murdoch and—"

"I'm aware I married a ridiculously capable woman, and have an equally capable staff. That is not the issue. What concerns me is—"

"What concerns *you*, sir, is the fact you, or rather we, must present ourselves again in society." She pursed her lips. "I have organized the best possible way to do this, under our own roof, with friends in attendance. Thus we may entertain as *we* choose. Is that not better, love, than attempting to resume polite company elsewhere, forced to dance to the *Ton's* tunes?"

Milton harrumphed, though Lizzie was, as usual, right.

"We will never be fully accepted, Jasper, but we must try to reenter society in small, deliberate ways. That begins tonight, so that tomorrow our guests all talk. They will spread word of your good health, wealth, and fortune. How your family now thrives. How your wife now—"

"Adores me?" Milton leaned in to kiss Lizzie's brow, then bent to kiss his daughter's tiny forehead. And then, before she could argue otherwise, he sat down beside his wife, released her other breast from her smock, and began to draw deeply from its tap.

Heaven.

***

Elizabeth sucked in a breath before she grinned. He was greedy, her husband, and she loved the bastard for it. "You will steal all her milk and grow fat," she chided, letting her free hand fall to his soft, dark curls. More and more he let her touch him without having to ask.

He let go, only to trace the swollen slope of her still-dripping tip. "You're altogether too tense from organizing this ball, wife. Therefore, as soon as you are done feeding wee Gemma"—his finger landed on their daughter's tiny nose, buried in Elizabeth's other breast—"you'll take yerself straight t' me chamber an' await yer master."

Elizabeth's insides flipped; they always did when his speech slipped—a portent of things to come. He commanded her in the bedroom even as she commanded his respect more and more outside it. He still tanned her bottom too, when least expected—yet most needed.

"Of course, sir," she acquiesced, her own lust rising.

He kissed her forehead once more before he slipped from the room.

Elizabeth leaned back, her breasts drained of all pressure. She took immense pleasure in her ability to provide for two such precious beings as her husband and daughter. Though she would derive even more pleasure if this ball went off without a hitch.

Four hours later Elizabeth was refreshed, dressed, and greeting their costumed guests.

"Lizzie, we'd not have missed this for the world!" The

Duchess of Allendale bussed Elizabeth's cheeks. Her Grace had come disguised as a pirate with her husband, the Duke, decked out as her first mate.

His mother, the Dowager, had also arrived, sans costume, along with the Duke's squire, one Sir John, and his wife, Lady Eleanor, who Elizabeth had learned was the Duchess's sister. She was impressed they'd made the long journey from Cumberland, until she learned their visit was, in fact, twofold.

"My cousin, Mercy Pendrake, is newly betrothed." The Duchess's face fell. "It is imperative I see her, and her father, before she is shipped out. You gave us an excellent excuse to journey to London, Elizabeth."

The Duke placed a hand on his wife's arm. "Banks has agreed to transport her, Charles. There is nothing we can do short of—"

"I know this, Roland," the Duchess bit back, "but it does not mean I am *happy* about it. Any of it," she grumbled as he steered her away.

Elizabeth turned to her next set of guests, her job tonight to prove to every person in attendance how well she and the Baron fared. United, they'd survived not only the Duke of Lennox's wrath following her disastrous behavior at his son's betrothal ball, but the *Ton's* subsequent severe reproach, not to mention lurid write-ups in all the London gossip sheets. She and Jasper had indeed committed social suicide, but it had allowed their relationship finally to thrive.

Elizabeth wanted the world to know their marriage was a success, even if Baron of Milton would never be welcomed in certain circles. She no longer cared. Her husband, after all, owned a large Barony in Scotland replete with well-kept castle and bucolic, rolling farmland. They could raise their children there, England be damned.

"Lizzie, you've outdone yourself." Lady Stanton beamed.

"The arrangements are simply stunning. Daisy and honeysuckle make such a fragrant combination."

Elizabeth smiled. Jasper had insisted on these two blooms. His 'devoted affection' and 'I love you truly' messages had not been lost on her.

"Thank you, Lady Stanton." Her erstwhile neighbor was dressed as a Bird of Paradise flower in a bold orange-and-purple gown. "I'm so glad you approve."

The lady eyed her critically. "You may not have given your husband an heir yet, Elizabeth, but daughters are cause for celebration too. Your own father, you know, doted on you and Bella when you were young. And now look at you both: married to such handsome husbands." She waved enthusiastically across the room at Elizabeth's blond brother-in-law dressed as a tawny lion. He stood beside her sister, a stunning fawn.

"You know I never doubted you," Lady Stanton's tone quieted. "Never doubted for a moment there was more to you than brains and books, Elizabeth."

"And I never doubted you wished me well, madam," she told her. "Though I may not always have agreed with your methods."

Lady Stanton threw back her head and laughed. "Nor I your husband's taste in dogs." She quelled her mirth. "Sir Wigglebottom was, of course, gratified to receive your invitation, Lizzie, but knowing there'd be a wolfhound prowling your fête, my boy chose to stay home. You must visit us soon, to make it up to him." Her plea was so genuine, Elizabeth caved.

"I shall call on your little darling first thing next week, Lady Stanton." And Elizabeth brightened at the thought of dragging Jasper with her.

***

"Might I steal my creator a moment, madam?"

Lady Stanton paled before Milton's dreadful visage.

"Why of course, Baron, by all ... means." She stumbled over her words, still staring up at him. "Quite the costume you have, sir. *Quite.*"

Milton nodded to Lady Stanton before he led his wife, dressed as Dr. Victor Frankenstein, in the direction of the dance floor. Not for nothing had he swallowed his pride and begged his erstwhile tutor, Paul Kilpert, to embark upon those necessary dance lessons. He'd done it for Lizzie, and to repair a friendship he'd sorely missed.

He'd also kept it a secret from his wife.

"Is it Gemma?" Elizabeth asked as he continued to guide her. "You were there when I fed her last."

"She is fast asleep in her crib. That is not why I am stealing you away."

"Then did Gerald ask for me? Milton, the dancing is about to start and as hostess I mustn't miss the opening—"

"Precisely." He was nervous as hell, but he'd not let her down. He'd let her down one too many times before. "You must not miss the first dance with your husband."

Elizabeth's brow crinkled adorably. "Jasper Audrey, have you been keeping things from me?"

"I simply wished to surprise you, as did Paul." Milton waved across the room at Kilpert, who responded with a grin and a flourish. He'd come dressed as England's Bard.

"Why you *monster*!" She playfully tapped his leg with her cane, dressed as she was in full doctor's regalia: elegant waistcoat, soot for sideburns, and hair slicked back in a bun below her top hat, her spectacles making her look all the more medical.

She tipped her hat in the direction of Kilpert, who nodded back. "I can't believe you two hid this from me." She kept her voice low. "Though I am terribly pleased you've reconciled with Paul. Only whomever did you cajole as practice partner? I must know whom else to blame for your deception."

"Ginny, of course." Milton grinned. "We've conspired these last two months, though it helped you were so preoccupied with planning this ball you paid little heed to your poor, neglected husband."

"Neglected?" She huffed. "Hardly, sir. You've been a perfect monster to me, just like Shelley's creature: willful, disobedient, demanding of affection, and—"

"An' you'll be punished later fer yer tone, wife," he whispered in her ear as he led her to the center of the floor.

"Will I?" she murmured back seductively.

The room suddenly stilled, the guests waiting for their hosts to open the ball.

It was a simple minuet, one he'd practiced often enough in the drawing room with Ginny to manage now publicly. Still, Milton's nerves flared; a formal dance was nothing like a simple sailor's reel.

He cleared his throat. "Friends, family, and esteemed members of society," he began. "It is with pleasure that I welcome you to our home, in celebration of much." He paused. "First, the birth of our daughter, Gemma." The guests all raised their glasses in cheer. "Second, the impending publication of Lady Milton's debut novel." Surprised applause covered his wife's kick to shin. Was that meant to be a secret? For Elizabeth had indeed written a novel all through her confinement, though she had yet to let him read it, the minx. "And of course, tonight's masquerade. You are all visions in disguise."

More applause erupted as Milton allowed the ensuing murmurs to ripple through their guests' ranks. "Many of you have known me for years, and I daresay of late you may have noticed a change." He looked about him to find one after another of his closest, oldest friends. "A change for the better I hope."

"'Bout time, Jasp!" and "Damned right, y' lowlife!" erupted from the crowd.

He took a breath. "I owe that change to the woman at my side, my wife, Elizabeth." He squeezed her hand. "She saved me, ladies and gentlemen, from a fate worse than death. She saved me from myself."

Lizzie looked shocked, or perhaps she was annoyed he had mentioned her book. Regardless, he forged forth.

"When we wed, I was not the gentleman Miss Winthrop needed or, I am sure, wanted." Milton thanked his lucky stars he was no longer that bitter, vengeful man. "But I stand before you today, before my wife, to renew the vows I made that day, this time with full conviction of feeling."

"Hear, hear!" more voices proclaimed as tears now clung to his wife's lashes.

"Elizabeth Audrey, I promise to love, cherish and obey you till death do us part." He gazed deep into her eyes. "Obey within reason, o' course." He winked.

She flung her arms about his neck and kissed him, her top hat and cane falling to floor. He hoisted her high in the air and held her there a moment, aloft. They were monster and creator, mirrors of their true selves, or perhaps mere symbols of their past.

Elizabeth raised her voice. "Enough talk, Baron, let the dancing begin!"

As the first strains of music swelled, Milton lowered his wife to the floor and executed each move of the opening minuet with poise.

For the rest of that night, he danced with no one but his brilliant, bespectacled Baroness.

The End

AFTERWORD

HISTORICAL NOTES

This story was built entirely around a minor character in *The Fox in his Henhouse,* Lord Redstocking, whom I initially imagined as a self-made British peer. He ended up a Scottish Baron once research decreed a bastard, no matter his wealth, could never purchase a British Baronetcy in 1839 England. In Scotland, however, money spoke louder than blood. Scottish law even allowed for female heirs to inherit titles, ensuring land and legacy could be passed down to a daughter. Thus 'Lord Redstocking' became 'Baron of Milton.' Incidentally, a real Scottish Barony of Miltonhaven exists, its current title holder from the *Newlands* family which originated from one *Jasper* Newlands, 1469. The current holder is also a *she,* Dorothy Newlands, who resides at Lauriston castle, the Barony's seat. Life imitates art, apparently, because I discovered these historical bits only long after drafting the story.

As for Milton's surname, Audrey comes from a pre-7th century female name, Aelforyd, meaning 'noble strength.' I wanted his mother's noble strength to balance his father's ignoble character. The gemstone jasper derives from Old French *jaspre* and Latin *iaspidem* and means speckled stone.

Common green jasper with red spots is known as heliotrope or bloodstone. The rarer blue jasper is sometimes called false lapis in reference to *lapis lazuli*. According to folklore, the stone draws out the truth to help its bearer see things more clearly—fitting, I felt, to Milton's journey.

Regarding our hero's obscene wealth, suspend disbelief, I beg. In 1813, the year Austen published *Pride and Prejudice*, Mr. Darcy's annual income was 10,000 pounds, making him a millionaire by today's standards. It seemed plausible a wealthy bastard like Milton could afford an astronomical five thousand pounds for Elizabeth's hand (actually two thousand since he forgave Lord Winthrop his debt of three). It also seemed possible that with his level of wealth he'd be able to import expensive French Letter condoms directly from France, even though access to this contraceptive was not readily available to the English until about 1850. Milton's wealthy 'patrons' like Mrs. Ogilvy may have also had access the general public did not.

Around the same time Jasper Audrey demanded his story be told, I came across a different kind of gem in my local library called *The Language of Flowers* by Margaret Pickston. This book is an out-of-print reproduction of an 1813 notebook of hand-drawn flowers and their meanings. I loved the idea of Milton communicating via bouquets instead of words, given the emotional baggage he carries. That baggage—childhood trauma, in truth—began when his father, the Duke, insisted Mary Audrey give up her newborn. It was common for mothers of illegitimate children to pay so-called baby farms to care for their children so they could continue to work, but such care was often so negligent infants frequently perished.

Rather than endanger her son, Mary bravely attempted to raise her child by herself. When she and Jasper finally escaped their pimp, Hieronymus Finch, she found community and support with other prostitutes:

> "...in nineteenth-century Great Britain and Ireland, prostitutes created communities of mutual aid, sharing income and childcare. A journalist observed at the time that '...the ruling principle here is to share each other's fortunes... In hard times one family readily helps another, or several help one... What each company get is thrown into a common purse, and the nest is provisioned out of it.'" (From: *Revolting Prostitutes: The Fight for Sex Workers' Rights* by Molly Smith and Juno Mac.)

This community was the impetus for Miss Li's house of ill repute. Why not turn a prostitute's collective into a thriving business model (whorehouse and clothing shop) with a savvy, foreign businesswoman at the helm? (Li will get her own story, her mixed heritage explained.) Of course, such business is still gritty and dangerous, no matter how well workers are treated. I'd no desire to romanticize prostitution in this novel, hence Elizabeth's assault and the blunt speech of Li's maids.

As for the removal of body hair, here I take full artistic liberty. In the 1800s, women's hair, including pubic hair, was a prized feature. Many an erotic Victorian serial (see *The Pearl: a Journal of Facetive and Voluptuous Reading*) waxes rhapsodic over a lady's silken hair down there, but prostitutes often shaved for hygienic reasons, given how rampant pubic lice and venereal disease were. They then applied merkins, or pubic wigs, which could be cleaned between clients. Since Milton grew up with prostitutes, I thought he might wish his wife to look similar. The poultice of wax Li's servants use to remove Lizzie's hair is accurate to the time period, as was a carbolic. And speaking of hair, Janie colored Harris's head and beard a coppery red using henna, a colorant as common in 1839 as it remains today.

A hairless body is simply another of Milton's kinks, along with his fascination for breastmilk. That idea came from a historical work of art I discovered based on the story of

'Roman charity,' in which a daughter feeds her jailed father breast milk to save his life. As for Milton's spanking kink, impact play was alive and well in 1839, though upper-class men were the ones more often paying lower-class women to spank them. It's unlikely 'safe words' were a thing back then (the term appears in the OED first in 1979, BDSM as a framework arriving even later in the 1990s), but I slipped this in to make Milton more agreeable to readers. There's history, and then there's our tolerance for it. Case in point: a woman's hymen as proof of her virginity is a myth, because not all women have hymens. But historically, ruling classes did check to ensure brides were 'intact' before marriage. Having initiated enough virgins himself Milton was, no doubt, aware of this, but I figured he'd choose to verify Elizabeth's virginity upon their first encounter just to shock her and—wicked fellow—cop a feel.

Annulment based on an unconsummated marriage is common to historical romance (see book one in my *Worthy Peers* series) but it is rooted in fiction. It was nearly impossible to annul or divorce in 1839 England. British women legally relinquished all rights and property upon marriage. Before the 1839 Custody of Infants Act they did not even have the right to keep their own children after a divorce. If divorce happened at all it was on a husband's terms. There is one notable example of a full parliamentary divorce granted to a woman, Jane Addison, in 1801, on grounds of her husband's adultery with her sister. This was considered incestuous; had he committed adultery with a woman unrelated to his wife, Jane would not have been granted the divorce.

Regarding traditions, I have no idea if London's working classes passed brides around the dance floor or sang *The Lusty Young Smith*, but I loved the song too much not to include it in Lizzie and Jasper's wedding party. Arthur and Bella's marriage over a smith's anvil, in contrast, was entirely plausible. Blacksmiths and other tradesmen were allowed to marry any two people at Gretna Green without a license until 1856, when one partner had to have Scottish residency. My research also indicated a smith could have forged a ring from a gold coin with the right tools. When Arthur knocks Bella out cold to kidnap her, he applied a type of 'soporific sponge' used as early as the 13th century. This was soaked in opium and laudanum and other drugs of the era, then allowed to dry. Once made wet and inhaled it could render a person temporarily unconscious. Arsenic was also a well-known poison easily purchased at any chemist's shop and typically used to kill rats. It acted quickly too; in thirty minutes effects were felt. There was no official regulation of sales until 1851.

Some of the books featured in this novel are worth noting, not only because Elizabeth is such an avid reader and writer, but because Milton was denied the education his hungry mind craved in youth. He reads for pleasure when we find William Blakes's *The Marriage of Heaven and Hell* poetry collection on his bedside table, and when Milton devours *Frankenstein* by Mary Shelley the parallels are rich. Elizabeth also gives Milton Charlotte Smith's popular gothic novel *Ethelinde or The Recluse of the Lake* (1789). Smith is not well known today, but she greatly influenced Jane Austen's writing. If you read book one in this series you may recall a quote from early Italian feminist Moderata Fonte (1555-1592) opens that novel. Fonte is the pseudonym of Modesta Pozzo, a Venetian writer and poet. The Duchess of Allendale gives Elizabeth this same book as a wedding gift, yet both women would have read it in the original Italian since no English translation existed until 1997. Fonte's writing predates Mary Wollstonecraft's *A Vindication of the Rights of Woman* (1792).

Last but not least, character dialects in this story are a mash up of mostly London Cockney with occasional Irish or Scottish flavor thrown in. See the glossary that follows for a list of Cockney expressions and other foreign words used in this book.

If you enjoyed Lizzie and Jasper's story, I hope you'll consider reviewing the novel on Amazon and goodreads—feedback means the world to an indie author. And if you enjoyed Arty and Bella's love story as much as I did, you can read deleted scenes at the link below. Incidentally, their game of truth or dare really was known as 'questions and commands' and originated in 1500s England.

Stay abreast of future *Remillard Romance* releases by following me on social media. Eventually, there will be a book three in this series.

Yours in romance both steamy and polite,

~Constance

constanceremillard@gmail.com
https://remillardromance.com
Newsletter: http://eepurl.com/jze9SE
Deleted scenes: https://BookHip.com/PVZRDQX

APPENDIX

Six lessons learned by Miss Elizabeth Winthrop:

1. Do not cross Baron of Milton (*unless he is in the wrong*).
2. Do not insult him by being late (*late to gratify, that is, when he demands it*).
3. Do not goad him (*into spankings. He alone determines punishment*).
4. Do not touch his person without permission (*though he may frequently permit you to do so*).
5. Do not try his patience by kneeing him in the bollocks (*else suffer severe and lasting consequences to one's bottom*).
6. Do not disobey him (*in the bedroom. Elsewhere being tolerated or encouraged*).

Meanings of flowers, in the order featured:

1. Yellow Marguerite (I come soon)
2. Blue Hyacinth (your loveliness charms me)

3. Red Tulip (I declare my love)
4. Cornflower (be gentle with me)
5. Iris (I send a message)
6. Wild Rose (pleasure and pain)
7. White Lily (my love is pure)
8. Yellow Pansy (thinking of you)
9. Red Ranunculus (I am dazzled by your charms)
10. Red Rose (I love passionately and desire you romantically)
11. Baby's Breath (everlasting love)
12. Daisy (I love you truly)
13. Honeysuckle (devoted affection)
14. Bird of Paradise (magnificence and freedom)

Quotes appearing from literary works:

- *Frankenstein or The Modern Prometheus* by Mary Shelley, 1818
- *The Worth of Women: Wherein Is Clearly Revealed Their Nobility and Their Superiority to Men* by Moderata Fonte, 1600 (English translation by Virginia Cox, University of Chicago Press: 1997)
- Poems by William Blake: *The Garden of Love* (1794) and *Proverbs of Hell* (ca 1793)
- Indirect reference to: *Das Märchen* or *The Green Snake and the Beautiful Lily* by Johann Wolfgang von Goethe, ca 1795
- *The Lusty Young Smith*, traditional English bawdy song ca 1719
- *Sing a Song of Sixpence,* 16th century English nursery rhyme
- *As I Was Goin' to St. Ives,* 18th century English nursery riddle

A GLOSSARY

OF FOREIGN WORDS AND PHRASES

Cockney and other period expressions in the order they appear in the novel:

- **to plant a facer** to punch the face
- **sixes and sevens** stupid
- **bees and honey** money
- **Cornwallis** slang for lord, not necessarily Cockney, but referring to a well-known British nobleman and military/political figure who played a role in the American Revolutionary War.
- **to natter on** to talk or gab too much
- **cobblers** men's testicles, derived from 'cobbler's awl' which rhymes with 'ball'
- **jam tart** sweetheart
- **addle-pated** foolish, scatter-brained
- **pot and pan** old man (meaning father or husband)
- **thrupney bits** (or threepenny bits) women's breasts. A threepenny was a stamp worth three pence.
- **crikey** slang for 'Christ', expression of surprise from 1820s/30s

- **blunt** slang for money, not necessarily Cockney
- **guv** 'guv'nor' is an informal term for boss or a person in authority, short for 'governor'
- **twists and twirls** girls
- **diggings** digs/lodgings/home, used by Charles Dickens
- **a bird** also means girl
- **yobs**. boys (spelled backward)
- **peelers/bobbies** policemen, named for Robert Peel, of Irish and British constabulary
- **to chaff** means to tease someone good-naturedly
- **rumdum** If you kept drinking after growing tipsy, you'd be 'rumdum' or stupefied drunk.
- **trouble 'n strife** wife
- **swell/toff/nob** all derisive terms for upper class nobility

Other foreign words and terms in order of appearance:

- ***Vingt-et-un*** French for the card game 21, a counting game of chance.
- **Croesus** a very wealthy 6th-century B.C. king, of Lydia, in what is now Turkey.
- **Rubens** a 17th century Flemish artist known for his voluptuous nudes.
- **Lombard** pawnbroker, from Italy's Lombardy region, where pawn shop banking originated.
- **phaeton** a sporty, open carriage, lightly sprung, on large, extravagant wheels which could be pulled by one or two horses.
- **French Letters** early term for condoms.
- **curricle** similar to a phaeton, but pulled by two horses and not as fancy.
- **hansom** a rented London carriage, like a taxi.

- ***kusottare*** くそったれ (Japanese) translates as 'son of a bitch,' old-fashioned.
- ***écoutez!*** French meaning: Listen!
- ***catin de la révolution*** harlot of the revolution (French)
- ***garçon*** French for boy
- ***bonne chance*** French for good luck
- **the Lady of the Lake** reference to the lady that hands King Arthur the sword Excalibur from the bottom of the lake; an enchantress also known as Viviane or Nimuë.
- **the riot act** from the 1714 British *Riot Act.* If twelve or more people grew unruly and did not disperse, the local authority would read aloud the *Riot Act*, giving them one hour to disperse.
- **flibbertigibbet** from Middle English *flepergebet* meaning 'gossip' or 'chatterer.' Today it means a silly, flighty person.
- **don't give a tinker's curse** to not care, from the reputation of itinerant tinkers being habitual swearers of worthless 'curses' (use ca 1824-54) .

ABOUT THE AUTHOR

Constance Rémillard has been a romantic for as long as she can remember, devouring books when young and now penning them with a vengeance in middle age. She's lived part of her life abroad, immersed in other languages and cultures, and another part outdoors, immersed in the botanical. She now resides with her family of humans, chickens, cat, and plants in the United States. She hopes you enjoy her stories as much as she enjoys writing them.

instagram.com/remillard.romance
facebook.com/Remillard.Romance
pinterest.com/remillardauthor
bookbub.com/profile/constance-remillard
amazon.com/stores/Constance-Remillard/author/B0C-S1TJ5V8
threads.com/@remillard.romance

ALSO BY CONSTANCE REMILLARD

The Dubious Mates Series

The Fox in his Henhouse (book 1)

The Bastard in her Boudoir (book 2)

Coming soon: *The Maiden on his Ship* (book 3)

The Worthy Peers Series

The Earl's Debt (book 1)

To Woo a Maid (a novella)

www.ingramcontent.com/pod-product-compliance
Lightning Source LLC
LaVergne TN
LVHW020647110826
845149LV00012B/1942

* 9 7 9 8 9 8 9 8 8 6 5 5 5 *